WILD FIRE

A Hawk Tate Novel

DUSTIN STEVENS

Wild Fire, A Hawk Tate Novel
Copyright © 2019, Dustin Stevens

Cover Art and Design: Paramita Bhattacharjee, www.creativeparamita.com

*The past will always come back to haunt
you. Whether it is to teach a lesson,
remind you of forgotten feelings,
or just to be a bitch.*
—Rosen

*When you are right no one remembers.
When you are wrong no one forgets.*
—Proverb

Prologue

Eight years.

Eight years had passed since I last looked at the man sitting across from me. Since I peered into those dark brown eyes, malevolence burning so strong they appeared almost black.

The time since had certainly brought about some changes. The hair that was uniformly dark and shorn down close had grown out a bit, revealing the gray now threaded along either temple. The front edge of it had receded a half-inch up his forehead.

The face that was full and youthful in his late thirties had now grown lean and angular, the throes of middle age and whatever horrors he'd been subjected to since our last encounter both readily apparent.

But the eyes - the hatred they possessed, the way they settled into a glare as he stared across at me - that much was unchanged.

As were the feelings that bubbled up within me as I met his gaze, staring directly back at him.

"Tate," he muttered, his expression revealing the word to taste like acid on his tongue. "The Hawk. The one that got away."

Seated upright in his high-backed leather chair, his entire upper body listed heavily to the side, contorted by his left arm reaching across his torso. Pressed tight into the soft flesh above his hip, he was fighting a losing battle to stem the flow of blood steadily working outward against his white linen suit.

In just the few minutes I'd been standing there, already the underlying stain had grown beyond the reach of his fingers. A couple more, and it would begin to sap his energy, his systems flagging, going into preservation mode.

Not that I had any intention of letting it get that far.

Doing so being a fate much, much kinder than this man deserved.

"*El Jefe,*" I replied, letting him hear the derision in my voice, both for him and the title he so ardently insisted on being called.

In my previous life, I spent more than half a decade chasing men just like him. People that gave themselves some unfounded moniker and then tried like hell to convince everyone around them that they deserved it.

That because someone referred to them in a certain way, it had to be true.

"So you remember?"

Of course, I remembered. I remembered the day his file first crossed our desk and the months we spent tracking and researching him. The sleepless nights running surveillance, and the evening we finally put an end to it all.

All memories from a different life. Things that I wished I hadn't been a part of, could banish from my mind forever.

Things that I had thought of incessantly for the last week, since the moment they were forced back to the fore, crashing down on me like a wave.

"Yes," I replied, the front tip of my weapon never wavering, extended straight out from my shoulder, hanging above the desk separating us. Shifting my hips, I turned and slowly circled around to the side of it, my footfalls landing heavy against the hardwood floor beneath me. "I remember."

Using his heel, the man spun his chair to match my movement, both of our gazes remaining fixed, our focus never once shifting.

A thin sliver of a smile creased his face, white teeth flashing beneath dark skin.

"So you also remember the question I posed to you that night?"

For a moment, my only response was the echo of my heels as I marched out the last couple of steps, clearing any barrier that might have separated us.

Not until I stood square to him, sizing him up, did I bother to respond.

"Yeah. And do remember my response?"

Part One

Chapter One

Normally, such a trip would require that Junior Ruiz be put into full walking restraints. His hands and feet would both be linked together by standard handcuffs, neither able to be separated by more than a foot at any given time.

Constricting him even further would be a chain wrapped around his waist, keeping his hands pinned by his hips before extending down and connecting to the short tether between his ankles.

The human equivalent of hobbles on a horse, ensuring that his total range of motion was no more than a few inches.

Trying to throw a punch would be foolhardy, telegraphing his intentions, bringing about unwanted attention from the guards flanking him. Running would be completely out of the question, brisk shuffling being the best he could hope for.

These were far from normal conditions, though.

And it wasn't like he was going far.

Bound only by a pair of manacles around either wrist, Ruiz walked between a pair of guards. Both the size of smallish NFL offensive linemen, they kept one hand attached to either elbow, their gazes aimed outward, scanning the area.

With each step their breathing seemed to grow louder, accentuating the sounds of their belts straining beneath the combined weight of their tools tugging downward and their enormous girth pressing outward.

One black and the other white, Ruiz knew both of them by sight the instant they had appeared in front of his cell. Saying nothing, warned not to draw any more attention than necessary, they had arrived and given a simple tap against the bars before stepping back.

Expecting their arrival, Ruiz had done what was expected without objection, rising and thrusting his hands through the slit in the front of his cage.

Their fourth such appearance in the last two weeks, Ruiz's cell-mate – a small, squirrely kid with buzzed red hair and a nervous tic named Burris – had barely looked up from the magazine he was flipping through.

Glancing to either guard in turn, he had gone back to the outdated issue of *Car Trader*, pretending to be interested in the going rate on a rebuilt engine for a 1985 Camaro.

Exactly as Ruiz had told him to.

Popping the door open just long enough to slide through, they had locked it back immediately in his wake. Moving faster than he would have thought possible a week before, they made a point of making very little noise, settling into their respective positions to lead him forward.

Positions they still maintained now ten minutes later as they marched deep within the underbelly of United States Prison Lompoc. Far removed from the traditional meeting rooms up on the main level, gone were any windows or cameras. Also missing were the traditional tile floors and bright lighting that was meant to put on a display for visitors, this underworld a sea of gray.

Nothing but concrete block and steel bars, everything left bare.

Forced to give his best guess, Ruiz would speculate they were two or three floors below ground. The air temperature was cooler, the smell of mildew in the air.

Not that he minded in the slightest.

Especially not given the information he was being summoned to receive.

Down here, deep within the confines of the facility, Ruiz abandoned his usual posture. He didn't keep his head on a swivel, always aware of who might be lurking nearby, anxious to take a swipe at him.

Walking on with shoulders square, he stared straight ahead, almost daring one of the yard punks to appear before him.

Moving in complete silence, the trio marched on for more than two hundred yards. To either side, doors of various colors and textures filed past, their contents a mystery Ruiz didn't have the slightest interest in trying to decipher.

Not once did the crew slow their pace, going on to the same destination as the previous three meetings before the white guard on the right squeezed his elbow. Just strong enough to get his attention, Ruiz slowed his pace accordingly as the man peeled to the side.

Pulling up in front of a plain slate gray door, he raised his balled fist and thumped twice on it. The echo of the blow traversed the length of the hall, joining the faint hiss of the exposed pipework above before receding.

All of it nothing more than theater, the kind of thing the bastards Ruiz had first been called to meet with weeks before insisted on performing.

The sort of thing that was fast growing old, no matter how enticing the carrot they were here to dangle might appear.

In the wake of the knock, the guard stood with features screwed up, his body turned to the side. Head aimed downward, he flicked a gaze to Ruiz and the second guard, all three waiting in silence.

Until, finally, a single voice called out from the opposite side, ordering them to enter.

Chapter Two

Kaylan Quick passed the edge of the white cloth napkin from one hand to the next three inches at a time, moving until she made it to one corner before shifting ninety degrees and starting over. One time after another, she bunched and straightened the linen grasped between her fists, her eyes wide, taking in everything around us.

A look I had decidedly never seen on the woman before.

And one - I had to confess - I couldn't help but find a bit humorous.

"Everything alright?" I asked, letting her see the bemusement on my face as she flicked her gaze back to me.

Leaving it there only a moment, she replied with a simple, "Hawk," before again giving the place a onceover.

The name of the restaurant was The Smokehouse, the newest spot in a town that some publications were saying was fast trying to make itself a player in the burgeoning domestic staycation industry. A direct result of the influx of expansion dollars flowing into the area surrounding Yellowstone Park.

Or so said the online article I had read two days prior after asking Google to recommend a good steakhouse in West Yellowstone.

If left to my own devices, I would have been fine with the hole-in-the-wall spot we went to for lunch on days I was in the office. Or even one of the chain restaurants on the south end of town.

Never let it be said that I am a slave to pretension.

"Okay, what's wrong?" Kaylan asked. Forcing the napkin down flat atop her thighs with both hands, she fixed her gaze on me, blue eyes opened wide. Atop her head, a mess of curls was piled high, blonde hair contrasting against the cranberry sweater she wore.

Feeling the smile on my face grow a bit larger, I asked, "Why does anything have to be wrong?"

Lifting one hand, she motioned to the scene around us, sputtering twice, attempting to find the words.

Not that she needed to. Already, I knew what she was hinting at, the two of us glaringly out of place, the bevy of sideways glances we were receiving making sure that much was known.

The website for the restaurant had merely stated that it specialized in locally sourced meats and produce. What they seemed to have omitted was that meant organic Angus products. Beef and bison steaks cut to more than an inch thick. Side dishes that were ordered standalone, rather than being part of the dinner.

All served on custom China by waiters and waitresses wearing vests and ties.

A harsh contrast to Kaylan and her curls, me and my beard, both of us wearing jeans and boots.

"Are you dying?" she asked, ignoring my question.

A couple of months ago, I had been shot while across the country in Tennessee helping my niece. In the moment, it had been painful as hell, even requiring a brief stay in the hospital to put together some of the underlying soft tissue. Immediately thereafter, the rehab had been cumbersome, and the Montana cold hadn't done any favors, but for the most part everything was back to normal.

"No more than yesterday," I replied.

Not seeming to appreciate my response, Kaylan's nostrils flared slightly. Leaning forward at the waist, she shot back, "Am I being fired?"

As a partner in the guide business I founded less than two miles from where we were now seated, I wasn't sure if that was even possible. For a variety of reasons, not the least of which being Kaylan was a whiz with all the things I hated.

Marketing. Outreach. Websites.

Customer interaction.

"Never."

"Are we shutting down?" she fired back, undeterred.

"No ma'am," I replied.

It was clear from the expression on her face that there was no less than a dozen follow-up questions she wanted to ask. Reasons we were now sitting where we were, what it could mean, her mind trying to wrap itself around the oddity of the moment.

"Are we," she asked, crinkle lines forming around her eyes as she lowered her voice, "*on a date*?"

Unable to stop myself, a sharp crack of laughter slid out, a single sound so loud it drew a handful more stares in our direction. Feeling the heat of them on my skin, I raised a fist to my lips, covering my mouth as I chuckled, shoulders quivering with the movement.

It was true that I did care about Kaylan. She and I were as close as I had been to anyone since my wife and daughter were killed six years before.

But it was also true that not once had that affection ever trended into romantic territory.

"Okay," she said, taking my reaction as response enough. "So, what is all this?"

Letting my hand fall into place, I sat back in my chair, feeling the sharp corners of the designer wooden seat digging into my kidneys. Looking around, I took in the mounted moose and elk heads on the wall, the sound of faint classical music in the air.

Everything painstakingly put together in an attempt to create a specific ambiance.

What that was, I wasn't sure.

Not that I for a second thought I was their target demographic.

"Call it an employee appreciation dinner," I replied. "Toasting another great season, all that good stuff."

On the opposite side of the table, I watched as the initial shock of the moment bled away, the Kaylan I'd come to know over the preceding years finally peeking through. Raising one eyebrow, she stared across at me, disbelief apparent.

"Really? Employee appreciation?"

"Come on," I replied. "It's not that hard to believe. We do this every year."

"No," Kaylan corrected, laying both palms flat on the table as she leaned in a bit closer. "Every year, we order pizza and watch football. Or we throw something on a grill.

"We've damned sure never done *this*."

Once more, I couldn't help but smirk, my head rocking back slightly.

She was right, as she generally tended to be.

"Okay, fine," I conceded. "*This* is proof positive that from now on, I leave all internet research to you."

Chapter Three

The salesman at the North Face outlet just outside of Seattle had sworn that the boots were guaranteed to be impervious to temperatures as low as twenty degrees below zero. He'd even made a point of taking them out of the box and pulling the pages from the bottom of it, pointing out the fine print embossed on the accompanying paperwork.

In the moment, Tres Salinas hadn't thought to press it further.

He was from somewhere far south of where he was now standing. Much further even than the driver's license from Northern California he now carried in his wallet. Cold weather was something he saw on television. An item on the morning news to be skipped past, audibly wondering why the hell people would subject themselves to such things when there were plenty of places in the world with sun and sand and warmth.

All things he would kill to be enjoying right now.

The temperature display in the car had said it was twenty-eight degrees as he'd parked and climbed out. Almost a full fifty degrees warmer than what the boots claimed to be successful at protecting against.

And still, now just one hour and a short hike through the woods later, he could barely feel his toes. With each passing moment, he could almost imagine the flow of blood to them being choked off, his skin turning to mottled shades of black and purple.

Not that there was anything he could do about that now. If such was the case, he would have to deal with it. Just as he would if forced to stand rooted in this spot all night, waiting until frostbite claimed all ten of them, rendering him a clubfoot forever more.

That's how important this was. How much it meant to him that he had been entrusted with doing it.

Lifting either foot no more than a couple of inches, Tres stamped them down against the forest floor. On contact, the sound of each was swallowed up by the two inches of fresh powder that had fallen in the last couple of hours, already obscuring his inbound tracks from view.

With luck, his exit would be just as clean.

He just needed a sign. A flare that it was time, allowing him to move forward.

With one shoulder pressed tight to the barren trunk of a hardwood tree, Tres allowed his weight to list to the side. Taking the stress of standing from his legs, he seemed to meld against the bark, using it and the cover of pine boughs pressing in tight from every direction to conceal his position.

Tucked into the dense forest, dressed in muted colors, nothing visible but a narrow oval framing his dark eyes, it was as close to invisible as he'd ever felt.

And sure as hell as cold.

Lifting his right foot again, Tres stared into the small window he'd created by clipping back a single branch. Affording him a square foot to peer through, he could see the home of his target ahead, the place just beginning to shut down for the night.

When he'd first arrived, the place had been lit up like a Christmas tree. Most of the lights inside had blazed bright, illuminating the quartet of people that called it home.

One by one they had blinked out, leaving just a couple behind.

If the last few nights of reconnaissance were to be trusted, it wouldn't be long now before the remaining lights were extinguished as well.

Sliding his gloved hands along the outer shell of the polypropylene snow pants he wore, Tres reached into the cavernous front pockets. The fingers of his right hand he ran over the hard outline of the Sig Sauer tucked tight into the bottom, feeling the gnarled ridges of the grip.

With his left, he felt a trio of much smaller objects. One was nothing more than functional, a basic cellphone awaiting final confirmation.

The last two were of a much more personal nature, totems chosen specifically, his own special touch. A closing statement on something that began years before.

As he did so, he couldn't help but notice the jolt of adrenaline that seeped into his bloodstream.

Soon, it would all be worth it. The long trip north. The endless planning. The interminable wait for this very night.

The damned cold that threatened to freeze his eyelashes together each time he blinked.

Soon.

Chapter Four

Neither of the guards bothered stepping inside the room alongside Junior Ruiz. Once verbal assent from within had been given, the same guard that had first banged on the door grasped the handle and pulled it wide.

There he waited as Ruiz passed through, feet barely making it over the threshold before the door was closed in his wake. Just like in his cell, every movement was done with care, an effort exerted to ensure that no excess noise was made.

Who they might be afraid of alerting down here in the catacombs, Ruiz hadn't the slightest. Not that he cared to press much on the matter, every single bit of his interaction with these men in recent weeks bordering on the absurd.

Abnormalities he was willing to overlook if they made good on everything they had been claiming thus far.

An eventuality he still couldn't quite force himself to believe, no matter how close that very thing seemed to be creeping.

Standing with his heels just inside the room, Ruiz paused. There he waited until the door was shut in his wake, his eyes adjusting to the bright halogen glow of the tube lightbulbs overhead.

The room was simple, in line with most every other space that prisoners inside Lompoc had access to. Made entirely of concrete block, the walls were bare and gray. The floor was polished concrete.

The sole furniture in the room was a single metal table. On either side of it rested a straight-back wooden chair.

The first time Ruiz had been summoned to the place, he couldn't help but shake the feeling that it was the sort of place where discussions that weren't meant to be seen or heard were conducted. A spot where sound was swallowed by the concrete walls and any spilled bodily fluids could be easily wiped away.

Eight years ago, when he first reported to Lompoc, such a thing wouldn't have surprised him. If not by prison officials or government authorities, then certainly by some subset of the population.

It wasn't like he had been a model citizen on the outside, the list of people that he had angered in some form over the years quite extensive, even if based several hours to the south.

To his unending shock, nothing of the sort had come to him, a fact he had always attributed to the small crew he had assembled around him and a few well-greased palms among the guards.

Only in the last couple of weeks had he come to realize the truth, the answers he'd received from the pair of men now before him making far more sense, no matter how much he might want to deny it.

"Good evening, Junior," the man in the center of the room said. Known simply as Jones, he was perched on the far side of the table. One hip on the tabletop, his opposite foot was still on the ground. Body turned toward his cohort, it appeared the two had been in conversation, only pausing at Ruiz's arrival.

Somewhere around forty, the man was the walking embodiment of the fabled government agent stereotype. From his pasty complexion to his light brown hair combed to the side, he was the sort of man that was seen but never remembered.

Ruiz knew, because on more nights than one he had lay awake on his bunk, staring at the ceiling, trying to place either of them.

Not only had he failed to do so, barely was he able to even conjure their exact faces to mind.

Saying nothing to the greeting, Ruiz flicked his gaze from Jones to his partner Smith in the corner. The Bad Cop to Jones's Good, he stood with his arms folded, a scowl on his face. Another from the agent assembly line, the parentheses around his mouth were a bit more pronounced, his hair a little darker than his partner.

Otherwise, they could have easily been siblings.

At least that way, they wouldn't have had to come up with two boring fake names to give him.

"Your shiner's looking better," Smith opened, the barb clearly meant to get under his skin, making a point.

In the wake of his first meeting with the men, finding out who they were and what they wanted, Ruiz's initial reaction had been to balk. Ingrained from years of habit, of being practiced in self-preservation, he had known better than to take a couple of white boys in suits at their word.

In the twenty-five minutes they had spoken that night, most of the talking had been done by the pair on the opposite side of the table. In the moment, Ruiz hadn't believed a word of it, thinking it was all nothing more than posturing to get him to agree to something against his best interests.

Rat on someone. Offer information about a competitor on the outside. Even pony up location details about some of his former cohorts.

Sitting in the very chair not four feet from where he now stood, he had listened to the plan they had in mind. He sat completely still as they explained that they had been running interference for him the last eight years. Keeping him covered, out of harm's way and off the radar of any officials running Lompoc.

Had even been the guiding hand in getting him assigned to the place, all while monitoring things on the outside, keeping his sheet clean just in case the day came when they would need his help.

Just eight years into a forty-year term, they knew he wasn't going anywhere. They knew they could take their time, considering all the angles, hoping it would never come to this.

But, finally, it had.

And now here they were.

Leaning back in the uncomfortable wooden chair, Ruiz had forced himself not to openly laugh. These two pasty bastards clearly thought quite highly of themselves, and locked inside an office building somewhere, they might even wield a tiny bit of power. Had maybe even talked themselves into believing that it extended beyond the front edge of the desk they sat behind.

But they didn't know the first damn thing about what went on inside the walls of Lompoc.

Sure as hell not about the life he had lived to find himself there.

Two facts he had not been shy about sharing with them, his reward being a quick end to the meeting and a pair of inmates waiting for him in his cell when he returned. Pretending not to see a thing, the same guards had waited while the young men put Ruiz through the paces. Any attempts to protect himself had more or less been batted away, the disparities in the two sides obvious.

While they might have all come from the same world, Ruiz was the guy usually barking orders. These two were the ones to carry them out.

Thick and tan, they wore the markings of affiliations existing south of the border. Deliberately chosen, their presence wasn't solely to deliver a beating, but to remind him of what could have been a daily existence.

A not-so-subtle demonstration of just how truthful the words of the men in the underground bunker had been.

Three days after that initial meeting, sore and bruised, Ruiz had been summoned back to the very same room. His features turned up in a scowl, animosity roiling through him, he had sat and listened to every word the men said.

At the end, again, he had balked.

And again, the same two young men were waiting for him when he returned, the remnants of their second visit now still lingering, bringing about the crack from Smith.

"You able to get what I asked for?" Ruiz said. Ignoring Smith entirely, he focused on Jones. Shuffling toward the table, he remained standing, his legs flush against the back of the chair.

Lifting his eyebrows slightly, Jones flicked a glance to Smith. "We did, as promised. Everything in writing."

Raising himself from the tabletop, Jones leaned forward to a satchel resting on the opposite chair. Sliding a hand down inside the top flap, he pulled out a sheaf of papers nearly a half-inch thick. Bound by a binder clip at the top, he slapped the stack down, the top page covered in dark ink.

"Have a look."

Tracking his focus toward it for just a moment, Ruiz allowed the disgust he felt to cross his features.

There was no point in reading it. Whatever there might be that was of any value to him was shrouded in legal terms and misdirection, all of it no doubt meant to cover their ass should anybody ever think to look into it.

All playing on the facts that his United States citizenship was at best a tenuous proposition and no matter how fluent he might be in English, it was still his second language.

Never before had Ruiz worked with the government – this or any other – beyond facilitating whatever payouts might be necessary for a given objective, but he'd heard enough stories to know how it generally went. Especially for people like him.

At the moment, they had a hard-on for him because he possessed something they wanted, something they couldn't achieve on their own.

Once that was over, his purpose served, he would probably find himself back in here, if not worse.

A fact that both sides knew intimately well, those first two beatings blatant reminders of as much.

Grunting softly, Ruiz shook his head to either side. "When?"

"Tomorrow, just like we said," Jones replied. "Noon. Full light of day, media crew on hand."

Again, a head shake. "We've been through this. No media, and I pick the time."

"Ha!" Smith spat from the back of the room. Inserting himself into the conversation for the first time since his initial barb, he walked forward, arms still folded. "Who the hell died and put you in charge?"

Glancing to Jones, a mocking grin on his features, he added, "I guess those two beatings weren't enough for this pissant to understand how things work here. You're not *El Jefe* anymore."

Bit by bit, the smile faded, his eyes flashing as he rotated his focus to glare at Ruiz. "The way this goes is, we speak, you obey. Or you get to know our friends very well."

Deep within, Ruiz felt his acrimony spike, this time making it all the way to his face. His nostrils flared, his cheeks warming as blood rushed to the surface.

There was no doubt the words Smith had chosen were deliberate, meant to incite this very reaction.

Not that he particularly cared, the time for getting hung up on such minutiae now well past.

"That might be the way it is in here," Ruiz replied, "but you two want me to go back *out there*. And believe me when I tell you, I know that world a hell of a lot better than you two *pendejos*."

Pausing, he matched the seething hostility of Smith for a moment before sliding his attention back to Jones.

"Now, if this is real, if you two want me to do this, you're going to have to let me do it my way."

"It is. We do," Jones inserted.

Unfazed, Ruiz pressed on. "Then that means I need to walk out that front gate under my own power. I can't have cameras looking over my shoulder, can't have my face splashed across every TV in the state.

"I do that, then I've got your stink on me. I'm toxic. You understand?"

Taking the information in, contemplating it a moment, Jones slowly tilted his chin back.

"And then nobody's going to touch you."

Not bothering to follow up, to confirm the obvious, Ruiz merely stared.

What the men were wanting from him was damn near suicide. Even with the contacts he'd maintained, the flow of information he'd been able to cultivate, it was a ludicrous plan with little chance of success.

But it was the only shot he had, the sole hope at not celebrating his seventieth birthday in the same bunk he'd spent the last eight.

Crazy or not, he had to take it. And both sides knew it.

"So tomorrow morning at dawn, I walk out of here," Ruiz said. "And you're going to have someone here to pick me up."

On the edge of his vision, Ruiz could see Smith throw his hands up. Turning away from the table, he rattled off a string of obscenities, none quite discernible.

"At dawn?" Jones asked.

"At dawn," Ruiz said. Leaning forward an inch, he said, "Whether you guys kept me alive in here or not, no matter how far from home I am, people around here still know me. They recognize me. And they'll be paying attention to how it goes down.

"You want this all to look legit, that's how it's got to be."

The ask was a big one. Ruiz knew that. But he also knew the world he was about to step back into.

He might have been away for eight years, but some things were timeless. Most of what he knew had been culled from the hand of those before him, their knowledge passed down from the generation before them.

People in their industry lived within a certain duality. They were forced to compete with the ever-changing times, but they also abided by a code that had predated all of them.

Would long outlast each of them as well.

"Dawn?" Smith said, stomping back into view. "Are you serious with this? Is this your idea of getting back at us because you took a few punches?"

Within, Ruiz could feel his hatred for the second agent pushing outward. Growing until it almost consumed him, it threatened to spill out of every opening.

But still he remained rooted in place. His molars clamped, he stared at Jones, imparting that what he was saying was non-negotiable.

If he was going to do this, going to step outside and serve as anything more than target practice, it had to be done right.

"Given the time of night, that could be tough," Jones said, "but I think we can make that work."

Much like the roiling hostility within, Ruiz gave no outward response whatsoever. Considering the enormity of what it was they were presenting him with, what he was requesting was minor.

At best.

"Anything else?" Jones asked.

Chapter Five

The lights from the roadside signage for The Smokehouse passed across the front windshield of my truck as I swung out of the parking lot. Bouncing across the seam separating the lot from the street, the entire rig shuddered slightly before settling out as we headed back south.

Not enough to be cause for concern.

But more than sufficient to set Kaylan moaning in the passenger seat beside me.

"Oh, dear God," she muttered. "Please be gentle."

The same crooked smile I'd worn through our earlier conversation - and again as her food arrived, and once more as she ate every last bite of it – graced my features as I glanced over. Propped up in the corner, the crown of her head was pressed into the frame of the door, her eyes closed, a hand placed gently atop her stomach.

In the half-glow of street lights filtering into the cab, her skin looked sallow, matching the strain in her voice.

"How we doing over there?" I asked.

"Why did you insist on ordering that dessert?" she asked, not once cracking her eyes open.

That dessert was the most decadent brownie à la mode I'd ever seen, the baked good more than two inches thick, the ice cream hand churned. Covering all of it was a homemade chocolate sauce so dense it resembled tar.

In total, no less than twenty-five-hundred calories.

And worth every last one.

"Because it was the only thing on the menu I recognized?" I replied, pushing a bit of levity into my voice. Extending a hand, I reached out, jabbing a finger into her thigh, "And because it was good?"

Peeling her hand away from her stomach, Kaylan swatted at me, just barely missing my outstretched finger before slapping her palm against the seat. "Don't touch me. I can already feel that chocolate sauce collecting on my ass."

Opting against saying anything more, I rode out the last quarter mile back to the office in silence. Given that it was a Wednesday night in early November, the streets were as barren as expected. A handful of vehicles were all that dotted the streets, even fewer lined up at the neighborhood gas station and the smattering of fast food joints along the way.

In a month, a new crowd would descend on the place. Ready to take advantage of the winter season, snowmobilers and cross-country skiers would arrive.

And then to take advantage of them, a new batch of vendors and services would prop open their doors, continuing the annual cycle that hit the area each winter.

But for now, life was blissfully tranquil, like a college town in the summer.

"You going to be alright to drive home?" I asked, dropping the turn signal and easing off the road. Trying to take it as slow as I could, I pushed forward into the gravel lot outside our office, sidling up alongside Kaylan's Sentra parked out front.

As I did so, the front lamps bounced over the exterior of the building, the place one I purchased six years earlier when first moving north out of the desert. A single story tall, it was cut from flat-front pine boards, everything except the green trim outlining the door and windows painted dark brown.

Stretched across the top was a rough-hewn wooden sign employing the same color scheme, announcing ourselves to all who passed by.

Hawk's Eye Views: West Yellowstone's Favorite Private Guide.

Never let it be said that anybody in our line of work had a problem with false modesty.

"Ugh," Kaylan said, cracking her eyes open. "We're there already?"

Posting a fist into the seat beside her, she wriggled her way upright, staring out at her car and the front of the building.

"I can just run you home," I offered. "Your car will be fine here overnight."

Even at the peak of tourist season, West Yellowstone wasn't the sort of place where one needed to worry about where they parked. All summer long, my truck more or less sat alongside the building as I ferried people through the sights, nobody ever so much as glancing sideways at it.

Added to that was the fact that Kaylan was a local. Everybody knew who she was and what she drove, an unofficial neighborhood watch employed to take care of their own.

"Naw, I'm good," she managed.

"You sure? I don't mind."

"Yeah, I got it," she said, reaching out and unlatching the passenger door. Cracking it no more than an inch, cold air flooded in, plainly obvious despite the vents shoving stale heat around us. "Thank you, for tonight. I might be miserable now, but it was worth it."

"You're welcome," I replied, opting against a handful of retorts. The poor girl was in enough pain as it was. "And thank you for another great season. You more than earned it."

Opening her mouth as if to respond, Kaylan thought better of it. Pressing her lips tight, she nodded once before shoving the door out wider and hopping down to the ground, her diminutive stature making the exit far from graceful.

"You sure you're good?" I asked, one last attempt to ensure she was going to make it.

"Yes," she said, her feet dragging over gravel as she turned to look

27

at me. Glancing up to the front of the building, she added, "Though I am going to use the restroom before heading out. Please don't wait for me."

Knowing better than to say a word, I smiled. Raising a hand in farewell, I merely offered, "Good night."

"Good night," she said, lingering a single moment to see if I would be foolish enough to add anything more before flinging the door shut.

Shifting toward the office, she lumbered up the trio of front steps, perfectly framed in my headlights. Fishing deep into her pocket, she extracted a wad of keys as she continued moving forward.

Selecting the one she wanted, she no more than had it inserted into the slot before the door exploded outward in an array of light and sound, lifting her into the air, seemingly suspended parallel to the ground.

All still under the watchful gaze of the twin spotlights protruding from the front of my truck.

Chapter Six

The last couple of nights couldn't be considered true dry runs. Not with the actual target out of town, leaving behind only his wife and two young children.

Instead, they were more like scouting missions. They allowed Tres Salinas to get close to the property in a way he probably wouldn't have if the man had been home.

Starting forty-eight hours before, he had spent an inordinate amount of time standing exactly where he now was. Watching the afternoon and evening coming-and-going of the family. Getting a feel for their bedtime rituals, committing it all to memory.

Adding it to everything else that had been gathered in the week before that, gaining an understanding of the family and how they conducted themselves each day.

If there was anything that had been drilled into Tres from an early age, it was the necessity of preparation. Nobody that was successful, that had ever achieved anything of value, had done so purely on luck or even talent.

They had gotten there by leveraging the latter to create the former.

And the only way to properly exert leverage was through sweat and determination. Going beyond what was expected.

Making the most of every opportunity, like the one bestowed upon him now.

Arriving in Washington a full week prior, Tres had done everything he could to make the target's life his own. Knowing the man's schedule and where he lived wasn't enough. He needed to be inside the family, to know where the wife would be and why. When the children took their bath each night and how early they rose in the morning.

He needed to have every contingency covered.

No matter how cold it got. No matter how tired he became.

The reward would be worth it.

Each day began at six sharp, with the wife rising in her second-floor bedroom. Not once had Tres seen her linger in bed, pummeling the snooze button for extra minutes. Instead, he suspected that with her husband gone she had spent the night tossing and turning, thinking of all that came the next day, awake long before the alarm summoned her.

An hour later, dressed and ready for the day, she would wake the children, the remainder of the morning a sprint to get them all out the door on time.

Given their remote location, no school buses went near the home. No garbage collection or paper delivery for that matter, either.

In lieu, she drove the twins – one boy, one girl, both nine – into town, dropping them off outside the front door of their school before making her way down the street to the local branch of the public library where she was the director.

Not that she needed to, what her husband made more than sufficient to keep them comfortable, especially in this part of the country.

A woman that insisted on pulling her weight, keeping herself busy.

A move Tres could respect.

Whatever errands the woman needed to run were done during the noon hour. Banking, groceries, dry cleaning, all of it conducted between twelve and one.

Two hours later, she walked the three blocks down to retrieve the kids from school, escorting them back to the library, where they took part in the daily after-school program.

Coloring. Storytime. If the signs posted on the bulletin board inside the front door were to be believed, a sing-a-long each Friday.

All of this, Tres had been forced to piece together through a series of quick passes through town. Brief swings where he was careful not to linger, knowing that someone of his particular skin tone would stand out in such a small town.

As would the stickers on the back of his rental car, perhaps the only thing less conspicuous than the California license plates on his vehicle still parked in the hotel garage outside the Seattle airport.

Maintaining strict nine-to-five hours each day, the woman and both kids were on their way by three minutes after the hour. From there it was straight home, where the kids retired to homework while she prepared dinner.

Evening meal at six. Baths at seven. Lights out for the kids by nine, the woman an hour later.

Next morning, rinse and repeat.

As Americana as baseball, apple pie, and all that other shit people liked to talk about.

Or so Tres had been told, his own upbringing about as far from all that as could be imagined.

Hands still entrenched in his front pockets, Tres tapped the pad of his right index finger against the butt of the weapon stowed inside. He felt the heft of it tugging just slightly against the drawstring of his pants, could already imagine the weight of it balanced in his palm.

Could practically savor the moment when finally, after so long, he could draw it. Hold it at arm's length, staring into the eyes of the man that had shifted his life irrevocably so many years before.

Let him know that the same thing would now befall his own family.

With his opposite hand, Tres rested his fingers atop the small flip phone wedged into his pocket. Ringer turned to vibrate, all he needed was a single pulse from it. A sole signal that the final hurdle had been cleared, he was free to move whenever the opportunity presented itself.

Tres felt his heart rate tick up slightly as he nudged himself away from the base of the tree. Inching forward, he peered into the small window carved through the branches of the pine trees, staring intently at the bedroom on the second floor.

To his surprise, the woman didn't appear there. She didn't cross in from the side, fresh from putting the children to bed. She didn't flip on the lights and begin peeling back the handful of throw pillows, readying herself for an hour of personal time before extinguishing the lights and heading off to sleep.

Neither did her husband.

Instead, they both appeared more than a dozen feet below, stepping out onto the back patio, each dressed in white terrycloth robes, champagne flutes in hand.

Chapter Seven

The last question Agent Jones had asked was exactly the one Junior Ruiz had been hoping for. Vague enough to be open-ended, it allowed him to pose what he was truly after, the one thing he needed more than any other, without having to say as much.

The instant the question was out, a fair bit of the wrath Ruiz harbored for Smith ebbed away. The previous comment about his eye, the theatrics about stating that the proposed exit wouldn't work, all of it fell to the wayside.

Replaced internally by a ripple, a series of palpitations rising through his core. A feeling he hadn't experienced in the better part of a decade, and as recently as two weeks before would have never imagined coming to pass again.

Hope.

There was not a single outward sign as Ruiz had stood and stared at the men. As he had put up the façade of considering the question, when in reality he was being careful not to overplay his hand.

"Everything we've talked about in here is written in there?" he asked.

"Jesus H..." Smith mumbled off to the side, following it up with something that seemed to be commenting on Ruiz's ability to read.

"It is," Jones confirmed, the man now also completely ignoring his partner.

"And that when I leave here, my debt is paid," Ruiz continued. "There's no way the DEA or the FBI or whoever the hell else you two work for can one day knock down my door, charge me with escaping, and drag me back?"

A slight flicker at the corner of Jones's mouth told Ruiz what he already suspected. He'd been careful to mention the two agencies he didn't believe they actually worked for, hunting for any form of a response, when in reality, he already had an idea who the men represented.

No way two men about to do what they were, proposing the plan they had, worked for most anybody else.

"It says that also," Jones confirmed.

Glancing down to the papers, his mind working quickly, Ruiz had waited a mandatory couple of seconds before finally dropping what he'd been waiting to all along.

"So when I step foot out of this place, everything from before that minute is considered moot?"

In the moment, Ruiz almost worried that he had been too obvious. That he had somehow tipped off his true intentions, that the men might get suspicious and call everything off.

Now, walking back to his cell, the same pair of guards on either side of him, he knew that wasn't the case. Whether the agents had suspected anything or simply didn't care was far from relevant, all that was being the answer they had given.

Striding forward, the corners of his mouth turned upward, Ruiz walked in silence. Barely did the comments lobbed at him from the cells filing by on their right even register, his mind in a handful of different places.

Third in order was the fact that this was his final night inside. His last eight hours of being forced to lay on a thin and frayed mattress, ignoring the jabs of pain in his back and neck. His final morning of having to face the showers, or the mess hall, or any of the other things that had demarcated the years.

Coming in at second was knowing that when he did take those

first few steps of freedom, it was with a completely clean slate, courtesy of the United States government.

The very same assholes that had put him here years before.

Both sat a good distance back from the top spot, the single thing dominating his thoughts.

What the agents were asking of him was ludicrous. Ruiz knew it, was fairly certain Jones and Smith did as well.

But the opportunity they were putting on the table was too good to ignore. Even if it did turn out the way Ruiz figured it might, if things went south within the coming days, they were at least granting him a taste of fresh air.

And to finally right the one enormous wrong that had hung over his head for so many years.

"Open Eight," the black guard called out. Deep and resonant, his voice echoed out, barely falling away before a metallic click could be heard the length of the hall.

The moment it did, the opposite guard stepped forward, sliding the front gate to the side. Allowing Ruiz to pass inside, he motioned for him to stick his hands back through the front bars, the final step in the process, the complete inverse of what they'd done an hour before.

Throughout it, Ruiz never once looked anywhere but straight ahead. His features were kept a stony visage, his gaze never alighting on any one spot for more than a couple of moments.

Even after the guards had removed his restraints and been on their way, he stood just millimeters from the steel bars. Rubbing his wrists with either hand, he stared at the frosted glass windows on the far side of the hall, seeing that darkness had fallen in his time below ground.

"Were you able to get your hands on a phone?" Ruiz asked, his voice barely more than a whisper.

"Yeah," Burris replied, matching the tone.

"And?"

"Just been waiting on you to give the order, *El Jefe*."

Chapter Eight

O ne would expect that with a background like mine, my mind would be impervious to witnessing violence. Between my years in the Navy, bouncing around on ships all over the globe, and then the subsequent time with the DEA working with one of the preeminent FAST – Foreign-deployed Advisory and Support Teams – crews scouring through Central and South America, that something like a front door exploding would barely register.

I'd spot the burst of flames, the hail of wood shards and splinters spurting in every direction, smell the smoke in the air, and I would be out of the truck before Kaylan even hit the ground.

The problem with such an assumption is that in every one of those previous situations, there was an accompanying awareness. An understanding that I was stepping forward into something where physical harm could befall me. Where people were standing opposite with a gun or a knife or a door rigged to detonate the moment the knob was turned.

Never something like this, though. Not on the front porch of the small and unassuming business I owned in an even smaller and more unassuming town like West Yellowstone.

Certainly not months after I'd even held a gun, ending the lives of the men looking to cause me harm.

Sitting behind the steering wheel, it was like having a front row seat at a drive-in theater, my headlights providing the optimal lighting for all that I witnessed. My jaw dropped, my eyes went wide as I sat and watched. My heart clenched in my chest, my stomach threatened to push out everything I'd just eaten.

But not until Kaylan hit the ground did what I was staring at truly resonate.

Only then did the rest of my senses catch up, shoving my logical brain to the side, allowing my baser instincts to take over.

The force of the initial blast had been enough to lift her into the air, shoving her back across the narrow expanse of the front porch. Showering her in busted splinters of brown and green, it dumped her hard on her back, her knees paired together and twisted to the side.

Thumping against the frozen boards, momentum folded her legs upward, knees almost touching her left elbow, before she came to a stop.

Not to move again.

"Kay-laaaan!" I called, separating her name into two syllables, the second extended several seconds as I pawed for the handle on the door. Shoving it open, I spilled out and swung it closed behind me.

Attempting to fight my way forward, the soles of my boots slid atop the gravel, pitching my upper body forward. Folded in half, I splayed my fingers wide, hands and feet all scrabbling against the loose stone, fighting for purchase.

"Kaylan," I muttered, shoving the word out between quick breaths. Head up, I padded forward on all fours, palms slapping against the cold planks of the second step leading upward.

Focus squarely on her, I used knees and elbows to hoist myself onto the front edge of the deck, spider-walking my way to my friend.

With each small step forward, each incremental gain, more details came into focus. From the blood streaming down her face to the bits of wood caught in her hair. The thick veil of splinters and sawdust covering the front porch to the acrid scent of chemical smoke in the air.

All of it registered with my subconscious. Skills that so often remained dormant rushed back to the fore, imparted from a lifetime of seeing things just like this.

Things that refused to ever be forgotten.

"Stay with me," I whispered, my entire being drawn tight. Making it up and over the three steps, I came out on the porch beside her, drawing a knee up beneath me along her right shoulder. Using it as a pivot, I spun myself so I was perpendicular to her, one hand going straight for the crease just beneath her jawbone.

A reach that never quite made it there, interrupted by the unmistakable ping of bullets slamming into the front grill of the truck above me.

Chapter Nine

Acting under the unexpected explosion of the front door, the shock of seeing my friend dumped unceremoniously on her back, I had made the mistake of believing there was no further threat. Not once did I pause to even consider what had caused the blast or to think that someone might still be lingering nearby.

Just like my attacker had made the faulty assumptions in thinking that it would be me that opened the door, and if I did somehow survive, I would still be standing directly in front of it.

At the first bark of a gun, the report roiling out into the night, reverberating from the pine trees lining the north end of the property, my body moved on pure instinct. Knowing only where the sound had come from, what the angle must have been for the rounds to hit the front of the truck square, I used my planted knee for leverage, hurling myself back toward the front of the office.

Keeping my body bent in half, I lunged out two elongated strides before tossing myself sideways against the wall. Careful to avoid the window to my right, I slammed into the wooden planks, the structure absorbing the collision without the slightest tremble, vertebra popping the length of my back from the impact.

As I moved, two more rounds were squeezed off, the bright orange glow of the muzzle flashes ignited in the gaping doorway beside me. Shifted in aim a few feet to the side, they slammed into the wall behind me, strong enough for me to feel the faint pulse of their impact, the boards thick enough to hold strong, swallowing them up, keeping them from punching through.

A moment later, the scent of gunpowder joined the putrid smell of chemical smoke, two more things about the moment that seemed so woefully out of place.

Not the least of which was me.

Body tucked tight against the side of the building, I remained pinned on one knee. Making myself as small a target as possible, I peered back to Kaylan, her immediate safety no longer my chief concern. In her unconscious state, my only hope could be that whoever this bastard was would assume he had gotten her, leaving her be, his focus squarely on me.

Who the hell this might be, I had no idea. My past is littered with people that I'd rather never see again, many with gripes real or perceived aimed in my direction, but it has been months or even years since I've crossed paths with any of them.

Who might now have tracked me into the mountains, have staged an elaborate scheme in the last couple of hours while we were at dinner, would be nothing more than speculation.

Same for what possible motivation they might have for doing so.

Not that it really mattered at the moment.

All that did was isolate the bastard, making sure Kaylan and I both made it far enough to even ask those questions one day.

Jerking my attention back toward the truck, I thought of the Winchester rifle that sat in a case behind the front bench seat. I considered the folding hawksbill blade that was tucked into the glove compartment, and even the tire iron that was squirreled away beneath the driver's seat.

None would be ideal, but any of them would be a welcomed addition. Any of them would give me something to go back at this man with, bringing the odds closer together.

As if sensing my line of thinking, wanting to point out how far away those items were, how there was no chance I was making it back across the open expanse of the porch again, another pair of shots rang out. Both aimed at the passenger headlamp, they found their target, the glass no match for the gas-powered rounds.

Smashing through, they shattered the underlying bulb, one-half of the illumination disappearing. Without the added glow, I could feel my pupils dilate, long shadows stretching across everything, the thin fog of smoke drifting across the single beam of light.

Back pressed flush against the side of the building, I tucked my chin tight to my shoulder. I tried to imagine who might be standing inside, what they were carrying, where they were positioned.

Best guess, the guy was using a single weapon. Each shot had had a clear report, cycling through the firing mechanism before barking out a second time.

Never was there any overlap, or even a change in the sequence, the way there might be if using multiple guns.

Based on sound and the sparks flying from the chrome of my front grill, the fact that the rounds hadn't made it through the wall behind me, the gun had to be a small caliber. Nine-millimeter, maybe slightly larger.

Which meant he could have anywhere from three to ten bullets remaining.

And the preferred position.

Kneeling at the base of the wall, I flicked my gaze from the doorway to the scene stretched out before me. I took in the short breadth of the porch and the truck sitting behind it, Kaylan laying prone in the foreground.

Right now, I did have the advantage of the man's attention. He knew where I was, that I was unarmed and pinned down. He also knew that his gun wasn't powerful enough to get to me, meaning at some point, one of us had to make a move.

That advantage evaporated the instant he got antsy, deciding to shift his target practice from my truck to my friend.

Rolling my head back, I allowed the base of my skull to touch the wall. I felt the cool of it pass through my hair as I drew in a deep breath, willing myself to calm down, to push past the initial shock of the moment.

Everything up to this point had been on his terms. He had caught me unaware by blowing out the door, had used my carelessness to put me in my current position. Whether planned or the best possible outcome of the sequence didn't really matter. What did was the fact that he was baiting me, counting on me to let fear or confusion or whatever else lead me into doing something stupid.

That ended now.

Chapter Ten

N ot once in the past week had Tres Salinas even noticed the hot tub sitting on the lower patio. Carved out on the underside of the master suite above, he'd barely considered the area as anything more than storage. A place where firewood was stacked, safe and dry from the elements. Where a plain metal shelving unit was pressed tight against the wall, loaded with old work gloves and gardening tools.

Twice Tres had threaded his way through the area, mid-day jaunts to get a feel for the layout of the property, without ever really thinking much of the blocky unit comprising the back corner of the area.

Not that there was ever much reason to. With the cover on and a few random towels strewn across the top, it looked like it hadn't been used in ages.

A faulty assumption if there ever was one.

Lips curled back over his teeth, Tres remained rooted in place as the couple stepped out from the house. Resembling a pair of specters in their bright white robes, he could just barely make out the faint din of their voices drifting through the cold night air, loud enough to be heard, but too soft to be discerned.

Backlit by the ambient light of the living room behind them, he watched as the man handed his champagne flute across to his wife and cleared the towels from the top of the tub. Once they were put away, he flipped open one end of the cover, light and steam rising from within.

Moving with practiced precision, he then slid the back end down to the ground, leaving it balanced on an edge, leaning against the side of the unit.

The first time Tres had ever seen the man was eight years prior. Dressed in full tactical gear, an automatic weapon in hand, plenty of California sunshine on his skin, barking orders to everybody within earshot, the man had seemed larger than life.

In the time since, that mental image had only grown stronger, Tres replaying the interaction over and again in his mind. With each retelling, the man's voice had grown a bit deeper, his jawline a touch more pronounced.

Now, standing in the woods outside his house, Tres couldn't help but smirk at how foolish he'd been. At how much what he remembered was nothing more than youthful ignorance, the mind conflating things in a way that simply wasn't true.

For the past week, Tres had been an unknown presence in this man's world. He had followed his kids to school every day, had watched his wife fall asleep at night and rise again in the morning.

He'd stood in this exact spot, less than forty yards separating them, a loaded weapon in hand, and never even been suspected.

Just as he was now.

As he had been a moment before, when the buzz of the cellphone he'd been waiting on pulsed against his thigh, managing to inject a ripple of adrenaline through his system.

Once the hot tub cover was stripped away and lowered into place, the man turned back to his wife. A smile on his face, he unknotted the robe from around his waist and let it slide from his shoulders, the form it revealed confirming every last thought that Tres had been having a moment before.

The man that had shown up that night, had turned his world on edge, wasn't superhuman. He wasn't larger than life, the perfect embodiment of everything a man should be.

He was merely a man. Someone that was just past forty and looked it. He was still in decent enough shape but wasn't winning any fitness competitions in the near future. He was an inch or so above six feet tall but wasn't towering over a room.

Tres felt his cheeks bunch beneath the ski mask as he stood and watched, a smile coming to his face. The middle and index fingers on his right hand flickered in rapid sequence, tapping at the butt of the weapon, adrenaline and anticipation surging through him.

No longer did he feel the least bit of apprehension. No more was he concerned about his approach or how to best proceed. Armed with the visual now before him, he knew there was no way he could fail.

Raising himself up onto his toes, Tres dropped his heels down, the snow continuing to swallow all sound. The cold that had gripped him just moments before seemed to bleed away, his focus on the man as he accepted his champagne from his wife and took hers, allowing her to strip out of her robe as well, before together they climbed onto the top edge of the tub.

Heart thundering in his chest, Tres slid his hand down around the grip of the Sig Sauer. Pulling it free, he tapped the elongated barrel of the sound suppressor screwed down onto the end of it against the outside of his thigh.

This was it. After everything he and his family had been through, at last it was here.

Barely able to contain himself, to make himself stay in place, he waited until the man and his wife both slid down into the water, their heads completely disappearing from view, before bursting out of the trees, a plume of powdery snow rising in his wake.

Chapter Eleven

I n an ideal situation, I would have a weapon. Not a long gun, like the Winchester stored fifteen feet away in my truck, but something small and versatile, able to be wielded in tight spaces. Fully automatic, so I wouldn't need to worry about reloading, or even injecting a new round into the chamber.

And I would have the high ground, or at least the proverbial equivalent. I'd be firing from a concealed position, safe in knowing my opponent couldn't see me, and even if they could, they couldn't possibly hope to get to me.

Basically, I would switch positions with the asshole currently squirreled up in my office, gun in hand.

Unable to do that, that left me with only one possible alternative.

Smoke and mirrors.

Keeping my back pressed flat against the wall, I leaned a few inches toward the door beside me. Listening hard, hoping to catch the slightest hint of movement across the hardwood floors, I lowered my hand to my foot tucked up beneath me.

Grabbing at the laces, I pulled apart the bow riding along the top of it before hooking a finger down inside, loosening the shoe. Easing my heel upward, I slid my foot free of it, the cold night air swirling around the sock, seizing on my toes.

Paying it no heed, I placed my stockinged foot back down into place and leaned forward a few inches, using the space to peel my coat down off my shoulders. Careful not to make a sound, I wrestled it past my elbows before tugging it free, sliding it from behind me and placing it down on the porch beside the boot.

Staring down at the twin items, I could feel my pulse pick up. Despite the frigid temperatures, perspiration came to my brow, my breathing becoming shallow.

The plan was worse than thin. It was foolish. I knew that, neither of the two objects before me the least bit lethal.

But it was all I had. If I was to stand a chance at surviving this, at getting Kaylan off this ice block of a porch and away to help, I had to do something.

Otherwise, it was just a simple matter of the guy sitting and waiting me out. I couldn't crouch and hope for the off chance that somebody would drive past and see the smoldering remains of the door. I couldn't bank on one of the rounds not eventually getting through and puncturing me in the back or the man deciding to open on Kaylan, waiting for help that likely wasn't coming.

Not on a night like this, not standing outside the office on the far north end of a deserted mountain town in November.

As my wife so often used to say, help comes to those that help themselves.

Grasping the collar of the coat in one hand, the heel of the boot in the other, I drew in a deep breath. Letting the icy chill linger in my lungs for a moment, I took one last glance to Kaylan, the image hardening my resolve.

I had no idea who this man was or why he was here, but I knew what his intentions were.

And I damned sure knew I wasn't going to let it go that way.

Using the tread on my one remaining boot as an anchor, I drove myself forward, taking no more than a single step before twisting into the gaping maw that was the front doorway. The instant my toes touched the threshold, I let out a deep and guttural roar, pushing the sound out with everything I had while simultaneously tossing the jacket high up into the air above me.

My body folded in half, stomach pressed tight to my thighs, I thundered forward, hearing a pair of shots ring out. In the confined space of the front office, the sound resembled cannon fire, pulsating against the walls, punctuated by two blinding flashes of light.

So close I could feel the wind from them, I heard as they slapped into the canvas coat above me, driving it backward before thudding into the wall.

Only then did I lift my gaze, for the first time spotting my attacker. Standing with his backside against the desk running almost the length of the room, bisecting the space, he was dressed in all black, everything but the top half of his face obscured from view.

Gripping a weapon with both hands, a thin tendril of smoke rose from the tip, his eyes widening as he spotted me moving in low.

Seeing his movement, knowing that there would be no stopping the next round he squeezed off, I snapped my right arm forward. Pushing it in a tight arc, using the heel of the boot as a leverage point, I flung it as hard as I could, aiming for the weapon steadily moving my way.

The throw wasn't perfect. It didn't twist end-over-end, colliding with the gun and knocking it from his hand. It didn't lift the front end toward the ceiling, a harmless shot firing into the sheetrock.

But it was good enough.

The man was able to squeeze off one last round, though it was faster than he wanted, before he was able to fully correct his aim. Tearing through the boot, it sent bits of leather spinning into the air, flinging the shoe across the room, a wounded duck coming in for a rough landing.

And then I was on him.

Coming in from such a low angle, I hurtled forward off bent knees, the full force of my weight, of my journey, of the anger I was feeling about whoever this bastard was and why he was here, hitting him square. Burying my shoulder into his stomach, I drove him straight back into the counter, hearing as his tailbone mashed against the front ledge of it.

A weak gasp passed between his lips as his body went slack for a moment, the gap all I needed to draw back, both hands immediately going for his wrists. Shoving them straight upward, I moved in tighter, raising my knee as hard as I could into the soft tissue between his thighs.

Holding him steady, I brought it up a second and a third time, my knee a piston, firing into his nether regions. With each contact, I could feel the strength seeping out of him, my grip on his wrists the only thing keeping him upright.

One last time, he fired off a round, weakly trying to push down against my hands, hoping to use the gun.

A move that was futile. He might have had the jump on me with better positioning and a weapon of choice, but he'd been too reliant on both. He'd assumed that coupled with those, all he'd needed was a bit of surprise and victory was his.

What he'd failed to take into consideration was I actually knew what to do once an initial plan went awry.

Hands still locked on his wrists, I rolled them down, pulling his forearms flush with mine. Squeezing hard, I slowly bent them inward, forcing his elbows out wide, opening a clear lane between us.

A lane he barely even seemed to register as I snapped my head forward, driving my forehead into the bridge of his nose. Hitting flush, the full weight of my two hundred and twenty pounds behind it, the thin bone disintegrated on contact, blood spatter flung across my face.

Any tensile strength that might have remained bled from his body, his knees turning to liquid.

Propping him up just long enough to take the gun from his hand, I relinquished my grip, letting him fall in a heap to the floor.

Part Two

Chapter Twelve

The locker room was so tiny, it could barely even be considered as much. Nothing more than an alcove carved into the back of a much larger space, it was comprised of only a single bank of metal lockers, their fronts laced with rusting lattice. Gone were the usual pegs that would allow someone to thread a lock through, as was any of the original paint.

Two even rows, five apiece, at most a couple of feet in height.

Why they were there, what purpose they had originally been meant to serve, was anybody's guess. The sort of thing that had been there for so long, everyone just sort of accepted their presence, not bothering to even consider what they were needed for.

A position Junior Diaz found himself in as he sat on the narrow wooden plank serving as a bench in front of them. With his head bent downward, he didn't bother to even glance up, his entire focus on the garments draped across his hands.

In the background, he could hear metal scraping. He could hear the faint din of conversation taking place nearby, not caring enough to even try to decipher what was being said or who was saying it.

The air around him was cooled in a way that only sitting inside a concrete basement bunker could be. Redolent with a handful of different scents, he could pick up the faint smells of water and mildew, concrete dust and grease.

A thousand others, if he really cared to try and pick them out.

But he didn't, his entire attention on the plastic sack balanced across his thighs and the objects folded inside. Items he hadn't seen or even thought about in eight years.

Not even in the whirlwind that was the last week or two, when things went from non-existent to ethereal to reality in record time.

For most people, the process of being sentenced and reporting to prison was an ordered one. A person was arrested and they stood trial, a long and drawn-out process that could extend for months or even years.

At the conclusion of it - if found guilty - they were given a date sometime in the future and told to report by then to begin their sentence.

Armed with so much time to think, to prepare, to plan, many of them arrived at the front steps of whatever facility they had been ordered to dressed as if arriving for Sunday church. Suits and ties. Polished shoes. The type of attire that they thought they could slip back into on the far end of their sentence and immediately assimilate right back into society.

The thinking being that rarely does someone see a person in a suit and tie and immediately think of the recently incarcerated.

Again, a process that occurs for most.

But not all.

Men like Junior Ruiz weren't so fortunate. They were deemed flight risks, or the crimes they were charged with were so severe, that the government considered the very thought of allowing them another moment of freedom an affront to national security.

For those unlucky few, there was no forewarning. No planning. No chance to present themselves in a way they would like to be viewed upon exit.

Instead, they were left with whatever they happened to be wearing at the moment of their arrest.

Garments such as the beige linen suit and the pink button-down shirt folded in the bag before him. Items that still bore the grass stains on the knees and shoulders from where he was forced to the ground and handcuffed. That no doubt still smelled of the champagne that was spilled across his lap and the sweat that seeped from his pores as he was driven across the desert.

Scents and marks that had had eight years to sit in a plastic sack. Eight years to grow stronger, embedding themselves forever in the fabric, a final harsh punctuation to the better part of a decade.

For him, there would be no stepping outside in fresh Armani or Brooks Brothers. There was no chance at presenting a spit-shined version of his former self, seamlessly blending back into the world around him.

There would be only these clothes and the memories they brought.

The resolve that now surged through him as he sat and stared down at them.

"Ten minutes," a voice said, jerking Ruiz's attention up to see the same guard that had handed him the bag moments before. Stomach straining against the front of his uniform shirt, he held a paper cup from McDonald's in hand, a half-sneer on his face. "Unless you want to stick around a little longer."

Where the man had come from, Ruiz wasn't sure. So lost in the memories wrapped in plastic before him, he hadn't heard the man approach.

Just as he wasn't sure if he was actually expected to respond, the best he could manage a simple shake of the head.

The clothes weren't what he would have picked. If given his preferences, he would have asked them to be burned in the incinerator long ago.

But they damned sure beat the orange jumpsuit he'd been wearing for the last eight years.

And he wasn't about to spend another minute in this place, regardless if he had to walk outside naked.

Chapter Thirteen

The sound of the ringtone shattered the silence of the hotel room, jerking Tres Salinas upright in his bed. Not the shrill, harsh bark of the standard phone found on every nightstand in the country, making good on the wakeup call he had requested before falling asleep, but the understated melody programmed into his cellphone.

The specific sound set aside for one caller and one only, the unexpected arrival of this distinctive din what had so radically altered his course just a couple weeks before. A tone he would recognize anywhere, association strong enough to pull him from the deepest of sleeps.

Even those coming on the heels of nights like the one he'd just had.

Snapping himself upright at the waist, Tres let the covers fall back from his bare torso, bunching around his hips. Reaching out with his right hand, he grabbed up the phone from the nightstand beside him, the white glow of the screen a harsh beacon of light in the otherwise darkened room.

The celebratory shots of whiskey he'd allowed himself the night before seemed to bore into his skull, making his brain feel two sizes larger than it was supposed to be.

Pinching his eyes shut to block out the glare, Tres thumbed the device to life, pressing it to his face.

Even here, within the confines of his room, he knew better than to put the person calling on speaker.

The risk of someone overhearing, of possibly even getting a word he might say or the sound of his voice on tape, was just too great.

"Sir," Tres answered, long past having to be told to never use names over the phone.

As they had learned long before, no electronic communication could ever truly be considered secure. Not with law enforcement agents the world over practically soiling themselves at the thought of their next big get.

"Is it done?" the caller asked, employing his usual phone voice. Low and even, it came out as little more than a hiss, Tres having to strain to hear him.

Though, again, he knew better than to ever say as much.

Or to even insinuate the man repeat something.

"It is," Tres replied.

Grunting softly, he asked, "Were there any problems?"

The presence of the target's wife in the hot tub made things a bit trickier for Tres. It had meant he had to stay a few minutes longer than necessary, had been forced to do something he really hated and put hands on a woman, though nothing that he would consider a problem.

"No," Tres replied. He thought of adding that it was almost too easy, that the man stepping out onto the covered porch and sliding into the hot tub had taken some of the joy from it, before opting against it.

This man was not a friend, and this was not a call to swap stories, a fact that was never once forgotten.

By either party.

Once more there was a grunt, a quick guttural click. "And were you seen?"

The target's wife had gotten a quick glimpse of him, but there would be nothing that she could identify, everything but his eyes shrouded in black. As he'd determined many times in the preceding week, there were no cameras on the grounds, same for the network of backroads he'd taken to return to Seattle.

Nothing that would have captured a single image of him before he arrived back at the airport car rental counter. By that point, he had stripped out of his winter reconnaissance togs and into jeans and Seahawks sweatshirt and ballcap, just another tourist dropping off his ride before catching a late flight.

Taking a shuttle all the way back to the main terminal, he had stopped for a slice of pizza and the shots that were now reverberating through the inside of his head before walking out the opposite side and catching an Uber back to the hotel he was now lying in.

In total, plenty of people had seen him, but not one would have had any reason to give him even a second look.

Not in a city as teeming with tourism as Seattle.

And definitely not with the look he'd tried so hard to cultivate, the tan complexion of his skin the only thing differentiating him from being a poster child as the average American male.

"No."

"Good," the man snapped, the closest he would ever offer to praise. Pausing, he fell silent a moment, seeming to contemplate his next words, before asking, "Have you heard from your counterpart yet?"

The first words uttered that weren't completely expected, Tres felt a crease form between his brows. Lifting his gaze to the flat screen directly in front of the bed, he could just make out the outline of himself sitting upright, the faint glow of the phone illuminating his silhouette.

To call the man that had headed north at the same time as Tres a counterpart would be a misnomer at best. The two had known each other for a while, had even been friendly when the occasion called for it, but in no way had they been working together.

A shared task, states apart, and nothing more.

Since departing a week before, Tres hadn't heard a single word from the man. The two had left in opposite directions, each with a specific target in mind and the instructions to complete what was asked and get back without being seen.

Beyond that, there was no interaction.

Not even any reason for there to be.

"No, sir. Was I supposed to?"

Ignoring the question entirely, the man muttered something too low to be heard. Based on tone, Tres would guess it to be an obscenity, pushed out in Spanish, the default setting whenever he was angry.

"Where are you now?"

"Just outside the city," Tres replied, still careful not to give away too much. "Planning to head south as soon as traffic breaks."

"Not anymore. There's something else you need to do first."

Chapter Fourteen

I've never been what one might call a coffee connoisseur. I derive no joy in drawing in the aroma, trying to determine what sort of beans were used, where on the globe they came from, or even how they were sourced. Never have I lingered for an hour or more at the dinner table, sipping on a Cafecito, letting it act as the perfect palate cleanser after a meal.

I just don't care that much.

To me, coffee falls into the same category as vehicles. I need it to perform the purpose for which it was designed, and beyond that, I am ambivalent. It doesn't bother me if it looks and smells like jet fuel, so long as it provides the requisite jolt of caffeine I'm looking for.

A task the third cup I've gotten from the hospital vending machine seems to be achieving with even less success than the first two. Much longer and it will be spitting out nothing more than muddy water, each mouthful of the swill managing only to heighten the frustration roiling through my system.

Agitation aimed at where I'm seated. At not hearing anything in the hours since I arrived.

At wondering who in the hell that man was that showed up at my office last night, blew the front door from the hinges, fired at me, and put my friend in this damn place to begin with.

Seated on the front edge of a padded chair, the lone person using the waiting room at such an ungodly hour, my hands were wrapped around either side of the paper cup. In the background I could hear the hospital beginning to come alive, mixing with the faint drone of the morning news cycle on the television above me.

Little more than a faint staccato, my mind tuned it all out, instead trying in vain to make sense of what happened. Again and again I asked the same questions that have been flitting across my consciousness since the moment I put down the intruder standing in my front office, no closer to finding answers now than I was then.

So badly, I wanted to be out of the place, on my way, knocking on doors, demanding to know what happened. I could feel nervous energy pulsating through my system, threatening to come spilling out at any moment.

But just as surely, I knew that I would not – could not - move. I would not leave my friend and partner alone, would not go anywhere until I knew that she was okay.

That there was zero chance that whatever happened wasn't actually aimed at her, or that somebody wasn't looking to return and finish the job.

Lifting the paper cup toward my mouth, I made it less than halfway there before abandoning the notion. Unable to force down any more of the sludge, I pushed myself upright, shoving out a sigh through my nose. Shifting to the side, I chucked the beverage away, barely noticing the thin stream of droplets that splashed out, dotting the top of the receptacle. ·

"Excuse me, Mister..."

Rooted deep in my own angst, focus completely drawn inward, I had failed to even notice the woman standing beside me. Had somehow completely missed her pushing through the double doors on the end of the hall and walking steadily forward, the sound of her voice being the only thing strong enough to catch my attention.

No wonder the man last night had been able to get the drop on me so easily.

"Tate," I replied, drawing myself upright. Rubbing my hands along either side of my jeans, I began to extend one for a handshake, making it only a few inches before realizing the woman still had both of hers thrust deep in the pockets of her lab coat.

Under the coat was a pair of dark purple scrubs, a lanyard identifying her as Dr. Jade Whitney hanging across her chest.

Looking like she had been awake as long as I had, her chestnut hair was pulled back into a tight ponytail, concentric rings underscoring her eyes.

"I understand you came in with Ms. Quick?"

"Yes," I replied, "she and I are business partners. We own a guide company down in West Yellowstone."

A series of faint lines appeared around one eye as she nodded slightly, processing the information, her thinking plainly obvious on her features.

All thoughts that - no matter how much they might sting - she wasn't wrong in having.

"And I understand you were there last night? When it happened?"

I could tell she was being deliberately vague. She was handing me a sanitized version of whatever had been relayed to her by the attending nurses that had wheeled Kaylan back hours before, they themselves getting the information from the officers that had escorted us up from the scene. Not wanting to assume anything, it was almost like she was an attorney, offering open-ended questions, intending not to lead my responses in any way.

An approach I could appreciate, even if I was in no mood for it.

"I was," I answered, shoving the words out quickly, making no effort to hide the underlying sigh that came with them. "Is she okay? Can I see her?"

Pressing her lips down tight, the doctor regarded me for a moment. It was clear there was so much more she wanted to ask, details from the night before she was aching to have, but to her credit, she didn't press.

An amount of self-restraint there was no way I would have been able to display in that moment.

"She is," Whitney began, "or rather, will be. Right now, she has second degree burns on her face and hands, and a linear fracture along the back of her skull."

Lifting my face, I felt my eyelids lower, my hands curling up into fists. Whatever angst I'd felt a moment before managed to climb even higher, mixing with the weak caffeine in my system, threatening to send me straight through the ceiling.

The burns would have been from the initial blast. If the smoke I'd smelled was any indicator, they were almost certainly chemical, meaning scarring would be likely.

The fracture would have been from being blasted backward, landing on the frozen porch. Already burned and lifted into the air, she'd been unable to do anything to break her fall, her entire weight coming down hard on her occipital lobe.

"We also treated her for a variety of cuts and contusions, dug out a tremendous amount of wood shards and splinters. For the time being, we have her sedated and will be keeping her for observation."

By the time she was done speaking, my shoulders were mere millimeters beneath my ear lobes. Every muscle drawn up tight, I held the pose a moment, clenching, wanting so bad to scream at the ceiling, before slowly pushing it away.

Already, it was clear what the doctor thought of me. No matter what the story that had accompanied Kaylan might have been, the woman was a professional, had probably heard every possible tale there was about how someone ended up in the emergency room with such an assortment of injuries.

Getting angry, making a scene, would only galvanize such opinions.

And more importantly, do absolutely nothing to help my friend.

Peeling my eyes open, I tilted my chin downward, meeting her gaze. For a moment, I said absolutely nothing, letting her see the gamut of emotions passing through me.

"Thank you, doctor," I whispered. "Is there any way I can see her?"

Chapter Fifteen

Like a naughty child being led to the principal's office, for some reason Dr. Whitney felt the need to escort me back to Kaylan's room. Doing so in complete silence, she stayed a step or two ahead, everything about her making it quite clear she still didn't know what to make of me.

Which, I suppose, was a valid stance.

Since leaving my sister-in-law and her family in Nashville months before, I hadn't done a single bit of grooming. Not on the inch-thick tuft of beard that protruded from my jaw. Certainly not on the hair that now hung in shaggy loops over the tops of my ears and across my forehead.

With my coat and boot now pieces of evidence shot full of holes, I was down to the backup attire dug from the storage bin mounted in the bed of my truck. Mud-streaked and ragged, they didn't exactly help to offset the shaggy appearance.

Nor did the stray droplets of dried blood still splattered across from my chest, remnants of my encounter with the man now locked up across town.

Even for Montana, I was a sight.

Keeping one step ahead and one step to the side from me at all times, she steered us through a series of turns. Covering more than a hundred yards in less than a minute, the journey ended abruptly outside a recovery room.

"Like I said, the patient is sedated right now," Whitney said, both arms clasped across her torso. "Please don't try to wake her or bother her in any way."

What the woman thought I was going to try to do, I didn't have any idea. Reflexively, I felt a pang of anger rise, the frustration I'd experienced in the waiting room resurfacing, before slowly ebbing away.

My fight right now wasn't with this woman. She was just doing her job.

And even if it was, she was here to help my friend. That had to take precedence over any wounded pride I might be harboring.

"Yes, of course," I managed. "Thank you for letting me see her."

Lifting her face just slightly, Whitney's gaze met mine. Her jaw sagged, as if she were about to respond, before closing, a simple nod her only response.

Shifting her shoulders to the side, she motioned for me to enter.

My first impression upon stepping into the room was that it strongly resembled the one I'd been housed in after being shot in Tennessee. And the one that I had visited a friend in down in Southern California.

And a thousand others around the country, all made by the same companies, all following the same basic parameters.

Small and rectangular in shape, the total space was no more than a dozen feet in length and a little over half that in width. Dominated by a standard hospital bed, the full array of associated monitors and apparatuses lined the far wall.

Across from me was a window with blinds closed, a shade pulled down three-quarters of the way, ensuring no small bit of early morning light penetrated.

In front of it sat a single plastic chair, the kind that was hell on the back and butt, meant to make visitors as uncomfortable as possible.

And - by extension - keep any time spent to a minimum.

Each of those details I took in with merely a quick glance. Even if

I did have the intention of sticking around, it would have to be in the waiting room. That much the doctor had made clear already.

Instead, my focus went straight to the bed. To the back angled upward to forty degrees and Kaylan resting atop it, her hands encased in thick gauze, the same for the majority of her head.

From where I stood, the only parts of her that even remained visible were concentric ovals around her mouth and eyes, everything else wrapped in white.

Taking a step forward, I felt the air slide from my lungs. In my adult years, I had seen my share of injuries. Battlefield wounds and damage much, much worse than what she had suffered the night before.

But much like the shock of watching the front door of my office explode outward, those were within certain contexts. I knew when my FAST team and I went on a mission that things could happen. It was understood that when a Navy patrol was out in hostile waters, we could take on casualties.

And so it wasn't quite as jolting when those things came to pass. No less severe, but there was a certain desensitization to it.

Forewarned being forearmed, and all that.

Even though the doctor had given me the full litany of her injuries, had told me what to expect, I was not at all prepared to see Kaylan splayed out in such a state. Not the woman that just ten hours before had been bemoaning how miserably full she was.

The same one that considered walking from our office down to the sandwich shop on the opposite end of the strip to be her daily exercise.

My legs seemed to go numb as I eased forward. Approaching the foot of the bed, I extended a hand, my every reaction to reach out, to touch her, to provide some form of solace.

Making it to within a few inches of the white bedding enveloping her, I pulled up short. Palm balanced above her knee, fingers spread wide, I held the pose, staring down at her, trying to make sense of what I was seeing.

There was no reason for Kaylan to be here. Not at all, and certainly not in the state she was in. Whoever had rigged that front door had meant for it to be me. They had hoped to catch me off-guard, render me helpless, and then finish me on the front porch.

No advanced warning. No pretense of a fair fight.

Damn near an execution, performed right beneath the sign that bore my very name.

Who they were, why they had done it, just two more questions I didn't have answers to.

"But I will," I whispered. For the first time since arriving, I felt resolve begin to seep in. Move past the frustration, the confusion, the shock of the last hours.

Letting it push through, I watched as my hand began to tremble. As thoughts, feelings, that I so often managed to keep tamped into place began to rise.

"You have my word, K."

Chapter Sixteen

My phone was vibrating against the plastic cupholder in the middle console as I jerked open the door to my truck. Going straight for it, I slid inside, slamming the door shut behind me.

It was enough to stop the frigid morning breeze from penetrating, but did nothing for the interior temperature hovering at most a degree or two above freezing.

Of everybody in the world, there wasn't but a handful that had the direct number to my cellphone. Of those, one was now laying in a hospital bed eighty yards from where I was sitting. Most of the others were still asleep, as they should be at such an hour.

That left only a precious few, none the type to be calling unless it was important.

"Tate," I said, thumbing the phone to life. Pressing the button on the side to send it to speaker phone, I balanced it across my thigh.

With both hands, I dug into the pockets of my coat in search of the truck keys. Each breath shot out before me in a white plume, ethereal zeppelins connecting me and the steering wheel before dissipating.

"Oh, thank God," a male voice said, shoving the words out in one quick bunch, underscored by a heavy sigh.

Just as fast, whatever relief there was evaporated. "Where the Hell have you been?!"

My search for the truck keys came to a momentary pause, a cleft appearing between my brows as I stared down at the phone.

The voice was one I would recognize anywhere. For years, it had been piped directly into an earpiece, providing me with intel and oversight on every DEA operation I ever took part in.

What didn't fit was the words he was saying, for tone as much as substance.

"Pally?"

Responding in kind, my stomach drew in tight. For more than a decade – a stretch both preceding and outlasting my time with the Administration - Mike Palinksy had served as the best ops man on the government payroll. A technological savant, there wasn't a security camera he couldn't get access to, a blueprint or schematic he couldn't dig up whenever we needed it.

Not once did he ever lace up a boot or fire a weapon, but that didn't make him any more dispensable than the rest of us.

Even after getting out and migrating to the private sector, I knew he still kept tabs on all of us. Forever his guys, he had certain indicators set up throughout various systems, flags meant to alert him should anything arise with one of us.

What I didn't know was how he could have possibly already gotten word about what happened at the office the night before.

Or how that would be enough to make him open with mentions of both God and Hell, two entities I knew for a fact he didn't believe in.

"Sorry," I muttered. In my haste to get inside last night, I hadn't even thought to grab my phone. "Left my phone in the truck."

"Son of a..." he muttered, his voice trailing away. "What have I told you about that? You finally get a twenty-first century model and *you leave the damn thing in the truck?*"

It was true that the man had scolded me many times for my indifference to most forms of technology. Just as Kaylan had. And most of my clients.

What didn't fit was why he was choosing this moment to berate me on it.

"Look, I was a little distracted when I got here," I spat back. With every word, each of the competing, disparate emotions I'd been carrying just moments before surged upward, all wanting to be heard at once. "Besides, hospitals don't let you take the damn things in with you anyway."

In response to my outburst, to the vitriol I was flinging back, the line went quiet. Outside, a rusted Ford pickup spewing an uneven tail of exhaust rolled up. Choosing a spot on the far end of the row I was on, it pulled to a stop.

Thinking better of climbing out just yet, the driver sat in place, content to remain in the warmth of the vehicle.

"You're at the hospital?" Pally eventually asked. Gone was the previous angst in his voice, as was the rush of relief and concern.

In their place was the same calculating calm that I had come to know.

"Are you okay?"

"I am," I replied, peeling back whatever hostility had been in my voice to match. "Kaylan is in bad shape, though. Tried to duck into the office last night to take a piss, had the damn front door explode in her face."

Most people would react to such news with something. Some form of a follow-up question, or an admonishment, or condolences. Concern, perhaps.

All I got back from Pally was silence.

"But that's not what you were calling about," I said, my mind piecing things together.

"No," he whispered. "I'm calling because Martin is dead."

Chapter Seventeen

For as clichéd and overwrought as movies got almost everything about the prison experience, Junior Ruiz couldn't help but feel a bit of déjà vu as he walked down the narrow concrete sidewalk toward the front gate. It was as if he had seen this part before, Hollywood depictions surprisingly accurate on this tiny detail.

Behind him stood a trio of guards, still close enough he could hear their voices, a vain attempt to pretend their eyes weren't boring into his back. That their position had nothing to do with where he was or what he was doing, their focus on making sure he got out without incident.

And maybe a lingering glance on who arrived to get him, that serving as data to be written down, entered into some government database, one more piece in his file no doubt.

A file that, if Jones and Smith were to be taken at their word, was about to disappear forever.

Tight to either side of the sidewalk corridor were the omnipresent chain link walls that had insulated him for so long. Rising well above his head and lined with razor wire, one wasn't sufficient. Instead, a strip of gravel had been inserted between two, enough space to ensure that if anybody was to decide to try going up and over, they'd still have to do it a second time before getting out.

Gaze locked straight ahead, Ruiz made a point not to look in either direction. He'd seen enough chain link to last him a lifetime, had witnessed sufficient faux camaraderie from the guards for much longer than that.

Focus locked on the gate before him, on the final barrier standing between him and what he'd craved for so long, Ruiz kept his pace even. He forced his features to remain neutral, not to reveal the tempest of thoughts and emotions swirling within.

One step at a time, he cut the distance from fifteen yards down to ten. From ten down to five.

As he drew within the last few steps, his pace slowed just slightly, the good folks at United States Prison Lompoc granting him one last indignity. One final bell toll to remind him of his time spent with them.

The automatic release of the metal latch on the gate. The same sound that had started and ended his every day. A noise he had heard more than fifty-five hundred times.

Echoing out into the cool early morning air, it preceded the door swinging wide. Spring-loaded and pressure-released, it burst out to a ninety-degree angle. Waiting at attention, it remained fixed in place as Ruiz passed through, never once slowing his pace.

A march that continued until he heard the door swing back closed behind him, the clear din of metal slamming against metal filling his ears.

Only then did he stop, raising his gaze toward the sky. Filling his lungs with the first free air he'd known in ages, he stared toward the heavens, the last gasps of stars just fading out in the face of encroaching morning.

A sight that more than once he didn't know if he would ever live to see again.

Damned sure not at this point, just days past his forty-sixth birthday.

"You expecting me to carry you the rest of the way or something?"

Tinged with just the right amount of shrill, the voice cut through the enormity of the moment. Landing deep in the cortex of Ruiz's brain, it aligned with memories from long ago, matching up perfectly, a sound he would know anywhere.

A smile pulled one corner of his mouth back as he lowered his face and shifted his attention to the side. Scanning fast, he spotted the black Chrysler with the fresh wax and polished grill sitting in the first stall.

And more importantly, the short woman with wide hips and glossy dark hair standing beside it. Backside resting just above the front tire, she stood with arms crossed, bright red lips pursed.

"Esmera."

It was true that his last condition before agreeing had been given just the night before. Meant to be taxing, the purpose of it had been twofold, Ruiz both wanting to set the men to scrambling and to test what they were truly capable of.

The answer - if her presence before him now was any indicator – being quite a lot.

When the topic of who would arrive to fetch him had first arisen, she was admittedly well on down the list. Focused almost entirely on the business side of his operation, Ruiz's first thought had been maybe one of his former lieutenants, perhaps one of the guys from shipping or even the fields.

Never would he have imagined them dipping into his family.

Much like he had brushed aside their wanting to wait until noon and bring in the cameras, they had done the same on this point. A none-too-subtle way of letting him know that while the majority of their heavy lifting was now over, it was not to be forgotten how strong their reach could be.

A thought that – as harrowing as it might seem – he was not about to let interfere with the moment.

Allowing the smile to grow larger, Ruiz began his march again, eschewing the sidewalk and cutting a diagonal path across the small patch of grass separating him from the lot.

The last time Junior Ruiz had seen his sister Esmerelda was the night he'd been arrested. Barely out of college at the time, she was now just past thirty. As the distance between them diminished, he could see that her form had rounded out some, but otherwise she looked exactly as he remembered.

Just as he'd hoped she would.

"Baby sister," Ruiz said. With each step, he allowed the smile to grow broader across his face, extending his arms before him.

"Big brother," Esmera replied, the same smile gracing her lips. Using her hips, she leveraged herself up from the side of the car before stepping forward, meeting him halfway. Going straight in, she slid her hands around his waist, burying her face in his chest as she pulled him in tight, clasping her hands behind his back.

Going rigid for just a moment, his every instinct programmed to avoid contact of any sort, Ruiz slowly pushed aside the reaction. His muscles relaxed as he wrapped his arms around her shoulders, drawing her in. Placing his nose against the top of her head, he inhaled her scent, lilacs and jasmine filling his nostrils.

Easily the best thing he had smelled since stepping inside.

Holding the embrace for several moments, neither wanting to move, Esmera was eventually the first to break. Releasing her grip, she stepped back, her cheeks wet, eyes puffy.

Blinking quickly, she lifted a finger to the corner of her eye, straightening an eyelash as she glanced from him to the front gate. "How old are those clothes?"

"You remember," Ruiz replied. "You were there."

"Yeah, I guess I was."

"My style needing an update?" Ruiz asked.

"More like a fireplace," Esmera answered, shoving out a wet chuckle. "You stink."

Unable to stop the single crack of laughter that spilled forth, Ruiz felt the smile return. Reaching out, he clasped her shoulder, giving it a squeeze, using the grip to steer her back toward the car.

"Yeah, well, guess what? You now get a nice, long drive home with me and my smelly clothes inside a warm car."

"Like hell," Esmera replied. Popping open the driver's door, she stood with one hand balanced atop it, watching him circle around the front. "I brought a whole bunch of rope. You're not messing up my car, I'm tying your ass to the hood."

Chapter Eighteen

Ramon Reyes couldn't remember the last time he'd gotten a full night's sleep. If forced, he would guess at some point five or six years before, though there was no way of knowing that definitively.

Long enough in the past that he wasn't sure what anything more than four hours of rest would even feel like. If it would be too much, leaving him feeling sluggish and lethargic, his system used to running on an elixir of adrenaline and caffeine.

At the moment, the latter of those two sat on a saucer in front of him, the smell of fresh ground Cuban roast wafting up at him. Rumored to be the strongest on the planet, he had long since bypassed the usual miniature cup in favor of a full-size mug, the beverage practically calling to him from the edge of his desk.

So badly he wanted it. To reach out and grab it, upending the bottom, taking down more than half in a single pull.

But he wouldn't. Not right now, with more pressing matters at hand.

Part of being in charge meant showing everyone that he was in control. Not just of the operation, but of everything, right down to his own impulses.

A fact that was true now, perhaps more than ever before.

Seated behind his desk, already Reyes was dressed for the day. Having barely slept the night prior, he'd been up long before any need for an alarm, showering and into the office overlooking the property hours before the sun.

Already, this was one of the busiest times he could remember since ascending to the top spot.

Now, this.

To look at him, there was no way of knowing that he had been awake ninety of the previous one hundred hours. Adorned in matching slacks and vest, a sharp crease ran the length of the sleeve of his dress shirt. Links held the cuffs in place.

His thick hair was recently barbered, gelled into place.

Rings and a watch adorned his hands and wrist. His skin bore the effects of a life spent in places perpetually graced by the sun.

Everything carefully selected and maintained, no small part of his role was to convey the proper image, even if at this point it was largely only to those he employed.

Seated perpendicular to his desk, Reyes sat with elbows braced on the armrests of his chair. One ankle raised to the opposite knee, his fingers were steepled.

His focus was on the phone before him, the receiver lying flat, the call switched to speaker.

"You get eyes on?" Reyes asked.

"*Si*," Hector replied over the line. Even speaking his native tongue, his thick accent was apparent. "Walked out five minutes ago."

Despite having expected the information, Reyes couldn't stop the small clench that tugged at his core. The same one that had surfaced a week before, it wasn't hard to pinpoint the exact moment it had first arrived.

What was infinitely more difficult was trying to ascertain when there might be any hope of it receding.

"Just him?" he asked.

"*Si*," Hector repeated. "Stepped out alone. Some *puta* waiting for him."

Reyes's brows came together slightly as he flicked his gaze across the desk to Arlin Mejia. The only man that spent anywhere near the amount of time Reyes did inside the office, he too was already dressed for the day in gray slacks and a black pinstriped dress shirt.

Unlike Reyes, though, he was starting to show the effects of the recent stretch they'd been on. His already-thinning hair was heavily oiled, his scalp peeking through the ridges left behind by his comb. Bags hung under either eye, his chin and nose both appearing especially pointed.

A combination of age, stress, and dehydration.

"A woman?" Reyes asked.

"*Sí*," Hector replied. "Younger. Short, thick."

"Esmerelda," Mejia whispered.

Rocking his head back slightly, Reyes accepted the information. The younger sister, she had already moved north by the time he onboarded, his only interaction with her being a small handful of events over the years.

Ones like the night that everything had shifted.

Letting the news settle, Reyes sat in silence, pondering this new development.

By all accounts, Junior Ruiz had gone completely quiet while inside. Nobody had reportedly been to visit him in a long time. His phone calls and letters had started as a trickle before drying up to nothing.

An outcome that Reyes could have only hoped for when first taking over years before.

According to the contact at Lompoc that was paid very well to monitor such things, Ruiz and his sister hadn't spoken in ages. Not even in the last week, when word first broke that he might be getting out.

Yet, somehow, there she was, the dutiful sibling standing on the curb, waiting to drive him away.

One more item that made zero sense in all of this. One more thing that now needed to be monitored, taxing an organization that was already spread thin, focusing on other areas.

"Anybody else?" Reyes asked. "Media or anything?"

"No," Hector replied. "Right before sunrise, not a soul around."

Again, Reyes shifted his gaze to Mejia.

The original sentence for Junior Ruiz had been forty years. Convicted for multiple drug offenses – the list including trafficking, distribution, and a handful of related other charges - the court had been seeking to make an example of him.

Prosecutors had gone after the maximum sentences. Judges had postured, taking every opportunity to grandstand against everything the man and the enterprise he worked in represented.

The media had had a field day, a major score in the decades-long war on drugs.

Now, just eight years later, twenty percent through a stay that was said to have no chance at early release, he was walking out under cover of darkness with absolutely zero fanfare.

Junior Ruiz. The man that had been one of the largest players in the market for over a decade, credited by many for ushering in the second boon of cocaine traveling north across the border. Someone whose footprint was so large, his exit had created a vacuum that resulted in a veritable free-for-all across Baja, an eventuality Reyes himself was still benefitting from, even it had forced him up into California years before.

No part of it seemed to fit.

"Where are you now?" Reyes asked.

"Half-mile back on the 101, headed south."

Nodding, Reyes superimposed the information onto the map in his mind.

As best he could tell, the stretch of land they were now on was easily the most remote portion of the entire drive. From there, it was straight on into the greater Los Angeles area, everything becoming a dense mass of city and suburban sprawl all the way to San Diego.

Close to twenty million people all stacked into a single corridor.

Every road, every hotel, every airport, being a possible destination, Reyes with no way of knowing where Ruiz was headed.

So badly, he wanted to tell Hector to speed up. Catch them from behind, run them off the road, and grab Ruiz. Put a gun to the back of his sister's skull and demand to know what was going on, how he had gained his freedom, before wrapping both up as nothing more than loose ends.

But that wouldn't be wise. Not with so many eyes cast his direction, watching to see how he would proceed. Not with a small handful of his own staff still holdovers from the old regime, people who cut their teeth long ago, back when Ruiz was still in charge.

And certainly not with whatever juice Ruiz had leveraged in gaining his freedom lurking nearby.

"Okay, Hector. Stay on them, report back if anything changes."

"*Sí*," Hector replied a third time, cutting the line.

In the wake of it, Reyes remained seated as Mejia raised himself from the chair. Leaning forward, he lifted the phone from the desk, returning it to its cradle.

Watching him, Reyes remained silent, continuing to work through things in his mind.

"You're built to withstand this," Mejia said, settling himself back into his seat. "The reign of Junior Ruiz ended years ago."

Shifting only his gaze, Reyes looked across at the older man. "This – all of this – was his. You know it. I know it. Every single person we do business with knows it."

Lifting his brows just slightly in a shrug, Mejia said, "The key word being *was*. But, like anything, time moves forward. Things change.

"Ruiz might have been *El Jefe* in 2010, but today he's just a name. A hand people will make a point to stop and shake before coming to see you."

Both of those things, Reyes already knew. Just as he knew that Hector was the best urban tracker around. He would stay on them as long as it took, keeping him apprised of whatever may occur.

Still, things didn't quite feel right. There were too many layers, too many moving parts, any one of them capable of bringing down all that he'd been working toward for the last eight years.

Lowering his hands, Reyes reached for the coffee still resting on the edge of his desk. Taking up the mug, he allowed a single swallow, feeling the nutty warmth run back over his tongue.

Body craving more, he returned it to its original saucer, carefully placing it back in the same spot.

Appearance was of the utmost importance.

Now, more than ever.

"You worked closely with him, right?"

"I wouldn't say that," Mejia replied. "I was a warehouse guy back then. Nothing more than a hired hand."

"Still, you know him," Reyes countered. "Must have heard about some of his contacts, seen how he did business."

Lifting his gaze from the steaming mug, he stared across at Mejia. "Best guess, what the hell is all this right now?"

Chapter Nineteen

After that first sentence, Pally continued prattling on. He fired off a handful of questions, all pertinent and useful I'm sure. But I didn't hear a single one of them.

All I heard was that first sentence. The bombshell that Shawn Martin - my friend, one of my mentors - was dead.

And it had happened at the same exact time that some guy had showed up at my office and tried to use an exploding door to get to me.

Hitting me every bit as hard as the shattered remains of the door had smashed into Kaylan, I felt the air slide from my lungs. My chest and my stomach both pulled tight, a dull ring settling into my ears.

My mouth dropped open, all else fading to the background.

No longer did I notice the cold. Or the smell of blood on my shirt. Or even see the hospital before me.

All I could focus on were those six words, playing on repeat.

"Stop," I whispered. Despite barely being audible, Pally fell silent immediately, giving me the moment I needed.

Things were moving too quickly. From seeing Kaylan tossed back to this instant, it was all going too fast. I was being too reactive, allowing instinct and emotion to take over.

I had to stop, to think about what was happening.

"Martin is dead?" I asked, going clear back to the beginning. Even if it was a foolish question, Pally's answer bound to be exactly the same as the first time he said it, I needed to hear the words.

I had to start there and work my way forward.

"Yes."

"When?"

"Last night," Pally said. "Serra called 911 just after midnight."

Serra was Martin's wife. A wonderfully nice woman that was also my friend, and a friend to my wife before her passing.

"Last I heard, they were in Washington, way outside the city," I replied. "That still the case?"

"Yes."

Grunting softly, I nodded, even knowing there was nobody there to see it. "Midnight there would be one o'clock here. Obviously, it wasn't the same guy, because he's still sitting in the West Yellowstone jail, but it couldn't have even been a team.

"No chance someone makes it from here all the way over there in that amount of time. Not without a damn private aircraft, anyway."

"Right," Pally agreed, "but even if they weren't working together, have to think these are connected, right? What are the odds of both of you getting hit within hours of each other?"

He didn't bother to continue the thought, though he didn't need to. He was right, and we both knew it.

No chance that this occurred, states apart, years after we both retired from the public sector, on the same night by coincidence.

I didn't believe in the damn things to begin with, and even if I did, this would have been a stretch.

"What happened?" I asked. No part of me wanted the answer, though I still needed to hear it. For comparison purposes, if nothing else.

A clatter of keys was the first response. A moment later, he said, "Details are sparse, but the gist is a single shooter approached the home on foot. Shawn and Serra were both out back in the hot tub.

"Guy waited until they both slid down, came tearing out of the woods behind their house. Plugged him in the back of the head, back-handed her with the barrel of the gun to keep her quiet."

By the time he was done, my eyes were clamped down tight. My hands had curled into tight fists, the clench in my core having migrated outward to my entire body.

There was a time not that long ago when nobody would have gotten within a quarter mile of Martin's place without him knowing it. When he was still on the job, spent his days staring at active threats, he made sure every inch of his property and the surrounding area was secure.

Even more so after what happened to my family, I'm sure.

The years since must have eroded some of that. Moving to the mountains, leaving the life, he allowed his vigilance to come down.

And apparently someone had been out there, waiting.

"Meaning the shooting probably took place even earlier," I said. "That was just the first she was able to make it to the phone."

Pausing, as if considering it for the first time, Pally said, "Yeah."

Silence again fell as we both sat and chewed on things. We each added what the other had shared, trying to make things fit.

"Diggs?" I asked.

"Out of the country on assignment," Pally said. "I reached out to him, same as you. He's deep in the muck, undercover."

"I got a message his way, but who knows when he'll get it."

After retiring, Carl Diggs had spent a year or so bouncing around in civilian life before deciding he missed it too much. Without a wife or kids, he'd been too untethered. He felt his skills were going to waste, his bank account suffering, and had decided to go into the private sector.

Soldiers for hire, if you were the one collecting a paycheck.

More commonly known as mercenaries to everybody else.

Of the original team, Martin was the lead, Diggs his deputy, me the swing guy. Pally was on comms, and a man named Don Hutchinson was our handler and overseer out of the Southwest Head-quarters.

To this day, nobody knew where Pally lived, myself included. Hutch had died two years ago at my hand.

That was everybody.

And, again, way too much to be considered coincidence.

My mind raced. It tried to put everything from the last hours in context, attempting to add in years of prior history and case logs from our past time together.

"Who the hell..." I muttered, thoughts spilling out, my head unable to hold them all in. "And why now?"

"I don't know," Pally replied, taking the internal monologue as questions aimed his direction. "I've got every system I have working on that as we speak."

I took his cutting things off there to mean that he hadn't turned anything up yet, which wasn't terribly surprising. Together, we had worked hundreds of cases, most involving multiple players. Layers and layers of people spread across many countries, all with associates and family members that would love nothing more than to garner our home addresses.

A ton of scattershot information to try and sort through.

"While you do that, I'm going to go back over to the sheriff's office and see what they've gotten out of the guy that showed up here," I said. "I doubt he's said a word, but I guarantee they've at least ran his prints by now."

We both knew that unless the man was in the system for something, they would be worthless, but it was a start. Someplace to go, something to do while I cleared my head a bit, trying to make sense of everything happening.

"See if you can get a picture, too," Pally said. "Text it over to me, I'll put it through the databases."

Again, I nodded. "Will do, though fair warning, I mashed the hell out of his nose last night. No promises on what it'll look like."

Grunting softly, Pally asked, "You break it? Lots of blood?"

I had hit that man so hard, there was still a dull throb in my forehead. Already, I could feel a small lump protruding beneath the curtain of hair hanging to my eyebrows.

I could remember the bridge of his nose shattering, ground to splinters against my skull.

"Yeah."

"Good."

Any other time, I might have chuckled, or at least cracked a smile. I knew the sentiment Pally was getting at, wanting to feel like we at least got in one solid shot for the good guys.

As it was, I just wished I had hit him harder. That Kaylan hadn't been there, so I could have really gone to work on him.

"Have you talked to Serra?" I asked.

"Not yet. I called, but haven't gotten through."

That made sense, the home probably rife with police, all wondering what the hell had happened in their sleepy mountain town.

"When you do, can you tell her I'm on my way?" I asked.

I just needed to check on Kaylan first, make arrangements to ensure she would be okay. Then I had to stop by the sheriff's, get what I could from them.

After that, it was time to head west.

Chapter Twenty

A town the size of West Yellowstone would never be able to sustain a hospital. With just fifteen hundred full-time residents, there would barely be enough people around to staff the place, let alone take advantage of its services.

Even during the peak of tourist season, when the town size swelled to almost double, many of them prone to profound acts of stupidity, it just wouldn't have been a good investment. For the community, or for the state that would inevitably have to bail them out.

Care for the area instead started with the clinic on the western edge of town. More than capable of handling most small injuries, I'd even been there a few times myself for things that had happened while out with clients.

Almost all of them, again, springing from some act of foolishness.

Anything larger - such as a door exploding in Kaylan's face - was sent straight to the hospital in Big Sky. Fifty miles north, it was a straight shot up US-191.

Fifty miles of faint morning light just starting to break through the cloud cover above. Fifty miles of dense pine forest and barren highway.

Almost an hour to sit in silence, berating myself for everything I had done wrong the night before.

In the face of an active shooter, my reptile brain had completely taken over. Logic and reason had been pushed to the side, over-whelmed by self-preservation. The most powerful of all evoked responses, it had driven my every action from the moment the man had opened fire as I was scrambling onto the porch until my forehead connected with his nose, rendering him neutralized.

There was no way around that. The body was programmed to react the way it did for a reason.

Kaylan and I were both alive because of it.

In the moments afterward, though, I should have been smarter. I should have realized that just because Kaylan was hurt, she wasn't the only friend at risk.

Nor was she the only one I had the responsibility of taking care of.

A quick call to Pally, telling him to sound the alarm. A simple text, not even needing to type out a single word, a basic 911 sufficient to alert them to be watchful.

Anything more than what I had done. So worried about Kaylan, about calling for help, I had been blind.

No better than the foolhardy tourists I was always swapping stories about with the other guides.

Based on what Pally was telling me, there was no way to know when Martin had been put down. Trying to determine an exact time of death would be close to impossible, making it difficult to ever know if a message from me might have saved them.

But it damned sure wouldn't have hurt.

Reaching for the middle console of the truck, I grabbed up my cellphone. Sliding it onto my thigh, I draped my left hand atop the wheel, alternating glances between the device and the road ahead.

More concerned with any wildlife that might dart out than encountering my first vehicle in over fifteen minutes, I thumbed through the phone. Bypassing the recent call log, knowing the person I needed to speak to wouldn't show up there, I instead went straight to the address book.

Finding the listing I wanted, I raised my gaze, checking the clock on the dash. Halfway past six, my finger lingered above the screen, considering whether it was too early yet to call, before hitting send.

Hours before, I had had the chance to reach out to my friends and hadn't. Someone had died as a result.

Not again, even if it did cost another friend a little bit of sleep.

Besides, something told me she wouldn't mind.

The shrill ringtone echoed over the line, filling the cab of the truck, overpowering the sound of the road passing beneath my tires. Sounding off twice in order, it was snatched up in the middle of the third ring.

"Hawk," Mia Diaz answered. The first time I had heard her voice in more than a year, she sounded slightly out of breath.

But definitely not like she had just woken up.

"Diaz," I replied. "Sorry to call so early."

A year and a half earlier, Diaz and I had first met as part of a case that had pulled me out of retirement. Dragged back into the fold by a woman that had hired me as a guide and then tried to leave me for dead in the park, it had been a whirlwind week.

One that had seen me and Diaz work together to bring down a major new player in the drug trade coming over the border and allowed me to track down the people that had murdered my wife and daughter years before.

As the acting director of the Southwest field office, she had gone out of her way to help me. Even though it had turned out to her benefit, she hadn't known it at the time, doing me a solid based on nothing more than reputation and common history.

Six months later, I'd been able to repay the favor, acting as a protection detail for a vital witness to a desert human trafficking and drug mule ring.

In the time since, we had spoken little, though that wasn't for any particular reason beyond we were both busy people.

It happens.

"Don't be," she replied. "You know this job doesn't really afford sleep. I was in the shower, about to head in."

I did know exactly what she was referring to. During my time, Don Hutchinson – Hutch – was the area overseer. Seeming to age in dog years, I more than once commented that I wasn't sure why he even bothered with the expense of renting an apartment.

It wasn't like he was ever there.

"What's up?" she asked.

Under different circumstances, I would imagine the question to be the sort of thing that one friend might ask another. A basic greeting, a way to say hello, inquire as to what was new in the other's life.

Now, I took it for what I imagined was much closer to her intent.

Why the hell I was calling her at what was five-thirty in the morning along the west coast.

"Last night, a man broke into my office," I said. Every word I kept free of inflection, wanting her to hear the account more than any underlying animosity I had about it.

Of which there was plenty, both at the man and myself.

"Rigged the front door to explode, waited inside with a nine-millimeter to finish the job."

Whatever movement there might have been on the other end of the line ceased.

"You okay?"

Grunting softly, I replied, "My partner Kaylan happened to open the door before me. The blast dropped her on her head, cracked her skull, burned the hell out of her.

"Gave me enough time to get to cover, eventually neutralize the threat."

Remaining silent a moment, processing what I'd said, Diaz eventually asked, "Neutralized? As in...?"

"No," I said, getting her insinuation. "He is alive, currently in possession of the West Yellowstone sheriff. I'm on my way there now, see if they have an ID.

"Pally also wants me to snap a picture of him so he can start running facial rec."

During our first go-round together, I had introduced Diaz and Pally via video conference. A couple times since, I heard she had even hired him as a private consultant.

Again, Diaz remained quiet a moment. She seemed to piece

together what I had just said, adding it to the fact that I was calling at such an unseemly hour.

"And you think it was related to this place somehow?"

Pulling in a deep breath, I again felt my core draw in tight. Tiny pangs shot through my system, scads of thoughts and feelings too numerous to be singled out.

Self-loathing. Frustration. Anger. Confusion.

Grief.

"Seven hundred miles west of here, Shawn Martin was killed behind his home at the same exact time." Pausing, letting the bile that rose along the back of my throat from merely saying the words settle, I added, "He was the lead on our FAST crew the whole time I was there."

This time, I heard the slightest exhalation. "Oh, shit."

"Yeah," I muttered, bobbing my head in agreement.

Most people would have moved immediately from there into apologies. They would have offered condolences, asked if there was anything they could do.

But most of those people hadn't made a career doing the sorts of things we had.

"Pally looking into it?" she asked instead.

"Digging as we speak," I said. "As soon as I get anything from the sheriff, I'm going to send it his way. Hopefully it can aid in the hunt."

On the opposite end of the line, I could hear movement begin anew. Bare feet sliding over hardwood floor. Drawers being opened and closed.

A woman moving with purpose.

"After that, I'm going to head over to Washington," I said. "Talk to my friend's widow, maybe poke around a bit, see if anything else shakes loose."

"Okay," Diaz replied, her voice a bit terser than even a moment before. "You get anything, shoot it my way too. Like I said, I'm heading into the office now.

"I haven't heard about anything new going down, but I'll make it top priority."

Chapter Twenty-One

Sheriff Sam Latham was as much a West Yellowstone fixture as the Conoco station in the center of town or the enormous gateway into the park along the eastern edge. First elected twenty-five years prior, he'd been the recipient of running unopposed in the wake of the sitting sheriff keeling straight back at his desk from a heart attack.

Considering that the next in order would have to use the same desk in the same office, no one else had wanted the job.

After that, nobody had thought to challenge the kid that had slid into the vacancy, watching him grow from a cocky twenty-something into the man now in his early-fifties standing beside me.

Coming in at five-ten and weighing right at one-hundred-and-seventy pounds, he had sandy brown hair finger combed to the side and a matching mustache.

More or less the embodiment of the average American male.

Pulled in in the middle of the night by the deputy that had first responded to my call, he was dressed in jeans and flannel. A cup of coffee in one hand, the thumb of his opposite was hooked into the rear of his jeans. Body shifted toward me, just a couple of feet separating us, his gaze was aimed at the pane of one-way glass running the length of the room beside us.

At the man that I had first encountered in the front of my office the night before.

Without the black ski mask and under the harsh glare of the fluorescent bulbs above, the man was a stark contrast to the one I'd first encountered. Gone was the cocksure arrogance or the sense of control he had originally displayed. Missing was any hint of defiance.

In their place was a clear withdrawal. A defeatist attitude that hinted that he didn't care where he was or what happened next.

That he already knew his fate, regardless.

Seated on the far side of the lone metal table in the middle of the room, both wrists were cuffed to the bar rising from the center of it. Gaze focused on the bare tabletop before him, he sat with his shoulders rolled inward, a classic defense posture.

Free of his original ski mask, he had dark hair cropped short, tan skin peeking through.

With the benefits of time and light, his nose looked even worse than I remembered, a twisted mash of bone and cartilage. Blood was still smeared across his cheeks and upper lip, ending in an upturned arc across the middle of his face where the ski mask had been.

As macabre a grin as I had ever seen, like something the Joker might have worn in an old Batman comic.

"He said anything?" I asked, glancing from the glass to Latham.

"Not a word," the sheriff replied. "Rules say we have to offer medical treatment in clear instances of injury, water after so many hours.

"Most of the time, the tough guys at least pull it together to curse at us or tell us to go away. This one hasn't said a damn thing."

My own experiences with the sheriff were fairly limited, in an official capacity. Once before, my office had been broken into, that too part of the same incident that introduced me to Diaz. His crew had handled it capably, and I'd never heard any local chatter complaining about him or his office.

Besides, it wasn't like the town was in Compton or Southeast D.C.

Personally, I knew him to be an affable guy, someone that had made an effort to integrate into the community. Deacon at church, PTA, wave-when-people-drive-by sort.

Basically, someone that would have no reason to lie to me right now.

"Anything on an ID?" I asked.

Pulling his mouth back into a tight line, Latham shook his head. "We ran his prints, but nothing came up in the system."

Shifting his gaze from the glass to me, he glanced back over a shoulder, ensuring we were still alone. "And not to sound like a racist here, but based on appearances..."

The first part of his statement I let go as the sort of thing people in Montana said, even if they didn't recognize the irony in it.

The latter, I couldn't help but agree with, especially knowing all that I did.

The man was clearly Hispanic. Considering that the bulk of the work Martin and I did together was in South and Central America, it wasn't a stretch to believe that whoever was sent north after us hailed from one of those countries.

Making the odds of getting a hit low, just as Pally and I had all but said earlier.

"How about my office?" I asked.

"Deputy Ferry is there now, keeping it secure," Latham said. "We put in a call to Bozeman right after it happened last night requesting a crime scene crew, but they said they couldn't get here until morning."

"You know how that goes."

That too, I was familiar with. It was extremely unlikely that anything had happened the night before to warrant them needing to be kept in town. The more logical response was that they had heard about the incident, determined that nobody had died, and decided it could wait until morning.

When the day shift came on, and it was much warmer outside.

"I don't suppose you recognize him now, under the light?" Latham asked.

After the first time my office was broken into, I had made a point of sharing my background with Latham. A professional courtesy, if nothing else, in the event that anybody else ever showed up in town.

Over the time since, it hadn't been an issue, the conversation never mentioned again.

Not that there had been reason to.

Taking a moment, as much to prove I was seriously considering the question as anything, I stared in at the man. I tried to see past the garbled nose and the smears of blood, focusing on the face beneath.

"No," I replied. "Definitely never seen him around here."

A non-committal sound slid from Latham's throat. "But before, maybe?"

"Maybe, but he looks young. Like he wouldn't have been much more than a late teenager back when I was still involved."

Not that that would necessarily mean anything. There was virtually zero chance whatever slight our team had committed was perpetuated on this guy directly. He was nothing more than a pawn, sent up to do someone else's bidding.

That's just how things were done.

"I checked in with my contacts on the drive back down this morning. They said they haven't heard of anything new going down, but asked that I take a picture and send it over. You mind?"

Lifting a hand, Latham motioned to the glass before us. Adding nothing more, he waited as I slid my cellphone from my back pocket and pressed it tight to the glass. Zooming in, I snapped off a trio of shots before pulling it back.

Head down, I worked my way through the various programs on my phone, attaching the images to emails addressed to both Pally and Diaz.

When I was done, I returned the phone to my rear pocket. "Thanks."

Grunting out a soft reply, Latham nodded before shifting his gaze back in my direction. "How's Kaylan doing?"

Chapter Twenty-Two

The air was redolent with fresh pine wood. The kind used for boxing and transporting wine, thin slats that housed the bottles, allowing them to breath.

A most vital aspect when operating under the intense blaze of the Southern California sun.

Mixed in with the smell was the cornucopia of usual scents that always accompanied Ramon Reyes's trips to the warehouse. Diesel fuel and exhaust from the forklifts that lifted and moved the pallets of wine. The sweet underlying smell of grapes that seemed to linger on the periphery, a result of the rare occasional breakage.

Sawdust. Manure. A hundred other things that also came with owning a vineyard.

Walking in tandem with Arlin Mejia, Reyes crossed out of the bright morning sun and into the shade of the warehouse that served as the shipping hub for his operation. Large enough to house the better part of a football field, the place was made entirely from corrugated metal. Gaps were cut from the ceiling, enormous paddle fans turning overhead used for ventilation.

Beneath their feet was brushed concrete, stripes of rubber from the forklifts streaked across it. In equal amounts were bits of mud and straw, Reyes careful to lift his feet over them, not wanting to ruin the polished look of his loafers.

Not so early in the day, with so much still left to do.

Given his preference, Reyes would still be posted up in his office. He would be staring at the phone, or − better yet − a video feed from Hector as he closed in on Junior Ruiz.

As he put an end to the newest threat to the empire Reyes was working so hard to build.

Such a thing would never abide, though. Not for someone like Reyes, that prided himself in being hands on. Always in control, not even wanting his people to see him diving haphazardly into his morning coffee.

They had to know that he was put together. That he had the best interests of all in sight, the work they were doing in service to someone that was working even harder.

That he had a plan, a vision for how things were going to run.

For things such as the warehouse they were now standing in, the vineyard spread for acres in every direction around it. All part of the relocation and expansion project he had undertaken in recent years, a concerted effort not just to stay with the times, but to be out in front of them.

To set the market, letting others fight in vain to keep up.

A clean start, on the north side of the border. A clear demarcation from the old regime with a new business model moving forward.

And a way to make sure he didn't make the same mistakes as his predecessor, dropping onto a radar that would one day land him in prison as well.

Keeping all such thoughts sealed tight, his features neutral, Reyes walked across the open end of the warehouse. Barely aware of Mejia keeping pace beside him, he moved by the small office carved out from the front corner. His stride never broke as he went past the steel holding tanks lining the wall, his focus unwavering as he headed for the cargo truck sitting along the rear wall.

With the rolltop door on the back-end pushed all the way up, a forklift sat just off the rear bumper. A full load balanced across the tongs, the machine held it six feet off the ground, a trio of men inside the truck making steady trips to unload it.

Moving with practiced precision, the men said nothing. Never did they slow, one trip after another after another.

With the temperature already starting to warm inside the confines of the warehouse, Reyes could see perspiration forming on their dark skin.

"Good morning!" Reyes called as he approached, drawing the attention of the men in the truck. In turn, each raised a hand to their brow, mumbling their greetings.

Never did they slow, the ritual one that occurred with practiced regularity.

In their stead, the man tasked with driving the forklift slid from his seat. No more than five-six in height, he was dressed in jeans and a blue canvas work shirt, a crumpled hat balanced across his dark hair.

Moving in a quick shuffle, he shot a hand down along the inside of his waistband, straightening his shirt, before thrusting the same hand out before him.

"*Buenos días, Signor.*"

"Good morning, Manny," Reyes replied, making a point of doing so in English.

It was no secret that every man there spoke Spanish, the native tongue for all present, Reyes included.

A fact that made it that much more imperative that they speak English whenever possible. The more they did, the more comfortable they became.

And the more comfortable they became, the wider the possibilities became for the operation, the less obvious they were to anybody that might be paying attention.

Ignoring that the man had just shoved his hand around the inside of his jeans, Reyes reciprocated the shake of his warehouse foreman. "How are things going this morning?"

"Good, good," Manny replied, the words heavily tinged with accent. "We'll have this truck loaded and headed to the airport within twenty minutes. The next one will be here on the hour."

"Headed where?" Mejia asked. His hands clasped behind his

back, he made no effort to step forward, to offer any kind of greeting to Manny.

Something Reyes was long past trying to force onto the two of them, so long as that was the extent of their open defiance of one another.

Especially in moments like this, while in the presence of others.

"Split load," Manny replied. "Half to Phoenix, the rest to Denver."

"How many bottles?" Reyes asked.

"Six hundred total," Manny answered.

Always careful to keep his responses muted, Reyes gazed past Manny into the open maw of the truck. Three hundred bottles served as a nice sale. A couple years prior, when they were just starting to dabble with this and looking to scratch out a platform, they would have been happy with a fraction of that.

Six hundred had to be one of their best loads ever.

Things were coming along. They were moving in the right direction, finally putting together what they deserved.

Which made handling the situation with Junior Ruiz quickly and efficiently all the more imperative.

Chapter Twenty-Three

Eight years, Junior Ruiz had called the inside of a prison cell home. Fifteen feet in length, half that in width. Every single day shared with another human being.

Arguably sixty square feet to himself.

And even that had felt less confined than the interior of the Chrysler.

"You alright over there?" Esmera asked. Glancing over from the driver's seat, she had one hand wrapped around the outside of the steering wheel. The opposite was running back through her hair, red fingernails flashing against dark locks. "I don't remember you being so fidgety."

For only an instant, Ruiz felt acrimony flash inside him. A quick flare that rose fast, making it as far as his eyes before dying out as suddenly as it had arrived.

Absolutely no good would come from lashing out at his sister. It wasn't Esmerelda he was upset with, it was the fact that she was right.

Once upon a time, the drive south wouldn't have bothered him in the slightest. The front seat would have been perfectly comfortable. The faint melodies on the radio a nice undercurrent to the ebb and flow of conversation.

Now, all he could concentrate on were the semi-trucks bunched tight to either side. The way cars seemed so close outside his window he could reach out and touch them, all moving at eighty miles an hour. The way his backside bunched against the padded springs of the passenger seat.

The myriad of questions that he still had, with no clear way of knowing when – or even if – he would ever get answers to them.

And everything he needed to do in the coming days, where to begin one of many things he'd been chewing on since first meeting Jones and Smith.

"Yeah," he replied. "Just didn't remember the drive being quite so long."

"It's usually not," Esmera said. "It's because they released you at the crack ass of dawn and that meant we hit LA right at morning rush hour."

Flicking his gaze to the dash, Ruiz took in the time, just minutes after eight, before shifting back to the world outside. Already, the sun was well above the horizon, streaming in over his sister's shoulder. Warming the confines of the car, he would guess that they would hit the mid-seventies by afternoon, if not a little higher.

The first time in ages he didn't openly loathe the thought of sunshine or the warmth it brought with it.

The choice to leave at dawn was his. Prudence would have said that he should wait until eight or nine in the morning, but prudence hadn't spent the last eight years pinned up tight. It hadn't constantly had an eye out, even in the presence of the closest things he had to friends.

Even if he'd known Esmera would be the one dragged out to come get him, he still would have picked the same time.

The car ride now through traffic was miserable. That much was obvious. As was the fact that his clothes stank. And that he had a lot longer to go on the path to reintegration than he'd ever realized.

But it was still better than sitting another minute inside.

"Ought to try making it twice in ten hours," Esmera added. "Longest two-hundred-mile trip of my life."

Ruiz rolled his attention away from the window. He bunched his gaze tight against the sun streaming through, extending a hand and balancing it on her shoulder.

Truth was, he hadn't quite known what to expect when he'd stepped out. As far as he knew, outside of a couple calls placed via Burris, nobody else was even aware of his release. The night before was the first time he'd even mentioned needing someone to come and get him, but that had been more for the sake of challenging them.

Not once had he actually expected it to be her, nor would he have even believed it possible.

So much so that in the moment he'd been surprised to see her standing there, but now with the benefit of hours in the car to consider it, he had to admit it was perfect.

Even if it had sparked just as many questions in her as the last week or two had for him, the open-ended statement she'd just floated likely the closest she would get to actually voicing them. Nothing more than a gentle nudge, letting him know anything he was willing to share, she was willing to hear.

A response couched in years of having a sideline seat to his business dealings.

"Two hundred miles," Ruiz said, repeating the last part of her statement. "That would mean we're headed..."

"Home," Esmera replied. Glancing over his way, she added, "San Diego. Or just north of it in Escondido, rather."

The last Ruiz had seen his sister, she was still in college at UCLA, living in the heart of Los Angeles. From there, she'd stayed in the city after graduation, working as an assistant at one of the myriad production houses in Culver City, before finally cashing out and heading south.

All of that he was intimately aware of, making sure his sister was watched over a demand he had taken great pains to ensure long before he went inside.

A fact he would never dream of mentioning out loud.

"Home," Ruiz whispered instead, repeating the word, placing it out there gently, as if tasting it for the first time.

Not in a long time had he had any concept of such a thing, all thoughts banished, pushed away in a desperate attempt at self-preservation.

"Yeah," Esmera replied. Turning her chin an inch toward him, she kept her gaze on the road, making sure her lane was clear, before chancing another glance his way. "I mean, if you want. I don't know what your plans are, but you're welcome to stay as long as you'd like."

This time, there was no hiding the parade of thoughts, feelings, that spiked within Ruiz. Beginning with shock, it immediately passed into surprise before finally ceding to something else entirely.

The relationship with his sister – with his entire family, for that matter – had been rocky, even in the best of times. Now almost a decade removed, there was no denying how much some things had changed, how many things he still needed to get caught up on.

Despite the appearance of happiness on Esmera's face as he stepped out that morning, there was no way of knowing just how she'd receive his sudden release. The fact that she was present was a start, but that was before considering whatever had been done to get her there.

"Thank you for doing this," Ruiz said. His voice low and even, he was careful to keep away any of the various emotions he felt. "I know these last years, things couldn't have been easy."

Shrugging her right shoulder, Esmera pressed her cheek against the top of his hand. Pressing it tight, she held the pose a moment before releasing.

"You're welcome, big brother. And no, they haven't been. But if that shiner you've got is any indicator, I'd say they've been hard on us all."

Letting his hand fall away, his fingers slid down over her arm before recoiling back to his lap. Turning back to face forward, he felt his features harden slightly. His vision blurred as he stared at nothing in particular.

He'd done what he could in case something like what happened eventually came to pass, but there were some things no amount of money and planning could accommodate.

Hearing his sister's words only confirmed as much.

There would be plenty of time for her questions. Maybe with enough of it, he might even begin to give her some of those answers.

The rest, he would still need to cull together for himself.

Until then, his focus had to be on other matters. On looking forward, trying to make the most of the situation that had been placed before him.

"Tell me about them," he whispered, ignoring her remark about the bruising still covering his face.

"Them what?" Esmera asked, dark hair flashing as she looked his way.

"The last years. And please, leave nothing out."

Chapter Twenty-Four

The drive from West Yellowstone to the town of Snoqualmie, Washington was listed as eleven hours. Even driving slightly above the speed limit, taking advantage of the lax stance of Montana Highway Patrol on any truck bearing local plates, the best I could do was ten.

Under most circumstances, I probably would have opted to fly. If the goal was merely to go for a visit, or even to get there as fast as possible, I would have driven the hour and change up to Belgrade. From there, I would have caught a quick plane over to Seattle, rented a car, and driven due east.

Assuming that flight schedules lined up, I could have been there in somewhere between five and six hours. Technically less than that, counting the time difference.

But these weren't most circumstances.

For starters, I knew Martin was already dead. That if someone had wanted Serra and the children gone as well, they would already be as well. Based on what little Pally knew, the opportunity had been there many times over.

In fact, the intruder had gone out of their way to render Serra unconscious without killing her.

Point being that my getting there four hours faster really wouldn't mean a great deal to the Martin family. As much as it probably didn't feel like it - probably wouldn't ever again - there was no immediate threat.

I also knew that whoever it was had likely put five hundred miles between them and the Martin house by now. This wasn't a thrill killer, wasn't someone that would get off on waiting around to watch the first responders arrive. Damned sure wouldn't stand by the driveway with concerned neighbors, wondering what happened, offering to be of service.

Largely because there weren't any neighbors. This wasn't a random incident, certainly not a stranger selected from a pack to fulfill some inner longing.

This was a carefully chosen and planned attack. Just like the one that had occurred at my office the night before.

All of that taken together meant that opting to drive was the best path. Still having no idea what I might find, who might be out there targeting our team, the truck gave me the option of bringing along whatever toys I needed. It ensured that unlike the night before, I wasn't caught empty handed again.

That whenever the next person showed up looking to finish the job, I wouldn't be left with nothing more than misdirection and luck to make it through.

Something that simply wouldn't be possible on an airplane.

The second benefit of driving was the time it afforded me. Nothing but hours of open highway. The ability to set the cruise control, point myself toward the western horizon, and get lost in my thoughts.

The last time I had seen Shawn Martin was six years before. On hand the day I had turned in my badge and gun at the DEA Southwest Headquarters, he hadn't tried to talk me out of it. Hadn't said a word, in fact.

He had known my wife Elizabeth. And my daughter Alice. He'd been one of the first to arrive at my house the night they were taken from me. Had sat with Diggs by my side through those first long days, when I was nothing more than a shuffling zombie, my cheeks encrusted with ash and soot, streaked by tears.

Just as he'd known what their loss did to me. The fact that there was no way I could ever go back to work, pretending that it wasn't the very reason they were gone.

Instead, he'd merely given me a hug. Not the sort of quick, one shoulder, side bump that people like to do today.

An actual embrace. The type that grown men so rarely share.

One that told me in an instant that he was there for whatever I needed, wherever I ended up.

Hour by hour I pushed west, crossing from Montana into Idaho. Another hour after that, I moved into Washington, breaking in Spokane for fuel and gas station food before getting on my way again.

A mile at a time, I watched the world peel by on either side, the sun catching me from behind, eventually moving out ahead of me as I drove. Around me, the landscape moved from mountain and forest to agricultural. Orchards and open pastures with enormous irrigation pivots pushed in tight along the road.

Barely registering any of it, I kept my focus straight ahead, the cruise control set as I moved on.

It's natural for someone to feel a strong affinity for the people that they directly worked with. To perhaps place them on a pedestal, using the crucible of intense shared experience to impart a status on them that wasn't quite earned.

I knew that. I wasn't boorish enough to believe that my experiences were tremendously different from thousands of other servicemen in various branches. That my judgement was somehow beyond reproach compared to theirs.

But I also knew that of the multitude of people I had encountered in my time in both the DEA and the Navy, Shawn Martin was one of the good ones. The top whatever percent. The type of guy that as much I might have hated the thought of my daughter one day dating, I would have hoped would be the one she brought home to meet us.

Same for his wife. And - I imagine - their kids, barely more than babies when I last saw them.

Even if nobody had shown up at my office the night before, I couldn't imagine any of the Martins to have been dabbling in anything illicit. To have crossed paths with anybody that might be willing to go to these lengths.

It all had to go back to our service in the Administration.

The only questions were who and why now, after all this time.

Exactly ten hours after rolling out of West Yellowstone, nothing more than a duffel bag and a gun case in hand, I pulled into the town of Snoqualmie. Dragging my phone over onto my lap, I called the navigational system back to life, raising the volume.

Following the instructions of the bossy automaton, I rolled past a small and quaint downtown. On the edge of it, I again stopped for gas, not knowing what the coming hours might hold and wanting to be prepared for anything.

In addition, I once more loaded up on a plastic sack of groceries. Protein bars and granola and Gatorade, easy fuel sources that could be eaten while driving if need be.

And the largest coffee the place sold.

Five minutes after that, I was back behind the wheel. My stomach too tight to even consider food, I left the sack in the passenger foot well. The coffee I took down in long pulls, starting to become faintly cognizant of the fact that I had just missed an entire night's sleep.

Something that would have likely been more apparent if not for the cocktail of adrenaline and confusion that had been powering my mind for the better part of a day and counting.

"In a quarter mile, turn left."

Doing as instructed, I took a narrow two-lane into thick forest. On either side, overgrown pine forest pushed in tight, almost blotting the afternoon sky from view.

"Your destination will arrive in one half mile."

Prickly heat rose to my face and back as I followed the instructions. Pushing the coffee into the middle console, I leaned forward.

Gripping the wheel tight in both hands, I steeled myself for whatever lay ahead.

Chapter Twenty-Five

According to the address Pally gave me and the visual on the screen of my phone, the Martin home sat back more than a quarter mile off the road. Accessible via an asphalt drive carved from the forest, it shot out from the road I was on at a ninety-degree angle. Visible for less than fifteen yards, it disappeared into a hard turn, effectively leaving anybody driving by with a view of nothing but dense trees.

That part didn't surprise me. It would have been one of a thousand tiny details Martin undertook to ensure his family's safety.

It wasn't like the man would bring them all this way out here only to have the place sitting right on the road, a neon sign flashing their name resting atop the mailbox.

What did surprise me was the cruiser sitting at the mouth of the drive.

Or, more aptly, the young deputy standing in the middle of the drive as I approached. Dressed in dark tan slacks and a matching winter jacket, a flat-brimmed hat was pulled low on his head.

Beneath it, red hair peeked out, offset by a thin moustache and pale skin.

Opie Taylor, in the flesh and all grown up.

At most, he couldn't have been more than twenty-five. The youngest man in the office, assigned to the worst possible detail.

Pushing down a handful of smart remarks, I unlatched my door and stepped out. Moving slow, I was careful to keep my hands visible at all times.

My gaze remained fixed on the young man as I did so. Even with the better part of twenty yards separating us, I couldn't help but note his rigid posture and the way his upper body twisted to the side, hand inching back toward his hip.

"Good afternoon," I said. Not wanting to trend into levity, I was sure to keep my tone even, my voice loud enough to be easily understood.

The young man flicked his gaze over me and the truck. "Afternoon."

"My name is Hawk Tate, I was a friend of the deceased," I said. Pausing, I added, "Served with him in the Air Force, long time ago."

Of the original team, Martin was the only one that had been in the Air Force. I was a Navy guy, Diggs a Delta operator with the Army.

Not that there was any way this kid could know that. Or that it really even mattered, the point of the statement to build camaraderie. To make the young man think we were all parts of the same circle, provide some form of equal footing, easing away a bit of the obvious trepidation he carried.

The military was something most law enforcement could identify with. Even those like this string bean, who would barely be able to stand under the weight of full field gear, wouldn't think to say anything against former Air Force buddies.

Mentioning the DEA, however, was a different animal. The history of local and federal agencies interacting was littered with stories both sides would just as soon forget.

Considering the statement for a moment in silence, the coiled stance of the young man relaxed just slightly.

"Sorry about your friend. I didn't know him, but my captain said he was a good guy."

Shawn Martin was a good guy. The kind that would have made a point to find the local police captain and introduce himself. Not just the way I had with Latham, but as a genuine offer to help should the need ever arise.

"Thank you," I replied. "He was that."

Flicking my gaze to the drive twisting away behind the cruiser parked before me, I saw nothing but dense woods. Aside from the young officer there didn't appear to be any signs of life, the initial crime scene crew likely having come and gone.

"Listen, I'm sorry to bother you," I said, "but Serra asked if I could come out and grab some things for her and the kids. They left in such a hurry after what happened..."

Whatever bit of hesitance had seeped out of the man a moment before seemed to return, his hand drawing back another quarter inch, his eyes bulging.

A stance I had to admit was fair. If standing in his shoes and a man that looked like I did showed up claiming to need access to a fresh crime scene, I would have likely reacted in the same way.

Widening my fingers just slightly, making it clear that they were empty and would remain that way, I added, "Last I talked to her, she was still at the station. Feel free to call and verify."

The ruse was weak at best, but it was all I had. It had been years since I'd had Serra's direct number, and I knew that any hope of getting into the house without her explicit say-so wasn't happening.

Not without resorting to overrunning this poor kid, a prospect that wouldn't have been an issue - even with him being the only one of us armed - but it would have created a whole host of other problems I didn't need.

Not right now, having no idea what else I might be delving into in the near future.

That left relying on educated inference, hoping that she was still with the local police or easily accessible. And that Pally had gotten through to her earlier and told her I was on my way.

"For her and the kids?" the young man asked, his voice betraying just a hint of uncertainty.

"Yeah, the twins," I replied. "Stevie and Samantha."

Cracking a thin smile, I added, "What can I say? Folks like the letter S."

Chapter Twenty-Six

The instructions on the call that morning hadn't been explicitly clear, but that was by design. Famously paranoid, the man never said a word that wasn't absolutely necessary.

All with good reason, as Tres Salinas was abundantly aware.

Over a phone, from a thousand miles away, every snippet was meant to be deliberately vague. It was to ensure that if anybody was listening – on either end – there would be enough wiggle room that any decent lawyer could get it tossed.

And more importantly, that nobody looking for the slightest hint of their intentions would be able to decipher them.

Not that Tres needed things to be any more obvious than they already were. The real information underlying the exchange had been shared a week earlier, before he ever left for Seattle.

If anything was to go sideways, if Tres's counterpart was unable to complete the mission in any way, such a call would be coming. And if it did, the new goal was to snip away the loose end.

Delivered one-on-one, it was a mirror copy of the talk Tres was certain the other man sent north had gotten in the event that he fell short.

After receiving the call that morning, Tres had attempted to get a couple more hours of rest. Finding it a futile gesture, his body still too charged from the night before, his mind unable to slow down, he had risen and gone straight to the shower before heading down to breakfast.

An hour later, his stomach full and his bag packed, he had called for an early checkout.

An hour beyond that, he was already east of Seattle. Taking advantage of morning traffic heading in the opposite direction, he had set the cruise control at a conservative four miles above the speed limit.

Not wanting to give anybody any extra reason to glance at the vehicle with the out-of-town plates, he had steadily worked his way across the state. Not until he reached Spokane, just miles from the eastern border, did he stop.

Going straight to the airport, he had performed essentially the same swap he had in Seattle. Leaving his car in the long-term lot, he'd picked up a nondescript sedan with Idaho plates, the lady behind the counter barely glancing up at him as she completed the paperwork and handed over the keys.

Looking strictly at the map, going on to Bozeman would have made the most sense. Infinitely closer to his destination, he could have gotten a rental at the airport there, done what he needed to, and swapped things back when it was over.

If not for common sense, he might have even done so.

The vehicle he was currently driving was registered in California, with plates that bore out as much. Plates that didn't raise a ton of eyebrows in Washington, but definitely would as he crossed into Idaho. Even more as he made his way across Montana.

Not exactly the best approach for trying to slip in and out of a place unnoticed.

After the week Tres had had - the long drive north, the days spent in surveillance - the trip was one of the very last things he wanted to be doing. But he understood it. He recognized the need for making a clean break, of finishing what they had set out to.

Especially given the changes that would soon be upon them.

Hours after leaving Spokane - and nearly half a day after getting the phone call in his hotel room - Tres rolled into the town of West Yellowstone. Like every other place he had been in the last week, it was his first time there, the place fitting with every preconceived notion he'd ever had.

Buildings that were made from logs with metal roofs and signs carved by chainsaws. Pickup trucks driven by guys wearing boots and cowboy hats.

Bone-numbing cold, the temperature staring up at him from the display on his dash, flashing on the roadside signs of every bank he passed.

Arriving just before dark, Tres made a slow and careful loop through town. Going just fast enough not to be noticed, he took in every detail of the small enclave, from the medical facility sitting on the western edge to the sheriff's office just off the main drag.

The small cabin on the north end of town with crime scene tape stretched across an open doorway.

Committing it all to memory, Tres pushed north out of town as fast as he'd arrived. Knowing better than to step out, to let anybody see his face before it was absolutely vital, he leaned on the gas.

Acting now would be the polar opposite of what he'd just done in Snoqualmie. It would be hasty, and it would be sloppy.

He refused to let that happen.

Chapter Twenty-Seven

I wasn't surprised to find that Serra was no longer at the house when I arrived. Given what had happened, it would have been a stretch for anybody to stay onsite where their husband had been shot in cold blood less than twenty-four hours before.

Every room, every item, would be an associated memory. Every noise would cause a flinch, the fear being that the shooter would return to finish the job.

From the moment Serra came to and found her husband dead, her chief concern would have been protecting the children. Both in the literal sense of keeping them alive, and in the grander view of shielding them from everything that had just taken place.

If forced to guess, I would imagine that she would return to the house at most once, ever. She would ask local law enforcement, or her family, or even me, to escort her up during daylight hours. A mad dash through the place, she would snag whatever she could for her and the kids, tossing it all in the car before leaving, never to return.

Anything beyond that would be left to movers.

Or auctioneers.

I also wasn't surprised that the on-the-fly tale that I put together wasn't enough to get me past the officer standing guard, but it was sufficient for him to take a step back and put in a call to the office. Even without having heard the run-up, the mere mention of my name was enough for Serra to offer her blessing to allow me inside the house.

Once such an edict was issued, the man before me visibly relaxed, as if relieved that he didn't have to act in some way. Stating only that I wasn't to impede on the crime scene itself at all, he happily stepped aside to let me pass.

Even offered his condolences for my friend and thanks for my service.

Handshakes and well wishes all around.

Both retreating to our respective vehicles, I had waited behind the wheel as he eased the cruiser to the side of the lane. Turning parallel to allow me a clear lane to pass, I raised a hand as I passed, the deputy returning the gesture before pulling back into position, effectively closing the gate behind me.

And ensuring that I had at least the next few minutes to operate without fear of someone walking up on me unexpectedly.

Nudging the gas just slightly, I followed the winding driveway. Behind me, the cruiser disappeared from view, swallowed by the thick tangle of pine and birch trees pushing in tight along either side.

To the front, the paved driveway cut an asphalt ribbon through the dense forest, visibility limited to no more than a few dozen yards at a time.

Classic Martin, if there ever was such a thing.

Feeling one corner of my mouth rise into a smile, I couldn't help but give a slight shake of my head at the thought of my friend.

Just as fast, the smile faded, replaced by the realization of how long it had been since we'd actually spoken.

A hundred times over I'd thought about the guys in the preceding years, maybe even considered picking up the phone and giving them a call. As was human nature, though, it hadn't happened. Always there had been an excuse. Some bullshit rationalization or belief that whatever I was doing was more important. Or that they wouldn't want to hear from me.

Or, whatever.

It was the same as it had been with the last of my remaining family until just recently, my niece being kidnapped the kick I needed to finally bridge that gap.

More of the self-loathing I'd been feeling since the incident at my office the night before rose through my core. Rising the length of my throat, it tasted bitter on my tongue as I nudged the gas a touch higher, pushing my truck almost a quarter mile before reaching a clearing carved out of the forest.

Obviously done for the purpose of construction, the space was the better of a hundred yards square. Positioned in the exact center of it was a home, anybody attempting to approach being forced to cover forty yards or more of open ground, regardless which direction they were coming from.

A two-story structure, it appeared to be made in one of the newer modern styles utilizing nothing but steel and glass. Boxy in nature, thick poles rose straight to the roof every ten feet or so, effectively cutting the front façade into eight equal pieces.

Of those, the two bottom corners had both been fashioned into outdoor areas, the one on the right serving as a front porch beside a concrete landing for car parking.

On the back end, I could see the hot tub where Martin had taken his last breath, the entire quadrant of the house sectioned off with yellow police tape. Most of the snow on the ground around it had been stripped away by the warmth of the day and untold amounts of foot traffic, leaving behind mud and matted grass.

Fighting to keep any emotional responses at bay, to not let them cloud my true purpose for being onsite, I followed the curve of the driveway.

Approaching from the south end, the side of the home was built much like the front. Instead of there being four equal sections across, there was only two in depth, the same glass and metal design comprising the outline, allowing for clear lines of sight.

Climbing out, I pushed the door shut just far enough to catch the latch. For a moment, I stood rooted in place, my gaze flicking back through the driver's side window, considering whether or not I should return for the gun stowed behind the seat.

Images of the night before passed through my mind, my initial response being to go back for it, before deciding in the negative.

There was no way the person that had done this was returning. Not right now, there being no reason to do so. Martin was gone. If they wanted Serra dead, they had ample opportunity already.

Same for the kids.

All my going inside carrying a gun would do was make things extremely uncomfortable should Deputy Opie decide to peek in on me while I was still inside.

Twisting my focus away from the truck, I instead concentrated on the world around me. I tried to listen for any sounds, hoped to pick up any out-of-place scents.

More than a minute I stood, waiting, analyzing, before finally giving up on it, the world completely still, as if it too was in mourning.

Turning for the front door, I ascended a trio of steps before passing inside. Coming to a pause with my heels just over the threshold, I waited to allow my eyes to adjust to the dim light, taking in everything around me.

Despite the modern architecture of the outside, the interior was meant to resemble more of a North Woods lodge. Directly in front of me was an oversized living space, split log furniture with Pendleton blankets on leather cushions. On the floor was a flattened bearskin. Overhead hung a deer antler chandelier.

Spread out wide to the right was an open kitchen and dining room. Same design as the living room, the kitchen table and bar stools all employed the same motif. Behind them, appliances of stainless steel lined the counter.

Whoever the last person out had been earlier had turned off the lights. Thin sunshine filtered in through the front windows, illuminating a line of dried footprints across the hardwood floor, likely left behind by Serra when she stumbled back inside, and dust motes drifting through the air.

Otherwise, there was absolutely nothing to intimate a crime had occurred the night before.

Again, my thoughts returned to the man currently sitting in West Yellowstone. So badly I wished that he had said something when we met in my office. Or I had walked in to catch him going through something specific.

That his damn face had registered in even the slightest way.

Anything that might give me a bearing on what this was all about or what I should now be looking for.

But none of that had happened. Not one thing to help me sort through all the cases we had worked and all the people we had no doubt pissed off over the years.

Right off the top of my head, more than a dozen different people came immediately to mind. People that we had put out of business or sent to prison or in some other way interfered with their plans.

People that needed someone to blame, something to fixate on in all the years since.

People looking to make a statement now.

Letting out a sigh, I again glanced around the space. The home that my friend had built with his family. The place that had been violated, that none of them would ever be returning to.

Surveying the scene, I figured I had twenty minutes. A full third of an hour before my snooping became too obvious to ignore.

As it turned out, I barely needed half of that.

Part Three

Chapter Twenty-Eight

Much like the front seat of the Chrysler that Junior Ruiz had ridden on all the way back from Lompoc, the sofa in the front room of Esmera's house was almost too soft. Utilizing overstuffed cushions and a brushed velvet covering, the piece seemed to swallow him whole, forming around his body.

It left him feeling like he was trapped, pinned in place.

A sensation he despised, eight years of ingrained response telling him to avoid. To jump up, find a wall and put his back to it immediately, never knowing who might want to prove themselves against someone like him.

Forcing himself to remain seated, to not let his sister see any such thought occurring beneath the surface, he instead cast a quick look around the place.

When he had first been sent away, his kid sister was still a senior at UCLA. Two hours north, she was in the center of Los Angeles, living the college apartment life.

Buoyed by the occasional cash infusions from both Ruiz and their mother, she had a nice place she shared with a pair of roommates. Also both young Latinas – one a fellow student, the other a recent graduate – the three had done everything that was expected of a trio of beautiful young ladies in the big city.

Hosting pre-parties every weekend before hitting the clubs. Saturday afternoons at the beach, sprawled out in the sand, making sure to be seen. Trips to the gym in full hair and makeup.

More than once during those years, their mother had pulled Ruiz aside to express concern for the girl. She had not been a fan of her going away to the big city for school, wanting her to try something smaller - or even more preferable - staying home.

She had worried that the life and all the trappings that went with it would be too much. That eventually Esmera would get hurt or end up pregnant or potentially something even worse.

Each time such worries were brought to the fore, Ruiz had walked his mother back. He assured her that she had raised a good daughter, that she was just being young and having fun, would eventually make her way back and settle into the life she was meant to lead.

A stance made easier to believe by the fact that he always had someone keeping an eye on her.

Never once had he mentioned that to either one of them, just as he would never mention continuing to do so in the time since, the place he was now sitting in having proved his faith in the young girl correct.

Now thirty years of age, gone was the blown-out hair and off-the-shoulder wardrobe. Missing also was the overdone makeup and bright nail polish. Even toned down were the loud banter and boisterous laugh, all things that had at one point been part of a calculated effort to draw attention. To fit into some sort of preconceived ideal.

In their place was a woman that had aged much more than just eight years in his time away. With the exception of the occasional playful barb, her words were carefully selected, her gestures minimal and withdrawn.

How much those changes could be attributed to his being away directly he could only guess at, though he couldn't imagine the time had been all that easy on her.

Certainly not with everything else that had happened as well.

"You have a beautiful home," Ruiz said, casting a glance about the place.

Aside from the sofa he was now seated on, there was a pair of matching armchairs. All three of the same style, they were arranged in a horseshoe, a coffee table in the center.

Opposite them was an entertainment center and a flat-screen television, a pair of electronic boxes of some sort on the shelf below them.

Framing it on the wall to either side were a collection of photos, the left a collage of who Ruiz assumed to be friends. A few he recognized as the college roommates, many of the others he'd never seen before.

On the right were family pictures, a series of regular snapshots all clustered around a single larger image in the center. Allowing his focus to settle on it, he felt folds of skin line up around his eyes, his core tightening slightly.

"Thank you," Esmera replied. "I bought it two years ago, after...well...you know."

Ruiz did know, his gaze not once moving, locked on the photo in the center of the spread.

"Market in San Diego proper is so ridiculous right now, didn't make sense to buy down there," Esmera continued, her words barely registering with Ruiz.

"Agents told me this area would be the next to skyrocket, so I figured I would do it before things got too expensive," she added. "You always were the one that told me to invest early in something."

Only barely did Ruiz even hear what she was saying. It faintly registered she was discussing her decision to buy the place, though she could have been addressing the weather, or fashion, or the local sports team.

All he could focus on was the photo.

Ruiz felt the corners of his mouth draw upward as he glanced over to Esmera. "I always liked that picture of her. From back before."

Her mouth partially opened, ready to continue discussing the area real estate, Esmera paused. A crinkle appeared for just an instant on her nose before dawning set in, her gaze tracking over to the same photo hanging on the wall.

"She was a stunner, wasn't she?"

Matching her pose, Ruiz drifted back to the picture.

To say their mother was a stunner would be a massive understatement. It assumed that she was merely the type of woman that could turn heads, when in fact she was more of what Ruiz would call a classic beauty.

The kind of woman who only became better over the years.

In a different time and place, she would have been a Hollywood icon. Mentioned in the same breath as Audrey Hepburn or Grace Kelly, her name would have been embossed on the Walk of Fame, her poster still hanging on walls across the country.

Instead, she had put all her focus into raising her children, first Ruiz, and later Esmera, the little girl that was technically her niece but was brought in with open arms and without a moment's pause.

"I'm so sorry I wasn't there," Ruiz said. "I can't even imagine what you must have gone through."

Flicking his gaze to his sister, he could see her eyes become glassy. Her jaw flexed, held rigid as she stared at the photo, her nostrils flaring just slightly as she pulled in breath.

"She always loved you," Esmera said, voice betraying the slightest crack. "Even after everything that happened."

Shifting her attention back over, letting him see the red tendrils threaded through her eyes, she added, "So many times she talked about driving up to see you. So much, she wanted to."

Still raw was the memory of the day he had found out about her passing. Funneled in through Burris, his young cellmate had done his best to offer the words kindly, but it hadn't mattered. They could have been delivered with flowers and candy, and it still would have been a sledgehammer to the stomach.

His mother, the woman that had raised him entirely on her own, had opened her home to Esmera when she was an infant and had nowhere else to go. The very same that had stood by his side, ever proud, even as she pretended not to know what it was he did for a living.

126

Or of the various things that were involved with such a venture.

Warmth rose to Ruiz's face as he met his sister's stare. Blinking twice, he pulled in air, letting the initial moment pass. "I know. But I just couldn't. At the time, the notion of letting her see me in a cage, wearing that jumpsuit. It was just too much."

The last words they had spoken were shouted in anger three years into his sentence. So frustrated with his lot, with having the same conversation with his mother over and over, he had expressly forbidden her from contacting him again.

Never would he have imagined it would be the last time they ever spoke. Just one more thing ripped away from him by those damn agents that had showed up that night.

And one more reason why it had been imperative he got the concession from Jones just twenty hours prior.

Even if everything went south from this day forward, if their plan proved to be nothing but wishful thinking, that much would be worth it.

"I know everything that's happened," he said. "First me, later with mama, it couldn't have been easy."

Pausing, he drew in a breath, adding, "I'm proud of you."

Pressing her lips tight, Esmera lifted the corners of her mouth. Staring back at him, she seemed to consider a handful of responses before finally settling on the one that Ruiz had been expecting since he first saw her that morning.

"I can't begin to tell you how glad I am to have you sitting here right now," she whispered, "so please don't take this the wrong way.

"But what the heck is going on here?"

Chapter Twenty-Nine

The suit was originally purchased from Brooks Brothers. A conscious decision to avoid Armani or Brioni or anything else with an Italian name that would stand out anywhere beyond the largest of American metropolitan areas.

Equally of concern was to avoid the light colors or linens meant to withstand warmer climates, just as obvious in most parts of the country.

Instead, Tres Salinas had opted for a simple charcoal two-piece. He had underlaid it with a white shirt and a bright blue tie, textured but not patterned.

In short, everything he could to blend in as much as possible.

As much as a man that looked like he did could in a place like West Yellowstone, anyway.

After being folded into his luggage for the last week, a pair of faint horizontal creases ran across the midsection and over the knees. Unable to do anything about them, not sure if anybody in a town such as this would even notice, Tres stepped out of his rental car at half-past-four in the afternoon.

In his hand was a briefcase, the interior stuffed with a legal pad and a few random documents. Of those, the majority was nothing more than the rental agreement he'd signed hours before in Spokane.

Not that he was in the slightest worried about somebody giving too much scrutiny. At most, they might peek inside, ensuring he wasn't trying to sneak in a weapon or some form of contraband.

Parked in the sole visitor stall outside the West Yellowstone Sheriff's Department, Tres stepped out of the rental car. Pausing, he stood ramrod straight, assessing the front of the building, pretending to ignore the cold wind swirling around his body.

Pushing inside the lapels of his suit jacket, rising under the hem of his slacks, it seemed to suck the air from his lungs, his body temperature plummeting fast.

Still, he gave no indication of as much. From where he stood, he couldn't see any cameras visible, didn't notice anybody peering out through the pair of windows lining the front, but that didn't mean they weren't there.

And from this moment forward, he had a part to play. An act to commit to.

Completing this newest charge was already going to be difficult enough. He didn't need to compound things through foolish error.

A thin layer of rock salt crunched beneath his dress shoes as Tres strode for the front of the West Yellowstone Sheriff's Department. A moment later, he passed through the pair of glass doors, feeling the blast of warm air as he moved inside.

Forcing himself not to linger, to maintain a stiff façade, he moved straight ahead, stopping only once he'd reached the reception counter just inside the door.

As he did so, a middle-aged man with receding dark hair and the heavy shadow of a beard matched his steps on the opposite side. Dressed in a mud brown department uniform, he moved with both hands on his hips, a wary expression on his face.

"Help you?" he asked, rolling his head slightly so as to peer the length of his nose at Tres.

Never before had Tres been to Montana, though the man and his posture were both in line with what he'd expected. Thus far in his first few forays around town, he'd yet to see a single person that wasn't decidedly Caucasian.

Seeing someone with brown skin must have really been a surprise.

Even more so for that man to be wearing a suit.

"I'm here to see my client," Tres replied. He was careful to keep his tone polite, masking any animosity he could already feel rising.

Spreading his feet a few inches wider, the man shifted his hands from his hips to across his stomach.

Sitting just above his folded forearms was a silver nameplate, **Deputy Ferry** stenciled across it.

"Your client?" Ferry asked.

"Yes," Tres replied. "Young Hispanic man I understand was brought in early this morning."

A flicker of something moved behind the man's eyes as the statement registered. His mouth shifted a bit to the side, his teeth jutting out over his bottom lip, gnawing at the edge of it.

Clearly, the man wasn't much of a poker player.

"Hang on just a second."

Rotating on the ball of a foot, the deputy turned in the opposite direction. Leaving Tres where he stood, he wove his way past a handful of desks and mismatched chairs before disappearing through a door on the opposite side of the room.

In the wake of his departure, Tres took a half-step back. He lowered the briefcase to the floor and thrust both hands into his front pockets, clenching his fingers, attempting to work some feeling back into the digits fast growing numb.

So much he'd love to have the snow gear he'd been wearing just twenty hours before.

Or even better, to get back on the road south, to a place where temperatures north of freezing weren't such an aberration.

Casting a glance around the place, Tres took in his surroundings, the office bearing out most every preconceived notion he'd had before arriving. On the floor was white tile that was started to yellow with age, the seams between them having expanded to cracks, or even gaps. The light fixtures up above used long tubes, filmy light and a faint hum both emitted in equal measures.

In the air was a cornucopia of scents, ranging from bad coffee to body odor.

In total, the sort of place that would make Tres take a long look at his service weapon every single day when he showed up for work.

Still going through his assessment, his focus was drawn by the sound of voices drifting in from the open doorway in the back. Pulling his hands from his pockets, he again took up his briefcase, standing at attention as Deputy Ferry appeared before him, a second man arriving right on his heels.

Older by at least a decade, he had sandy brown hair and a matching moustache, the same brown uniform covering his frame.

The moment the two were inside the office, Ferry moved to the side, allowing the second man to take the lead. Striding directly forward, he made no effort to hide his open appraisal of Tres, waiting until the front of his thighs were almost flush with the desk before speaking.

"Good afternoon, I'm Sheriff Latham."

Delivered as if it was supposed to mean something, that the title was one of importance in West Yellowstone, Tres nodded.

Again, he was here to play a part, no matter how much it might pain him to do so.

"Hello sheriff, my name is Juan Perez. I am an attorney here to speak with my client."

The name was the Spanish equivalent of John Smith, as vanilla as existed in Hispanic culture.

Not that Tres had any concern that it would be noticed as a blatant misrepresentation to these men. The closest he could imagine either had ever been to the language would be Taco Bell.

Just as the deputy had a moment before, the Sheriff shifted his weight. He settled his hands atop either hip, the ring and pinkie fingers on his right hand grazing the top of a Beretta handgun.

A position Tres didn't pretend to think was by accident.

"Your client?" the sheriff asked.

"Yes," Tres replied. "Luis Mendoza. Hispanic, twenty-five years of age."

Unlike the name Tres had given a moment before, this one was real. Already he knew that the moniker would turn up absolutely nothing, the man from somewhere deep in the heart of Mexico, not a single known tie to put him anywhere near the operation.

Just as he knew that if things went to plan in the coming hours, who the man was would cease to be of use to anybody moving forward.

Turning at the waist, the Sheriff shot a glance to his deputy. "Luis Mendoza," he repeated, the name clearly one he hadn't heard up to that point, wanting to make sure that it was heard and recorded.

At least Mendoza had had the good sense to keep his mouth shut.

Shifting back to face forward, Latham said, "And you are, again? I'm sorry, I'm not real good with names."

Forcing himself to chuckle, to not let it be known that he saw right through the ruse, Tres took a half-step forward. He thrust his hand across the desk separating them, his features completely neutral.

One of the reasons he had been chosen for the trip up north was because he was adaptable. He prided himself on being just as good standing out in the forest as he was dressed in a suit and telling some ignorant rubes exactly what they wanted to hear.

The detour might have been a pain, but it was necessary. He would do what he needed to here before finally turning back south, leaving the cold and the condescension and everything else behind.

"Juan Perez," Tres repeated, accepting the man's reluctant shake and pumping it once before releasing. "I apologize for my delay, but I am based out of Seattle and the trip took longer than expected."

Bobbing his head just slightly, the sheriff remained silent. His eyes narrowed as he worked through what was just shared, Tres practically able to see the wheels turning as he tried to make sense of things.

"Seattle. Right," the man mumbled, his mind clearly elsewhere before blinking himself back into focus. Once more, he shifted to look back at Ferry before saying, "Absolutely, counselor. We do have Mr. Mendoza in custody right now, be glad to let you speak to him.

"I just have one question first, and then I'll take you straight back myself."

Having expected as much – if not worse – Tres slowly drew in a breath. He held it, making sure his vitals stayed even, before slowly exhaling, his gaze never wavering.

"Please."

Leaning forward a couple of inches, the man's eyes narrowed slightly. "He's been in custody since midnight last night. Hasn't made a phone call, hasn't said a word.

"So how in the world is it you managed to show up here now?"

Chapter Thirty

Leaving the house and getting back past the officer standing guard over the front drive hadn't been easy. Not because the young man and his fledgling facial hair posed any real threat, but because I had to fight to keep my emotions in check, my features neutral as I did so.

Filled with adrenaline and vitriol, with sudden dawning and the urge to be moving, it was all I could do to step out the front door and not immediately tear down the driveway. To stop to offer thanks for letting me pass and accepting the young man's condolences once more for my fallen friend.

To offer one last wave out the window as I departed, finally leaving the Martin home behind.

Not until I was effectively around the bend, out of sight from the world, did I allow any of the thoughts I had to surface.

"Ruiz," I hissed, shoving the word out between my teeth, each syllable laced with venom. With one hand atop the steering wheel, I clenched it tight, veins running across the belly of my forearm.

Not trusting myself to utter another sound, I knew that a torrent of obscenities would be the next words out of my mouth. Not wanting to give the man even that much, already the taste of his name like acid on my tongue, I instead jerked my attention out the window, watching the thick woods slowly pass by.

The last time I had heard the name Junior Ruiz was the better part of a decade before. The previous instance he even crossed my mind, at least half that long ago.

My body rigid, I drove with pure muscle memory, the truck coasting without my active input, my focus turned elsewhere, my mind racing. Scads of questions rushed to the surface, adding to the mix that had already arrived the night before.

Things that didn't make sense, for a multitude of reasons. Notions I had no way of answering.

If memory served, Ruiz had been sentenced to somewhere between forty and fifty years in prison. Of the many cases we worked, that one always stood out in my memory, largely because it was far below what we had asked for.

Though still a hell of a lot longer than whatever had passed since then.

Unfurling the fist that was my right hand, I slowly unzipped the front of my coat. Reaching into the inner pocket, I slid out my phone, balancing it on a knee.

Calling the screen to life, I moved through the recent call log, going down only a pair of listings before finding what I wanted and hitting send.

A moment later, after only a single ring, Pally's voice appeared.

"You find Serra?" he asked.

"Junior Ruiz," I replied, ignoring his question for the time being in favor of the reason I had called. "Junior sonuvabitching Ruiz."

Just hearing the full name out loud, I again felt my core draw tight. Ire rose like bile along the back of my throat, my left fist almost aching for something to lash out at.

On the opposite end of the line, Pally took only a moment before asking, "Ruiz? Are you sure?"

Reaching the end of the road Martin lived on, I eased up to a stop sign. Seeing nothing in either direction, I remained sitting there, letting the engine idle as I focused on the conversation at hand.

"Positive," I answered.

Before stepping foot into the Martin home, I had promised the deputy that I wouldn't go near the crime scene. And I hadn't.

Because I hadn't needed to, the message left behind right out in the open, the sort of thing someone would only notice if they knew to be looking for it.

In the background, I could hear Pally fall back to the computer. A clatter of keystrokes echoed over the line, the man furiously working, no doubt in seek of answers to the same questions now filling my head.

Continuing for almost two solid minutes, it ended abruptly, culminating with a loud exhalation before all sound bled away.

"I'll be damned," Pally whispered, the words drawing my attention down to the phone.

"What?"

"I'm going to have to call you back."

Chapter Thirty-One

The only sign that Ramon Reyes was more than twelve hours into his workday was the fact that his cufflinks had been unfastened, sleeves rolled to mid-forearm. On the underside of the cuffs of the designer dress shirt was a print design of black and white, the patterned formation a perfect match to the slacks and vest he wore.

Always, a man like him had to live up to the position he held. He needed to look the part, act the part, the smallest details often meaning the most.

Just denying himself from leaping on the first cup of coffee for the day wasn't enough. He needed to exude confidence, display to everyone in his charge that he was on top of things.

Even if in reality there was a tempest of thoughts and emotions roiling through him, all aching to be expelled.

With the rolling office chair he'd been perched in that morning pressed tight to the desk to clear space, Reyes walked a steady path across the breadth of his office. Head down, his hands were clasped behind him, his steps measured and even.

Lips pursed, he thought on everything that was already underway, on what it could mean moving forward.

Right now, the business was flourishing. Things were being taken care of. Not two hundred yards from where he stood, the work that was currently underway in the warehouse was finally making headway. The last year or two of trial-and-error, of attempting to put things together, was finally yielding results.

Demand was up. Profits were increasing.

Soon, they would be the sole provider of their particular product. They could effectively set the market in a new and burgeoning area.

A marked shift from the old ways, from the methodologies of Junior Ruiz, was finally coming to fruition.

A fact that made what was occurring now a hundred miles north all the more curious.

And the timing as potentially bad as it could be.

"Time is it?" Reyes asked, glancing across the desk to Arlin Mejia back in the same chair he so often occupied.

Late in the day, the skin under his eyes sagged, the front of his slacks were rumpled. Given his age, he seemed to be aging in dog years, his prior time spent in the elements as a warehouse worker bore plainly on his features.

That being just one of many reasons why he'd been selected for his current post.

"Almost five," Mejia responded, not needing to so much as consult a watch. "Two minutes."

Nodding slightly, Reyes resumed his steady pace.

The first word Reyes had received that Ruiz was about to be offloaded was just a week before. Coming far outside of the traditional channels, it had started in a much more organic manner. A fellow prisoner inside Lompoc had gotten word, looking to use the information to curry favor with Reyes.

A first-time informant, Reyes had met the original intel with obvious suspicion, waiting until it had been thoroughly vetted before acquiescing to the man's requests.

Even now, Reyes had no idea how the guy found out what he did, thankful only that he had.

Even more that it had turned out to be true.

His original reaction to the news was to be quick and decisive. To end Ruiz the moment he exited, ensuring that the possible return of the old guard could have no effect on what had been amassed.

Grab one of the local guys with mouths to feed and no clear way of doing so. Promise them a pot of money and guaranteed protection for their family moving forward.

Or even hire a professional, someone paid to pull triggers and keep their mouths shut for a living.

Just, anything that came with no concern of anybody ever drawing a connection. With never having to worry about the trig-german pointing a finger at him.

Nothing but sitting back and watching as whatever concern there might have been was brushed aside.

That first idea hadn't gotten far off the ground, though. As delicious, as enticing, as the thought might have been - one more solid statement to put on his resume, an act to hold up to anybody else that might challenge him - prudence won out.

No amount of good behavior in the world could reduce a sentence from forty years down to eight. There had to be some reason Ruiz had been released, something more than deals cut and favors exchanged.

That being where the real opportunity lay for Reyes.

Halfway through his untold numbered pass across the back of the office, the phone sitting atop the desk burst to life. Offering a single shrill pulse, the sound was enough to jerk Reyes's attention toward it.

Pausing in the middle of his lap, he watched as Mejia leaned forward and slid the phone receiver to the side. Placing it face-up on the desktop, he hit a single button, shifting the call to speaker, before retreating back to his seat.

By the time he made it into position, Reyes was back across from him.

Choosing to stand rather then retake the chair, Reyes leaned forward. Both palms pressed into the front edge of the desk, he could feel the yoke of his dress shirt strain across his shoulders as he stared down at the phone.

"Hector?"

"*Si.*"

The last time they had spoken was three hours prior. By that point, Ruiz had pulled into a house outside of Escondido, a small outpost forty miles north of San Diego.

Barely more than twice that from where they now stood.

"Anything?" Reyes asked.

"No," Hector replied, the vowel sound drawn out to twice the normal length. "Since they got here, nobody has come or gone."

Lifting his gaze, Reyes took in Mejia across from him, the man's focus on the phone.

A handful of quick follow-ups immediately sprang to mind, each dissipating as fast as they arrived, the previous response answering much of what Reyes wanted to know.

Pushing himself back from the desk, Reyes folded his arms across his chest. He thought on things a moment, considering each angle anew.

Nobody coming or going was somewhat surprising, but not entirely. Just hours into his first day of freedom, it made sense that a man like Ruiz would hole up. He'd want to shower and change, get his feet back under him before ever allowing anybody to see him.

And if his behavior on the inside was any indicator, there weren't many left that would even want to. Years had passed since he'd received a visitor. Ditto for any phone calls incoming or outgoing. Same for basic mail.

His father had been gone for decades, his mother passing on a few years before. His sister lived in Escondido, ensconced in a regular life so boring Reyes had stopped keeping tabs on her long ago.

A handful of Reyes's employees had once worked for Ruiz, though they had been thoroughly vetted.

Who else that left that might have any interest in visiting Ruiz – if they even knew he was out – Reyes could only speculate on.

"Orders?" Hector asked.

Optimally, Reyes would tell him to figure out a way to get a listening device inside the house. Or to tap whatever phone Ruiz was using.

A way of monitoring the conversations that were being had, both in person and over the phone. A peek behind the curtain on what had landed him such an early exit and what he planned to now do with it.

Doing so, though, would tip his hand too much. If caught, it would give the appearance to Ruiz and anybody else that might be watching that he was nervous. That his own affairs weren't seen to, even so many years later.

And as he knew all too well, in this particular business, appearance was everything.

"Stay on him, but keep your distance," Reyes replied. "If you need to be relieved for anything, let me know, and we'll get somebody there to spell you."

Chapter Thirty-Two

Given the time of year and being so far north, the sun was already well into its descent by the time I pulled into the lot of the Snoqualmie Police Department. Bouncing over the seam separating it from the street, the single remaining headlamp on my truck threw a glow across the brick façade of the building, leveling out as I slid into a diagonal visitor space along the front.

Making no effort to shut off the engine just yet, I instead reached for my cellphone tucked away in the middle console. Dragging it over onto the seat, I again went to the recent call log, dropping down past Pally and hitting send.

A moment later, Diaz was on the line.

After speaking to Pally earlier, I had decided to wait before placing the second call. Fighting back a potent mix of anger and confusion, I decided to spend the ten-minute drive back into town composing myself before speaking to anybody else.

Pally would have understood what I was feeling. I'm sure he heard the strain in my voice, matching it with his own, the revelation we had discovered a lightning bolt from the clear blue sky.

Expecting anybody else to get that, to not be offended or worse if I was to explode, was another thing entirely.

A decision that proved to be prescient, most of my drive spent alternating between mashing my left palm into the top of the steering wheel and my right fist into the seat beside me.

A healthy amount of screaming had been involved as well.

Now that several minutes had passed, most of that initial torrent of acrimony was now tucked an inch or two below the surface. Not gone by a long stretch, but tamped down enough that I could explain what I had found, what it might mean, with something approximating a level head.

At least, that was the hope.

"Hawk," Diaz opened, using the same greeting she usually did.

Much the way I had with Pally before, I cut straight to it, bypassing any form of salutation.

"Junior Ruiz," I said, the mere mention of the name causing my left hand to curl into a fist.

For a moment there was no response, nothing but dead air, before Diaz said, "What about him? The picture you sent me this morning was definitely not Ruiz."

The second part of her statement was unequivocally true. The guy sitting at the West Yellowstone Sheriff's Department right now was at least fifteen years younger than Ruiz, if not more. He was also several inches taller, several pounds lighter, and had a nose that was now much less functional.

Not that Ruiz would have ever been there to begin with.

Guys like him never touched anything that might result in blood or leave behind fingerprints. They were always puppet masters, the ones that were sure to take credit, but never got their own hands dirty.

Him showing up at my office would have been unheard of, for a variety of reasons.

As was any notion that I would have left him alive after the fact.

"Right, but he's the one calling the shots."

Again, silence fell for a moment before Diaz asked, "What makes you say that?"

"*Plata o plomo*," I whispered, just barely audible.

Finally putting to words what I'd known since standing in the living room of Martin's home, I felt my eyes slide closed, another spike of venom welling within me. With it came the urge to again swat at the steering wheel, my jaw clamping down tight.

"Hawk?" Diaz asked. "What was that?"

Allowing the tension I felt to slowly unfurl, I peeled my eyelids open. Gaze locked on the plain brick façade just beyond the front of the truck grille, I said, "*Plata o plomo*, which as I'm sure you know, means —"

"*Silver or lead*," Diaz finished. "Expression rumored to be made famous by Pablo Escobar back when he was running Colombia. Either take the bribe or take the bullet."

"Exactly," I replied. "And like you said, it was nothing more than a rumor. The sort of thing that somebody probably made up and attached to Escobar, trying to inflate the myth.

"Damned sure not the sort of thing anybody ever said."

Even as I explained to her what I'd found, I kept my gaze locked forward, right hand clenching and releasing in equal measure.

How the hell I expected to walk inside in a moment and speak to Serra Martin with a clear head was anybody's guess.

"But Ruiz did?" Diaz asked.

"He did," I replied. "He said it to us the night we stormed the *quinceañera* he was hosting and arrested him."

Once more, I shoved a slow breath out through my nose. "And he said it just now at Shawn Martin's house."

The display was small. So much so that unless someone was familiar with the expression, had been through the paces we had, they wouldn't have recognized it. Nothing more than a single bullet standing upright and a silver peso leaning against it, some might even think it had been placed there deliberately by the Martins.

Some sort of homage, perhaps souvenirs gathered from a trip taken long ago.

As such, they might have even thought that the smudges in the dust underlying them and the prominent placement in the center of the entertainment center housing their television were both merely accidents.

I had had no such compunctions, recognizing it instantly.

Five minutes later, I was back outside, having seen everything I needed to.

Accepting the information in silence, I could imagine Diaz working through what I'd told her. If she had questions about what I was saying, any objections to the story I was laying out, she didn't voice them.

Instead, the first words out of her mouth were the same ones I kept returning to as I tried to make sense of all this.

"Isn't Junior Ruiz in prison?"

Bobbing my head in silence, I let the last sentence hang a moment, chewing on what I knew, no closer to answering the question than I had been standing in the Martin's living room.

Junior Ruiz had been sentenced to forty years in prison. Five counts in total, all involving the production and international distribution of cocaine. Because he didn't have any prior convictions, and his lawyer agreed to plead guilty in exchange for leniency, the judge had cut twenty years off the maximum total, a move I didn't agree with at the time and did even less now.

Especially considering that potential sixty turned out to be eight, less than fifteen percent of what we originally wanted.

Eight years for a man we spent six months chasing, turning up egregious acts of moving copious amounts of product. Six months of uncovering things much worse, the cascading structure of his organization ensuring he was always a degree or two removed from the major acts.

International trafficking. Money laundering. Using human mules. Murder.

All the requisite things that came with running an operation like his.

"Any word from Pally?" Diaz asked, the first words shared in over a minute.

"No," I answered, glancing down to the screen to ensure no calls had been missed while we were talking. "Last we spoke, he said, *I'll be damned* and disappeared."

Considering that for a moment, Diaz said, "I mean, I thought..."

Knowing already where she was going, knowing she was circling back, much the way I had been for almost a full day now, I countered, "And he might well be. It wouldn't be hard to send someone after me and Martin like that, even if he was inside."

Which was true. We'd both seen it done many times before.

The part that didn't fit was the timing.

"Okay, but then why now?" Diaz said. "An anniversary of some sort?"

"June, 2011," I replied, leaving the statement open-ended, knowing she would understand what I was getting at.

This was a long way from being any sort of commemoration. As best I could tell, it was just a random day, there being no reason for men to have gone after us when they did.

And it wasn't like they'd just been waiting for us to drop our guard. My office has the exact same set-up it did when I opened doors. Any forms of home security are exactly as they've always been.

"You happen to notice if the same message was left at your place?" Diaz asked.

In the haste of the night before, I hadn't thought to search my office, the immediate threat standing right in the middle of the room.

"No," I admitted. "Definitely wasn't on the front counter. Maybe on my desk in the back?"

"Or still on his person," Diaz offered. "Orders to wait until it was done before leaving them behind."

Considering that a moment, I lifted one shoulder in a shrug. Whether the man had them or not was irrelevant at this point. The message had been received, one just as poignant as if it had been two.

The onus was now on me to figure out why.

Chapter Thirty-Three

The phone was waiting in Esmera's box when she'd gone out to
the curb in the early afternoon to check for the daily mail delivery. Purchased three days earlier via a phone call placed through
Burris, it rested on a small stack of bills and the usual litany of local
grocery store advertisements, inconspicuously wrapped in a cardboard
box from Amazon.

Brand new, it was still in the original packaging, Junior Ruiz not
even bothering to unwrap it. Instead, he'd merely unfurled the
charger tucked away in the bottom and plugged it into the wall.

Now two hours later, the battery symbol displayed through the
plastic film adhered to the screen showed it to be almost fully charged.
Prepaid and loaded with the necessary SIM card, all he had to do was
power it up and he was ready to go.

His first tiny baby step back into the world.

And, more importantly, that much closer to the two things that
had been burning just beneath the surface all day, each crying out for
his attention.

Having swapped his post from the overstuffed sofa in the living
room to the hardback chairs by the kitchen table, Ruiz sat with his
elbows resting on the polished oak before him. Much more comfort-

able on the grooved wood of his chair, he waited with his fingers laced together, his gaze aimed straight ahead.

Before him rested the phone, the charging cord snaked out from the base of it, disappearing over the side of the table.

"Hey, I'm going to run over to the store and grab a few things for dinner," Esmera said, appearing in the open doorway across from him. Still dressed as she had been that morning, her hair was pulled up behind her, a thin sweater enveloping her shoulders.

In either hand were her car keys and a couple of cloth sacks, the name of some local market stamped across the canvas material in green block letters.

"The call yesterday came as such a surprise, I wasn't exactly expecting company."

The last words she said with a hint of a smile, bits of color flushing her cheeks.

Lowering his hands from his chin, Ruiz replied, "You don't need to do all that. After what I've been forcing down the last few years, whatever you've got here is just fine."

"That's the problem. I don't have *anything* here." The smile grew larger on Esmera's face as she patted at her midsection. "Been trying to cut back. You know what mama always said happens when we reach thirty."

Ruiz did remember. More times than he could count, he'd been warned about the family genetic predispositions and the way metabolism tended to plummet after they reached a certain age.

Much like his sister, once upon a time he had been rail thin, a full slate of abs on display every time he looked in the mirror.

Muscles that had seemed to disappear a month before he exited his twenties, never to be seen again.

Even if not his sister by birth, his mother had always imparted the same thoughts in Esmera, reminding her that a healthy midsection was a universal Ruiz trait.

"Don't I know it," he replied, leaning back and patting his own stomach.

For an instant, he considered offering to go with her. He could push the cart, load sacks into the car, carry them in for her once they returned.

Take advantage of the time they'd been gifted.

Even revel in being around someone that he didn't need to perpetually be wary of, free of any lingering concern what their true intentions might be.

As fast as it arrived though, the notion faded, his gaze drifting back toward the phone sitting before him.

Seeing his attention shift, Esmera tracked his focus. Eyes landing on the phone, the smile faded, just a hint of teeth peeking out between red lips. "You need anything? Something specific you want?"

"No," Ruiz replied faintly, "whatever you come up with will be great."

Meeting her glance, the two paused for a moment.

The conversation earlier, replete with questions far outnumbering the answers that were available, had managed little more than to leave them both frustrated. Not necessarily with one another, but with the situation as a whole.

What it meant, now and in the future.

At the conclusion of it, both had retreated to their respective corners of the house - Esmera to her bedroom, Ruiz to the kitchen chair – to regroup. To ponder things.

Things that neither had dared touch in a long time, figuring them to be nothing more than wishful thinking. Longing for all that was lost, could never be again.

"See you soon," Esmera eventually managed, adding a small nod before drifting from the doorway.

Tracking her movement, Ruiz listened as she made her way through the kitchen before exiting out a side door. A moment later, the garage door kicked to life and a car door slammed, followed in order by the engine turning over.

Visage completely unreadable, Ruiz sat in place, waiting until he heard the garage door begin its descent before extending a hand. Taking up the phone before him, he thumbed the device to life, pausing as it vibrated twice in his hand before a series of logos and startup messages passed across the screen.

Beneath the table, his left leg began to bounce up and down like a sewing machine on the highest setting, the pace matching his elevated heart rate. Warmth came to his face as he stared at the screen, the phone finally powering to life and settling on a home page before him.

Scanning the thin smattering of icons across, he jabbed a finger at the small picture of an old-fashioned receiver in the corner. Pulling up a basic calling feature, he input the number he wanted to dial from memory.

Pausing, he stared at the numbers scrawled across the screen. His leg continued hammering out a steady beat as he stared at the digits, the green button at the bottom practically calling for him to press it.

To make the connection and check on where things stood, if all had transpired to plan.

Finger hovering over the screen, the thought dancing across his mind, Ruiz muttered, "Dammit," before shifting his thumb and canceling out of the program.

Dropping the phone back into place on the table, he stared at it as the screen faded and then eventually blacked out.

Handfuls of thoughts, of next steps, of future actions, all flitted through his mind. Extensions of everything he'd been thinking since first meeting Jones and Smith weeks before, he allowed them to swirl in his mind for several minutes.

One at a time he considered each, working his way through what they might mean, before pushing himself to a standing position. Crossing the small kitchen, he went to the counter and found a stack of blue post-it notes and an ink pen.

Writing at a diagonal, he jotted a quick note before pulling the top sheet from the stack. Pressing the adhesive against the pad of his thumb, he dropped the pen back into place, his pulse rising yet again.

Turning to face the front windows, he could see the late afternoon sun peeking out around the edges of the shades drawn low.

As much as he wanted to place that phone call, there was something more important he needed to see to first.

And he had waited long enough.

Chapter Thirty-Four

The six years that had passed since I last saw Serra Martin seemed to have gone by the way one might expect. Stepping from her mid-thirties into her early forties, her features had become a bit sharper, enhanced by what looked like some unnecessary weight loss. A couple of stray grays had started to appear in her hair.

Otherwise, she looked exactly as I remembered her from our last encounter, standing alongside the gravesite of my wife and daughter.

Right down to the red-rimmed eyes and the black blazer she wore.

Spotting me the instant I passed through the front door, she leapt from the conference room table where she was seated. Striding directly out of the window-lined room, she hooked a sharp turn, going straight for me and burying her head in my chest.

Sliding both arms around me, she squeezed tight, fingers clawing at the back of my coat.

Responding in kind, I wrapped my arms around her shoulders. I lowered my chin to the top of her head, grazing her hair.

Just as we'd stood the last time I saw her.

Then mourning the loss of my partner, now doing the same for hers.

"Hey, Serra," I whispered.

Neither of us said another word for nearly a full minute, each embracing the other, oblivious to the handful of stares from the room behind us.

Standing there, dozens of thoughts moved through my mind. Offers of condolences, telling her I was sorry for having been gone so long, merely saying hello after so much time.

One at a time, I pushed them away.

Sometimes, with people having shared history, there really isn't the words.

The other members of our team had been together when I first arrived in the Southwest. They'd had two or more years in before me, had ascended together, assimilated into each other's lives.

In the time since, I also knew they'd remained visible to one another, doing what I had failed to and making a point of maintaining contact.

A point that couldn't help but cause some bit of shame to rise as I felt Serra release her grip and slowly pull back. Making it as far as her hands resting on my waist, she looked up at me, moisture underscoring her eyes.

"Thank you for coming. I know it was a long way."

"Of course," I replied softly.

"Pally said you had a visitor, too," Serra whispered. Her gaze traced over my face as she did so, landing on my forehead.

Lifting a hand, she lightly brushed aside the hair hanging across it, revealing the small lump and faint bruising from the head butt I'd delivered the night before.

"Yeah."

Eyes lingering another moment, she pulled her hand away, my hair falling back into place. Retreating a step, she placed both arms across her torso, hugging herself tight.

"Hawk, what the hell is going on right now?"

Chapter Thirty-Five

The conference room felt more like a fishbowl, much in line with the rest of building, which resembled a small-town diner more than a police department. Square in shape, the entire interior utilized support poles and low partitions rather than actual walls.

Everything and everybody in plain sight.

The only two spaces with even a modicum of privacy was the office for the police captain in the corner and the space we now sat in. Even at that, both had glass walls, not bothering with blinds or shades of any kind.

Where an evidence locker, or holding cell, or any of the normal trappings of a police department were, I hadn't clue, such questions far from the most important at the moment.

Seated on one side of an elongated oak table, my bottom rested on the last few inches of a leather padded rolling chair. Directly beneath the overhead vents, my coat was off, sweat forming beneath the hair swaying across my forehead, my elbows on the front edge of the table.

Positioned beside me at the head of the table, hands folded in her lap, was Serra. Gaze aimed down at her fingers, she watched as they writhed continuously, constantly moving, twisting and wrapping themselves over one another.

Behind me, I could still feel the weight of a handful of stares coming from the police station staff, no doubt curious who the grizzly guy that had just arrived could possibly be.

Which was fine by me. I had both an airtight alibi for the night before and zero patience for anybody that would even think to insinuate otherwise.

Resting on the far end of the table was a silver coffee pot and some upturned mugs, probably left over from prior conversations earlier in the day, nothing remaining but the faint aroma of dark roast.

I had been the first to speak. Recognizing that Serra might not have been in any state to launch straight into another retelling of the night before just minutes after my arrival, I had offered to kick things off.

Needing neither prompting nor agreement, I had explained in quick but thorough fashion what had taken place. Beginning with Kaylan inserting a key into the front door, I took her through the confrontation with the man inside and the night spent at the hospital. I'd also shared returning this morning to find that no ID had been made and snapping a picture that as yet had turned up nothing.

Throughout my story, Serra had done her best to be unflinching, only occasionally allowing herself to respond exactly how I anticipated before walking in. At mention of Kaylan getting tossed, she flinched visibly. When I told her of encountering the man in the front of the office, she winced, her face scrunching, shoulders shuddering slightly.

In the wake of it, neither of us had said a word for several full minutes, Serra superimposing the new information onto the parts she already knew, me running it back through my head, placing it against the questions I still had.

Not until she had everything in place did Serra finally lift her gaze. Looking my way, she pressed her lips tight together, drawing in a quick breath.

"I've already been through this a couple of times, so forgive me if it comes off sounding rehearsed," she began.

"Since hanging up his badge three years ago, Shawn had been consulting with a company over in Seattle. Private sector, running security for office buildings across the country.

"Most of the time, he was in the city a couple of days a week, worked remotely the rest. Every now and again, he would have to be on the road, going to help with an installation or to troubleshoot a problem."

Flicking her gaze upward, she continued, "This past week, he was down in Houston."

Careful not to react in any way, already I could guess what the police behind me were probably thinking. Just in the first couple of paragraphs, already Serra had mentioned what most investigators would see as a primary motive.

Martin had been a consultant for a company that worked in security. There could be upset clients or someone that was looking to gain access to one of the facilities he oversaw.

A hundred red herrings that would keep them guessing for ages.

"Yesterday, he landed back in Seattle early evening. Made it home in time to have dinner with all of us, spend some time with the kids before putting them to bed."

At mention of their children, a veneer of moisture came to her eyes. Shifting her gaze to the side, she stared resolutely out, her head quivering just slightly as the moment drifted past.

"A few days ago, the client had taken them out for dinner," Serra began anew. Unlike a moment before, her voice was softer, the narrative sapping her strength bit by bit. "Steaks and lobster, and at the end, champagne."

Again, she lifted her focus, looking over to me. "You know he was never much of a drinker. That night when he called, we joked about it, how he was down there enjoying the high life while I was here with the kids.

"Got to be this thing, so we hatched a plan that as soon as he got back, we would get a bottle and sit out in the hot tub together."

Fixing her attention on a spot in the middle of the table, I watched as one corner of her mouth lifted.

Far and away the saddest smile I had ever witnessed.

"So we did. Or, at least we tried."

Once more, she paused. Her lower lip quivered, her cheeks bunching slightly. Moisture pooled along the underside of her eyes, her hands clutched in the pit of her lap.

Remaining fixed in such a position, she waited a full thirty seconds before again drawing in a deep breath through her nose, the effort accompanied by the sound of phlegm catching.

"We were both underwater when it happened. We'd both set our champagne along the side and slid in, going straight to the bottom. Like always, we had a contest to see who could hold their breath the longest.

"And, like always, I won."

The last word was not even loud enough to be considered a whisper. Nothing more than a murmur, her face crinkled again, remaining as such for several moments.

This time, gravity proved to be too much, forcing the moisture collected along the underside of her eyes down over her cheeks.

Never did she attempt to stop it, not even wiping away the twin trails cleaved across her skin.

"When I came up, the water around me was already red, the jets just swirling it around, dyeing the entire thing within seconds."

Flicking her gaze up, she added, "At that point, I didn't even see what had happened. All I saw was the blood and screamed. That's when things went black.

"Wasn't until I came to that I saw Shawn floating beside me."

Start to finish, the story represented what was essentially a worst-case scenario. It hinted at a combination of skill and luck that would make gleaning anything beyond what I already knew almost impossible.

Someone had clearly been tracking their movements, just as they obviously had been mine. They'd known exactly where to be, aided by the Martins deciding to get in the hot tub and even submerging themselves in the water.

From there, they'd been able to use surprise and stealth to perform the act, virtually undetected.

"Did you happen to see anything?" I whispered.

"No," Serra said, twisting her head slightly. "I was mid-scream when something hit me in the back of the head, and everything went dark."

The statement told me two things instantly. The first was that the placement of the wound was why I hadn't noticed anything. To look at her head-on, one would not even know she had been hit.

Until she mentioned it, I'd almost forgotten it even happened.

The second was that the attacker had made a point to spare her. Not only by refusing to simply shoot her, but from the fact that he likely had to prop her upright to keep her from falling face-first into the water as well.

Both things further guaranteeing that Martin was the target, the point likely being the message I'd found on the entertainment center.

"The kids?" I asked.

Sliding her focus from one side of the table to the other, Serra shook her head slightly. "That was the very first thing I did after coming to and checking Shawn. Before I even called 911.

"Scrambled upstairs to find them both sleeping. Didn't look like the..." she said, pausing before saying the word *killer*. "Like they even went into the house."

So many more questions came to mind, things that if I was running a basic interview on someone I might want to ask, but in this instance, there was no point.

Asking if Shawn had seemed worried, had mentioned anything troubling, was futile. If he had, he would have taken necessary measures. At the very least, he would have made sure his family was safe.

Sure as hell wouldn't have made himself an obvious target by climbing into a hot tub unarmed.

So was asking about the kids, both likely with her parents, or officers, or a trusted friend, Serra making sure they were cared for.

Odds were, the attack had come from just as far afield as the one that had landed on my doorstep. It had been a sneak approach, at a single individual, with the point of making a very specific statement.

Reaching into the front pocket of my coat, I slid out the two objects I'd found at their house. Placing them side by side on the table, I was careful to keep them tucked close to my body, hidden from view by anybody in the police station that might be walking by.

The only things I had touched from the home, I knew they wouldn't be missed, apparently not even noticed on the first pass by investigators.

"Serra, have you ever seen either of these things before?"

Lifting her gaze slightly, Serra used her heel to roll herself forward a few inches. Eyes narrowed, she peered at the two items, staring for a moment before lifting her gaze to me.

"No," she replied. "I mean, not those two specifically, I don't think. Why?"

"They were found on the mantle of your entertainment center a half-hour ago," I replied. "Are you absolutely sure you've never seen them before?"

"Like I said, pesos and bullets were around all the time back when you guys first started, but not since the kids were born. And damned sure not on our mantle."

Chapter Thirty-Six

The official recommendation from the doctor was that surgery was needed. The blow that had crushed Luis Mendoza's nose had managed to splinter the delicate bone structure, creating a trio of long fissures the length of the bridge. Given the direction of the hit and the time that had passed since, the underlying cartilage had also been mangled in ways that were never intended.

A combination that was at first and most obviously extremely painful. Even more concerning, though, was the underlying formation. The septum had been deviated, effectively blocking the passageway, meaning that drawing air in and out was an impossibility.

Once the initial findings were disclosed and the x-ray board along the side wall turned off, the doctor turned to the room. A middle-aged man already fast losing twin battles with a receding hairline and an expanding waist, he delivered each word as if sighing.

A tired man just wanting to go home.

A home, Tres Salinas got the impression, that was just as hectic as the clinic, the man's features and demeanor both seeming to exude exhausted resignation.

A look that mixed perfectly with the motif of the clinic as a whole.

The room they now stood in was standard examination fare, or at least what Tres would imagine the Montana equivalent to be. The few times he had ever been inside such a space, it had always been at an emergency department of some sort, usually at a county hospital or worse.

The kinds of places where anything less than a gunshot wound barely earned a passing glance from any of the attending personnel.

Where something like the state of Mendoza's nose might earn a question or two from a gawking child, but nothing more.

A far cry from that, this place could almost pass for an elementary school room. Larger than needed, a hospital bed was fitted against one wall, Mendoza currently sitting on the edge of it, feet hanging down.

On the opposite end were an array of cabinets, a wash basin serving as their centerpiece.

The wall to one side was replete with framed prints of outdoor wilderness scenes. The other had a pair of windows, their blinds closed, the faintest hints of cool air seeping through them.

All things Tres took in, filing away in the back of his mind. Information that was vital to his true interests, even as he stood playing the part for a little longer.

Forcing himself to pay attention, to at least feign interest in what was happening, he listened as the doctor went on to state that he would prefer to put Mendoza in an ambulance and transport him directly to some town called Big Sky. Seeming to know that two of the three men before him weren't from the area, he then went on to explain it was a town fifty miles north.

The closest location with a major facility equipped for facial surgery, the doctor was certain they could get him in by morning.

The longer they waited, the more likely the concern for permanent damage.

Throughout every word the doctor stated, Tres continued to do as expected. Dressed in his charcoal Brooks Brothers suit, he had lugged his briefcase in from the car with him, the item now heavy with one extra provision.

A provision that was currently equipped with a full magazine and a sound suppressor screwed down on the end. Practically calling to

Tres, it had taken everything he had to listen intently as an examination was made and the doctor stated his case.

Especially as he endured the steady onslaught of sideways glances from Deputy Ferry, the man barely capable of keeping his wariness from spilling out.

The only thing that wasn't quite as obvious was the source of it, be it racism or simply a distrust for anybody that wasn't born and raised into the tiny map dot they called a town.

But now, at last, after forcing himself to remain resolute, to not do anything foolish, he was being rewarded with an opening.

"Absolutely not," Ferry replied, jumping in, anxious to be the first to respond to the doctor's suggestion. "This man was arrested last night for destruction of property and attempted murder. Do what you can to stabilize him, and then he is going back to his holding cell."

Feeling a spike of ire that had nothing to do with the role he was playing, Tres glared at Ferry.

"The law clearly states that my client is entitled to medical treatment for any obvious injuries. Common sense says there is an injury and the doctor here has now confirmed it, recommending surgery."

What the law actually stated, Tres had not a clue. He'd heard something similar spouted by a blowhard attorney once on one of his previous trips to the emergency room.

It had worked then, just as it had worked back at the Sheriff's Department.

No use trying to come up with something new on the fly now.

Looking from Tres to the doctor, blood rushed to Ferry's cheeks in response. His eyebrows lifted, the rosy pallor moving to encompass his forehead, his features a harsh contrast to the brown uniform he wore.

"An injury he received while in the act of committing a felony," Ferry spat back.

Seeing the obvious state the man was in, unable to keep himself from taking an additional jab for sport, Tres countered, "Or so you say."

Flicking his gaze to the deputy, Tres made no effort to walk the comment back. Instead, he merely stood and gazed at Ferry, watching as the man's features trended from pink to crimson.

His mouth sagged as he pulled in air. His chest swelled in kind as he raised an index finger, thrusting it out before him, a tirade ready to be unleashed.

The mere thought of which made the gun tucked away in Tres's briefcase call even louder.

Fortunately for both men, the words never made it as far as the surface.

Seeking to diffuse the situation, the doctor took two strides forward, standing directly between them, interrupting their line of sight.

"Gentlemen, please." Keeping his body at ninety degrees, he made no effort to look at either one. Gaze aimed straight ahead, he kept his attention on the cabinets along the far wall, making Tres and Ferry both look at the side of his head. "Let's remember, we're all professionals, and we've already got one injury to deal with here."

Delivered in an even monotone, he waited several moments, allowing the opportunity for either side to object further. When none came save the near-panting of Ferry, he added, "I have made my recommendation. I realize there is more to this than simply a medical diagnosis, though, so I'll leave you two to hash it out."

Moving slowly, he eased back into his original position. The slip-on shoes he wore scuffled across the tile floor as he retreated a step before turning, headed for the door.

"Please let one of the nurses in the hall know when you've decided what you want to do. Either way, we'll need to prepare the patient for transport."

Chapter Thirty-Seven

Every single thought I'd had listening to Serra tell her story was mixed into an amorphous blob in my head. Added to it was a hundred other questions I'd already been harboring, a combination of what happened at my office and what had happened in Baja eight years before.

Forming a sum total that felt like a hurricane circulating within my skull, I paused just two steps beyond the front door of the Snoqualmie Police Department. Sensing the cold evening air hit me flush, I could feel it picking at perspiration I didn't even realize I had.

Filling my lungs with it, I allowed my chest to expand, the chill cooling me from within. Like a bull about to charge, I pushed it out through my nose, a plume of condensation extended almost a foot before me.

What was happening was a mess. Nothing short of a shit show.

And I couldn't help but think that it had a long way to go before it got any better, let alone was finished.

In front of me, a truck rumbled past, engine revving hard. Lights sweeping by, it disappeared as fast as it had arrived, leaving me standing in silence beneath the overhead light of the front door.

Positioned on a corner at the far end of the main drag through town, already I could see businesses shutting down for the night. Instead of the glow of interior lights, most ambient illumination was now provided by stanchions equally spaced the length of the street.

Standing there, it wasn't hard to imagine the place decked out in Halloween regalia just a week prior. Just as clearly, I could imagine six weeks later bringing about red and green, everything done in anticipation of Christmas.

As Americana as existed, a visual carefully curated and maintained, bringing in tourists by the droves.

An effort that was completely lost on me, the scene barely even registering. Instead, I stood with features scrunched, my thoughts still inside the conference room not ten yards behind me.

"Bad luck and timing," I muttered. "Two things that can destroy all the preparation in the world."

To anybody listening, they would probably think I was speaking in some sort of code. Broken sentences, meant to obfuscate.

In reality, nothing could be further from the truth, largely because I wasn't really trying to communicate. Merely thinking out loud, I was replaying what Serra had shared, bemoaning what it likely meant.

Making no attempt to move, I continued to chew on things, in no particular hurry to head to my truck. Without a clear next step, it was better for the time being to stand in the cold, letting it work on the mixture of emotions sitting just beneath the surface.

The obvious grief for my friend and his family. The confusion of Junior Ruiz and what he could be playing at. The adrenaline and hostility of having received his message.

The initial reaction of wanting to tear straight ahead into the night until I found him, extracting every answer I needed before paying full retribution for what he had done.

In the absence of doing that, trusting it would be nothing more than wasted energy, I waited and processed, staring out, looking without actually seeing.

Entranced in thought, peering into the night, I barely even felt my cellphone buzzing against my ribcage. Not until the fourth or fifth pulse did it register enough for me to blink away the confluence of thoughts at the front of my head. Snapping myself back into the moment, I jammed a hand down inside my coat. Pulling the device out, I stared down at the screen, eyes narrowing slightly at what I saw.

My first thought had been that Pally was finally hitting me back, filling in the blanks after his sudden disappearance earlier.

After that in order came Diaz, having done some digging after what I'd shared before stepping inside.

In the busyness of the last hours though, I had completely forgotten there was a third person I was waiting to hear back from, that name the one staring back up at me.

Latham

Accepting the call, I lifted the device to my face. Drifting to the side, I rounded the corner of the building, walking on until I was on the far side of my truck before saying, "Tate."

Lingering just past the door, I leaned against the bed. Keeping my head aimed forward, I managed to clock the interior of the police station in my periphery.

"Hawk, Sam Latham, over here in West Yellowstone."

"Hey, Sheriff," I replied. My voice I kept low, not even considering going to the speakerphone. "I'm glad you called, I was actually going to reach out here shortly."

With everything else that had just happened, circling back with him wasn't real high on the list, but it was there.

That was all he needed to know.

"That's why I'm calling," Latham replied. "Wanted to let you know, we got an ID. Luis Mendoza."

"Luis Mendoza," I repeated. Letting the name linger a moment, I tried placing it. Both parts fairly common – especially in many of the countries we had been in – the full title didn't really bring anybody in particular to mind.

"Doesn't ring anything," I said. "You eventually got him to talk?"

Earlier that morning, standing behind the one-way glass, the man had been the poster child for defiance. Or, at least what he thought such a thing should look like.

Even with his nose mashed down into a nub, blood still crusted on his clothes, he'd sat and stared resolutely ahead. He had apparently refused water or medical aid.

There was a chance that now, twelve hours later, the pain or dehydration had gotten to him.

But something told me there was more to it than that.

"Not exactly," Latham said. "His lawyer showed up a little bit ago, told us who he was and asked to speak with him."

My grip on the phone tightened as pinpricks started in my core and rippled upward, rising to my scalp in record time.

"His lawyer?"

"Yeah," Latham said. "Guy named Juan Perez. Little on the young side, didn't get here until late in the afternoon. Said he was coming over from Seattle, which was what took so long."

All previous concern for who might be nearby, for who may be listening, bled away. Turning my focus to the side, I stared at the windows lining the outer wall of the police station, my own reflection faint against the backlighting of the building interior.

Every concern, every innate response that had risen a moment before, began to explode at once. Like fireworks dancing across my mind, they appeared behind my eyelids each time I blinked, as if I'd been staring directly into a bright light.

Juan Perez was the effective Spanish equivalent of not even having a name. Dozens of times before we had been handed the moniker by people that didn't want to answer questions. Or were simply hoping that the Americans down in their corner of the world wouldn't know the difference.

Taken alone, it would be cause for concern. Partnered with the facts that he was young and confessed to having come over from Seattle meant something much worse.

"Did Mendoza call for him?"

"Asked that too," Latham replied. "Said he had called and told him before the fact he was about to do something and might need help."

By the last few words, hints of disbelief seemed to be creeping in. As if hearing them out loud unlocked their true meaning, Latham barely made it to through the sentence.

Drawing in a sharp breath, he asked, "You think it's bullshit?"

I didn't think so.

I knew so. Emphatically.

People like this weren't used to running unsuccessful plans, but even still, they always had a failsafe.

Odds were, two people had been sent north in tandem. One had gone for Martin, the other for me. If either were to come up short, the other was to make their way across the gap and ensure that all holes were cauterized.

"Where is Mendoza now?" I asked, already knowing that the name was fake, that no amount of searching would turn up a thing.

"He's just inside," Latham said.

"Inside where?"

"West Yellowstone Med," Latham replied. "Lawyer took one look at things and demanded that he be moved for treatment on that nose."

"Is anybody in there with him?"

"Yeah, Ferry," Latham replied.

With each exchange, the feeling passing through me grew more pronounced.

"Where's the lawyer?" I asked.

As if finally putting together everything I'd asked, the events of the last eighteen hours aligning in his mind, Latham said, "He's in there with them. You don't think..."

Chapter Thirty-Eight

Arlin Mejia held the base of the bottle in one hand, the rounded curve cupped into his palm. The neck of it he laid back against the indent of his opposite thumb, presenting it as if he were a waiter in a high-end restaurant.

Extending it out over the desk, he pitched forward a few inches at the waist, holding it above the oak top. "Manny just sent this over from the warehouse. This is the first of the new vintage, complete with the redesigned label."

Seated with his body turned to the side, one leg raised to the opposite thigh, Ramon Reyes glanced up from the miniature laptop balanced across his thigh. On the screen was a spreadsheet detailing the latest transactions, numbers playing out exactly what they had discussed that morning.

Shipments were increasing. In the last six months alone, demand had gone up by a factor of three.

With the introduction of this newest line, it wasn't difficult to imagine even greater growth in the year ahead.

Shooting out a hand, Reyes closed the screen of the laptop. Without the bright glow of the spreadsheet, the office seemed to grow much darker, his focus so intent he had barely noticed that late afternoon had slipped into evening.

Placing the device down on the desk, he slid off the pair of wire-rimmed glasses that nobody outside of Mejia ever saw him in, dropping them bottom-up atop the computer.

Not bothering to rise, he extended a hand, accepting the bottle.

"How many?" Reyes asked.

"This is the only one right now," Mejia replied, retreating back into his customary seat. "Manny said that once we give final approval, they can begin rolling them out. Could be ready to ship as soon as this weekend."

Grunting slightly, Reyes drew the bottle over, balancing it across his thigh.

To look at it, there was nothing particularly remarkable about it. Standard size and shape, the glass had been darkened to the color of wood smoke, a wide bottom funneling upward to a half-inch neck. More than a foot in height, the top was enveloped in a wax seal.

On the side was a square white sticker, announcing that it was a 2019 Cabernet Sauvignon. Along the top was the name Fruit of the Desert Vineyard, the moniker given to the spread they were now seated on.

Serving as the centerpiece was a re-creation of a pencil drawing they had had commissioned of rows of grapevines extended into the distance, framed by scattered cacti and a rising sun in the background.

A bit heavy on the cheese factor perhaps, but that was hardly important.

Every single thing listed on the label save the name of the place was fictitious. And even that was only for shipping and tax purposes, needing to maintain the veneer of a legitimate business entity.

And just like the label, the liquid rising to just millimeters from the top was disingenuous as well, closer to grape juice than any Cabernet that a human would ever actually drink, let alone purchase.

"Outside looks good enough," Reyes said. Giving the bottle a complete revolution, he saw nothing glaring that would cause anybody to take a second glance.

"Dogs?"

"Passed two different tests," Mejia replied. "One a German Shepherd, another a schnauzer. Placed the bottle in the middle of the warehouse floor, neither animal even paused."

Grunting once more, Reyes lifted the bottle. Giving it one more full turn, he passed his gaze quickly over the exterior, going through the paces he knew were expected of him, before setting it down beside the computer.

"And the product itself?" Reyes asked.

What the bottles, or the labels, or the boxes they were shipped in, or any of the other crap that came with their new venture, looked like, Reyes didn't much care. None of it actually mattered, little more than window dressing for the new direction of their enterprise.

That was where his concern really lay. Making sure that they hadn't gotten overly creative, their attempts to work below the radar didn't accidentally undercut their entire purpose for being.

"Clean," Mejia said. "Early returns show this works out even better than the Sauvignon Blanc."

Flicking his gaze up from the bottle, Reyes felt his brows rise just slightly. The Sauvignon had been by far their biggest seller. It alone seemed to be driving the sharp incline in distribution, responsible for most of the numbers on the spreadsheet he was just consulting.

If what Mejia was now saying was true, that could mean big things for them moving forward.

"Tell Manny it looks good. Begin filling orders as soon as possible."

Leaving the bottle in place, Mejia nodded. "Will do."

For a moment, neither man said a word. Each stared at the bottle, contemplating what it would mean, putting it in context against the various other machinations currently swirling around them.

The ascent to where the organization now sat had been an arduous one. Beginning more than half a decade before, it had been a steady slog, a battle fought on multiple fronts.

Developing their new product. Staving off attempts at encroachment from other organizations. Carving out their own territory.

Forming a network. Complying with everything necessary to give the impression of a legitimate business entity.

Rinse and repeat, day after day, for what felt so long.

Making what was happening now with Junior Ruiz all the more important, a toehold on a precipice they could tumble from under the slightest nudge. A feeling that Reyes hated, as much for it at face value as for the simple fact that even after so many years it still got to him so much.

The sooner it was behind him, Ruiz and any threat he represented snuffed out, the better.

"How long before Hector checks in again?" Reyes asked.

Showing no surprise at the question, Mejia replied, "Twenty-three minutes."

Nodding slightly, Reyes leaned his head back against his chair. He allowed his gaze to lift to the ceiling, watching shadows play across the inset woodwork.

"No point waiting. Go ahead and call him now."

Chapter Thirty-Nine

Not once since Tres Salinas had arrived in West Yellowstone had Luis said a word. Not sitting in the holding cell at the Sheriff's Department. Not as Tres demanded he receive medical treatment for his shattered nose.

Not even as the doctors and nurses had examined him, at that point content to let Tres act as his spokesperson.

The closest thing there had been was a flicker behind his eyes the first moment Tres stepped inside the interrogation room. A look of momentary buoyancy, as if help had arrived. A flash that was extinguished just as fast, realization setting in.

Much like it would have if the situation had been reversed, Tres the one sitting in the holding cell when Luis arrived.

Despite the silence, Tres held no preconceived notions. Just because Luis had pushed himself to the periphery, that was only in the presence of the sheriff and his deputies. For the purposes of the initial medical examination.

The entire time, his eyes had been moving, tracking the conversation, always aware of what was occurring.

Just as Tres was aware that from this moment forward, his focus could not only be centered on Deputy Ferry.

"There is no way we are sending this man up to Big Sky," Ferry stated. Barely waiting until the door had closed behind the doctor, he positioned himself as one point in a triangle, equidistant from Tres and Luis both.

Shoving his hands inside the bottom hem of his jacket, he placed them on his hips, peeling the coat back to make sure the breadth of his belt was visible. A classic power stance, it was obviously meant to exude dominance, his feet spread apart, toes pointed wide.

What it really did was show Tres that he was not carrying a baton or nightstick of any kind.

And that his gun was still secured.

At no point was Tres going to be left alone with Luis outside the confines of the interrogation room where they'd already met. A solid block room that locked from the outside, it had one-way glass overlooking everything and probably microphones embedded in the walls. Even if he was somehow able to do what he needed to, there would be no getting out of the room.

Let alone the building.

The same applied for anywhere else in the world they might be, the odds of ever being left alone with Luis nil. Even if he was posing as a lawyer, there would always be some amount of law enforcement present, in observation if not direct interaction.

In the hour and a half that he had already been there, this was the first time that the sheriff hadn't also been in the room.

Based on the debate that was now happening, things didn't promise to change for the better moving forward. The options were either for them to go straight back to the holding cell, or for the officers to load Mendoza up and take him up the road to Big Sky.

A large hospital with plenty of people and cameras covering every square inch of the grounds.

Never was he going to get a better chance than what he had right now.

A conclusion Mendoza had to no doubt be reaching at the same moment.

"You heard the doctor," Tres replied. "He is of the opinion that this could cause permanent damage."

The words slid out without much thought. The sound of his own voice became distorted, even to his own ears. His focus shifted, not from the conversation at hand, but to the room around him.

The night before, he had had the benefits of being tucked into the woods, staring at a target that had no idea he was present.

Now, he was in an enclosed space. His weapon was stowed inside a briefcase a few feet away. One opponent was standing across from him, a weapon on his hip that would take at least a moment to retrieve.

A second opponent was just beyond reach, most likely even more dangerous than the first, weapon or not.

Tres could feel a sheen of sweat appear on his face. The t-shirt he wore beneath his suit stuck to the small of his back, his mind putting together a plan, his features remaining absolutely still.

"Permanent damage?" Ferry scoffed, giving an exaggerated eyeroll for effect. "This is Montana. Every man here has had a busted nose at one point or another. It's not like he was in a motorcycle accident or something."

The words landed, though they barely resonated. In their stead, Tres could only feel his pulse increasing. The adrenaline that always seemed to precede violence seeped into his system, every sense becoming heightened.

He just needed to figure out the best way to leverage the situation. Right now, he was staring at an armed deputy. In his periphery was a man he could imagine was aching for any opening to slide away.

And once he did, there would be no doubt he was gone forever.

Mind racing, Tres took a step back. Continuing to face forward, he bent at the knee, hand extended for his briefcase resting upright on the floor.

"It seems we aren't getting anywhere with this conversation, so maybe I should call in the sheriff and get his take?"

Time seemed to slow as Tres felt his fingers slide over the brass handle of the case.

The instant his fingertips felt cold metal, he caught a flash of movement, eyes flicking to see Luis rise from the edge of the bed.

Moving in one quick pulse, he pushed off both palms, flinging himself forward, feet extended.

Focus aimed squarely on Tres, he appeared to hang suspended in the air. Time seemed to slow as he landed, both feet smacking the tile. The instant they did, his body twisted to the side, both hands curling into balls.

In unison, a few feet behind him Ferry's mouth and eyes all formed into congruent circles, surprise and realization hitting him hard.

An inch at a time, Tres saw it all, as if watching how things were about to play out.

A scenario that lasted only a moment before things snapped back into place, everything returning to real time, a sensory overload smashing down at once.

Grasping the handle of the briefcase, Tres yanked it up in one fluid motion. Bringing his other hand in behind it, he held it like a shield, extending it at arm's length, getting it into place just as Luis's fist came crashing down.

The force of the blow twisted the makeshift block in Tres's hands, his arms acting like shock absorbers, feeling the weight of it travel clear to his shoulder. Spinning his body out to the side, he held tight, using it to direct Luis on by, opening a gap between them.

The instant he was past, Tres's first thought was on popping open the hinges. On getting inside, grabbing hold of the suppressed Sig Sauer, and doing to both of these men what he had done to Shawn Martin the night before.

But there was no time. No space.

No chance to get inside before one or both of them was on him, taking him down or alerting someone outside what was happening.

For the time being, this was what he had, forced into close quarter combat while wearing a suit.

So be it.

Shuffling to his right, his focus shifting, Tres grasped the briefcase on either edge. Aiming for the deputy, he swung it in a sharp under-handed angle, rotating it so the short side was square with the man's chin.

Twisting upward, he pushed on, swinging with all he had, Ferry jerking himself into motion just in time to lean back a couple of inches.

Enough to keep the blow from landing square, the leather binding caught the front edge of his chin. Snapping his jaw shut, the sound of his teeth smacking together echoed out, accompanied by a low grunt.

Following the force of the impact, his face went toward the ceiling. Stumbling a half-step back, his weight rose to his toes, his eyes seeming to dim, his weight uneven.

Recognizing the lack of balance, the uneven sway, Tres pushed aside the thought of Luis for a moment. Needing to half his opposition, to put the deputy down, he moved in again. Drawing the case straight back to his shoulder, intent to use it like a poker, he aimed to drive it directly through Ferry's cheek.

Propelling himself off his back foot, he hurtled himself forward, teeth clenched, preparing for impact.

An impact that instead came in from the side, Luis slamming crossbody into him, shoulder hitting him square in the ribs.

With his hands raised by his head, the briefcase parallel to the floor, there was no way for Tres to protect himself. No chance at him even steeling for impact, his entire core left exposed to the shot.

The air was driven from his lungs on contact, a pair of pops ringing out as the thin bones of his bottom ribs snapped. Stars erupted before his eyes, pain receptors firing the length of his body as the two of them tumbled backward.

Smashing into the bed Luis had been seated on a moment before, they rolled in a tangle over the edge of the mattress, arms and legs flailing before landing hard on the tile floor.

Hitting first, the flat side of the leather briefcase still gripped in his hands slapped down hard, a resonate boom echoing through the room. So close to Tres's ear, it felt like it might shatter the drum, a dull buzzing settling in.

His eyes going wide, pain hurtling the length of his body, Tres made no effort to move. Taking an instant, willing himself past the initial burst of battle, he drew in air.

Blinking through the fog, the sheen of moisture on his eyes, he peered from the briefcase beside him to Ferry. Still somehow upright, he swayed in place, weight passing from one foot to the other. Both hands on his right hip, he pawed at the strap of his weapon, trying in vain to free it.

"Lath..." he whispered, shoving the broken word out with a puff of air.

"Latham," he managed a second time, trying to find his voice. Eyes squinted up tight, he peered down at the weapon on his side, trying to pull things into form.

Little by little, Tres could feel his focus return. Things around him returned to place, snapping back into order.

Any moment, the initial shock of the blow to Ferry would recede. His vision would clear, letting him retrieve his weapon.

He would find his voice, able to call out for aid.

Behind him, Tres could also hear Luis grunt, his shoes sliding against the tile floor, fighting for purchase. With his nose shattered, he breathed loudly through his mouth, hands and feet scrabbling as he tried to get moving again.

Tres could allow neither to happen. Either one and any hope he had for finishing the task or getting away was gone.

As were all the years he'd spent in preparation. All the effort and menial tasks and everything else he'd been through.

The life he'd left behind when this moment arose.

The truly big events that still lay ahead.

Left hand still wrapped around the handle of the briefcase, Tres drew the same elbow up beneath him. Dragging the case closer, he balanced his weight on his arm, using it as a fulcrum point.

Clamping his teeth against the pain he knew was about to arrive, he twisted his body backward, flinging his elbow over his shoulder, scything it at Luis behind him.

Without seeing a thing, he felt it mash into the man's chest, dropping him back flat to the floor.

Coupled with landing exactly where he wanted, it also did just as he'd imagined, feeling like a hot knife was jabbed directly into his side.

An audible gasp passed his lips as he pulled his arm back, cocking it across his body before firing it a second time, a piston with the added benefit this time of seeing where it was directed.

Using his knees as a pivot, Tres lifted his entire upper body from the floor. Acrimony spiked from the pain shooting through him, at the situation he was now being forced to deal with.

Eight days earlier, they had both been sent north. They'd been given a single target, aided by the fact that their prey had no reason to believe they were coming.

As easy a situation as could possibly arise.

And still, this man had failed.

Not just that, but he had done so in such spectacular fashion that he had gotten beat up and arrested, causing Tres to now be here trying to clean things up.

Aiming the tip of his elbow at the matted mess that was the man's nose, Tres saw the ceiling flash by in his periphery. Working up as much centrifugal force as possible, a low cry seeped between his teeth, moisture rising to his eyes from the pain jabbing into his core.

Body parallel to the ground, he waited what felt like seconds before his elbow finally found its target.

The shot wasn't perfectly aligned, his uneven posture and his own injuries making that virtually impossible, but it was close enough. Landing just left of center, it drove into the twisted bone and gristle of Luis's nose, sliding across the bridge of it, grinding the underlying structure into a splintered mess.

Doing just as it was intended to, the shot was enough to ignite every nerve ending in Luis's face. Signals shooting straight up to his brain, they overwhelmed him on contact, his eyes rolling back. His head smacked hard against the tile, his body going limp as Tres fell atop him.

Laying belly-to-back, he stared straight up at the ceiling. His entire right side felt like it was alternatingly being set on fire and dunked in ice water, everything tingling at once, pulling the air from his lungs.

For only an instant, he lay flat on Luis, fighting to get his bearings. The lights above distorted, twisting into double before realigning, adrenaline alone allowing him to jerk his focus back to Ferry.

If the deputy had been smart, had been in a right state of mind, he would have left the moment things broke out. He would have moved into the main of the medical facility and started yelling, calling for Latham, and orderlies, and the local fire department, and whoever the hell else might be in the surrounding area.

Beyond the edge of the tussle between Tres and Luis, he would have had no trouble drawing his firearm, using it to either warn them or make them stop.

But he wasn't. The shot from the briefcase had been just enough to scramble things, reducing him to his baser instincts. It rendered him into a state of tunnel vision, clear thought and manual dexterity both falling to the side.

Instead, he was still standing in the middle of the room, working to get his weapon free, trying to call out in muted gasps for aid.

Rolling forward, Tres braced himself against Luis's body. Pushing off, he drew his knees up beneath him, his own mind beginning to winnow inward as the pain in his side intensified. Briefcase still in hand, he pulled it across his body, shuffling forward.

Across from him, Ferry raised his gaze, the snap on his holster finally giving way. Sliding his hand around the grip, his features pinched in tight, his elbow jerked back by his side.

Repeating the same movement he had used just moments before, Tres swung the briefcase back down past his knees. Bending at the waist, he added his right hand for extra force, clutching tight with both hands and swinging through in one fluid arc.

Much like the start of the fight just minutes before, things seemed to slow down. Tres could see as the front edge of the briefcase came up before him, his gaze tracking the barrel of the deputy's gun sliding free.

His molars came together, sweat and saliva dripping down over his chin. Every muscle seemed to work in concert, his body twisting upward, a human cyclone moving across the interior of the examination room.

All of it ending as the briefcase this time found it's mark, catching Ferry clean under the chin. Lifting him in the air, it deposited him flat on his back. Folded in half, the toes of his shoes hit the floor above either side of his head before slowly unfurling, leaving the man laying flat on his back in the middle of the examination room floor.

Chapter Forty

Forty-five minutes had passed since the call with Latham. Three-quarters of an hour with no word, a trio of calls back to him all going unanswered.

Twenty-seven-hundred seconds for my mind to race, taking everything that had happened in the last day and adding this newest development to it, tons of new questions arising.

No clear way of answering any of them. Even less chance at tamping down the adrenaline, the anxiety, the competing emotions roiling through me.

In the wake of the first call, I had stood in the Snoqualmie Police Department parking lot for nearly ten minutes. Retreating back a couple of steps, I had opted to lean against the side of the truck, not wanting to climb inside, knowing that everybody within the station was likely still very aware of my presence.

Shoving my hands into the front pockets of my jeans, that had lasted only a couple of moments. Unable to feign inertia, to even contemplate standing in one spot like that, I'd started pacing. Using the body of the truck as a makeshift barrier, I'd marched a path back and forth from the brick wall of the building to the rear bumper, never once slowing my pace.

With every step I took, more thoughts, more ideas, had tumbled in. Most of them little more than sentence fragments, they'd poured forth in a stream of consciousness, my mind barely able to grasp one before the next in order pushed in behind it.

Hands swinging free to either side, I'd alternated clenching them in a slow sequence, squeezing one until lactic acid burned in my forearm before switching to the other.

The entire time my phone had rested on the top rail of my truck bed, the ringer turned on high, me practically willing it to life, almost begging for somebody to get back to me.

Latham. Pally. Even Diaz.

Anybody that could make sense of what I was facing. Or at the very least give me a heading on where to go to find answers.

At the conclusion of those first ten minutes, sweat beginning to form along the small of my back despite the cold, I'd come to the realization I needed to be moving. While the SPD might have allowed me in as a friend of Serra and the deceased, there was no question that every person in the building had had a keen interest the entire time I was there.

Never did a moment pass when at least one person didn't have eyes on me. No doubt my name and face had been run through every system they had access to.

Just like they were no doubt watching me in the parking lot, my continued lingering, pacing, doing nothing to acquit me of any doubts they had.

Even if I had done nothing wrong, the longer I stayed where I was, the more I gave them reason to grow suspicious.

A fact that - at the very least - would cost me time I didn't have.

Equally important was the simple reality that for as long as I stayed in Snoqualmie, I was getting no closer to whoever had killed Shawn Martin. Or was now in West Yellowstone posing as the attorney for the man that had attacked me.

Or Junior Ruiz.

My first move from there was to duck back inside the station. A quick trip to tell Serra that I had to go, but that I would return soon.

A plan of action she seemed to already be well aware of, accepting the news with nothing more than another hug.

No admonishments of being careful, no pleas for me to wait it out and let the police do their jobs.

Fifteen years, she and Shawn had been married. Perhaps more than anybody outside of those of us on the team itself, she knew how these things went. She was aware of the threats that existed in this world.

And the lengths we would go to as a result of them.

From there, I had gone straight back to my truck. Pulling my phone from my pocket, I'd checked the screen again, hoping in vain for there to be a missed call waiting for me. Or a text message informing that more information was forthcoming.

Something.

Anything.

Finding nothing more than the same blank screen that I'd been staring at since hanging up with Latham, I swung in behind the wheel. Starting the engine, I'd allowed the heater to begin piping in air around me, the temperature slowly thawing as I kept the phone in hand.

Thumbing through the various apps on the home screen, I landed on the navigation system, my first thought to head west. Inputting the Seattle-Tacoma International Airport as my destination, I could probably be there in an hour and change at most, even with evening traffic.

Catching a flight south, I could be in San Diego by midnight.

Just as fast, I dismissed the notion.

In the coming day or two, there was no doubt that was where I would ultimately end up. That's where Diaz was, less than a couple hundred miles south of where Junior Ruiz had been locked up, roughly the same north of where we had apprehended him.

I still had no way of knowing if he had gotten out. And if he had, what strings he had pulled, favors traded, or even deals cut to make it happen.

What I did know was either way, there was zero chance he was leaving the area.

Everything I could recall about the case originated and existed in that one four-hundred-mile corridor. Every contact we ever considered, every bit of surveillance we ever ran.

Even most of the business he conducted, the man making a mockery of border patrol as he crossed back and forth with impunity.

Equally important was the timing of it all, something finally creating the leverage he needed to go after Martin and me both. He'd had time to plan, to reach out to his cohorts, to put things into motion.

And some reason for acting when he did.

Regardless of the particulars, my running straight down south would be exactly what he wanted. It would mean I showed up alone and outgunned, making it easy for him to finish exactly what he had tried to the night before on my porch.

I refused to be so foolish. This was now a lot bigger than just my anger or my ego or whatever else one wanted to assign to it.

It was about Serra standing inside the police station fifty feet away, devastation splayed across her face at the loss of her partner and my friend.

Kaylan lying in a hospital bed, mummified in gauze for making the mistake of trying to use the damn restroom after dinner.

For all of that, Ruiz would pay. And in order for that to happen, I needed to be better prepared.

Using the backspace feature on my phone's keyboard, I removed the airport as my destination of choice. Instead, I asked for it to direct me back to the freeway, pausing just long enough to ensure I knew the route before wheeling out of the parking lot.

According to Google Maps, the drive from Snoqualmie back to West Yellowstone would be ten hours. Ignoring any listed time estimates, I'd leaned hard on the gas, the drive away from the city easy. Moving opposite any form of evening traffic, I pushed the gas as fast as I dared, staying a full ten-to-twelve miles above the speed limit.

Once I made it to the freeway, I set the cruise control and headed due east across the state, retracing my path from earlier in the day. My nerves pulled taut, I clenched the wheel tight in both hands, willing the miles to pass quickly.

All of which meant that by the time my phone finally burst to life in the middle console, the ringer still turned up as high as it would go, I nearly shot straight through the roof of the truck. Body surging on an elixir of every chemical I produced, my heart rate spiked as I fired a hand out, snatching up the phone and thumbing it to life without so much as a glance to the screen.

Balancing it in my lap, I could see the glow of the faceplate in the windshield, my focus alternating between it and the road before me.

"Tate."

"Hawk," Pally replied.

Recognizing his tone in an instant, I riffled back through my mind to our previous conversation, pushing aside the mess that had most recently occurred with Latham.

"What'd you find?" I asked.

"A shitstorm."

A clatter of keys followed the statement. Remaining silent, I repositioned myself in the seat, raising up a bit higher behind the wheel.

"Okay," he said after a moment, all sound falling away on the other side. "Here's what I've got so far. And believe me, this is spotty as hell, so don't bother asking questions."

The advance warning did nothing for the myriad feelings working inside me, though I again remained silent, allowing him to continue.

"Apparently, at five o'clock this morning, the front gate to USP Lompoc opened wide and one Junior Ruiz stepped through."

Delivered without inflection, the words still managed to make my jaw drop and my eyes grow wide, palpitations rippling up through my core and passing into my chest. For an instant it was the same as when I'd first learned of Martin's death, a dull hum settling into my ears, all else fading away.

Unlike that last time, things snapped quickly back into place, my mind fighting to keep up, to focus on what Pally was saying.

"Eight years into a forty-year sentence," he continued. "No official court order, no evidence anywhere of him turning state's evidence.

"Just, done. Free and clear."

Flicking my gaze up to the green metal signs passing by along the side of the road, it was all I could do to register the words flitting by.

Barely did I even see any of the vehicles moving past me in the opposite direction.

Instead, my full focus went to what Pally had just shared.

For most of the afternoon, I had known who was behind this. The
bullet and the coin left at the Martin house was simply too poignant to
ignore.

Still, that was a far cry from finding out everything that happened
last night was a mere hours before he became a free man.

"Any chatter?" I managed to get out.

"None," Pally replied, seemingly expecting the question. "And
believe me, I've been looking everywhere. Whoever orchestrated this is
operating in some rarified air."

For every question I'd had just moments before that was now
answered, it seemed handfuls more surged in to replace them.
Together they congregated at the front of my mind, all adding to the
enormous tangle that had been there since first leaving The
Smokehouse.

Before I could so much as voice a single one, the color on the faceplate of my phone shifted. Drawing my attention downward, I
glanced to my lap just long enough to see I had an incoming call, the
familiar string of digits telling me that at long last, Latham was getting
back to me.

Raising my voice slightly, I cut in before Pally could share any
more, my heart rate again managing to lift a bit higher.

"Let me hit you right back. I've been waiting on another call to
come in, and something tells me he won't be so easy to get ahold of
again."

Chapter Forty-One

The call from Pally had been a bombshell. Completely unexpected, it was like a thunderbolt from the clear blue sky. Barely was I able to process what he was telling me and pay attention to the road, being extremely fortunate that the route was straight and traffic non-existent.

There was no way to know what the second incoming call might hold, but before I even attempted to accept it, I knew I needed to get off the highway. Every minute that I continued moving away from the city put me that much closer to the vast expanse across the center of Washington, much of it with cell reception that was patchy at best.

As much as I hated the notion of stalling my progress for even a moment, right now I needed to get on the horn and gather more information while I still could. And I needed to do so without worrying that some volatile mixture of anticipation and anger was going to cause me to end up in a ditch or as a greasy spot along the interstate.

Turning on the flashers, I made sure I was several feet removed from the rumble strips lining the highway and jerked the gear shift up into park. I left the engine running and accepted the call. Lifting the phone to just inches from my lips, I snapped, "Tate."

A bevy of voices was the first sound to respond. None of them seeming to be aimed in my direction, they were little more than background chatter, like the person calling me was standing in the middle of a crowd.

A fact that proved the wisdom in my choice to park before accepting the call, my left hand wrapping around the top of the steering wheel and squeezing tight.

"Hawk?" Sheriff Latham asked after a moment, as if he hadn't heard my original greeting. "You there?"

"Yeah," I said, raising my voice, the phone coming a bit closer to my mouth. "Sam, you there? Can you hear me?"

"There you are," he replied, the cacophony of background noise receding a bit. In their place came the sound of boot heels on tile, as if he were marching away to find a quiet place to speak.

"Sorry it took me a while to get back to you. Things got a little crazy around here."

Flicking my gaze to the rearview mirror, I watched as a pair of headlights appeared. Sitting up high and square, they looked to be on a semi-truck, a long-haul trucker moving across the state, probably singing along to the radio, thumping along with the beat against the top of the steering wheel.

Feelings I could only guess at right now, my own temperament on the extreme opposite end of the spectrum.

"How bad?" I prompted.

"You ever seen a monkey shit fight at the zoo?" Latham replied.

The clamp of my left hand grew tighter on the steering wheel, knuckles white beneath the skin. "Aw, hell."

"Yeah," Latham agreed, "and that would be an improvement at the moment."

The last time I had spoke to him, he'd gone tearing back inside to find out who was there posing as the attorney for the man that had tried to kill me and nearly did get Kaylan. Based on his demeanor and the cryptic phrasing of his first couple of lines, it had gone exactly as I'd originally feared.

"How many dead?" I whispered.

Latham let out a long sigh, the simple sound seeming to bear out a mix of resignation and self-loathing. "One. Luis Mendoza, the guy that you called us about last night."

The name was a complete fabrication and we both knew it, though neither objected to its use, needing to refer to him as something.

"How?" I asked.

"Shot between the eyes," Latham replied. "Small caliber, looked like he was already on the floor when it happened, most of the blowout on the tile beneath him."

Picturing what he was describing in my mind, I tried to envision how they might have ended up in such a position, the list of possibilities preciously thin.

"Ferry?"

"Unconscious by the time I got there, but alive," Latham said. "Thank God."

"Thank God," I echoed, adding what I was just told to the mental imagery I'd already put together. "Anybody else?"

"No," Latham replied. "There was a doc that was in there for the initial examination, but he'd stepped out after giving his diagnosis to let them decide how to proceed."

My focus aimed out the front windshield, I tried to put myself into the scene Latham was describing, gleaning as many details as I could while I had the chance.

"Nobody heard anything?" I asked.

Another long sigh met my ear. "Not until it was too late. When I went running inside, there were two orderlies banging on the door, asking if everything was alright.

"By the time we made it in, the damn side window was standing open and Juan Perez was gone."

Clamping my teeth down tight, I peeled my lips back, sucking in air. Beginning with my left hand, my entire upper body clenched, muscles knotting into tight balls. Keeping them that way until a faint burn traversed the length of me, I slowly released, wanting nothing more than to replay the scene from earlier and begin flailing at the seatback beside me.

Once, twice, I pulled in deep breaths, forcing my heart rate to slow, my mind to make sense of what I was being told.

"Did you happen to see which way he went?" I asked. "A license plate on the car he was driving?"

"No," Latham replied. "Some sort of sedan. Silver. Had the window stickers of a rental, though beyond that, I didn't even think to..."

Letting his voice trail away, it was clear that he was now doing what we all had at one point or another. The crushing weight of guilt was closing in, making him analyze everything through the benefit of hindsight, every misstep becoming that much clearer.

Just like I'd spent all last night doing in the wake of what happened on my front porch.

Knowing better than to offer any sort of condolences, any empty platitudes about how it wasn't his fault, I instead focused on the matter at hand. On anything that he might be able to add that would help us moving forward.

"You guys are out at the clinic on the west side?" I asked.

"Yeah," Latham muttered.

"That means he'd either have to go back through town or west into the mountains, right?"

Chapter Forty-Two

The look on the man's face had been nothing short of priceless as Junior Ruiz walked up to the unassuming blue Honda parked five doors down from Esmera's house. Sitting on the opposite side of the street, the guy had at least had the good sense to be looking the other direction, using the mirrors for coverage instead of staring directly at the house.

Not that it had mattered. After a lifetime spent doing what Ruiz had, he was accustomed to being aware of his surroundings at all times.

Especially after spending the last eight years in jail, nearly every single person he came in contact with someone capable of coming after him at any time. Even a few years removed, *El Jefe* would be a major get for someone looking to make a name for themselves, more than a couple having done just that over the years.

Not that it had ended well for any of them.

And not like he hadn't had a bit of a head start on this particular sighting.

Exiting the front door of the house, Ruiz had kept the post-it note pressed against his index finger. The rest of it remained tucked into his palm, his bare feet not making a sound as he padded down the sidewalk.

Drawing even with the Honda, he had turned and stared directly at the man through the passenger window, seeing the shock register on his features.

Middle-aged, with dark tan skin and a heavy thatch of curly black hair on his head and lining his jaw, his eyes had gone wide, his mouth sagging open. Upon being spotted, his right hand had shot out, pawing at the tangle of keys hanging down from the ignition.

Despite every internal reaction being to crack a smile – if not openly laugh – at the display before him, Ruiz had kept his features neutral. Making a hard left, he'd crossed out into the street, walking directly up to the passenger window.

Giving no effort for the handle, he merely curled a single finger, using a knuckle to tap on the glass. Using his left hand, he made a circular motion, gesturing for the man to roll it down.

A move that the guy seemed to sit and openly contemplate for several moments before eventually doing just that.

"*Sí?*" the man asked, his voice heavily accented.

Still on his face was a hint of the surprise he'd been wearing when first spotted, no matter his best efforts to keep it hidden. Twisted up in the front seat, he kept his right hand on his thigh, ready to reach out and turn the keys in the ignition if need be.

His left he kept hidden from view, most likely with some form of weapon tucked away between his seat and the door.

A position Ruiz had to admit was reasonable, if extremely unnecessary.

"You're one of Reyes's guys, right?" Ruiz opened.

Knees bent, he glanced along the street in either direction. On both sides, homes much like Esmera's were crowded onto small plots, the development meant to maximize what little usable land the desert landscape provided.

All single story and designed in the old Spanish mission style, they had stucco exteriors with red tile roofs. The yards were filled with rock gardens and succulents of various colors.

Very few had grass or trees to speak of, the murderous cost of water in the area forcing people to try alternative forms of land-scaping.

Pausing, contemplating the question, the man said nothing, merely sitting and staring.

Pulling his attention away from the neighborhood, Ruiz had looked back at the man. Shaking his head slightly, letting the annoy-ance he was beginning to feel be noticed, he said, "You've been on me since leaving Lompoc, right? Parked in the third row? Followed us clear down the 101 to the 5?"

A single muscle twitched in the man's face as he stared back, his features otherwise hard, giving away nothing.

Not that Ruiz needed him to. He'd spotted him the instant he walked out the gate that morning, less than a minute after he'd seen Esmera. Just as he'd known he was a quarter mile back throughout the entire drive, that being the reason he hated spending so much of it boxed in on the highway, feeling like it made it too easy to set a trap.

There was no need for Jones or Smith to be following him. They knew where he was going.

Ruiz had known word would get out about his release. In a place like Lompoc, information as a currency was worth its weight in gold. People would be lining up to get on the horn and tell whoever they thought would care that he was leaving.

But of the myriad people that might be interested, Reyes would be the only one sufficiently paranoid and with enough to lose to actually have someone waiting for him.

If not of his own accord, then with the help of a small nudge.

Extending his hand before him, Ruiz peeled the note from his finger. Mashing it onto the headrest of the passenger seat, he'd made sure it stuck before retreating a step.

"Tell your boss to give me a call at that number. I'd like to talk to him."

Saying nothing more, he'd turned on a heel and walked away. Retraced his steps across the street and down the sidewalk, entering through the front door and going back to the same seat he'd had in the kitchen when Esmera left.

Settling down on the hardwood chair, he'd stared down at the phone, his pulse raised just slightly. Fingers laced before him, he'd been prepared to wait as long as it took, suspecting that Reyes would drag it out most of the evening, trying to assert some level of dominance over the situation.

To his surprise, it took just twenty minutes, the phone springing to life before him.

With the ringer turned up, the sound was loud and shrill inside the quiet confines of the house. Shifting only his eyes, Ruiz had looked down at the screen, the word **RESTRICTED** stamped across it.

Letting it go to three rings, ignoring the small jolt that moved through his core, Ruiz extended a hand. Lifting the phone, he accepted the call, pressing it to his cheek.

"Mr. Reyes."

"Mr. Ruiz."

The last time Ruiz had heard the voice was eight years prior. At the time, Reyes had been with the organization less than two years, a mid-level employee that he had taken on as a favor to an influential member of the community.

A nephew in need of work. That sort of thing.

In the moment, never would Ruiz have imagined him being the one to rise in his wake, nothing more than a cocky kid just north of thirty.

Yet another point in favor of the cliché about time changing everything.

"I take it you wanted to speak with me," Ruiz said. "And this seemed easier than having you leave a man outside my sister's house."

Said without change in tone, Ruiz knew it would still manage to get his point across, letting Reyes know that he had been onto his presence all day.

On the opposite end of the line, Reyes paused. Choosing his next words carefully, he eventually settled on, "Can you blame me? Quite a curious thing, wouldn't you say?"

To call all that had transpired *curious* would be a gross understatement, though Ruiz wasn't about to state as much. Not now, and certainly not to this man.

"I wouldn't say that," he replied. "I served my time, kept my head down, and the review board determined that was sufficient."

A faint snort could just barely be heard, quiet enough not to be obvious, but plenty loud to be heard.

"Just like that?" Reyes countered. "Eight years into – what was it – a forty-year sentence?"

Every word used was meant to be a barb. No doubt, the intent was to elicit a response, get Ruiz's ire up, provoke him into disclosing something foolish.

All tricks that long predated them both, so easy to spot they were almost laughable.

"All I know is what I told you," Ruiz said.

Again, there was a small snort. "Right."

Handfuls of responses came to mind. Remarks Ruiz could make, banter that could be lobbed between the two men.

None of it would really serve any purpose, though.

"The reason I gave you my number was to suggest a parlay," Ruiz said. "A chance on neutral ground to sit and discuss things. Air any grievances. Make it so you're not looking over your shoulder for me, and I don't have one of your guys parked outside my front door."

In the wake of the offer, Ruiz fell silent. In response, nothing but dead air came back for the better part of a minute. Long enough that he could picture Reyes on the other end, features scrunched up in thought, trying to determine how to respond.

Determined not to add another word, to give the man as much time as he needed, Ruiz sat completely still. His focus glazed over, entire attention on the phone and whatever words came next.

"A parlay," Reyes eventually said, the word sounding closer to a question than a statement, disbelief, disdain hanging from it. "To clear the air."

"That *is* still how things are done, is it not?" Ruiz replied.

Again, a pause. "It is."

Ruiz could tell there was more the man wanted to say, additional things he was thinking. Remaining silent, he waited as Reyes continued, "But this one will be different from others. There will be no meeting on neutral ground, some place where you can get your people in place or bring in an army.

"You want to meet, you have to come here to me."

Regardless of what tradition dictated, Ruiz had expected the move, yet another attempt by Reyes to exert himself as the dominant party.

"When?" Ruiz asked.

"Tomorrow night. Ten o'clock. You will receive the address one hour before."

The line cut out the instant the last word was delivered. A small sound was all that could be heard, though the finality of it was more than enough to signal that they were done.

Slowly pulling the phone back from his face, Ruiz looked down at the screen, seeing that the call had lasted less than five minutes, most of that spent in silence.

Still, it had given him far more information than he had any right to hope for prior to receiving it.

Using his forefinger, Ruiz cleared the call from the screen. Going back to the keypad feature, he punched in a new series of digits, inserting them from memory before hitting send.

Letting it ring just once, he hung up.

Keeping it in hand, he stared at the screen, counting seconds.

Ultimately, he made it no further than six before it lit up again, a call coming in from the same number he'd just dialed. Feeling the corner of his mouth curl back, he accepted it, returning the phone to his cheek.

"Burris? It's me."

Chapter Forty-Three

The name Juan Perez was clearly bullshit. It was nothing more than a lowest common denominator, the type of thing someone that had spent their life in northern Mexico or southern California would tell people in Montana, figuring that they wouldn't know the difference.

And to some degree, they might even be right.

If not for the fact that there were at least a few residents that had spent significant time in other parts of the world. Places where Spanish wasn't just a spoken language, it was the only language.

Spots like those that I spent almost a decade working throughout before retiring north to the mountains.

Pulling back onto the road in the wake of the call with Latham, I had pushed the gas hard. Bringing the truck back up to speed, I'd gotten the cruise control set again before calling the phone back to life.

Gone were my initial reactions in the aftermath of leaving the Snoqualmie Police Department. Also nudged aside was whatever hostility I'd felt after speaking with Pally and Latham, not completely gone, but momentarily shoved out of the way in favor of caution.

Anger, venom, wrath, were all good things. Things that at some

point in the near future I would need in abundance. Guiding princi-
ples that would help me whenever I finally encountered Ruiz.

Until then, though, I needed to keep them in check. I needed to
have a clear mind, sorting through what I knew, assessing what was
available.

Namely, the man that had just left West Yellowstone. Who he was,
what his connection to Ruiz was.

How I could use him to get exactly where I needed to be.

Step one of that had to be getting a positive ID. Latham had said
that the man was driving a rental car, which would have required a
driver's license and a credit card. Even if the name he'd given at the
sheriff's department was bunk, there was a chance that he had used
authentic items to rent the car.

And in the more likely event that they too were fake, there was a
chance that whatever alias he was working under was in the system.
More information that could be searched for, pointing me in the right
direction.

Alternating my attention between the road and the cellphone in
my lap, I made my way back to the recent call log. Leapfrogging the
top listing in the list, I dropped down a single entry before hitting
send.

Throwing the line to speaker, I turned the volume up as loud as it
would go, the ringer drowning out the sound of pavement passing
beneath my tires. After a pair of rings, it was snatched up.

"Hawk."

"Pally."

"I'm still digging on Ruiz," he said, his voice a bit detached as he
worked. "Your call give you anything?"

Along the side of the road, a green highway sign passed by
announcing distances to various cities stretched out along I-90.
Closing in on halfway across the state, Ellensburg was just a few miles
up ahead, Spokane a hundred and seventy beyond that.

From there, it was a quick trip across the panhandle of Idaho
before closing back in on West Yellowstone.

With luck, I should arrive sometime overnight.

"More shit," I replied, relaying the story of what had transpired at the medical center. As I shared, I could hear the sound of computer keys fall away, replaced by complete silence.

When I was done, he said nothing for several moments before finally exhaling slowly.

"Yeah, that is some shit."

Unable to disagree, I felt my eyebrows rise slightly as I bobbed my head. Flicking a glance to the rearview mirror, I could see the vitriol I'd been trying to keep under wraps come a little closer to the surface, my features drawn tight.

If ever I was going to relay my idea, ask him to begin looking into things, it had to be soon.

Otherwise, there was a decent chance I might descend into pounding the seatback beside me, no matter how hard I fought to keep myself under control.

"Maybe not," I replied. "Or, at least not completely. Remember that time in Rio? When you were able to-"

"Access the public works and pull traffic camera footage?" Pally asked, jumping ahead.

"Yes," I replied. "I was thinking...Latham said that after the guy shot Mendoza and took out the deputy, he jumped in a rental car and took off.

"I know you don't know the area well, but from where they were, there's only one road. Now, he wouldn't want to go west, because he has to assume there would be a BOLO going out looking for him, and that road would just take him out into the mountains."

Seeming to follow along - most likely having a map already pulled up on screen before him - Pally said, "And that would limit his options."

Pausing, he considered it for a moment before adding, "But I thought Latham didn't get his license plate number?"

"He didn't," I said, having considered that too, "but this guy wouldn't have known that. He'd probably even assume the opposite, meaning he'd want to get back through town as fast as possible. Either find somewhere to ditch the car, or better yet, drop the rental off wherever he got it and disappear back into his own ride."

For a moment, there was no sound. Nothing but the familiar

thrum of the highway as lights appeared along the south side of the highway, the town of Ellensburg fast approaching.

Flicking my gaze to the dash, I saw that I still had plenty of gas from filling up in Snoqualmie, the sack of snacks still rolling around on the floor. Combined, they dismissed any thought of stopping, the speedometer staying pinned at eighty-two as I hurtled forward.

"I'm assuming since you alluded to Rio, there are traffic cameras in West Yellowstone?" Pally eventually asked.

"There are," I confirmed. "New ones put in last summer to monitor traffic coming in and out of the park."

"Any idea who oversees them?" he asked.

"Not exactly," I confessed. "I would guess the Park Service, though there's a handful of other organizations that could lay a claim to them.

"West Yellowstone Sheriff, Montana Highway Patrol..."

"Even the FBI," he said, citing their primary jurisdiction of the federal lands inside Yellowstone. "You say those are the only cameras?"

"Definitely."

"Shouldn't be a problem," he said, not the slightest hint of concern in his voice. "And what am I looking for?"

"Silver sedan, Idaho plates. Hispanic male, mid-to-late twenties in age. Probably the only man in town wearing a suit and tie."

Grunting in reply, I could hear Pally go back to working on the keyboard. "And here I thought you might have a challenge for me. Timeframe?"

"Latham ran inside about an hour and a half ago. The clinic is just outside of town, so he'd have passed through maybe five or ten minutes after that?"

"Got it," he said, more keystrokes audible behind him. "When I have something, you'll have something."

The line cut off without another word, Pally going to work, leaving me alone with my thoughts in the darkness.

Chapter Forty-Four

"The threat has been contained."

With the phone switched to stereo Bluetooth, the sound of the man breathing on the other end was plainly obvious. Drawing in deep and even breaths, it sounded like he was just inches from Tres Salinas's ears, loud enough that he reached out and lowered the volume on the radio dial.

"Are you sure?"

"Positive," Tres replied. "Put a bullet between his eyes myself."

Headed north on the sole state highway leaving West Yellowstone, Tres had one hand draped over the wheel. The other sat trembling in his lap, his body coming down from the adrenaline of the fight, fighting to recalibrate.

Making that even more difficult was the pain in his ribs, every breath feeling like a hot poker being jabbed into his serratus muscles.

Offering some sort of guttural noise that Tres took to be positive, the man asked, "Any other damage?"

"Had to slap around some low-level flunky a little bit to get the opening I needed," Tres replied. "No other deaths or even serious injury."

Again came the same noise, as if the man was clearing his throat. "Any word on the target?"

Rounding a bend in the road, a car approached from the north. Low-slung headlights that were spaced tight together, the vehicle looked like some sort of sports car. Closing fast, it threw halogen light across the rental Tres was in, illuminating the interior, highlighting the spots of blood spattering the front of his dress shirt.

"None," Tres replied. "I did a drive-by on his office, but the place was blocked off with police tape. Otherwise, I just went after our guy and got out."

"Good," the man said, his voice low. "Where are you now?"

"Moving north," Tres said. "Going to swap rides and then head back down."

"Good," the man repeated. "Be sure to check in before arrival."

"Will do," Tres replied. Knowing the last statement was a signal of closure, he cut the line, silence falling in the car. Tossing his cellphone onto the passenger seat, he shifted his body back to sitting upright. Seizing the wheel in both hands, he stared straight out, lifting his shoulders just slightly, stretching as much as his body would allow.

The events at the medical center weren't exactly how he would have liked things to go. Under optimal conditions, he would have been given a few minutes alone with the man that was supposed to be his client.

Time when he could have fired a bullet or used a knife or a garrote or a damn cyanide capsule. Anything that would have allowed him to complete the task and get away cleanly, without raising an alarm.

Such a thing was never going to present itself, though. For all the faults of the hillbillies that were playing cops, they had at least had the sense never to leave him alone.

So he'd had to improvise.

Peeling his right hand away from the wheel, he grabbed at the lapel of his suit coat. Holding it open, he saw the spots of blood dappling his white dress shirt, already dried and hardened, closer to black than red in the semi-darkness of the car.

Shooting him wouldn't have been his first choice – not after the man had messed up such an important assignment – but it had gotten the job done. All things considered, that was the best Tres could hope for.

Lifting his gaze back to the road ahead, he noticed a faint glow begin to rise above the treetops before him. The sign he'd been waiting for since pulling away from the clinic, he felt a tiny bit of the clench in his stomach release.

Growing ever brighter, it served as a beacon drawing him in, lighting the way to Bozeman, the town he'd been yearning to see for the better part of an hour.

The answer he'd given on the phone a moment before about being close to swapping rides wasn't entirely true. Still a few hours east of where his car was parked, there was no way he could risk making it that far and crossing multiple state lines.

Not with the very real possibility that the sheriff had gotten his license plate, probably had half the state now looking for him.

What was true was he was about to make a swap of sorts. Once he got to Bozeman, he could find a shopping center. From there, all he needed to do was spot another vehicle with Idaho plates and make a quick trade.

Between that and peeling away the suit he was in, switching back into the Seahawks gear he'd been wearing the night before, he would become effectively invisible. Just another random sedan out for a drive, passing through on his way back home.

Nothing to concern himself with before making it back to Spokane, grabbing his own car, and turning due south.

Never to return.

Chapter Forty-Five

F or a good hour after hanging up with Pally, I was too wired to even begin coming down. Armed with a combination of adrenaline and anger, confusion and anticipation, there was no way I could get my body to slow.

Not after all that had happened in the previous twenty-four hours, the truncated timetable seeming almost too much to even believe. To think that just a day earlier I had been sitting at a table with Kaylan enjoying the most decadent fudge brownie monstrosity ever put in a bowl, the two of us laughing at the uptight folks sneaking glances our way, seemed inconceivable.

Adding to it the way things had escalated, beginning with the explosion on the front steps of my office, including seeing Serra Martin for the first time in years, and now culminating with a second trip across the Pacific Northwest, bordered on the absurd.

And that was before saying anything of Junior Ruiz or the henchmen he somehow had traipsing across two states.

By the time I had made it two-thirds of the way across Washington, much of that initial angst had started to bleed away. Not because I reached any form of resolution in my mind, but because simple physiology began to take control.

I hadn't slept in well over thirty hours. In the time since, my body had been yo-yoing through caffeine and adrenaline bursts, needing precious rest soon if I was going to be any good to anybody.

Doing the best I could given the situation, I had slid down a couple inches behind the steering wheel. Shaving a mile or two off the cruise control setting, I'd put myself into a low energy state, letting the flat and straight nature of the road and muscle memory push me on through the night.

A state I remained in, gleaning any bit of rest I could, allowing the hum of wheels on the blacktop to become white noise, until the sound of my phone shattered the relative still of the truck cab. Snapping me from my trance with the first shrill bark, I blinked three times in succession. Raising a hand, I rubbed at my eyes, sliding myself back upright.

Without bothering to look over at the phone, knowing it had to be one of three people, I jabbed out a single finger, accepting the incoming call.

"Tate."

"Pally. Where are you?"

Blinking twice more, I took just a moment to let the voice register. Giving a quick shake of my head, I expelled any lingering grogginess, alternating my gaze between the glowing faceplate and the highway before me.

"An hour from the Idaho border."

"On which side?"

A crease appeared between my brows as I considered the question a moment before recognition of what he was saying, of the last conversation we'd had, landed.

"Washington. Why?" For as much as the last hour had managed to push aside whatever chemical elixir my body was operating under, in just seven words Pally was able to draw it back to the fore. My body temperature rose, my pulse picking up just slightly. "What did you find?"

"Like Rio all over again," Pally replied.

The sting we had carried out in Brazil had gone well beyond merely being a success, coming in as a veritable coup. A joint operation with the local field office, we'd managed to seize more than a thousand kilos of product and two million dollars cash.

And more importantly, we'd pulled a couple of known cartel leaders that were funneling proceeds to known terrorists off the board.

Saying whatever he had found was like that was no small praise, words I knew he would not offer lightly.

Again, I sat up higher, lifting my bottom from the seat. Running a hand over my face, I could feel bits of moisture underlying my beard and the hair draped across my forehead.

"Hit me."

"Okay," Pally began, his voice taking on the detached tone he always employed when relaying information, "the cameras in West Yellowstone are run by the Park Service. They are saved to a depository in the cloud and kept for a period of one week before being wiped clean."

Neither of the pieces of information he gave me came as a surprise. The intersection was well within city limits, meaning the highway patrol wouldn't care. Same for the sheriff's office, which always had at least one patrol car roaming the streets.

The cameras would be meant to monitor anybody entering the park, footage archived for the same period as the standard pass people were granted upon entry.

"And you were able to find our guy?" I asked.

"Way, way better than that," he said. Hitting a couple of keystrokes, I heard the sound of a rolling desk chair sliding across a hard surface.

"Tres Salinas," Pally said.

Pulling up there, he gave me a moment to pass it through my mental repository, the name bringing up absolutely nothing.

"Real or alias?" I asked.

"We'll get to his alias in a minute," Pally replied. "For now, we'll focus on this, his real name. Got it from pulling his image from the traffic cam footage and running it through facial recognition."

The move was one I hadn't thought of before, not knowing what the resolution on those cameras might have been, though I had to admit it was a good call. A man could have all the fake identification he wanted, but changing his face on the fly would be much more difficult.

"In the system?" I asked.

"DMV," Pally replied. "United States citizen, born in Chula Vista, California in 1993."

Running the math, I landed on him being twenty-five or twenty-six, depending on the month he was born. Much like Luis Mendoza.

"Any known affiliation? Anything?" I asked.

"Nope," Pally replied. "Outside of the driver's license, has surprisingly little footprint on American soil. Never attended high school here, not so much as a credit card in his name."

On the opposite side of the highway, a trio of semi-trucks moved by in a miniature convoy. One after another, the glare of their lights infiltrated the cab of my truck, bright enough that they lingered with every blink even long after they were gone.

What Pally was describing wasn't terribly surprising. We'd seen it a number of times before, especially with people that might somehow be affiliated with the drug trade.

"Passport baby," I muttered, referencing the term that was given to people that entered the United States for the purpose of giving birth, imbuing their child with citizenship rights. From there, they likely took them back over the border, keeping all other activities quiet moving forward, ensuring that both had an easier timing moving between the two countries.

"Definitely looks like it," Pally agreed. "Which brings me to the alias. At one o'clock this afternoon, the car he's driving was rented from the Avis counter at the Spokane International Airport."

My lips parted just slightly as I took in the information, adding the mash of disparate facts already floating through my mind.

"Spokane," I whispered, having seen the name flash by on a dozen or so different road signs as I cut a path east across the state.

"Exactly," Pally said, "which is why I asked where you were. Once I had a time of rental, it wasn't too hard to take a peek at the cameras on their short-term parking lot.

"Lo and behold, fifteen minutes before picking up the sedan, he pulled in driving another equally nondescript vehicle with California plates."

For the untold time of the day, information Pally gave me landed heavy and hard, fireworks exploding across my mind. My eyes went wide as I considered it, my subconscious forcing my foot forward, causing it to press down a bit harder on the gas.

"You don't think-"

"He's headed back there to make the swap?" Pally finished. "I don't know. At some point though, he'll either have to ditch it or switch them out."

Flicking my gaze to the clock on the dash, I considered the hour, running the math in my head.

West Yellowstone and Snoqualmie were roughly equidistant from Spokane. I couldn't imagine him running much faster than me, not wanting to draw attention after everything that had happened at the clinic.

If I hurried, I stood a chance at intercepting him.

At the same time, there was no way of knowing if he would even make a run on Spokane. A handful of different factors would play into it, beginning with if he thought Latham got his plate number and including how many viable shots he had at nabbing another.

"Has the rental been returned anywhere else?" I asked.

A quick sequence of keys rang out before Pally said, "Nope. Avis still has it listed as rented, not expected to be returned until tomorrow."

The fact that Salinas had gone back through West Yellowstone told me something. It showed he was planning to go north, which didn't mean he had to be headed back for his car, but it hinted at it strongly.

Best guess, he was doing exactly what I was now doing. He'd brought his own vehicle up because it was the easiest way of transporting things he might need. Clothing. Surveillance equipment.

The gun that killed Shawn Martin.

While at least part of that was with him now, I couldn't imagine him wanting to leave any evidence tied to multiple offenses unattended in an airport parking lot. Especially knowing he needed to ditch the car he was now driving anyway.

Just like there was no chance I was willfully ignoring the chance to get at this guy, even if it did turn out to be nothing more than a couple of hours sitting in a parking lot.

"You've got eyes on the car with the California plates in Spokane now?"

Chapter Forty-Six

Despite the man's extreme proficiency in a variety of skills that were beneficial to the organization, basic communication was not one of them. Sitting in the chair normally reserved for Arlin Mejia, Hector sat ramrod straight, his hands repeatedly running down the front of the black cargo pants he wore. Beads of sweat were plainly visible on his cheeks and forehead, underscoring the twist of scruff spread across his jaw.

They even stained the underarms of the royal blue t-shirt he wore, a damp inverted triangle having formed just beneath his chin.

Seated across from him, Ramon Reyes took full measure of the man. Leaning forward in his own chair, his elbows were spread wide to either side, fanned out almost like wings. Forearms lying flat on the desktop, his cuffs had been returned to their usual position, his fingers laced before him.

To look at him head-on, there would be no indication that anything had gone wrong. Still as fresh as the moment he first stepped into the office fourteen hours earlier, his eyes were clear. He spoke evenly, tone never rising or falling.

All in spite of the spiking mix of thoughts he had locked inside.

"Did he give any indication as to how he knew you were there?" Reyes asked.

Hands continuing to move down his thighs, Hector cast a glance to Mejia standing off to the side, arms folded, a deep frown accentuating the lines of his face.

"No," he said, his thick lilt distorting the response just slightly.

"But he just walked straight out the front door, down the sidewalk, and came right over to you?"

"*Si.*"

Flicking his gaze over to Mejia, Reyes considered the information a moment.

"Was he armed?"

"No."

"Did he make any threats?"

"No."

Pushing out a long breath through his nose, Reyes used his elbows to leverage himself back away from the table. Moving until he rested flush against the padded leather behind him, he kept his fingers laced, balancing them in his lap.

Twice already they had been through every second of the interaction with Junior Ruiz. First with Hector telling the entire story, and then again with Reyes breaking down every aspect in excruciating detail.

Now they were just to the point of belaboring things, Reyes realizing that his questions were starting to take on the appearance that he was merely hoping for the answers to change.

As a standalone encounter, Reyes might have been able to accept things at their face value. Perhaps Hector had gotten a little too close and been spotted, or Ruiz's release from prison had made him a bit more cognizant of his surroundings than usual.

But coming on the same day as him becoming a free man more than a decade before it should have even been a possibility, Reyes couldn't square it.

"And after he left you the note," Reyes said, shifting his eyes down to the small piece of blue paper in the center of the desk, "he just turned and went back inside?"

Mouth open to respond, Hector contemplated his answer for a moment before twisting his chin an inch to the side, his eyebrows rising just slightly. "*Sí.*"

Once more, Reyes felt a series of pinpricks rise through his chest. Little bits of light flashed through his mind, his brain attempting to line up what he'd just discovered, hoping that this one tiny aspect would somehow fit.

Like so much else in the last weeks though, it simply refused.

Snapping his heels up under him, Reyes drew himself to full height. Pulling his hands back and clasping them behind him, he said, "Thank you, Hector. I appreciate you coming down to talk with us."

Jerking his gaze up to follow the unexpected movement, Hector's jaw sagged a bit more. Only his eyes moved, the whites of them flashing against his dark skin and beard, flicking from Reyes to Mejia.

"If we need anything else, we'll be sure to be in contact."

Taking another moment, slow realization set in for Hector. Closing his mouth, he dipped his chin half an inch before twisting sideways over the arm of his chair.

Without a word, he turned and departed, nearly sprinting out of the room.

Rooted in place, Reyes watched as he left. He even stood still and tracked the man's progress on the stairs outside his office, waiting until he heard the main door below open and slam shut before turning his attention to Mejia beside him.

Shoulders visible sagging, he pulled his hands around to his waist, shoving them into the front pockets of his slacks.

"What the hell do you make of all that?"

Taking a step forward, Mejia seemed to consider his usual seat, making it as far as the veneer of Hector's sweat still spread across the leather before thinking better of it. Choosing to remain standing, he kept his arms folded, the frown in place.

"I mean, how many times have we used Hector before?" Reyes asked, not waiting for an answer to his opening inquiry.

"Several," Mejia conceded. "Double digits, anyway."

"And has he ever been spotted before?"

"Never. When it comes to this sort of thing, the man is practically a ghost."

Turning perpendicular to his desk, Reyes began to pace. With each stride across the floor the soles of his shoes let out a distinctive din, tapping against the polished tile floor.

Making it as far as the wall, he turned on a heel, retracing his steps.

"Exactly," Reyes said. "A damn ghost. And yet, somehow Ruiz walks right up to him on the street, lets him know he's been aware of him all day."

Offering a guttural click from deep in his throat, Mejia bobbed his head twice in agreement. "You think he has help?"

"Don't you?" Reyes asked. Pulling a hand from his pocket, he extended it before him. "Guy gets released after eight years, strolls out at five in the morning, not another soul around? Somehow just knows the best tracker we have is watching him?

"Somebody's pulling strings for him, don't you think?"

Again, the same sound could be heard. Shifting his attention to the desktop between them, Mejia took a moment, considering the question, before saying, "I think the days of *El Jefe* are over. Whatever is going on here, whatever he is trying to play at, is nothing more than the dying gasps of someone that doesn't yet realize time has passed them by."

On the back end of a loop across the space, Reyes turned his shoulder just inches from the wall. Looking back in the opposite direction, he stared at Mejia, running what the man had just said through his mind.

"And this business with the parlay tomorrow?"

"Optics," Mejia said. "The man has been inside a long time. The last anybody saw of him, he was pinned to the ground at a party he was hosting and carried away.

"That's a bad look for someone like Junior Ruiz. So bad that the very first thing he'll want to do is begin running damage control on his image."

Keeping his gaze on Mejia another moment, Reyes shifted his focus out through the wide opening lining the back end of the office.

Past the vegetation bunched tight around the house they were in, he could see the warehouse they'd been in earlier in the day, a series of security lights illuminating it on the far end of the spread.

Moving under their glow was a pair of guards, each on opposite ends of the structure. Matching them on the backside was another pair Reyes knew, keeping the same spacing, walking in the same even stride.

Eight years ago, none of this would have seemed possible. Not the spread they were currently operating from, or the new direction the business was moving in.

Not even the country they currently called home.

Stuck in the old ways, Ruiz had been content to do things as they always had been.

"So you think this is nothing more than peacocking? Ruiz trying to give himself some whiff of legitimacy? Maybe try to get in on the fringes, make it look like he's still somehow involved?"

His gaze still on the warehouse, Reyes pulled his attention from the warehouse, switching his focus to Mejia standing behind the desk.

"Like I said," Mejia replied, "the days of *El Jefe* are over. You have nothing to worry about."

Chapter Forty-Seven

The way most car rental agencies worked was through barcode scanners. A simple sticker affixed either in the bottom corner of the front windshield or inside the driver's side door. Rarely did attendants even bother to notice license plates, using their handheld device to scan in a return, print a receipt on the spot, and hand it off.

A process made even quicker and more efficient in a place like Spokane.

Especially late at night, with temperatures hovering right around thirty degrees.

Even at that, Tres Salinas had opted against going through the process. There simply wasn't any need to. The car had been rented under a false name and credit card. The inside had been wiped down, any trace of him eliminated.

There was nothing that could lead anybody back to him.

And it wasn't like he could see too many people getting in a fuss over it, the car parked less than three hundred yards from where he'd first picked it up.

Changed out of the suit he'd been wearing in West Yellowstone, Tres was back in the jeans and Seahawks sweatshirt. Covering his top half was the down coat he'd worn the night before, the heavy lining managing to keep his upper body warm, cold air swirling around his ankles and rising beneath the cuff of his pants.

Everything else he'd bothered to take with him on the short jaunt was wadded into a single duffel bag. Hanging from a strap over one shoulder, he could feel it bouncing against his back as he walked as fast as he darted across the short-term parking lot.

A far cry from most of the airports he'd been to in his life, there was no tower structure protecting him from the weather. No bright lights or endless rows of vehicles.

In their stead was merely a single open expanse, completely exposed to the elements. Spaced at even intervals were sodium lights on stanchion poles, a few stray snowflakes floating down beneath their filmy glow.

The trip to West Yellowstone couldn't quite be considered a success, though it was far from a disaster. His interaction with the sheriff and his deputy was much more than he would have liked. The entire scene at the medical clinic was a debacle of the highest order.

Having to stop and swap license plates with a mid-sized SUV with those annoying stickers of a stick figure family in the back window was something he'd rather never have to do again.

His ribs hurt like hell.

But the simple fact remained, Luis Mendoza – and any chance he ever had at pointing a finger at the people who had sent him – was dead.

Of everything, that was most important.

Threading his way between a pair of pickup trucks sitting up high on oversized tires, Tres emerged to see the car he had driven north from California parked in the row before him. On the passenger side, a hunter green sedan had parked too close to him, no more than a couple of inches separating the vehicles.

To the left was an open space, a bald patch in the light film of snow covering the ground showing whoever was there to have pulled out recently.

Keeping his pace even, Tres extracted his left hand from deep in the pocket of his coat, the cold seizing on his exposed fingers. Sucking in a sharp breath, he reached around beside him, grabbing the bag and pulling it forward, balancing it atop his hip.

Coming up alongside the car, he stopped beside the rear door and unzipped the side pocket of the bag, thrusting his hand down inside.

Splaying his fingers wide, barely did he touch the cold metal of the keys when he saw it.

Nothing more than a flash of movement, a quick reflection moving across the window beside him, pure instinct caused Tres to snap his body downward. Adrenaline leaked into his system as he jerked his attention up, catching a flash of metal as it swung down at him in a hard arc.

Jerking up his left arm, he twisted the bag out in front of him, using it as a shield against the incoming blow.

Just barely able to get the front edge of it there in time, the duffel caught enough of the incoming object to deflect it from crashing directly down on Tres's head. Pushing the trajectory several inches to the side, hardened steel instead smashed into the top of his shoulder.

Feeling the joint separate on contact, bright lights erupted before Tres's eyes. His mouth gaped, sucking in a sharp intake of air. A loud buzz sprouted in his ears, spiking fast before evening out.

Barely able to keep himself upright, Tres spun with the force of the blow. Dropping to a knee, he twisted to his right, dropping the duffel behind him.

Pain hurtled the length of his body, sweat instantly rising to his features. Right arm pinned tight to his side, he used his left to try and push himself upright.

Staggering, he made it no further than a couple of steps before a second blow landed. This one coming in from the opposite direction, it was a boot buried square in his midsection, a vicious kick that lifted him from the ground, flinging him against the side of his car.

Coupled with the existing injury to his rib, an electric shock surged through his entire midsection. His breath seized tight as bright lights flashed across his vision.

His right shoulder mangled, the arm virtually worthless, there was no way for him to break his fall as he tumbled down, landing hard on the frozen asphalt. Again, every pain receptor in the joint ignited, every muscle and nerve ending he had seizing tight, almost paralyzing in the hold it had on him.

Under the combined weight of the blows, he lay sputtering on the ground, his mind unable to compute everything that was happening. Locked in survival mode, it told him only to breath, to do something about the searing agony gripping him.

Seeing a pair of feet appear before him, it was all he could do to lift his gaze. To see the man standing there, a tangle of hair and beard covering his features.

The look on his face pure venom as he stepped forward and lashed out with another kick, this one sending his world straight to black.

Chapter Forty-Eight

It took everything I had, every iota of self-restraint I could muster, not to end Tres Salinas in the Spokane International Airport parking lot. To not just step forward with the tire iron and start lashing at his unconscious body curled up against the rear tire of his sedan.

To not use the studded soles on the hiking boots I wore and just go to work on him. Beginning with the smaller bones in the hands and feet, I'd then go after his wrists and ankles, knees and elbows, systematically continuing what had started with his shoulder.

All the while making him pay for what he had done to Shawn Martin.

For what happened to Kaylan, even if he wasn't the one directly responsible for it.

As much as I wanted to do all that, for as much as the bastard deserved it, I had managed to hold off. Not from some last second intervention of my conscience and damned sure not out of some sudden concern for fellow man.

Because right now, I needed answers from him.

Answers I had no way of getting if he was dead.

Instead, I had left him folded up beside the car on the frozen pavement. Moving off at a jog, I'd made my way back to the truck and fired it up, swinging around and sliding into the vacant parking stall beside his car.

Working with the radio and the headlights off, I tried to be as quiet as possible. The combination of the day of the week and the time of night was able to give me some coverage, ensuring the lot was desolate as I worked.

Heart racing, sweat coated my features as I left the engine running and climbed out. Each breath extended before me in a white cloud, my internal temperature running much hotter than the air around me.

Tiny pinpricks lit up my face and forehead, the cold nipping at the moisture covering my skin.

Leaning over the side of the truck bed, I popped open the toolbox running the width of it. Cold to the touch, the hinges let out a small moan as I shoved it upward, reaching into the bottom for a roll of duct tape.

Snapping it up, I jogged around the rear of the bed. Starting with Tres's wrists, I bound the entirety of his hands and lower arms behind him into one solid silver cocoon, ensuring there was no way he could get them free. With his shoulder so severely disjointed, I doubted he'd even be able to lift them, the man's upper body rendered basically useless.

Once that was done, I moved to his feet and did the same, beginning with his ankles before encapsulating the shoes he wore. When that was done, I made a few passes around his knees, clamping them together as well.

The last thing to be mummified was the lower half of his face, working around the mangled remains of his nose from my kick a moment earlier. Without needing to break the tape into strips, I wound it around his head a half-dozen times before tearing it off.

Whenever it was time to revive the prick, there would be no small amount of hair and skin to come with it.

A fact I have no shame in admitting made me smile.

Vaguely aware of the clock, I unspooled nearly the entire roll, waiting until I was sure he was rendered immobile before tossing the remainder of the tape into the truck bed.

From there, I hefted the man off the ground, hoisting him to a shoulder like a bag of mulch and dumping him in as well.

To say it was a gentle landing would be a misstatement, his forehead bouncing off the spray-on liner, a new gash opening above his left eye.

A worthy addition to the busted nose, uneven stripes of blood moved across his face as his body settled into position, balanced on his mangled shoulder.

As good a place as any.

Snatching up the man's duffel bag from the ground, I jogged back around the truck and slid in behind the steering wheel. Chucking the bag into the passenger foot well, I checked the clock on the dash, less than three minutes having passed since moving the truck.

Jerking the gear shift down into reverse, I backed away and headed for the exit, waiting until I was on the main drive leading away from the airport before sliding the phone back onto my thigh. Moving from pure muscle memory, I used my thumb and forefinger to navigate through the call log, finding what I needed and hitting send.

A moment later, Pally's voice piped in, the first ring not even complete before he answered.

"Well, that looked fun."

Under the extreme mix of thoughts and feelings running through me, it took a moment for me to place what he meant. Once I did, a half-smile appeared, my head shaking an inch or two to either side.

"You saw?"

"Watched the whole damn thing."

I should have suspected as much. He'd been the one to tell me where Salinas's car was parked. Cleary, he'd had a real time feed of everything.

To have expected him not to tune in would be nothing short of selfish.

"The video?" I asked.

"What video?" he replied, an unspoken assurance that he and Salinas and I were the only three that knew about what had just taken place. Already the camera feeds had been scrubbed clean, a five-minute loop of inactivity filling any gap.

Glancing to the rearview mirror, I could see that the man's body had rolled over flat on his back. With his hands pinned behind him, the uneven surface caused him to shift a few inches to either side, his eyes still pinched shut.

Just staring at him, knowing I was in the same space, had just shared the same air, as the man that killed my friend caused acrimony to rise within me. White hot and acrid, it rivaled what I'd felt standing in Russia almost two years before, staring at the man who had killed my wife and daughter.

"For a second there, I thought you were going to kill him," Pally said, the words pulling my attention back to the call.

"Would you have blamed me?"

For a moment, there was no response. Nothing but silence, punctuated by a slow sigh.

"No," he eventually confessed. "Though that would have made things a lot more difficult moving forward."

Setting my jaw, I bobbed my head slightly, again flicking my gaze to the rearview mirror.

This man deserved absolutely no quarter from me. What he did, the greater scheme he was willingly participating in, made him culpable for anything that came his way.

And still yet might soon be arriving.

But to merely succumb to those urges, to lash out in pure rage, would do no good. It wouldn't bring us any closer to Junior Ruiz, wouldn't help answer how he'd gotten out or why he'd decided to come for us when he did.

It wouldn't have given peace of mind to Serra or Kaylan.

All it would have managed to do was feed my own desire for vengeance.

"Which is why I didn't," I muttered. "Though I still can't make any promises moving forward."

"Nor should you," Pally replied. "There's a lot we don't know yet. No way of foreseeing how this all plays out."

Pally wasn't being as forthcoming as I was, but in his own way, he was letting me know he was of the same mind.

This son of a bitch had killed our friend.

That would not pass lightly.

Chapter Forty-Nine

A small turnout along the side of the road, the spot was one I'd been to a few times in the past. Still a couple of hours from making it back to West Yellowstone, it abutted the Beaverhead National Forest. The last place I knew to have reliable cell coverage before the road officially moved into the back country.

Pulling the truck to the side of the road, I killed the lights and the ignition. Grabbing up my cellphone, I slid from the interior of the truck, stepping out into the night.

Well past midnight, the world was completely silent. Enough cloud cover existed to block any stars or the moon from getting through. Any other ambient light there might have been was swallowed by the towering lodgepole pine trees lining either side of the road.

Aside from the ticking of the cooling engine block, there was not a sound. The sole smells were of pine needles and ice crystals.

Everything clean and pure, very much my element.

Exactly as I would have spent the day if not for the unexpected visitor that had arrived the night before.

Circling around the side of the truck, I rested both forearms along the top edge of the bed. Gripping my phone in hand, I pressed a single button on the side, using the glow of the screen to check on Salinas.

Despite more than an hour passing since I'd dumped him into the bed of the truck, his eyes were still closed. Having rolled over onto his opposite shoulder, his entire body quivered with the cold, the down coat he wore enough to keep him alive, but little more.

Not that I cared, my interests in his state purely for the purposes of information gathering at the moment.

If frostbite took every appendage he had in the process, so be it.

Pulling the phone back, I took a step away from the side of the truck. Using my thumb, I called the phone log back up on the screen. Scrolling down through, I bypassed a handful of conversations with Pally and Latham before finding what I wanted.

Three rings later Diaz was on the line, answering just as she had eighteen hours before, regardless of the late hour.

"Hawk."

"Diaz," I replied. Taking a few steps, I kept my back to the truck, my boots crunching against the gravel beneath my feet. "I need to ask you something, and I need it to be as far off the record as humanly possible."

"Hold on," she replied, her voice even. No other reaction of any kind came with the words, any surprise she might have felt completely hidden.

The even cadence of hard-soled shoes against a floor could be heard, ending with a door closing.

"You're still at work."

"I am," she replied, letting out a sigh as she fell back into her seat. For the first time all day, I heard the slightest hint of exhaustion creep into her tone. "Pally's been keeping me appraised of what he's found. I've been doing what I can from here, looking into all this with Ruiz."

Feeling my brows rise just slightly, I asked, "Any luck?"

"Not really. Just a lot of closed doors. Layers and layers of red tape."

At some point in the near future, I would want to know exactly what she meant. I'd sit down across from her and we could share notes, bringing each other completely up to speed on things.

But that point wasn't right now.

"On your end?" she asked, seeming to think the same thing.

Twisting over a shoulder, I peered toward the truck sitting silent and the man I knew to be tied up in the back, no part of him visible as he lay in a twisted heap.

"I found Tres Salinas."

Taking a moment, presumably to place the name and what I was referencing, she said, "Salinas being the man who killed Shawn Martin."

"Yes. And who killed the guy that came after me and beat the hell out of a local deputy."

The last words betrayed a bit of the angst I was feeling, Diaz doing a much better job of keeping her emotions in check than I was.

"And by *found*," she asked, seeming to seize on that very thing, "you mean...?"

This time, it was my turn to pause. To consider what she was asking and her post as a ranking official in a government agency. Someone that could take what I was about to share and put me away for a very long time with it, service record be damned.

The first words I'd said to her was asking if we could speak far removed from the record. I had to believe that her rising and closing the door, continuing to speak to me thereafter, was a tacit acknowledgement of as much.

Or that, at the very least, our friendship would be enough otherwise.

"I mean, I intercepted him trying to dump his rental car and pick up his original ride at the airport in Spokane," I said. "And that he is currently encased in duct tape in the back of my truck, and we are about to go out into the woods for a little chat."

"And when you're done?"

Again, there was no hint of shock or surprise, no attempt to talk me out of anything.

Answering her question exactly would be impossible. Not until after I got done with Salinas would I know my next steps, whatever he disclosed doing a great deal in determining how things proceeded.

Something told me, though, that wasn't exactly what she was getting at.

Just like I doubted she cared that before I left the area again I needed to check on Kaylan and find a few hours of rest.

"That's why I'm calling you."

Chapter Fifty

Much like the front seat of the Chrysler, and the sofa in the living room, the bed in Esmera's guest room was much too soft for Junior Ruiz. After eight years of sleeping on a twin-size mattress that was little more than two inches of carpet padding, the pillow top mattress had too much give. Each time he began to drift off, his eyelids fluttering shut, it would begin to feel like he was being swallowed up.

Falling into an abyss, the overstuffed mattress coming up around him, threatening to pull him down.

After the first time he'd woken with a start, he'd shrugged it off. He had assumed it was just one of many small things he was going to need to get used to, forcing a laugh at his elevated pulse and the beads of sweat along his forehead.

Nothing a quick trip to the bathroom and a few gulps of cool water couldn't fix.

The second time it occurred, he'd recognized things for what they were. Grabbing a pair of the infinite throw pillows lining the headboard, he pulled the comforter to the floor, sprawling out on the area rug at the foot of the bed.

Fifteen minutes later he'd been asleep, not moving again until a faint buzzing managed to penetrate his senses an unknown number of hours later. Cracking open his eyes to see something besides the top bunk above him for the first time in ages, it took several moments for his bearings to reset.

For him to feel the shag loops of the rug beneath his fingertips, the softness of the comforter sprawled across him.

To see the first stripes of morning sun penetrating the blinds covering the window, the closest thing to an actual sunrise he'd witnessed in years.

Blinking twice, he exhaled slowly. Raising both hands to his face, he rubbed vigorously at his cheeks, feeling the skin move beneath his palms, before finally focusing on the sound.

Faint and persistent, it continued for thirty seconds before pausing. Gone for just a couple of short beats, another round started immediately thereafter, Ruiz finally raising his head from the pillow beneath him.

Swinging his gaze around the room, he took in his new surroundings, everything looking different in the light of morning, before landing on the phone resting on the nightstand by the bed.

"Alright," he muttered. Peeling back the comforter, he rolled forward onto a knee, snatching the phone off the distressed wooden top before dropping back down into position on the floor.

Not quite ready for the day to begin, he rubbed the thumb and forefinger of his left hand over his eyes, his right raising the phone to his cheek.

There was no need to check the screen. As far as he knew, there were only two people alive that even had the number.

And there was no way in hell Ramon Reyes was calling a minute earlier than he had to.

"Yeah?"

"*El Jefe*," Burris replied, his voice little more than a whisper. "It's me."

Every word uttered thus far was pointless, Ruiz knowing his own name and who was on the other end of the phone. One of many things he'd learned to ignore in the four years since Burris had been assigned to his top bunk.

A small price in the name of unflinching loyalty.

"You good?" Ruiz replied.

"Yeah," Burris answered. "They haven't filled your spot yet. It's a little lonely, but I don't have to worry about anything."

If the measures Ruiz had put into place, the protections he had secured before stepping out, were honored, there would never be any cause for concern.

Burris's reward for such loyalty.

"Good," Ruiz said. "Any word yet?"

Prisoners at USP Lompoc were not technically permitted to have cellphones, but that didn't keep them from being able to secure them easily enough. Smuggled in in a variety of ways – from visiting family members to guards looking to make a little extra cash – Burris was almost always in supply.

But that didn't mean he was always at liberty to speak, the inmates that most often got caught being those that were foolish enough to flaunt them.

The last time the two had spoken was almost twelve hours earlier. The majority of the time since was considered lights out, meaning Burris would have been alone in his cell, but if patrols were extra heavy or something had gone down, he might not have had a moment to check in.

To say nothing of the people he was trying to contact being slow to respond or having delays on their end, as was the case the last time they talked, no official word having yet been given.

"Martin is gone," Burris said. No lead-in, no voice inflection what-soever. A simple transaction, as easy as if he were delivering the weather.

Dropping his hand away from his face, Ruiz blinked rapidly, small spots appearing behind his eyelids.

Shawn Martin had been the man in charge the night he was arrested. He'd been the one barking orders and brandishing his weapon, fully enjoying his place in front of the crowded outdoor area.

The one that had made a point of taking Ruiz to the ground and cuffing him in full display of everybody present.

And one of several that had turned down the offer Ruiz had made.

"Who did it?" Ruiz asked.

"Tres."

Not a response Ruiz was expecting, he felt his eyes bulge slightly. "Tres?"

"That's what he said," Burris replied.

The last time Ruiz had seen Tres, he was but a child, still in his teen years. To have been entrusted with such a task now meant things had progressed rapidly in his time away.

Or the circle of people that could be counted on had shrunk to be much smaller than Ruiz realized.

"The others?"

"One was out of the country. Soldier working in a swamp somewhere, completely unreachable."

As fast as the partial smile had risen at the mention of Martin being put down, Ruiz's felt his mouth droop. One of the men being out of the country meant he wasn't a threat, but it also made for a task that would have to be dealt with later.

"Which one?"

"They didn't tell me his name," Burris said. He didn't add that he'd been coached never to ask or to write anything down, his role simply as a conduit, a way of making sure there was never a clear line to be drawn between Ruiz and his contact.

"And the other?"

"Got away," Burris said. "They sent a new guy after him, but he wasn't able to finish it."

The frown on Ruiz's face deepened, this time moving into a full scowl. Glaring up at the window above him, he saw the sun outside growing stronger, a series of shadows beginning to form across the ceiling, the temperature in the room rising in kind.

Errors like this could not be abided. Not only because a target had been made aware of their presence and still managed to get away, but because it was sloppy.

It sent a poor message at a time when every move was critical.

"New guy?"

"Yeah," Burris replied. "Tres went over after he finished his job, made sure he didn't talk."

Ruiz didn't press further about what exactly that entailed, his own instructions on the matter having been very clear from the beginning.

Eliminate the target, leave no loose ends.

A fact that made the inclusion of Tres at all quite curious.

"The target?"

"Eagle," Burris.

Folds of skin appeared around Ruiz's eyes. He thought on the list a moment, running through the names in his mind. Three in total, there was Martin - the leader of the group - followed by Diggs and Tate.

Others had joined them, local muscle meant to put up a show of force, ensure things didn't escalate, but for his purposes, those were the three that mattered.

"Eagle? You mean Hawk?"

"Yes!" Burris said, his voice rising just slightly before instantly falling back to a whisper. "Hawk, that's what he said. Sorry."

Outside his door, he could hear Esmera shuffle by. Lifting a hand, he covered the mouthpiece, waiting until she made her way into the bathroom and the overhead fan kicked on before pulling it away.

When he spoke again, his voice was lowered to match Burris's.

"And where is he now?"

Chapter Fifty-One

I was already parked behind the West Yellowstone Sheriff's Department by the time I saw the familiar Bronco I'd watched Sam Latham drive for years pull into the lot. Coming off the main drag, he looped out wide around the building, eschewing his marked parking spot on the corner that was plainly visible for anybody that might be passing by.

Something told me he wouldn't want many other people in town witnessing this.

If there was anywhere else within reasonable distance to do it, I would have told him to meet me there. Anyplace that I thought we could do what we needed to, that I could explain what happened without it immediately raising suspicion, I definitely would have opted for it.

As it stood, I was going to have a difficult enough time pulling off what I was about to attempt here. Especially considering I absolutely could not afford to be getting bogged down at the moment.

Not with things finally starting to come together.

And so much still left to do.

Standing along the rear tailgate, I watched as he circled the building and pulled in a few feet away. Sliding in at an angle, the front nose of the

Bronco stopped just inches from the side of the building. Glancing over, he offered a small wave before killing the engine and cracking open the door.

With one foot on the ground and the other on my rear bumper, I stood with both forearms draped over the rear tailgate. Despite the cold, I appreciated the chance to be out of the cab of the truck, the assorted scents of wood smoke, blood, and even a bit of charred flesh clinging to me.

Spots of blood speckled the front of my jeans and the backs of my hand.

My eyes I knew to be tinged with red, smoke and an extended lack of sleep beginning to wear on me.

The sound of frozen metal being wrenched open echoed across the asphalt as Latham pushed his way out of the driver's side door. Already in uniform, ready to start the workday, he hitched his brown pants up a bit higher as he regarded me standing there, the questions he had plain upon his features.

Questions I'm sure I would have had if in his position as well.

"Hawk."

"Sheriff," I replied. "Thanks for meeting me."

Snapping the door shut behind him, he ambled my way, the cold already having drawn most of the blood from his face.

What I was about to show him no doubt would manage to remove the rest.

"Way you sounded on the phone, didn't seem there was much of a choice."

My brows rose a quarter inch and my mouth parted about the same. Thinking better of any oral response, I instead lifted my hands, extending them as they hung draped over the side of the tailgate, motioning for him to take a look at what I'd brought.

Continuing to move forward, Latham came up on the side of the truck. Lifting his arms to match my pose, he made it no closer than a couple of feet away before stopping, his body jerking as if electrified.

Arms frozen in the air before him, he stood rigid, staring down into the bed. Mouth gaping, a look of sheer terror was on his features, his brown eyes fixed on what he saw.

None other than the man that ran off from him the day before.

Or, at least what remained of him.

After getting off the phone with Diaz, I stood alongside the turnout for a full ten minutes wrestling with the advice she'd given me before deciding she was right. No matter how much I might have wanted to kill this man, to take him out into the woods and do the most violent and reprehensible things I could think of, ultimately, he – and by extension Ruiz – still would have won.

They would have managed to pull me down to their level, getting me to act out of emotion and nothing more.

I have no delusions about who I am or some of the things I've done. I am aware of the lives I've taken and the stains that I can never wash away.

But taking this man out into the woods and sacrificing him - or more aptly, *executing* him - was a bridge I wasn't willing to cross.

That still didn't mean there weren't a lot of things that I needed from the man. How we got there depended entirely on him.

A process that he now bore plainly, despite being wrapped back up in his black down jacket.

"Jesus, Hawk," Latham managed. Looking my way, he took another step forward, one hand rising to cover his nose.

"After this man left the medical clinic yesterday, we were able to pull a visual of his license plate from the cameras at the intersection over there," I began, motioning with my chin a block to the south. "Ran that through the system and determined the vehicle had been rented from the Spokane Airport."

As I talked, a hint of the shock on his features receded, though he still managed to stay a few feet back from the truck bed.

"I happened to be moving east across Washington state, so I stopped in to wait for him."

Flicking his eyes to the truck bed, he asked, "And all that?"

All that had occurred from taking him deep into the Beaverhead and having a little discussion with him. A talk that began by leaving the duct tape in place, stripping away much of the clothing he wore, and tying his hands high above his head.

After that, I'd built a small fire, stuck the blade of my hawksbill folding knife into it, and went to work.

Not exactly an interrogation technique our government would ever prescribe to, but it had been effective.

And did serve the dual purpose of letting me take out some of the wrath I'd been carrying around.

With plenty still left over for Junior Ruiz.

"Most of that was done before I got there," I lied. "Looked like he'd been in a car accident or something. Probably figured you guys were chasing him and was trying to flee in a hurry."

Disbelief was plain across Latham's features, though to his credit, he kept it bottled in. Taking another step forward, he lowered his hand from his face, growing accustomed to the scent.

"So he's alive?"

"He is."

Coming around the end of the tailgate, Latham assumed a stance similar to mine. Little by little, I could see the initial shock passing, his mind unfurling what he knew and what he saw before him.

"Didn't think I'd see this bastard ever again," he muttered. Regarding the man another moment, he twisted his focus up to look at me. "And no offense, but damned sure didn't think you'd be the one to bring him here."

He didn't fully articulate what he meant by the comment, but he didn't have to.

The thought had definitely crossed my mind.

"How's Ferry doing?"

Shifting his gaze back to Salinas, Latham said, "He'll be okay, just got knocked around a little. Wounded pride more than anything. Tried to tell him to stay at home for a couple days, but he wouldn't hear of it."

Extending a finger, he added, "This will help, though."

Nodding slightly, I pushed away from the rear bumper. Standing to full height, I leaned back at the waist, stretching my back, the ache of having now missed two consecutive nights of sleep beginning to wear on me.

A fact I planned to remedy in the very near future.

"The guy's real name is Tres Salinas, driver's license has him at an address in Southern California. That duffel bag there has everything he brought back with him from Montana.

"I don't know if he ditched the gun he used on Mendoza or not, but you might have the murder weapon sitting here as well."

Knowing better than to go rummaging through the bag, to even consider contaminating evidence or putting any of my own finger-prints anywhere near it, I hadn't touched it since tossing it in the truck in Spokane.

Cocking an eyebrow my way, Latham said nothing, the question he was thinking obvious.

I moved right past it just the same.

"As you can guess, the DEA also has more than a little interest in speaking with him. I imagine they'll be in touch this morning, prob-ably send someone down from Billings."

I didn't feel great about dropping a potential jurisdictional pissing match on his doorstep, but there wasn't much choice in getting around the matter. Salinas was now wanted for at least two murders in two different states.

And that was just in the last thirty-six hours.

"You think it's safe leaving him here?" Latham asked.

"Yeah," I replied. "I can't imagine anybody else showing up. This guy was their backup."

Not to mention, nobody else could even know where he was. I had the man's phone, the device turned off and the SIM card removed for the time being. His car and everything except his duffel bag was still in Spokane.

Seeming to ponder the statement a moment, Latham gave one final nod before twisting back to look my direction. A myriad of thoughts and half-sentences seemed to pass over his features, his mouth working twice before finally he simply said, "Thank you."

Dipping my chin, I replied, "Yeah, well, it doesn't quite come free of charge."

Chapter Fifty-Two

There was no bullet or coin waiting on the counter in the front of my office as I stepped inside. Whether Luis Mendoza had them on him when I arrived the first time or if it was something special Tres Salinas decided to add as a middle finger to us at the Martin house, I couldn't be sure.

Not that it much mattered anymore.

The point had been made.

And in the process, painted an enormous target on everybody that had been involved on his end.

A quick scan of the rest of the office showed there to be nothing else out of place. No wanton destruction or messages scrawled on the walls. Nothing with special symbolism propped up in a place where it would be impossible to miss.

From what I could tell, nothing missing either.

Outside of the ragged hole in the front of the building, police tape in a sagging X across it, and the arctic chill in the air it created, there was no sign that anything had even occurred.

If only.

Stepping around into the back half of the building, I had cranked the heat as high as it would go and set about making myself as decent for human interaction as possible. Just barely had I been able to get through the encounter with Latham, my scent and the various things clinging to my clothes making it difficult to be anywhere near me, the choice to meet outside not by accident.

Even sitting in the cab of my truck was hard, forcing me to run with the windows down and the heater off.

Stripping out of the same clothes I'd been wearing for two days straight, I went to the small bathroom carved out on the far end of the building and spent ten minutes standing under the hottest water I could handle. Bent forward, I pressed a forearm into the tile beneath the shower head, letting the water pound on the top of my head.

Focus straight down, I waited until the water swirling into the drain between my feet ran clear before stepping out. Wrapping a towel around my waist, I brushed aside the steam from the small mirror on the wall.

Using the old pair of scissors that usually resided in the top drawer of my desk, I went to work on my beard. Holding it away from my face in clumps, I trimmed it a uniform half-inch around the length of my jaw, tossing the clippings into the trash can beside me.

Once that was in order, I moved up a bit higher, peeling back some of the shag hanging over my ears and forehead.

The instant I was done, I tossed the scissors down and stepped back into the shower, this time scrubbing down with the cheap combination soap and shampoo I kept stocked. Starting with my head, I worked my way down steadily, going into my fingernails and every crevice I could find until all remains of my encounter with Salinas in the woods were gone.

From there, I turned the water temperature up even higher, letting the suds sluice away, remaining in place until my entire form seemed to glow pink from the heat.

Basking in the residual warmth of the shower and the steam still hanging in the air, I changed into the spare clothes I kept in the office, more than once having returned from a day in the park looking no better than I had this morning.

Start to finish, I spent just over half an hour in the office. Time I didn't really have, but it seemed like a wise investment as I now stood beside Dr. Jade Whitney. In the same position we'd been in just over a day before, we waited in the hallway outside of Kaylan's room, both of us peering in through window inset in the top half of her door.

"How's she's doing?" I asked.

From where I stood, there seemed to have been moderate improvement from the day before. Some of the gauze that had encased her had been removed, though the bevy of tubes and instruments attached to her were still in place.

Eyes closed, she was reclined at an angle, head lolling to the side.

"Vitals are strong," Whitney replied. "She was awake for a few minutes last night, seemed to have about the level of cognition that would be expected."

What exactly that meant I wasn't sure, though I knew better than to press. Just seeing me show up this morning, the doctor had been only nominally more receptive than the first time we'd met.

The fact that she was allowing me back here at all was a bit of a surprise.

"Any idea what kind of timeframe she's looking at?"

In my periphery, I could see her look my way, dark ponytail swinging behind her.

"Not really," she said. "Everybody responds differently, recovers in their own time. And we obviously don't see a lot of cases like this."

Whether that last line was meant as a barb my direction or not, I couldn't be certain. And couldn't much concern myself with at the moment.

I was here to check on my friend, to watch over her until Latham could honor the request I'd made and get somebody to stand guard until I knew for a fact that no further threat existed.

Now that I knew for certain Junior Ruiz was at the root of all this, I knew just as certainly that he would not hesitate to send someone here if he thought it would be a way to get to me.

"Like I said though," Whitney continued, pulling me from my thoughts, "she is already showing signs of improvement, and none of her injuries are life threatening."

Nodding my head slightly, I pressed my lips together. Meeting the doctor's gaze, I passed along my unspoken thanks before turning my attention back to the window.

"You're welcome to go in if you'd like," Whitney said. "But like I asked yesterday, please don't wake her. Right now, rest is the best thing for her."

Again, I dipped my chin, a nod of understanding. This time I didn't bother looking over, not even as I sensed her take a step back, and then another, before eventually turning and moving off in the opposite direction.

Just like I didn't bother pointing out that I had no intention of waking her.

Right now, rest was the best thing for me as well.

Part Four

Chapter Fifty-Three

The evening sun was more than two hours in the past, having pulled most of its warmth with it. Just days into November, finally the late summer that had gripped the area throughout the last six weeks was beginning to relent, granting a long-awaited reprieve to the omnipresent heat.

In its stead, the ambient temperature hovered somewhere in the upper sixties, a faint breeze blowing in from the west. Crossing the fields surrounding the homestead, it brought forth the faint scents of loam and mulch, sage and jasmine.

Smells Ramon Reyes was still only beginning to get used to, despite the years that had passed since they relocated to the new location.

With the floor-to-ceiling windows that comprised the outer wall of his office pushed open, Reyes stood on the adjacent balcony. Perched with his palms pressed into the white stucco of the top railing, he gazed out over the spread before him, imagining what it looked like the first time he had been in this spot.

How different the view had been in their last post, a couple hundred miles south in Baja.

Each a snapshot from a different time, both by the calendar and in terms of the organization as a whole.

Behind him, the lights within the office were on. Blazing forth, they swept past him, throwing his shadow onto the ground below. Stretching far into the night, the outline of his head was positioned like that of an arrow, pulling his focus toward the warehouse standing in the distance.

Surrounding it he could see four visible guards, all patrols beefed up to double their usual size for the night.

A bit overkill perhaps, but this was to be his first encounter with Junior Ruiz since the man was taken away all those years before. He needed to set the correct tone, both for Ruiz and every person in his employ.

Only recently had their newest business venture begun to really turn a profit, trending in the direction they'd worked toward for so long.

He would be damned if the sudden arrival of his predecessor derailed that.

"It is almost nine," Arlin Mejia said, his voice arriving a moment before he did.

Flicking his gaze to the side, Reyes remained in position, watching as a second shadow emerged on the ground before him. "Is everything in order?"

"Yes," Mejia replied. "The guards are all in position."

"And the holdovers?"

"Everybody who ever worked for Ruiz – myself excepted, obviously – has been sent home for the evening."

Grunting softly, Reyes pushed himself upright. Turning, he leaned his backside against the stucco railing, his arms folded.

On the opposite side of the balcony, waiting just outside the threshold of the office, Mejia stood with his hands clasped before him. Dressed in his traditional dark dress shirt and slacks, a suit coat had been added to the ensemble for the evening, the front buttoned.

"How do you see this going?" Reyes asked.

If given his preference, the meeting would not be occurring at all. He, and the organization he now oversaw, had moved on. It had grown, shifting from the cowboy days of the old cartels, when exorbitant bribes and heavy casualties were the price of doing business.

Any means justified in reaching the ends.

There was no place for a man like Ruiz in today's industry, let alone what Reyes had built in his wake. No need to offer him face time, to even let word get out that the two had gotten together for a parlay.

A sign his competitors would almost surely take as a show of weakness.

His immediate reaction to hearing Ruiz's request was the same one that he had had when Hector first mentioned seeing him walk out of jail the day before. To put a bullet in his head and dump his body in the desert, the man to survive as nothing more than a name from the past.

A thought that still seemed appealing, no matter how much he knew it would only serve to undermine his standing.

"However you would like it to," Mejia said. "The most important thing here being to remind him *you* are in charge. He is no longer *El Jefe*. You are no longer some employee."

Reyes had known exactly how Mejia would answer even before he asked, though he still appreciated hearing the words.

More than once he had seen similar situations play out. Instances where no matter how high an employee ascended through the ranks, they were never actually seen as anything more than what they had originally been.

Like some younger sibling, always relegated to second tier status.

A dozen other questions all came to mind in order, things he wanted to ask, thoughts he'd had since first discovering Ruiz was about to be free. Each and every one he pushed aside, there being no point in asking them.

Whatever he needed to know would come forth soon enough.

"Make the call."

Chapter Fifty-Four

Junior Ruiz wasn't sure which part of the scene before him he found more humorous. The enormous gate with brick columns and a polished gold finish that blocked the entrance to the driveway of the address he'd been given. The motorized golf cart sitting on the opposite side of it, ready to receive him.

Or the bevy of guards lining it, all with automatic weapons held across their waists. Dressed in black suits and sunglasses despite the hour, they looked like a team of miniature Hispanic Terminators for hire, all staring directly at the rented SUV he arrived in.

Fighting the urge to openly laugh, to allow his lips to curl back in a smile at the unnecessariness of it all, he instead turned off the engine and stepped out of the car. Hands empty and held to his side, he waited as one of the guards stepped forward, clearly the designated leader of the group.

Shifting his rifle to one hand, he cradled it into the crook of his elbow, leaving the barrel pointed toward the sky. The other he used to jerk open the front flaps of the suit jacket Ruiz wore, brusquely feeling along his ribs and waistline.

Finding nothing, he grabbed a shoulder and turned him to the side, completing the impromptu frisk before taking a step back.

"Mr. Reyes has asked that you leave your vehicle here. The cart will take you the rest of the way up to the house."

Resisting the urge to make a comment, to crack wise at the bluster of everything going on, to maybe even inquire as to what their boss felt the need to compensate for, Ruiz offered only a nod. Lowering his hands to his side, he left the rental where it was, keys still in the ignition.

Falling in behind the same guard, they marched through the narrow opening in the gate, taking up spots beside each other on the front seat of the cart.

Rifle still tucked into his elbow, the guard angled himself toward Ruiz, gripping the bottom of the steering wheel with one hand. Saying nothing, he punched the gas hard, the cart lurching before leveling out, sending them hurtling down the paved drive.

Wind hitting him full in the face, Ruiz sat and stared straight ahead. On either side, he could see palm and fruit trees flying by, the place a veritable agricultural haven, a far cry from anything else he'd seen so far south.

Largely ignoring it, he instead focused on the home growing steadily larger before him. Two stories in height, it looked like a cross between a Spanish mission and a southern plantation, a mix of white stucco and towering columns.

A central section provided the bulk of the front façade, matching wings extending wide to either side. Scads of windows lined both floors, every last one seeming to have the lights on, the place lit up like a beacon, likely visible even to most aircraft flying above.

Yet another move Ruiz couldn't help but smile at.

The last Ruiz could remember of Ramon Reyes, he was a product of nepotism. Someone that had traded on his family name and his uncle's political position to garner jobs and contacts he had no business being near.

Spots much like the one that he had landed with Ruiz.

Unaccustomed to having to do anything on his own, he had accomplished little in his time there. Treading water, he waited on more to be given to him instead of taking responsibility and going after it.

All things that made his being the one to emerge after Ruiz was sent to prison that much more shocking.

And the extreme pretension on display before him not surprising in the least.

Keeping all such thoughts tamped down, Ruiz fixed his gaze straight ahead. He waited as the guard followed the drive to the front corner of the spread before looping out wide, pulling the passenger side of the cart up parallel to the front steps.

Hopping off the front seat, he secured the rifle with both hands, using the muzzle to motion Ruiz out of the cart as well.

"Go."

Doing as instructed, Ruiz stepped down onto the first step. Taking a moment, he brushed the dust from the drive in off his suit, waving the front lapels of his coat.

Once he was reasonably certain the charcoal material looked something close to its original color, he began his ascent, a new pair of guards waiting on the top step for him.

Their expressions hidden behind mirrored sunglasses, the one on the left took the lead. In moves that made the entire sequence appear it had been rehearsed many times over, he turned for the door. Pushing the oversized gate open, he jerked his head back over a shoulder, signaling for Ruiz to follow him.

Marching inside, he made it no more than a few feet past the door before turning, his rifle angled toward the ground before him.

Taking it as a signal to move forward, Ruiz took a couple steps further. Behind him, he could hear the other guard enter as well, the enormous door swinging shut in their wake, the sound echoing through the cavernous space.

Using a wide and open floorplan, the front foyer rose the full two stories above them. Hanging down from the ceiling was an enormous chandelier, dozens of bulbs illuminating everything in a bright glow.

Around them, every last touch had been made for the place to resemble something from an architectural magazine. Paintings in gold filigree frames lined the walls. Narrow tables with expensive pottery and sprays of flowers were positioned in even intervals.

Rising from either side of the floor was a sweeping staircase, the effect to create an inverted horseshoe, one unending piece arc with a wrought iron railing.

All of it meant to convey a very specific look. A geometric design meant to sweep the gaze upward, funneling it inward to a central figure now standing ten feet above them.

His features neutral, both hands clenched the top of the railing in a death grip as Ramon Reyes stared down.

Yet another thing that gave Ruiz the urge to smile.

"Ruiz," Reyes said, voice much louder than necessary in the quiet of the foyer.

"Reyes."

Chapter Fifty-Five

The air outside San Diego International Airport was approaching forty degrees higher than when I'd flown out of Bozeman that afternoon. After catching five hours of sleep in the chair beside Kaylan's bed and spending another hour sitting by her side as she continued to rest until the first shift of the protection detail Latham had put together arrived, I'd made the short jaunt from Big Sky to the airport.

Taking off at three in the afternoon, I'd caught a direct down to Los Angeles and then a short hop to where I was now standing, arriving with a duffel bag carrying little more than a change of clothes and a toothbrush.

Items I'd only brought along because I'd heard many times over never to travel completely empty handed, as it only managed to raise suspicion.

Something I sorely did not need at the moment, with no idea how the coming days might play out.

The instant I stepped out into the night air, I could feel the warmth swirl around me. On contact, it managed to lift my body temperature, a thin veneer of sweat rising to my face despite the recent loss of so much hair.

Peeling away my coat, I stood in a t-shirt and jeans, the smell of the sea nearby filling my nostrils. Pulling it in, I waited on the curb, needing just a couple of minutes before a nondescript black sedan sidled up beside me. Appearing to have rolled off the assembly line specifically designed for government vehicles, it eased to a stop without a sound.

Remaining where I stood, I watched as the tinted passenger window buzzed down to reveal Mia Diaz behind the wheel.

"Somebody call for an Uber?"

Making no effort to hide the smile that split my features, I pulled the door open and slid inside, the two of us negotiating an awkward front seat hug. Holding it only a moment, we both pulled back, each openly assessing the other.

A year and a half had passed since the two of us had been in the same place, yet somehow, she seemed to have pulled off reverse aging. The same dark hair still hung in ringlets to her shoulders. A heart shaped face still featured sharp cheekbones and full lips.

Unlike the last time we'd encountered each other, though, there was a bit of color on her skin, the tan obscuring any sort of bags that might be underscoring her eyes.

"You look well," she said, checking the rearview mirror before easing us away from the curb. "Healthy, and all that."

"So I look fat," I replied. "Thanks."

Glancing my way, she said, "Or that you seem surprisingly upright and uninjured for someone with such a high propensity for being shot at."

Immediately setting myself to launch back into a rebuke, I pulled up, unable to mount much of an objection.

In the five years following my departure from the DEA, I had lived a life that bordered on hermetic in Montana. Summer months were spent as a guide, taking tourists into Yellowstone. Winters, I was holed up in a cabin I built myself outside a map dot called Glasgow.

Not a single regular human interaction besides Kaylan six months of the year.

During that time, not once had a single round been fired my direction. Nor had a punch or kick been thrown. The closest I'd come to an altercation was when a hiking party I was with stumbled onto the fresh kill of a mountain lion.

Over the last two years, I had managed to break out of the funk, slowly reacclimating to the world around me.

A trend that had somehow also seen a sharp uptick in the amount of physical violence I was privy to.

Choosing not to comment on Diaz's last statement, I instead offered, "You look good as well. Nice to see you finally remembered that you live in Southern California."

Alternating her attention between me and the road, a crease appeared between her brows. Seeming to consider the statement for a moment, I saw as dawning set in, her eyes widening slightly.

"Oh, you mean this," she said, motioning to her face. "No, this was from a case that we just wrapped a few days ago. Idiots trying to pass bricks of product through the slats in the border wall in broad daylight."

A sharp crack of laughter spilled out in response, the sound gone before I even realized it. Extra loud in the small space, I made no attempt to walk it back, shoulders shaking slightly with chuckling.

"You're shitting me."

"Like I said – idiots."

Linking up with the freeway, she pushed us south, sweeping past downtown and the first buildings taller than three stories I'd seen since being in Nashville last spring. Even with the clock now pushing past ten, many of the windows in them were still aglow, the workday lasting long enough to soon be running into the next one.

Peeking between the occasional gaps in the buildings, I could see the ocean in the distance. Out there, a handful of liners moved slowly along, everything from barges carrying supplies to the local Navy base to cruise liners ferrying passengers off to exotic locales.

Neither of which seemed too appealing at the moment.

Letting the curve of the freeway funnel us to the east, I shifted my focus out through the front windshield, our twin reflections just barely visible against it, lit up by the control panel of the dash.

"Thank you for picking me up. I could have easily gotten a rental."

Rolling her head along the seatback, Diaz flicked her gaze my direction. Holding the pose long enough to let me know I was being ridiculous, she said nothing, shifting her attention back to the road.

When I had left the DEA, Hutch was still the director of the Southwest field office. In addition to overseeing our FAST team, he also coordinated more than two dozen other agents, all covering a variety of topics and investigations throughout the region.

Although I was the first of our core to step aside, within two years both Martin and Diggs left as well. A year later, Pally transitioned into the private sector.

Without us, Hutch had migrated east, taking up a permanent post with the Administration's headquarters in D.C.

In the wake of his leaving, Diaz had been inserted as the acting director. Long after the fact, I caught wind that the rumor at the time had been it was because of her gender and ethnicity, the powers-that-be tapping her early on to be one of a handful of poster children for the new direction of the organization.

Having worked with her myself on multiple occasions, I knew that to be bullshit, nothing more than the sour grapes of people that hadn't been good enough to keep up in their own right.

Folks who needed an excuse because they couldn't hold a candle to the new girl.

"Okay, well at least let me thank you for helping me last night," I said.

Again, she rolled her head my direction. A hint of confusion was visible before she grasped what I was alluding to. "I didn't tell you anything you didn't already know."

"Yeah," I agreed, "but it doesn't mean I didn't need to hear it."

Especially from someone I trusted.

Keeping her attention rolled my way, she dropped her gaze to my hands, no doubt clocking the assortment of scabs covering my knuckles.

"How did it go?"

"He's alive."

"And the information you were hoping to get?"

Tres Salinas hadn't been quite the fount of data I was hoping him to be, but that was because he simply wasn't privy to the highest levels of decision making.

Based on what I put the man through, there was no way he could have possibly been holding a single thing back.

"Nothing about how the hell Junior Ruiz is suddenly a free man, if that's what you're asking. You?"

Dropping her blinker, Diaz shifted us into the outer lane. Changing freeways, she adjusted our direction to the southeast, pushing out toward the desert and the DEA office tucked away well beyond the city limits.

As she did so, the traffic around us grew thinner. City lights fell further behind us, the late hour and government tags allowing us to move with impunity.

"Same," she answered. "Lot of dead ends and brick walls."

Resetting the cruise control, she cast another glance my way, the numbers of the dash casting a faint green hue across her face.

"But that wasn't specifically what I was asking," she clarified. "Did he have anything you were looking for? Anything that could help us?"

For just a moment I let the question linger before turning to meet her gaze.

"Salinas was there the night when we took Ruiz down. Turns out, it was a *quinceañera*.

"For his sister."

Chapter Fifty-Six

The pair of guards that had led Ruiz through the front door knew to stay behind in the hallway. As did the pair that were standing on either side of the doorway leading into the office.

All briefed well in advance, there was no need for verbal commands. Nothing that even intimated that this wasn't how things were normally conducted, Ramon Reyes operating with complete control at all times.

Forming a half arc, they stood silent, sentries with assault rifles resting across their waists. A personal private army, all in matching attire, right down to the reflective sunglasses they wore.

A move that might have been a touch overkill, but did manage to convey the message Reyes wanted.

That Junior Ruiz was in over his head. Whatever time he might have had was gone, the operation moving ahead while he rotted away in prison.

Careful to stay a few paces out ahead, to let it be known that Ruiz was a guest and the two were not equals, Reyes stepped into the expansive spread that was his office. Essentially the nerve center for everything he did, it spread wide in either direction.

More than fifty feet from end to end, the outer edges were decorated much the same as the foyer downstairs. Everything picked out by some expensive interior decorator, paintings lined the walls depicting ocean and countryside scenes, the type of things that are noticed more for their framework than the images they conveyed.

Beneath them were sitting chairs and end tables, none of the items ever touched save by the occasional maid that came through to dust.

In the center of the space was where Reyes's personal influence began to be noticed. Modeled after countless images he'd seen of the Oval Office, he'd been insistent on a pair of sofas sitting across from one another. Both made of matching leather in a deep burgundy hue, the bodies of them were overstuffed, decorative nail heads lining the edges.

Separating them was a polished coffee table sitting atop a floor rug.

The proverbial greatest homefield advantage in the world, recreated right in his own office.

Taking a step to the side, clearing a view for Ruiz to see how business in the modern age was conducted, Reyes said, "As I'm sure you heard, we relocated here several years ago."

Turning over a shoulder to see Ruiz taking things in, Reyes continued circling to his right. Moving out around the sofas, he headed for the back end of the office, the place where the bulk of his waking hours were now spent.

The main feature of the office - the part that Reyes had noticed the very first time he stepped foot on the property, solidifying his decision to purchase - was the rear wall. Made from a series of floor-to-ceiling glass panels, they had been spread wide for the evening.

Along either edge, gossamer curtains swayed with the soft incoming breeze. Beyond them, a balcony looked out over the grounds, an expansive view aided by lights blazing around the property.

The perfect summation of what he was trying to build, the image he was meaning to convey. A place where he could oversee everything that was occurring, a watchful eye on all aspects of the business.

Just as they could do the same, looking up and knowing he was there, working every bit as hard as they were.

Exactly six feet in from the track the windows normally sat in was the desk Reyes had had specifically designed. Cut from oak painted solid black, it measured eight feet across, a full two more than any other available for purchase.

Behind it, the high-backed leather chair he'd also had designed to fit the desk was pushed in tight.

Across from the chair was a pair of padded visitor seats. Both comfortable and of a high quality, the only difference between them and most others was that the legs had been cut an inch shorter by design.

A nominal difference, but enough to ensure that anybody sitting across from him was forced to stare upward. To subconsciously realize who was in control from the moment they arrived.

Another trick he had learned from studying various leaders around the world, this one coming from someplace on the opposite side of the globe.

For some – men like Ruiz, for instance – such purchases would probably be foolish. Unnecessary posturing. An obsession with minutiae.

To Reyes, they were so much more than that. Small details that, when added together, greatly enhanced the whole. Helped to take things further than anything Ruiz had ever managed to build on his own.

Every item, every placement, was done with an exacting eye, a means of maximizing whatever advantage he thought could be gleaned.

"Looks like you've done quite well for yourself," Ruiz said.

A conscious sidestep of the opening comment, Reyes felt folds of skin form around his eyes.

Eight long years, he had wondered if this day would ever arrive. How far in the future it might be, how things may play out.

Never would he have imagined that it would come so soon, but that part he could do nothing about.

Stopping along the side of the desk, Reyes placed a hand on the corner of it. Turning back, he regarded Ruiz a moment, sweeping his gaze the length of him.

And making no effort to hide it.

He'd heard it said that prison years were hard years, and if the man standing before him was any indication, the maxim held true. Having passed from the tail end of his thirties to the back half of his forties, he appeared to have aged far more. His hair, once thick and dark, was now pulling back at the temples, threaded with gray.

Deep lines framed his mouth and eyes.

A small paunch pushed out the front of the blue dress shirt he wore tucked tight into a charcoal suit that was clearly pulled off the rack somewhere that afternoon.

"Could you blame us for making some changes?" Reyes asked. "After all, you were the ultimate cautionary tale. Adapt or die.

Get with the times or spend the rest of your days in prison."

With each word that passed his lips, Reyes found an inability to keep his true feelings from rising to the surface.

So badly, he wanted to rush forward on the man before him. To pick up a chair and beat him with it or order in the guards standing outside the door and have them empty their rifles into him.

For years now, he had been fighting against the specter of Junior Ruiz. Someone that had been martyred that night, the stories about how he stared down a dozen or more government agents growing with each retelling.

When in reality, there was nothing of the sort. Nothing but the man now standing before him, out of shape and out of sorts, completely passed by.

"So that's what all this is?" Ruiz asked. "Adapting?"

Opening his mouth to respond, Reyes pulled up. A thin smile graced his lips, his head tilting slightly to the side. "Not just adapting. Thriving."

Glancing to the standing clock along the wall, Reyes couldn't help but notice that already five minutes had passed. Three hundred seconds in the same space as the man he had usurped.

And still he had no idea why he was there.

"Join me for a drink? I'll show you what I mean."

Chapter Fifty-Seven

Junior Ruiz might have been surprised that Ramon Reyes was the one to rise up in his wake, but he wasn't the least bit shocked to find out this way how he was running things. A child of fortune, someone that had never wanted for a thing in his life, had no concept of actual work, would fixate on the unnecessary.

The parts that were entirely stylistic, void of any actual merit or value. Things like an excess of guards. And a gold-plated front gate.

Even the outfit the man now wore – replete with fitted patterned dress shirt, vest, and crocodile skin shoes – that looked more like what a young child would believe a successful person in the drug business should wear than anything a grown man would actually put on.

Noting that the tone and delivery of Reyes's last words were more directive than question, Ruiz watched as he turned away. Heading for the open windows behind him, he passed over the metal track where the glass frames normally sat, a shadow falling over him as he stepped outside.

Standing, waiting until the darkness swallowed him up, Ruiz followed suit. Taking in his surroundings, careful to miss nothing, he stepped outside just far enough to get beyond the edge of the inner lights before pausing to let his eyes adjust.

Not quite the full length of the interior office, the balcony ran more than thirty feet across. Extended ten feet out from the building, potted plants rested in the corners, some sort of grassy spray rising up from them. Filling the space between them and the rear of the house were bench seats, thick cushions resting atop wrought iron frames matching the railing from the main staircase.

Set up in the right corner, hidden behind the stack of window panels and curtains still moving softly in the breeze was a small table. Lined atop it was an assortment of alcohols, bottles of various heights, their tops capped with oversized stoppers.

Based on everything else he'd seen thus far, Ruiz hated to even speculate how much money had been wasted on the spread. A quick glance at the labels on display showed them to be some of the more high-end products he had ever heard of.

And even a few he hadn't.

Standing beside it was a single man. Shrouded in shadow, he was almost hidden in the dark suit he wore, his hands clasped before him. Somewhere north of fifty years of age, his thinning hair was combed straight back, his narrow shoulders drawn inward.

Staring straight ahead, he kept his focus fixed on Reyes, not once so much as glancing at Ruiz.

"What can he get for you?" Reyes asked, bypassing any attempt at introduction. "Tequila? Rum?"

The last alcohol Ruiz had tasted was champagne. The very same liquid that had stained the suit he wore home the day before, an offering at the *quinceañera* he'd been hosting when arrested.

Without question, any of the offerings atop the table would be divine. Drinks that under different circumstances, Ruiz would attack with aplomb, relishing every moment.

But now was not the time, any desire for such things completely lost on him.

"I'm actually okay right now."

"You sure?" Reyes pressed. "We've had some of the best stuff in the world flown in for occasions such as this."

Already, Ruiz could feel his patience for the self-importance on display wearing thin. With it, his ability to keep such feelings hidden was dipping quickly.

Even if the last eight years had been a daily lesson in maintaining a neutral face at all times.

Ignoring Reyes's questions, he took a step forward, heading for the edge of the balcony. Resting his palms on the wide stucco railing, he looked down at the grounds before them, the spread vast as it sprawled outward in every direction.

A near copy of the landscape he'd ridden through on the cart minutes earlier, it looked to be an unholy mash of jungle and orchard, the scents of various fruits riding in on the breeze.

Underpinning them were various other smells, all of it pushed forth with each puff of air.

"Impressive, isn't it?" Reyes said. No small amount of self-satisfaction permeated his voice, the words bordering on smug.

Stepping up alongside Ruiz, he assumed a similar stance. Just a couple of feet separated the men as they stared out, surveying the property before them.

"Far cry from what we were doing down in Baja," Reyes added.

The nails on Ruiz's fingers flashed white as he pressed his fingertips down into the railing before him. Clenching his breath, he felt his entire body go rigid, his gaze fixed outward.

Not so much for the barb about the previous operation, but for the use of the pronoun *we*, Reyes somehow insinuating that he had played any role in the operation there.

Or that what was now spread around them was a result of anything but the years Ruiz had put in before him.

If Reyes noticed in the slightest, he gave no indication. Intent on continuing the tour that had never been asked for, he extended a finger. Starting on the far edge of the horizon line, he pointed at a pair of outbuildings.

"The problem before was, things were too small. Antiquated. People wrapping bricks by hand? Drug mules? Tugboats going up and down the coast? Things of the past.

"Here, I've got spaces set up and dedicated to packaging, shipping, product design."

With each category he rattled off, he jabbed a finger at a particular structure. Working his way inward, he went until his hand was held straight before him, culminating with the enormous warehouse sitting a few hundred yards from the rear of the house.

Despite the hour and even at such a distance, a quartet of guards matching the ones downstairs was plainly visible. All shuffling listlessly from side to side, none covered more than ten or fifteen yards of ground, all watching for an enemy they knew was never arriving.

"To say nothing of that," Reyes continued, "my newest achievement, the thing that is about to make me the biggest name in the cocaine business for the foreseeable future."

Clearly there was more he wanted to say. Gloating to be done over how much their respective fortunes had shifted in the preceding years.

Barely able to pull up short, he paused, his mouth still open to deliver his next lines.

Again, the forced smile appeared.

"But enough about me." As fast as it had arrived, the smile faded, Reyes's features hardening. His hand dropped to his side, his body turning.

Placing a hip against the balcony rail, he folded his arms before him. "I want to hear about you. What you've been up to these last few years."

Leaning forward an inch, he added, "Why the hell you think we have a single thing to *parlay* about."

Pulling his focus from the grounds around them, from the gleaming warehouse structure designed to draw attention, Ruiz shifted his gaze to Reyes. Moving slow, he allowed the mask he'd been wearing since arrival to peel away.

The malevolence he felt for the man before him settled behind his eyes, one side of his nose rising in a bit of a snarl.

"You know, I've had eight years to think about this moment. More than two thousand nights lying awake, imagining exactly what I would say if I ever got this chance."

Matching the pose and seemingly the wrath that Ruiz felt, incredulity flooded across Reyes's features, his nostrils flaring.

"But now that I'm standing here, you know what I realize?" Ruiz continued. "I don't have one thing to say to your sorry ass."

His focus so intent on Ruiz, on the venom flowing through his system, Reyes never noticed the man step away from the makeshift bar in the corner. Not once did he hear a sound as the man unbuttoned his suit coat and slid a revolver from the small of his back.

A look of surprise never even got the chance to cross his face as the gun was placed to the back of his head and the trigger pulled.

Making no effort to pull back, to distance himself from the spray of blood and bone and brain matter that exited above Reyes's right temple, Ruiz stood completely still. He watched as most of the face of the man that had tried to take his place was removed, spray cascading over the rail of the balcony and down the side of the house, a red streak atop the white stucco.

Ignoring the blood that striped the front of his suit, the few stray droplets that landed on his cheek, Ruiz waited as Reyes's body pitched forward onto the top rail. As gravity slowly won out, muscle memory unable to keep him upright.

Even as he slid down to the floor, landing in a twisted heap.

In the quiet of the balcony, the shot seemed especially pronounced. Echoing out over the grounds below, it spread quickly, reverberating onto the treetops before returning in a faint echo.

Standing so close to the explosive sound, a faint buzz sprouted in Ruiz's right ear, though still he remained still.

His gaze fixed on the remains of Reyes, he slowly raised his focus to the man before him. To the way he remained with the gun extended at arm's length, a twisted curl of smoke rising from the end of it.

Regarding him for a full moment, a hint of a smile played at the corner of his mouth.

"It's good to see you, Arlin."

Slowly, the gun was lowered. Falling against Mejia's right thigh, he matched the thin smile.

"Good to see you too, *El Jefe*."

Chapter Fifty-Eight

Even at ten minutes before seven in the morning, traffic was already starting to line up heading into San Diego. Beginning on the outer edge of the urban sprawl that had steadily worked its way outward since I moved away six years prior, it was obvious that within a half hour the place would be a veritable parking lot.

My only hope was that we made it to the tipping point and were heading opposite the heaviest flow by then.

Sitting in the passenger seat, a pale blue folder rested atop my lap. Stamped with the same DEA logo that they seemed so intent on imprinting onto every office supply in the building, I peeled back the cover to find the face of Junior Ruiz staring back at me.

Dressed in a pink dress shirt and tan suit jacket, he glowered at the camera beneath disheveled hair, disdain seeming to ooze from every pore.

A stance I could attest was pretty accurate, having been standing right beside the photographer when it was taken.

One more image, one more memory, I would just as soon do without.

Sliding the paperclip away that was holding it in place, I shifted the photo to the opposite side of the folder, flipping it over so as to not have to look at the man another moment.

Already, my hostility was running high. It wasn't like a visual staring back at me was going to do much good.

Beneath the photo was more than a dozen sheets of paper, standard writeup for closing a case. Beginning with the top page, there was a basic overview, the name of the target, time, date, and location all noted.

Flipping the sheet back, the next several in order were all detailed transcripts of what had taken place. Arranged in a chronological timeline, they walked through the various steps of the investigation, beginning with what first put him on our radar and continuing through everything that secured the need for action.

"Eighteen months," I whispered, riffling through the sheets. One item after another was detailed in order, some I was an active part of and remembered clearly, others I had only been appraised of after the fact.

"What's that?" Diaz asked. Most of her features hidden behind thick sunglasses, she looked my way, early morning blaze reflecting across the lenses.

"A damn year and a half we tracked this bastard," I said, matching her gaze for a moment. "Look at this."

Lifting the stack of pages, I let them pass against the pad of my thumb, all falling back into place.

"And they just let his ass walk out after eight years?"

"Oh, I can do you one better than that," she replied. Shifting her focus back to the freeway, she worked her way between a pair of semi-trucks, leaning on the gas to get by them.

"You know how generally when somebody gets out of jail, there is a specific sequence? They have a parole officer assigned, put down a name and address where they can be reached, said officer goes and checks out the place..."

The prison system wasn't one we worked with extensively, though I was familiar with how the process went. A continuation of whatever work we had put in, we were often kept appraised of the various steps, letting us know when one we had apprehended made it back out on the streets.

An eventuality that didn't happen often, but we needed to be aware of when it did.

"Yeah."

"None of that listed here," Diaz said. "Just one day, the magic parole board fairy waved a wand and poof, the guy was able to walk out a free man."

Handfuls of responses came to mind. Vitriolic barbs. Angry rants. Full-on venting.

One at a time, I pushed them aside. Much like the photo of Ruiz now flipped upside down, I knew that succumbing to them, voicing whatever I was feeling, would only end badly.

Pressure I couldn't release, causing me to either implode or do something very stupid.

Turning my attention back to the pages before me, I shuffled forward to the part of the narrative outlining the night in question. A joint operation between us and a team from the field office in Mexico City, there had been ten of us that stormed the grounds that night, the entire thing as close to textbook as an operation could go.

Never before joining the DEA had I even heard the term *quinceañera*. From what I could gather, it was something akin to a bat mitzvah in Jewish culture or a debutante ball back where I came from.

An event to mark an official passage of a child into adulthood.

Specific to Spanish and Hispanic culture, the *quinceañera* was a celebration of a young girl's fifteenth birthday. A time when she was officially anointed a woman, one of the largest milestones in her life.

An event that, if the pained cries of Tres Salinas were to be believed, was held in his sister's honor.

"I read through that file after you called with a name a couple days ago," Diaz said, drawing my attention upward. "Seemed like a hell of a ballsy play."

She didn't add anything more, though she didn't need to. Already I knew exactly what she was getting at, my focus rolling forward as I stared out the windshield at the traffic growing steadily thicker around us.

Allowing my eyelids to sag slightly, I put myself back in the moment. Having relived that day no more than a hundred times in the last forty-eight hours, I could still hear the sound of a mariachi band drifting through the air. The smell of roasted goat still filled my nostrils.

More than three hundred people were on hand for the celebration that afternoon. All decked out in their Sunday best, they had gathered at the estate of Junior Ruiz, turning the place into a veritable town square.

Games on the lawn for children. A stage and dancefloor for entertaining. Enough tables and chairs to accommodate everybody without feeling cramped.

"Biggest damn party I'd ever seen. Hundreds of men, women, children, all packed into a spread that must have been five acres or more."

Even with the narrative report open on my lap before me, I didn't bother to look down. Every detail of that day was seared into my mind, one of the last major scores I was a part of, washing out not much more than a year later.

"Middle of August, hot as hell, everybody sweating so bad we could barely grip our weapons. Thousand ways it could have - and maybe even should have - gone to shit."

Without commenting, Diaz signaled, drifting over into the right lane.

Overhead, signage announced a freeway split, the road we were just on leading into the city, our new route sweeping us toward the north.

"In the days leading up to it, Martin and the lead from the Mexico City office had gone back and forth. The other guy had been some military hard-ass type. Wanted to wait for nightfall, bring in a huge contingent. Full-on SWAT tactical team with riot gear and tear gas."

"Jesus," Diaz muttered beside me, the word just barely penetrating my train of thought.

"Martin wouldn't hear of it. Kept telling him if we wanted to do that, we would have picked any other night. Just lined up our best against Ruiz's best and had a damn shootout."

Yet another reminder of how politics within the Administration really worked, I remembered sitting in the small house we'd commandeered in Baja for the operation. Ten grown men, all hopped up on testosterone and adrenaline, counting seconds, waiting for the signal to go.

"Kept telling the guy the crowd was actually the best coverage we could ask for. Go in there with a small team under the light of day to keep everybody from panicking. Make it very clear we didn't want violence, we were only there for Ruiz."

In my periphery, I could see her curly hair shift as she shook her head.

"And with it being that kind of gathering, so many innocents around, Ruiz wouldn't be likely to let it get ugly," Diaz inserted.

"A full-on *Godfather* type thing."

"*On this the day of my daughter's wedding*," Diaz recited, quoting the movie without bothering to attempt a Brando accent.

"Exactly," I agreed. "Even if it wasn't his daughter, he was the figurehead. *El Jefe*, as he liked to go by."

Nodding slightly, Diaz let it pass without comment. Falling silent for a moment, she seemed to chew on what I'd just described, both hands gripping either side of the wheel before her.

"I mean, logically the approach makes sense..."

"But if it goes south, it goes all the way south?" I finished, flicking a glance her way. "Believe me, we were all aware. More than once the three of us had private conversations standing outside that house, but Martin was convinced he was right, and we trusted him enough to have his back."

As the youngest man on the crew, it wasn't my place to push back. If anything went sideways, most of the flack that came down would be siphoned off long before it made it all the way to me.

Even knowing that, that he would be the one brought under scrutiny later, forced to testify whenever the case made it to court, Martin had not backed down.

"We rolled up on that place with ten men that day," I continued. "Outside of a pair of old ladies cursing at us in Spanish and some kids screaming, there wasn't a bit of trouble.

"Not a single shot fired or drop of blood spilled."

Returning my gaze to the file before me, I flipped to the last page. Seeing it had nothing more than what I had already been carrying around in my head for years, I dropped the papers back into position and flipped the file closed.

"In all the years of running with the FAST unit, it was the cleanest bust we ever executed. Nobody got spooked. No one got trigger happy or tried to make a run for it."

Falling silent, I clocked a mileage sign along the side of the road informing us that Miramar was just two miles ahead.

"Does make you wonder though, doesn't it?" Diaz asked.

"What's that?"

"Why the hell this is how Ruiz decided to retaliate."

Chapter Fifty-Nine

The city of Escondido sat thirty miles north of San Diego, a straight shot up the I-15. One of countless smaller dots on the map filling the space between San Diego and Los Angeles, it was a place I had heard of many times but never actually been to.

With good reason.

Appearing to be little more than a suburb that had grown larger than it ever intended to, the place resembled a bunch of strip malls holding hands. One street after another of the same sorts of small businesses grouped together, interspersed with fast food joints and open lots of sand and gravel.

All of it weathered into a uniform state of faded color, years of being blasted by the desert elements having taken a toll.

The better part of a day's digging still hadn't turned up many of the answers we were looking for. Despite the combined efforts of Diaz and Pally, neither had been able to break through whatever invisible barriers existed in the cyber world to determine how or why Junior Ruiz had been given his walking papers.

A fact that – based on my combined experience with the two – led to me believe that no such thing existed. That whatever had come together to put this all into motion had occurred in the realm where things were discussed but never committed to writing.

Where backtrails weren't just hidden, they were never created.

"So how does this go?" I asked.

Holding Diaz's phone in my left hand, I had the screen tilted up so she could see it. Scrawled across it was a map with a thick blue line pointing the way, an automated voice telling us each time we needed to make a turn.

"How's that?" she asked, glancing from the screen up to me before moving her attention back to the road.

"Esmerelda Ruiz," I replied. "What if we get up here and Junior is sitting on the couch in the living room?"

"He won't be."

"But what if he is?"

We both knew I was just playing devil's advocate, that there was no way what I was asking could come to pass, but it was a scenario that at least needed to be discussed.

The last three years of prison records displayed that not a single letter or phone call had been made or received by Ruiz. Not on birthdays or holidays. Never to inform him of a death or birth or engagement.

During the first part of his stay, interaction with the outside world had been limited, but it existed. The occasional visit from his mother. A call coming in from his sister.

After that, absolutely nothing.

Without that, or the usual paperwork that Diaz had alluded to that normally accompanied a release, it made the obvious choices for where to go next a bit thin.

"I talked to the office down in Mexico City last night while you were flying," Diaz said. "After Ruiz was taken away, Baja became the Wild West for a while. Lot of smaller players tried to step up, few bigger names from other parts tried to move in.

"Got the impression it was pretty ugly."

More than once we'd seen similar situations play out. The kind of thing that long after the fact, armed with the benefits of time and distance, made me wonder if what we were doing was really even a good thing.

Sure, we were removing a criminal from the streets. We were eradicating whatever evils he might have been responsible for, but it wasn't like we could do anything about existing demand.

Or human nature, for that matter.

We might have taken Ruiz out, but how many lives were lost because of it, if the people of Baja were any better for it, were questions we'd probably never know the answer to.

"His crew?" I asked.

"Guy didn't have anything definitive on file," Diaz replied. "Seemed to think they had disbanded, kind of scattered to the winds. Few familiar faces popped up in various places, but nothing concentrated."

That too I took without surprise.

The nature of the business and all that.

"In one thousand feet, turn right," the phone instructed.

Slowing the car a bit, Diaz drifted into the right lane, a bus stop lined with torn paper signage passing by. Behind it stood a taqueria with a name I'd never heard of before, a ragged line of customers already stretched out the door.

Above, the morning sun pounded down, a glare so bright it was almost white moving across the windshield.

"Ruiz had to go somewhere," I said, bringing the conversation back around to my original question.

"Yeah, but he won't be here," Diaz said. "At most, he would have asked her to pick him up. Wanted to make everything look legit, but he wouldn't have risked involving her in whatever he's got going on."

She didn't bother expounding on the last sentence, trusting I already knew what she was playing at.

Despite the radio silence Ruiz had undergone the last few years, there was no way he was suddenly granted his release and the message was left on Martin's mantle without him planning something big.

Almost like he'd been given a clean slate, a fresh start, and he was making sure to right old wrongs before embarking on it.

Easing into the turn, Diaz accelerated forward. The assorted businesses and throngs of people that had lined the major thoroughfare behind us fell away, replaced by residential streets. Along either side, single-family dwellings of similar architecture passed by, the exteriors and vehicles parked in the driveway putting it solidly in the middle class.

A far cry from the hacienda spread we had poured into that night eight years before.

"In five hundred feet, your destination will be on the left."

Chapter Sixty

The body of Ramon Reyes had already been taken away. One of the advantages of being on a spread that was so heavily rooted in agriculture, there were plenty of pieces of heavy machinery to make it easy. Within an hour of it taking place, a hole had been dug in one of the back fields. Body dropped in, it was filled in with dirt and covered over with assorted plant debris, no sign left behind that anything had ever taken place.

Overnight, one of the house staff had come through and scrubbed the stripes of blood and brain tissue away from the stucco railing of the balcony.

Now eight hours later, the only signs that anything had even taken place was the scent of gunpowder and the copper tang of blood in the air.

Already both were faint, the sort of thing someone would only notice if they knew to look for it.

And had smelled it enough times before to recognize it in an instant.

Standing a few feet down from where he'd been the night before, Junior Ruiz stared out over the fields below. Morning sun on his skin, it brought a thin veneer of sweat to his skin, the moisture touched by the occasional puff of breeze passing through.

Cigar in hand, he drew in a deep lungful of the sweet smoke, holding it for several moments, savoring the flavor before pushing it out in a plume before him.

"I had almost forgotten how good those things smell," Arlin Mejia said, stepping out onto the veranda. Hands clasped behind him, he was already dressed for the day.

Pulling up a few feet away, he stopped just short of the balcony rail, his gaze running parallel to Ruiz's.

"And I'd almost forgotten how good they taste," Ruiz commented, glancing down to the hand-rolled smoke wedged between his index and middle fingers.

One of the few vices he'd ever allowed himself, he'd picked up the habit when just a teenager. Something that his father had supposedly done years before, it was one of the few positive memories of the man his mother had ever imparted.

That alone being enough to get him started.

Simple enjoyment being enough to keep him going thereafter.

"Reyes," Mejia said, letting his distaste for the very name show in his delivery, "never abided such things. Man wouldn't drink a cup of coffee in the morning without getting into a damn staring contest, as if we were all supposed to be impressed by his restraint or something."

Cocking an eyebrow, Ruiz glanced over to the side. Never before had he heard of such a thing, but based on what he knew of the man, he couldn't say he was shocked.

Much like the opulence of the spread they were on, the ridiculous attire he wore, it was all part of some cultivated image. An exterior intended to spackle the enormous holes beneath. Things like Mejia, a lifetime employee of Ruiz, ascending so quickly to become Reyes's right hand. Or the way that an informant had appeared from nowhere to inform him that Ruiz was being released. Or that Ruiz had walked right up to Hector on the street, fully aware of his presence.

That the practice of parlay had fallen by the wayside long ago.

All things that someone focused on the proper aspects of the business should have picked up on right away.

Lifting the cigar, Ruiz motioned to the warehouse in the distance. Swinging his hand around in a half-arc, he included the various satellite structures around the property.

"Walk me through this. What the hell is all this stuff?"

A mirthless chuckle was Mejia's first response. "What you are looking at is the Fruit of the Desert Vineyard. A fully functional winery producing a Sauvignon Blanc and, as of yesterday, a Cabernet."

Feeling his eyebrows lift, his ire spiking in kind, Ruiz remained silent, refraining from asking the obvious question of why someone involved in the cocaine business would go through the time and expense of setting up a vineyard deep in the desert.

"After what happened with you," Mejia continued, "and all the press the situation at the border has been getting lately, he was afraid that just running a straight-up operation here like we had in Baja would be problematic."

Waving a hand before him, Mejia added, "So he came up with this system. Dissolving the incoming drugs into the wine during the production process."

A time or two over the years, a similar thing had been pitched to Ruiz. The reasoning behind it was pretty simple. By putting the cocaine into the wine, it received the double benefit of undergoing far less scrutiny and becoming much easier to mask.

Unless a dog was trained to sniff for the altered scent, they would never pick it up.

Border patrols and customs agents would likewise have needed to be briefed on how to assess liquids, relying on spectral light scanners to determine that what was inside wasn't strictly wine.

"Jesus," Ruiz muttered, shaking his head slightly.

"Yeah," Mejia agreed.

While those things might have made for a reasonable opening to a pitch, the problems with such an approach were too numerous to be ignored.

Trying to retrieve the drugs upon arrival. People overdosing from drinking the wine by mistake.

The cost and oversight of setting up a vineyard and running it like a legitimate business.

Turning away from the spread, Ruiz put his back to the wall. Folding his arms, he kept his right hand cocked upward, the cigar a few inches from his chin.

"Who is supplying the product?"

"New group, out of Peru. Only arrives when we're ready to produce a new batch. Comes in on ships, gets trucked here, is put straight into vats.

"Total time in its raw state, less than a couple hours."

"Total net?" Ruiz pressed.

"After everything?" Mejia replied. "Forty percent."

Feeling his eyes bulge, Ruiz glanced away. He let his gaze drift through the windows still standing open along the back of the office before glazing over, lost to the gentle ebb and flow of the thin curtains.

When he had last been in control, the average net per kilo was somewhere close to seventy percent. Costs they covered included shipping in both directions, along with packaging and manpower.

And of course, the need to always have the right people looking in the wrong direction.

Whatever was going on now meant that an additional thirty percent – double what he had been running at – was being dumped into extras.

Bullshit like the agricultural oasis they were standing in or the winery that was currently operating behind him.

"That shit stops now," Ruiz said. Blinking twice, he brought himself back into focus. Glancing over to Mejia, he gestured over his shoulder with the cigar. "All that back there. The excessive guards running around with AK's. Whatever other unnecessary expenditures he's got going on."

There was no surprise at the command. Not even a word of dissent.

Nothing but one corner of Mejia's mouth creasing back in a smile, his scalp becoming visible as he dipped his head in a nod.

"Absolutely, *El Jefe*."

Stuffing the cigar into the corner of his mouth, Ruiz nodded. The number of things he needed to see to, the sheer volume of conversations to be had, was nothing short of overwhelming.

All of it becoming an exercise in prioritization.

One he'd had years of time to sit and perfect.

"Now tell me about the other project we've got going. The one from up north."

Chapter Sixty-One

I knew the name Esmerelda Ruiz simply by virtue of her being the younger sister of Junior. A student at UCLA at the time we began our investigation into him, she was about to start her fifth year there when we made the move on his place, needing a couple of extra semesters to finish up a degree in marketing.

Attached in the file we amassed on Ruiz and his family were a few surveillance photos, the girl fitting every last trope that existed about pretty young college coeds in Los Angeles. Hair and makeup always in abundance. Clothing that was always sparse by comparison.

Beyond that, there hadn't been much effort put into the girl. We were aware of her existence, of the fact that she was still close to the family, received plenty of financial benefit from them.

Also, that they kept an eye on her from afar.

Otherwise, neither side seemed to be too involved with the other. On one side a child off enjoying college, opposite that a family intent to let her do so.

If she was even there the night we brought in Ruiz, I had not a clue.

What I did know was that the woman standing before me only vaguely resembled the one from the file.

Rooted just inside the threshold of the front door, Esmerelda Ruiz was dressed in a fuzzy blue robe checked with a white overlay. Looking like she was late in the stages of getting ready for work, her hair was twisted into dark curls, large loops hanging along either side of her face.

Makeup had already been applied, a much lower volume than in years past, now meant more to accentuate than to draw attention.

In the eight years that had preceded, I wouldn't say she had aged as much as grown up. Transitioning from early twenties to somewhere around thirty, the dewy look of youth was gone. Replacing it was someone with a bit of life experience, her features touched with world weariness.

A look I had no doubt she had earned every bit of.

And one I was all too familiar with myself.

"Can I help you?" she asked. Standing with one shoulder against the edge of the door, part of her remained hidden from view. Her posture hinted she wanted nothing more than to slam the door shut and throw the deadbolt.

"Good morning," Diaz said. Pulling her credentials from her hip, she wagged them in front of her, "Agents Diaz, Tate, with the DEA."

Noticing what she had done there, how she had managed to sidestep directly lying about my title or reason for being present, I kept my focus on Esmerelda.

If she caught it at all, she gave no indication.

Glancing between us, a bit of color drained from her face, her lips parting just slightly.

"Okay."

"May we come in?" Diaz asked, returning the wallet to her side. "We'd like to ask you a couple of questions."

Again, she looked between us. "About?"

"About the recent release of your brother from prison," Diaz replied.

Content to let her take the lead, to not overstep my being allowed to be here if I could avoid it, I flicked my gaze from her back to Esmerelda.

Much like the first time we worked together, I knew Diaz had other matters that needed her attention piled up on her desk. I also knew that her choosing to help me was about much more than just our being friends, the death of a former agent and the possibility of an enormous get in the form of Junior Ruiz also factoring into her presence.

"I don't know anything about that," Esmerelda replied. "And I'm sorry, but I really need to finish getting ready for work."

Shuffling a couple inches to the side, she closed the door just slightly, narrowing our field of vision into the home.

"You don't?" I asked, inserting myself for the first time into the conversation. "You weren't the one that picked him up yesterday from Lompoc?"

Pally had managed to pull the footage the day before from the cameras covering the prison parking lot, even sending over a printout of the two of them embracing beside the Chrysler now parked in the driveway.

The gap between her lips widened, a slight exhale pushing them apart. "I did, but I don't know anything about him getting out."

"So you weren't aware that it was more than thirty years before scheduled?" I pressed.

Her jaw sagged a bit more as she looked at me. Her olive complexion grew pale, her body rigid.

"Like I said, I don't know anything about that. He called last week and asked me to come pick him up, so of course I did."

The records showed no such call had been made. The last call to anybody Ruiz had made was more than six years prior.

For the time being though, I opted not to press it.

"Is your brother here now?" Diaz asked, pulling Esmerelda's focus back her way.

"No," she replied, giving a shake of her head. Once more, she made a slight move to the side, hiding a bit more of herself behind the door. "And like I said, I'm getting ready for work. I have a nine o'clock meeting that I really can't be late for."

Ignoring the comment, the not-so-subtle gesture to get away, Diaz remained in place. "Is he staying here with you?"

"No," Esmerelda repeated. "He stayed here one evening, but took off yesterday and hasn't been back."

"Do you know where?" I asked.

"And with who?" Diaz added.

"No," she managed to whisper.

"Do you know how to get ahold of him?" I asked.

Frozen in place, her mouth hanging open, Esmerelda stared at each of us. A slight crinkle passed over her face as if she might break, arriving and fleeing in a span of seconds.

"Look," she said, a hint of finality permeating the word, "I don't know anything about Junior's dealings, now or then. I know he called me a few days ago and asked me to come get him.

"Being my big brother, the only family I have left, I happily took off work and went to get him. He came over, we had a nice dinner, shared some laughs, and then he went on his way. Where he is now or what he's doing, you'll have to ask him."

Moving a few inches again, making it clear she was about to close the door for good, she added, "If you'd like to know any more than that, you'll have to come back with a warrant. I'm going to be late for work."

Chapter Sixty-Two

Every single part of Tres Salinas hurt. Not just the low lull of aches and pains. The deep-seated, persistent agony of a body having been actively abused.

Harsh and angry, it penetrated the darkness that he was under, grabbing him by the throat and pulling him toward the surface. Ripping him from deep in a state of unconsciousness, it jerked him upright in the bed he was laying on, his eyes popping open into uneven slits.

Bits of light popped around him like bubbles being shattered, the faint glow of an overhead bulb nearby penetrating his gaze like a knife to the front lobe.

Wanting so badly to scream, to raise his face toward the heavens and bellow with everything he had, he only barely managed to keep it in. To force himself not to react, to acclimate to the state he was in.

Which was to say, like he'd been dropped into a vat of acid. After being lit on fire. And hit by a car.

The last thing Tres remembering with any clarity was being out in the woods. After getting snatched while trying to retrieve his car from the airport parking lot, he could recall coming to some time later. Stripped of most of his clothes, his wrists and knees and ankles were bound with duct tape. His arms were pinned above his head, fastened to a thick pine branch.

Somewhere deep in the forest, the boughs of the trees around him were so thick he couldn't even see the sky. No moon or stars above, the sole source of light the small fire put together in a bed of rocks on the forest floor.

And beside it, the bastard that had nabbed him from the parking lot. The one that Luis Mendoza had been sent north to eliminate days before.

The very same one that Tres had seen with Martin that night years before, recognizable despite the tangle of hair enveloping his features.

After that, what Tres could call to mind was spotty at best. Beginning with the heated blade of a knife, the man had gone to work on him, peppering him with questions. Whenever an answer was refused, the knife was brought into play. Any answer that he didn't care for or thought was a lie, more harm was done.

Back and forth things had gone for some unknown amount of time, Tres doing his best to hold out, to resist as much as possible.

Right up to the point where the man had decided to get creative, visiting the toolbox in the bed of his truck.

From that point forward, the gaps in Tres's memory were more pronounced, each one punctuated by a flare of bright light.

Flares that all seemed to correspond to the pain now gripping his body, the various bandages encasing him corroborating most of what he remembered.

Setting his jaw, clamping his molars down tight, Tres attempted to push past the pain. He drew in breath slowly through his nose, willing his mind to move beyond the litany of injuries covering his body.

Lowering his face to stare straight ahead, he forced himself to take stock of his situation, to see where he was, determine how he might have gotten there.

Based on what he could recall, the state of his body, it was a wonder that he wasn't dead already. Considering where they were the last he could remember and some of the things the man was saying, he couldn't believe that was by accident.

Just as he wasn't surprised to see the walls around him made from concrete block. Painted over dozens of times before, the glow of the lights outside his cell reflected off the shiny surface, making them look almost liquid.

Lining the front of the space was a grate of iron bars. Beneath him was a cot mattress no more than a couple of inches thick, a flat pillow and cotton blanket so threadbare it was almost transparent.

Affixed to the wall beside the bed was an aluminum toilet, one solid metal piece without a handle or seat.

All of that together with the facts that he was alone and the place was silent also told him that he wasn't in prison. More likely a holding cell of some sort, a place to wait for him to wake up before turfing him to wherever he was going next.

Turning himself sideways, Tres attempted to lower his feet to the floor. Both completely mummified in gauze, he swung them a few inches over the side before remembering some of what happened the night prior and thinking better of it.

Knowing they were still in no shape to be bearing weight, he instead rested them on the edge of the bed, leaning back against the wall behind him.

Feeling the cool of it pass through his shirt, he stared straight ahead. Eyes barely more than slits, he peered into the darkest corner of the room, doing his best to avoid the harsh agony of the light penetrating his skull.

There he remained, forcing himself to clear his mind. To get past the physical damage, beating back the impulses traveling the length of his body. To fight his rising body temperature, his heart rate climbing in the face of what he knew he needed to do next.

"Hello?" he managed, his throat dry and raw, distorting his voice. Tilting his chin just slightly, he lifted his face an inch. "Hello?"

For a moment, there was no response. Nothing but the sound of the wind outside howling past, audible even through the concrete brick behind him.

"Hello?" he called a third time, his voice rising just slightly. Taking everything he had, it felt like a razor had hurtled the length of his throat, one more pain added to the collection.

So sharp it brought moisture to the underside of his eyes, he clenched tight, holding his breath, willing the moment to pass.

A moment that culminated with what he'd been waiting for, the sound of footsteps finally appearing.

Slow and persistent, they grew closer in an uneven amble. Every one seemed to be accentuated by the groan of various implements and metal chains, the kind found on a utility belt worn by law enforcement.

Little by little, the sounds grew more pronounced, finally ending as a figure came into view.

And someone that – outside of the bearded man from the woods the night before – was the last person on earth Tres wanted to see.

"Well, hello yourself," the deputy that Tres had last left dumped in a pile on the floor of the medical clinic said. A narrow bandage was pressed across the bridge of his nose, dark circles underscoring each of his eyes.

Despite the words he used, a glare covered the rest of his features, malevolence oozing from every pore.

"Finally wake up, Juan Perez? Or do you prefer to go by your actual name, Tres Salinas?"

Mouth still clamped shut, Tres stared straight back at the man. He made sure not to react in any way, to not let the needling that was being tossed his way get to him.

The assumption he had made before was correct. There was no way that he would have simply been left in the woods for dead. Not only had he been brought in on purpose, he had been brought back to this very spot.

And his real name had been used.

All things that couldn't add up to anything good.

"Let me guess," the deputy sneered, "you want to see your attorney?"

Reactions of every sort exploding just beneath the surface, Tres leaned his head forward and offered only a pair of words.

"Phone call."

Chapter Sixty-Three

The point in driving all the way to Escondido was never to get Esmerelda Ruiz to suddenly open her home to us. It wasn't under the delusion that her brother would be there or even that she would tell us where he was.

If she had, it would have been wonderful, but it would have effectively made her the first person in her position in our cumulative time with the DEA to do so.

Not that either of us blamed her for staying quiet. The bonds of family are thick and run deep, nowhere more so than in Latin culture. The odds were better of her opening fire on us than giving up the older brother that had just returned to her life after almost a decade away.

The goal in going up there was to tap into that. To set a trap, knowing exactly how she would probably react, and then using that to put things into motion.

With the time being half past nine, the sun sat much higher in the sky above. Even with it being the opening week in November, already the temperature was halfway between seventy and eighty degrees, with the promise of it only getting warmer the closer we got to afternoon.

Coming in straight through the front windshield, the sun far outpaced the cool air being pushed out of the vents. Unacclimated after months spent in Montana, I could feel a film of sweat resting beneath the hair hanging across my forehead.

Already, moisture underscored my beard, my neck just beginning to itch.

Ignoring all of that, I watched as San Diego grew closer before us. Our second pass through of the morning, most of the earlier traffic had already cleared. Along with it went most of the negative energy that seemed to radiate up from the asphalt, people finally making it to their destination.

A process that had ended for now, only to begin anew in six hours, the only difference being the direction it was traveling.

Folded into the front seat, I stared out, ruminating on the meeting we'd just had before pulling my cellphone onto my thigh. Balancing it there, I worked through a series of screens before finding what I wanted. Hitting send, I shifted the volume to speakerphone, turning it up loud enough to be heard over the thrum of the road beneath us.

Hidden behind her mirrored shades, Diaz glanced over only once from the driver's seat. "Pally?"

"Yeah," I grunted.

"Unless, of course, she really did have a meeting at nine she needed to get to."

Snorting softly, knowing the comment was a barb at the blatant lie Esmerelda had been trying to pedal not long before, I refrained from answering, letting the sound of the ringtone pipe in instead.

After just three rings, it was snatched up.

"Are we a go?" Pally asked, his voice a bit detached, as if he were in the process of doing multiple things at once.

"Just left," I replied. "We never made it past the front door, so I don't know if she had a cell or landline or what, but-"

"Already on it," Pally said. "One of each, been tracking them all morning. She hasn't made any contact yet, but as soon as she does, we'll have a number."

And with that, a location to trace.

Of the various people in Junior Ruiz's life, there were only two that he had maintained even limited contact with while in prison. One of those was his mother, who had passed a number of years before.

The other was Esmerelda, the person that had picked him up from prison and given him a place to stay his first night out.

The one that would always have a way to contact him.

And would damned sure call to alert him about a pair of federal agents already showing up to look for him.

"What about that other number I gave you?"

Two nights before when I'd nabbed Tres Salinas, the only phone he'd had with him was a cheap model that was clearly a prepaid, picked up with the intention of operating as a burner. Containing not a single text message, the sole listing in the call log was for a number in Southern California.

In total, there were just a handful of interactions between the two. Calls going in both directions, often at random times.

More than likely a contact overseeing the operation, someone radioing updated orders or for Tres to check in with for progress reports.

"Nothing yet," Pally replied. "I ran the number and it also belongs to a burner, part of the same shipment as the one you confiscated.

"Looks like right now it's turned off. No way of knowing if it'll come back online, but if it does, I'll be on that too."

Glancing over, I saw Diaz meet my gaze. Seeming to have nothing more to add to the conversation, she turned back to the road.

"Alright, thanks a lot, Pally. Keep us posted on anything that turns up."

Chapter Sixty-Four

The car sitting at the curb didn't have government plates, but it might as well have. A standard sedan not far from the one we had just climbed out of, it rested parallel to the front door of the Southwest Headquarters office, oblivious to the stretch of red paint along the sidewalk lining the front of the building.

Solid black in color with windows tinted almost dark enough to match, it reflected the overhead sun, giving it an ominous quality. At once a beacon, drawing our attention, and a warning, telling us to stay far away.

"This can't be good," Diaz whispered, stepping up from the parking lot onto the front walk.

"Nope," I agreed, not bothering to voice the second thought that came to mind, my hope being whatever news this car had been sent to dispatch was aimed more her direction than mine.

For the better part of three days, I had felt like I was running a race with no clear idea where the finish line was. After the initial encounter with the man at my office, I had spent half a day sitting vigil over my friend, trying frantically to put together what it could be pointing to.

The next morning, I had gotten a message, telling me about

Shawn Martin's death. A tiny breadcrumb, forcing me on a multi-state drive that revealed the bullet and the coin sitting on his mantle.

Almost a full twenty-four hours to figure out the who.

Another twelve after that tracking down what few leads I had in an effort to ferret out the why. A process that was still ongoing, just now beginning to finally bring me to what I ultimately needed.

The where.

Sixty solid hours I had been at this. I'd covered four states, put down two hired assassins, saved one friend and consoled another. I was calling in favors I didn't have, leaning on folks for time and effort they couldn't spare.

The time for more confounding factors was over. Already, it was all I could do to contain the angst I had. Every part of me had wanted to shoulder my way through the door at Esmerelda Ruiz's house, sit her on the couch and demand she get her brother on the phone.

To hear his voice, find out exactly where he was, and then track down the man that was trying to wipe out our team eight years after the fact.

Any further delays to that happening, and I could no longer be held accountable for my actions.

Walking on the inside of the sidewalk, Diaz reached the front door first. Passing straight through, she held it just long enough for me to enter behind her, the two of us crossing the front foyer together.

Finding nobody out of the ordinary waiting, no one that could explain the sedan outside, I allowed Diaz to lead us to the reception desk positioned in the center of the space. Behind it sat a young woman in her late twenties, a puff of curly blonde hair pulled into a ponytail behind her head. Any wisps held back by a thick white band, she was wearing a navy dress with an open white dress shirt.

At the sound of our approach, she looked up from the screen of some handheld electronic device, a smile bearing hints of both recognition and embarrassment at being caught.

"Good morning, Director."

Ignoring the greeting entirely, Diaz hooked a thumb over her shoulder. "Who is that, and why are they parked right there?"

Much like her steps since spotting the vehicle from the parking lot, each word was clipped, delivered quickly.

The smile the girl wore faded as she leaned to the side. Peering past Diaz, she looked through the glass front of the doors to the sedan sitting in plain sight.

"Oh, that is for Agents Jones and Smith," she said. "They said this wouldn't take a few minutes."

Flicking a glance my way, Diaz set her jaw, letting the look on her face relay exactly what she was thinking.

The initial feeling we'd both had on approach wasn't quite right. Not in that we were wrong, but that it was much, much worse than either of us had initially anticipated.

"Jones and Smith?" Diaz asked, letting her disbelief for the names or what they could possibly want hang from her words.

"Yes, ma'am."

"Did they say who they were with?"

Any remaining hints of the smile faded completely. All color seemed to flee with it, the girl casting a glance between us.

"No, ma'am."

"What they wanted?"

Whether she was unable or simply didn't want to repeat herself, the girl pulled up just the same. Jaw sagging, she gave us each one last look before lowering her eyes slightly, staring at the desktop in front of her.

"They're waiting in the conference room for you now." Raising her gaze to me, she added, "Both of you."

Chapter Sixty-Five

Junior Ruiz didn't mind that the operation had been moved north of the border. Considering the amount of competition that had sprung up between the various cartels working out of Baja and the assorted pitfalls in perpetually negotiating an international barrier, it was only a matter of time before he'd made such a move himself.

The weather down south was wonderful, there was no denying that. As was the fact that every person he considered family – by birth or by circumstance – was concentrated in a geographic area no larger than fifteen miles across.

The spread they had was great, and the post they occupied right off the coast aided considerably in the shipping process.

But the amount of money he was beginning to expend in keeping local government and police at bay was becoming astronomical. As were the assorted losses in manpower, many of those newer to the trade having seen too many action movies, believing the only way to garner a toehold in that world was with a lot of guns and hired muscle.

Beliefs that saw most of them eradicated pretty quickly, but not without cost.

And all that was before even factoring in global changes that had occurred in recent years. Ranging from heightened fuel prices to increased border scrutiny, it made a great deal of sense to be located where they now were.

What Ruiz didn't like, would soon need to go about fixing, was the particular spread that Ramon Reyes had put together.

An exercise in extremes, the place was designed to service a front business that never should have existed.

Standing on the same veranda where he'd officially taken over the night before, Ruiz stared out at the grounds around him. The thick tangle of palm and fruit trees up close, acre after acre of grapevines stretched off into the distance. The various tractors and machines he'd seen moving over the grounds throughout the afternoon. The irrigation system keeping everything alive.

The assorted outbuildings and the enormous warehouse sitting directly across from him. All eyesores. Things that could draw unwanted attention from anybody that might become curious and start looking around.

Reasons for health and agriculture inspectors to come around. People with eyes and ears and devices with video capability, making it that much easier for things to slip out.

Standing in the same spot along the balcony, Ruiz allowed the warmth of the stucco railing to pass through his palms. In his face was a faint breeze, ruffling his hair, filling his nostrils with the scents of apple and damp earth.

Letting his gaze sweep from one side of the property to the other, he made mental notations on all that he saw, things that would need to be relayed to Arlin Mejia soon. Items that would require their immediate attention as they reformed the business back into their own design.

Completing his pass, he turned his head back to face forward, his gaze landing on the even rows of grapevines stretching out before him. Extending out far enough to drop over a dip in the distance, he allowed his focus to glaze, working through all the last few weeks had held.

Of the promise of the weeks ahead.

Rooted in place, lost in his thoughts, the faint buzzing of his phone resting on the stucco between his hands barely resonated. Completely out of place in the scene he was immersed in, it wasn't until more than a half dozen bursts had sounded out before they finally managed to penetrate his thoughts.

Drawing his focus down, a deep V formed between his brows as he stared at the screen, taking a moment to recognize the number staring back at him before snatching it up. Turning away from the railing, he passed back through the open windows into the office, the breeze and the bright light of day disappearing behind him.

The number he had left with his sister was given with the strictest instructions only to contact him if absolutely necessary. Promising that he would be in touch in the very near future, the expectation had been clear that she was to avoid reaching out if at all possible.

The fact that she was doing so now, after barely more than half a day, caused his stomach to draw tight. Marching just past the desk, he paused, pressing the phone to his face.

"Esmera?"

"I'm sorry," she shot back, barely waiting to hear his voice. Mixed with heavy breathing, it sounded as if she'd been crying, her voice on the cusp of hysterics. "I know you told me not to call, but they just left a little bit ago and-"

"Wait," Ruiz inserted, cutting her off mid-ramble. Not wanting her to get too far afield, to let whatever was gripping her take over completely, he raised a hand before him. Mimicking an exaggerated breath, he said, "Calm down. Take a breath. What's going on?"

Heeding his advice, Esmera pushed out a long sigh. Whistling through the mouthpiece, the sound rocketed through Ruiz's ear before disappearing.

"I'm sorry," she said again, "I know you told me not to call unless it was important, but-"

Once more, Ruiz interrupted her, stopping her before she got too carried away. The feeling in his core grew more pronounced, the myriad things that could have put her in such a state, have worried her enough to ignore his request not to reach out, crossing his mind.

"It's okay, Esmera. Just tell me what happened."

"Okay," his sister replied. Taking another breath, she seemed to compose herself for a moment before saying, "This morning, before leaving for the office, a pair of agents showed up at the door."

"Agents?" Ruiz asked.

"Yeah," Esmera said. "They showed me their badges and everything. Said they were with some organization, but I can't remember right off hand. To be honest, I was trying to keep from freaking out."

Ruiz had assumed this was how it was going to be the moment the offer was first extended to him. By gaining his freedom, he would be forever beholden to them, the terms of their agreement changing whenever the other side felt like it.

He just hadn't expected it to start already.

"That's okay," Ruiz said, feeling some of the angst he'd held just moments before begin to flee. "Those are the guys I met with before being released. I'll give them a call later today."

Esmera accepted the information in silence, considering what was said, before asking, "Are you sure?"

Raising a hand to his brow, Ruiz turned back to the windows behind him. He looked out past the balcony railing to the warehouse in the distance, midday sun reflecting from the metal roof. On either side of it he could see horsetails of water sprouting in various directions, the sprinkler system fighting an ongoing battle against the desert heat.

He had plenty of problems to deal with already. He didn't need Jones and Smith adding to them.

"Yeah," Ruiz said. "I'm sure. Goofy bastards probably just got lost on their way to get matching haircuts and pick up some more cheap suits. Nothing to worry about."

On the other end of the line, he heard a sharp intake of air. Pulling his hand from his forehead, he moved his focus back to the call, a trio of horizontal lines appearing across his brow.

"Esmera?"

"They weren't wearing suits," his sister whispered. "And they definitely weren't both guys."

Chapter Sixty-Six

Both men were staring at the door as we entered the conference room, as if they knew we were coming. Looking to personify the stereotype of the fabled government agents in every way, both wore black suits that had clearly not been tailored to fit their builds. White shirts and solid black ties completed the ensemble.

Each with hair buzzed above the ears and the neck, they both had shoved it to the side, the only discernible difference being that the one standing was a shade or two darker.

If I were to guess, I'd peg them both in their early forties.

Most of all, the first thing that jumped out at me was they both looked a little soft, like most of what they did included barking orders from behind a desk.

"Good morning," Diaz said, pushing into the conference room. Like she had at the front, she paused to hold the door just an instant, letting me catch it before heading on in. "Sorry to keep you waiting, but I didn't know we were expecting anybody."

Delivered without any inflection, the word choice was deliberate, relaying the exact thought we'd both shared on the short walk from the front desk. Regardless who these guys were, the intrusion was neither expected nor appreciated.

Right now, we had far more important things to be doing than tiptoeing around bureaucracy.

Neither of the men made any effort to step forward as I filed in behind her. While I closed the door in my wake, they both merely stared back, each maintaining their respective position.

Letting everyone stay exactly as they were for a moment, the man sitting eventually spoke, forcing something approaching a pleasant countenance onto his features.

"Good morning," he said. "My name is Agent Jones. Here with me is my colleague, Agent Smith. You'll have to excuse our sudden appearance."

The names he rattled off without the slightest hint of irony, as if we were both supposed to accept at face value the blatant fabrications.

Even Tres Salinas had tried harder with his Juan Perez pseudonym.

Pausing there, he glanced expectantly between us, the silence extended long enough that Diaz eventually said, "Okay, I'm acting director here, Mia Diaz. With me is my colleague, Agent Tate."

Across the room, the man named Smith smirked slightly, loud enough to be heard, but soft enough he could pretend to mask it.

Lifting my hands, I grasped the padded leather top of the rolling desk chair before me. Already, I could see how the interaction was going to go. Coupled with the assorted emotions roiling through me, it was best to have something to clamp onto, a way of dispelling some tiny bit of the animosity I felt.

"DEA?" I asked.

In unison, both men flicked their gaze my way. Fixating on me for several moments, regarding me as if I were a dog that had somehow managed to speak while sitting beside the dinner table, neither said a word before turning their attention back to Diaz.

"The reason we're here this morning," Jones said, "is to make you aware of a very difficult situation currently unfolding and to ask for your help."

My grip on the chair before me grew tighter at his blatant dismissal of my question. My knuckles flashed white as I squeezed, every muscle in my upper clenching at once.

"And what situation is that?" Diaz asked.

The smile remained in place on Jones's face as he began to speak. Pulling up short, he drew in a short breath, glancing down to the table for a moment.

"Well, I think we all-"

"Stay the hell away from Junior Ruiz," Smith said, jumping in and finishing the sentence. Hands shoved into the pockets of his slacks, he stood a couple feet back from Jones, peering over his shoulder.

A look that appeared every bit an open challenge.

One that I would love nothing more than to answer, the fact that I was a guest in Diaz's office being the sole thing keeping me from tossing the chair out of the way and going straight across the table after him.

Never in my own experience before had I encountered what this had all the hallmarks of, though I had heard a few stories over the years. Instances where somebody from one of the bigger agencies – or namely, *the* bigger agency – would show up and start making veiled threats.

Suggest a new course of action. Hint at what would be in the best interest of all parties. Dissuade someone from whatever it was they were doing at a particular time.

"Right now, this office is not looking into Junior Ruiz," Diaz replied, taking a bit more of a diplomatic approach. "Last I heard, the man was still in prison."

Making no effort to hide his reactions, Smith again scoffed. Louder than his previous one, he twisted his body to the side, seemingly to bite back some remark, before turning to stare our way.

"Sure you don't," he said, shifting back to face forward. "And I suppose all those inquiries you've been making lately are just...what? Looking to write a book? Maybe sign a documentary deal with Netflix?"

At most, I would peg the man at no more than five-ten. Maybe one-hundred-and-eighty-five pounds on a good day, in full clothes, after a big meal. Where he got off thinking he was the heavy in the room, that his brandishing a scowl and a little bit of attitude somehow made him the alpha, was beyond me.

Though again the urge to show him just how wrong that supposition was rose within me.

"We recently ran a sting on an operation in Baja with some of his former associates," Diaz replied without missing a step. "I tried pulling his files to look into them and found I couldn't gain access.

"Naturally, that made me a little curious."

Lifting his eyebrows, Smith muttered, "Curious."

Accompanying the word, he made a show of taking a step back away from the table.

The moment he did so, Jones leaned forward, resting his elbows on the edge of the table, a dance that had clearly been rehearsed between the two of them before.

"I believe you can understand and appreciate that we're all on the same side here. We both want the same things, even if we're going about getting them in different ways."

Whatever goodwill Diaz had, any decorum that being in the conference room of the headquarters she oversaw demanded, evaporated. Unable to conjure the requisite propriety to banter back, she merely stood beside me, both of us silent.

"And right now, that means that we must ask this office to stand down with regards to Junior Ruiz."

Falling quiet, he waited as his colleague stepped in behind him, taking the cue that it was again his part to speak in their little performance.

"And just to be clear," Smith said, extending a hand our direction, "we're not actually *asking* anything. Just go back to believing Junior Ruiz is in prison, and understand that if he were to get out, it would be for a damn good reason."

Chapter Sixty-Seven

Tres Salinas's request for a phone call was summarily dismissed. The deputy that first fielded the request had thrown back his head and laughed in a mocking tone, letting it be known how ridiculous he thought the entire thing.

In the name of adding extra insult to the situation, he had then walked to the far end of the building to fetch the sheriff. At that point, he'd shared the request that had been made, both of the men getting a good chuckle out of the ordeal.

A response that prompted Tres to do the only thing he could, making a move he really didn't want to but had no other choice on, prompted by the deputy himself just moments before.

"Lawyer."

Both still finishing off the laugh they'd had at his expense, the sheriff had managed, "Yeah, we'll get right on that," before the two had drifted away.

As they left, he could hear them continuing to banter back and forth, loud enough to be heard without being deciphered before erupting into laughter again.

In the time after their departure, Tres had been forced to stay in the holding cell, fighting against the combination of pain gripping his body and anxiety hurtling through his mind. Time after time he'd sat and repeated the single word over and over, well past the point where his broken nose had started to bleed from the pressure of yelling and his throat was raw.

Past moisture rising to his eyes from the sheer overload of everything being put upon his system.

So long he had repeated the process, saying it time and again, until at last his wait ended just after noon. A full three hours after making the formal request, the same deputy had arrived and ordered him to stick his hands through the open slot on the front of his cell.

Clamping his wrists in cuffs tight enough to break the skin, he had marched him down the hall into the interrogation room, right into the same seat where he had first encountered Luis Mendoza two days before.

With a second set of handcuffs, he tethered Tres to the ring rising from the middle of the table before stepping to the side and opening the door.

"Come on in," he muttered, his graveled voice letting it be known he still wasn't over what had happened at the clinic, hating every moment of what he was doing.

The young man that stepped into the room looked even younger than Tres. Clearly the lowest ranking attorney from the public defender's office that could be found, he met Tres's request for counsel, though only just barely.

Dressed in a pair of khakis and a sports coat, he had a thick shock of fawn-colored hair and oversized glasses with square frames that made his eyes look twice their natural size. Weighing no more than one-hundred-and-fifty pounds, his footfalls were silent on the floor as he stepped inside, pulling up halfway to the table. Mouth dropping open, he audibly gasped at the sight of Tres.

A move that, given the reflection staring back at Tres from the one-way glass on the wall, he couldn't rightly disagree with. Especially with the fresh streaks of blood running from either nostril, mixing with the carnage still strewn across his features from two nights before.

"My god," the young man said. A briefcase in one hand, he raised the other to his mouth, covering his gaping lips. "What happened? Did these men do this to you?"

"We apprehended the suspect after he was in a car accident while fleeing a scene," the deputy replied. Extending his index finger, he jabbed it up at his own face, pointing to the bandage on his nose and his twin black eyes.

Injuries which were minor by comparison.

"A scene in which he did this and murdered another man in cold blood."

Eyes somehow managing to grow even wider, the young man turned to regard Tres. Remaining in place, he made no effort to come closer, a look of marvel on his face, like a spectator at a zoo that had just witnessed a caged animal attack a handler.

Of the few things Tres knew about the American justice system, the requirement that they honor his request for an attorney was at the top. They could deny him certain comforts, could easily keep him away from a telephone, but if they didn't put him in the presence of counsel, any chance they had at making charges stick would be nullified.

A fact he was reasonably certain they would want to protect more than anything else at this point.

Had he actually needed the young man's services, if he'd been forced to rely on them in any way for his health or wellness, he would have known at a glance that he was in trouble. That any hope he had of ever walking free again would be in vain.

But he didn't need such a thing. Not at this point.

All he needed was someone to do what he couldn't. To help him finish the task that had been assigned and relay a message.

He had made a mistake. Not in getting caught, but in going off-script at the Martin house. Taken alone, it was no big deal. A little farewell gift to the team that had forever altered the lives of so many.

But given the way everything else had gone in the last couple of days, it had proven to be much, much more than that.

Making it all the more imperative he get word where it needed to be.

Shaping his thumb and forefinger as if gripping a pencil, Tres shook his right wrist, rattling the handcuffs against the rink holding him in place.

"Pencil and paper, please."

Chapter Sixty-Eight

The inside of Diaz's office was almost identical to the way I last remembered it. Which was almost identical to the way it had been five years prior, neither her nor Hutch being the sort to bother with decorations or personal touches of any kind.

Instead, the place was a collection of remainder government supplies, all somewhat battered, all still bearing the metallic bar codes from whenever they'd first been handed out.

Aside from the missing stink of whatever herbal concoction Hutch was always guzzling, as far as I could tell, the biggest difference was the concentrated energy now crammed into the small space. In the wake of our meeting a few doors down, both of us were practically bouncing off the walls, wanting to scream and thrash and kick all at once.

Neither of us able to sit down, to possibly be motionless after the events in the conference room, we resided on either side of her desk. Jutting out from the wall, the piece served to bisect the room, giving us each enough space to pace back and forth.

Between us on the desk sat my cellphone, the item going off three different times in my pocket while we met with Jones and Smith.

Unable to pull it out at the time — and not about to step away from the meeting and tip the numbers balance in their favor — I had chosen to wait.

Now back in the quiet of her office, the door pulled shut behind us, the phone buzzed just a single time before being snatched up.

"Where the hell have you been?" Pally snapped in greeting, his voice threaded with annoyance.

"You don't want to know," Diaz muttered in response, the angst in hers even higher.

Ignoring them both, knowing the only reason he would have answered in such a way, I asked, "What did you find?"

Pausing, it seemed he wanted to press us, to ask what had happened on our end in the brief window since we last spoke, though he let it go for the time being.

"Esmerelda Ruiz called her brother," Diaz said, jumping ahead, putting together where Pally was taking things.

"Yes," Pally said, "eleven minutes ago. She called from her cell-phone to a prepaid number. They talked for six minutes and then the phone was turned off, hasn't come back on since."

Nor would it. The phone having served its purpose, it would now be destroyed, exchanged for another or relayed to someone else to serve as the in-between.

Flicking my gaze up to Diaz, she nodded slightly, an unspoken acknowledgement of what we both already knew.

"Were you able to get a location on it?" I asked.

"Also, yes," Pally said, "but that's not all. About the same time, the other number you gave me came to life. At exactly noon, it popped on for ten minutes and received an incoming call."

Pulling to a stop behind the lone visitor chair opposite Diaz, I stared down at the phone. I could feel a cleft appear between my brows as I considered the statement, working through what I knew.

For the phone to have come to life right at noon denoted that it was an agreed-to time. Outside of those specific moments, the device stayed off, meant to protect whoever was holding it.

"A call from...?" I asked. Adding the information to what I knew, I forced my mind to make sense of what I was being told. To put the disparate information into something I could handle. "Surely they didn't let Tres Salinas use a phone."

Across from me, Diaz had pulled up close to the edge of the desk, pressing the front of her legs against it. Glancing from me to the phone, she leaned forward, balancing herself on her palms.

"Nope," Pally replied, "but he found a way around it anyway. The number was from a landline at the Gallatin County Public Defender's Office."

For the second time in the last fifteen minutes, I felt like I'd been kicked in the shorts. Jerking my focus to Diaz, I raised my chin a few inches, letting her see the vitriol that was filling me.

Lifting a hand before me, I curled my fingers back into talons, squeezing so tight my hand quivered. My lips peeled back in equal kind, every inclination telling me to grab something and throw it against the wall.

Or even through it.

"An attorney wouldn't be able to be a part of something illegal," Diaz said.

"But if a client asked them to relay a message that seemed benign," I continued.

"Something that was coded," Diaz said.

Much like when I was standing outside the Snoqualmie Police Station, somebody listening may have thought we were the ones speaking in code.

In reality, we weren't really conversing at all, merely thinking out loud, both working this through to completion.

Even if we both already likely knew where it was going.

Anybody that had the foresight to set a predetermined time to talk would also put together a specific phrase or system of alerting each other when things went awry.

Already, we knew that Ruiz was aware that agents were snooping about. Our decision to visit Esmerelda that morning had expected as much.

But this took things a step further. It made it known not only that I had survived, but that Tres was being held in custody.

Two facts that would certainly alter their behavior moving forward.

"What happened with the line after that?" I asked.

"Cut out again," Pally said. "Just like Ruiz. Turned off, SIM card destroyed, whatever else, but not until I got an address on it."

Lifting just my eyes to Diaz, hands resting atop either hip, I asked, "Yeah? Where's that?"

"Same exact spot as Ruiz."

Under most circumstances, what was just shared would be good news. It would be the final string tying every assumption and piece of evidence we'd cobbled together into a single coherent bunch.

The person that had been calling the shots on the assassination attempts, the message left behind at Martin's house, and the release of Junior Ruiz all came together, confirmed by the two men now standing side by side.

All facts thrown into complete disarray by the visit from Jones and Smith a moment before and the directive that had been handed down.

"Thank you, Pally," I said. "That's hellacious work."

"Don't thank me yet," he replied. "As we speak, I'm pulling up records on the property, tapping into zoning reports and satellite imagery.

"Within a half hour, we ought to know damn near everything there is about wherever they're holed up."

Across from me, Diaz smirked. Shaking her head slightly, she said, "All this, minutes after we've been told to stand down."

For the first time since the call connected, the sound of activity on the other end ceased. The rolling desk chair stopped moving. All motion across a keyboard fell silent.

"You guys were told to stand down?" Pally asked.

"Yeah," I replied.

"By who?"

I flicked my gaze up to Diaz, who responded with, "They didn't say."

Gleaning exactly what was meant, Pally hissed, "Bastards." Pausing, he fell silent a moment, contemplating the information, before saying, "That's a shame. Any minute now there's a care package set to arrive that might have something different to say on the matter."

Part Five

Chapter Sixty-Nine

"I'll be a son of a bitch," I whispered, pulling to a stop inside the threshold to the conference room. Just inches from where I'd stood earlier in the day and resisted the urge to fly across the table at Jones and Smith, I now stared in the same direction, barely believing the sight before me.

Feeling my heart rate tick up slightly, I took a step to the side, seeing the lone man standing along the opposite wall turn.

A long, slow movement, as if meant to draw out the drama of the moment.

"That's no way to talk about your mama," Carl Diggs said as a means of greeting.

The third on-the-ground member of our team, Carl Diggs was three years in by the time I showed up. Half a decade older than me in age, in a former life he had been a part of Delta Force, proficient at handling every firearm ever produced.

My first thought upon meeting the man had been that it looked like he was carved from solid obsidian. Always he prided himself on standing exactly six feet in height and weighing exactly two hundred pounds, nice round numbers that could be rattled off in an instant.

With each step around the table I took, it appeared that the figures

DUSTIN STEVENS

still held true. At a glance, the only difference I could see was that the buzzcut that had previously adorned his skull had now migrated south into a goatee.

The rest remained the same, right down to the thousand-yard stare currently fixed on me.

"Pally said you were deep in the muck."

"I was."

"Brown or green?" I asked.

Arching an eyebrow, the gesture was enough to let me know that was classified, not supposed to be shared.

"Green. And I still almost got here faster than you."

Green meant that he had been in the jungle and not the sandbox. Either somewhere in eastern Asia or one of the hundreds of islands between here and there. Far enough that he would have had to call in some serious favors to get here for sure.

"Yeah, well, I'm sure Pally told you I got a visitor that night too."

"Only one?" he shot back. No small amount of derision in his tone, he remained rooted in place, staring at me, holding it for almost a full thirty seconds before finally his head quivered just slightly.

An instant later, a thin smiled cracked his features, a sliver of white offset against his dark skin and the goatee encasing his mouth.

"Was a day when Hawk Tate didn't get out of bed for less than three."

The same smile found my face. "There was also a day when that chin hair sat up a little higher, so I guess time's been rough on us all."

Diggs's expression grew into a grin as he finally took a step in my direction. Hands falling by his side, he replied, "Yeah, Father Time can be a real bastard, can't he?"

"Yes, he can," I agreed, meeting my friend along the side of the table filling the room. Sharing a quick hug, we clapped each other on the back, openly appraising one another before taking a step back.

"Good to see you, brother," Diggs said.

"You too. Damned shame this is what it took to get us here."

"Got that right," he agreed. The smile faded a bit as he asked, "How's Serra doing?"

316

Scrunching the side of my face, I gave him a non-committal shrug. "Exactly like you'd expect her to be."

Knowing just what I meant, he nodded slightly.

"And you?" he asked.

The answer to that was loaded to say the least. So much had happened in the last couple days, there was no way to possibly fill him in right now on just that part.

To say nothing of the host of emotions roiling through me, aching to be expelled at any moment.

Or of the years that had slid past since we'd last seen each other.

"I take it you're the care package?" I asked, sidestepping the question for the time being.

"Care package, cavalry, whatever the hell else is needed right now. Just tell me where to point and shoot."

Opening my mouth, I began to respond. Opting against it for the time being, not knowing just how much he had been briefed on, I instead reached into the front pocket of my jeans.

Sliding my fingers around the two objects I'd been carrying since leaving the Martin household, I placed them both down on the table beside us. Starting with the bullet, I leaned the coin against it, exactly as I had found them on the mantle.

Leaving them there, I said absolutely nothing, watching as the same thought process I had been through in Washington two days before played out on his features.

"You have got to be shitting me," he whispered, his eyes flaring as he glanced up to me.

"Nope," Diaz said, stepping into the room behind us. The sound of her voice pulled both of our attention her way, seeing her standing with a sheaf of papers tucked against her ribs.

Marching around to our side of the table, she dropped the stack down. Extending a hand before her, she said, "Mia Diaz."

"Carl Diggs," he replied, accepting the shake. "You're the one that took over for Hutch, right?"

"Still have the smell of that God-awful tea he was always drinking stinking up my office."

Releasing his grip, Diggs rolled his head back just slightly, the faint smile returning.

"I used to call it steaming elephant piss."

Eliciting a smile from me and Diaz both, we left the topic there. None of us wanted to get any further into the backstory of Hutch, what he had done or what I had been forced to do in response.

Never could anybody say I'd been in the wrong, but that didn't mean we wanted to dwell on it either.

Turning back to the table, Diaz laid a hand flat on the stack of papers. Flicking a glance between us, she said, "As much as I hate to cut the reunion short, Pally just sent over Part Two of his care package.

"We've got a hell of lot to do, and not much time to do it."

Chapter Seventy

"Ramon Reyes."

Diggs said the name out loud, the inflection on it indicating neither a question nor a statement. More of an audible inner thought, wanting to hear it, giving it some life so as to better contemplate the meaning behind it.

"Either of you guys ever heard of him?" Diaz asked. Seated at the head of the table, her body was turned a few inches to the side. Gripped in one hand was a Styrofoam coffee cup, the lower half of her arm flat atop the table.

"Doesn't ring a bell," Diggs said. Matching Diaz's pose, his body was turned sideways on the opposite side of the table. Slouched down in one of the matching chairs, he was reclined back as far as the seat would go.

Left elbow propped on the arm of it, the same hand kneaded his forehead, his eyes pinched almost shut as he stared at the far wall, considering the inquiry.

"You?" Diaz asked, flicking her gaze over my direction.

Sitting directly across from Diggs, I was pulled up tight to the table. Torso only inches from the polished metal, both elbows were propped before me, chin resting on fingers laced together.

Beneath them was a cup of coffee to match Diaz's, the scent wafting up at me, dark roast calling out for my attention. Already on my second cup, I was making the conscious choice to ignore it for the time being, not wanting to spike the adrenaline and anticipation I was already feeling too high.

In time, but not just yet.

"Maybe?" I confessed, rolling the name around much the same as Diggs had a moment before. Realizing how much my coming words were about to sound like Latham's a couple of days before, I added, "I know for a fact we tracked at least a handful of Reyes's over the years-"

"Ramon's too," Diggs inserted.

Letting the comment go with little more than a nod, I continued, "But knowing if this guy is one of those without a visual..."

The file that we had from the night of Ruiz's arrest was meticulous. Done in the same manner as all of the paperwork Martin touched, every detail was committed to writing. Each step of the process that led up to the raid, a complete recounting of every minute that we were onsite.

If ever it went to court, if someone in Ruiz's camp claimed bad faith, it would be ready for admittance directly into evidence.

But that didn't help us much now.

Not when what we needed were photographs. Clear images of every last person that had been present. The kind that would have made identifying Tres Salinas that much easier.

Or a full roster of the guest list that night. Anything that might give us some bearing on who Ramon Reyes was and how he might be playing into all of this.

Stuff it was easy to sit and bemoan not having with the benefit of hindsight but would have been impossible to attain with such a small attachment on the ground that night.

Not that such a thing did anything to alleviate the growing agitation inside the room.

"How about you?" Diggs shot back from the opposite side of the table. Tilting his head toward Diaz, he asked, "Anything on your end?"

"Nope," Diaz said. "Ran him through our database, reached out to field offices in Mexico City and Tegucigalpa. Nobody in the region has anything on him."

Spread on the table before us was the sum total of everything Pally had been able to cull together in the last hour. Since hammering down a location on both Ruiz and whoever it was that Salinas had been communicating with, he'd concentrated his entire focus entirely on that.

An effort that had yielded a great deal, most of it grossly at odds with what we were expecting.

"Fruit of the Desert Winery," Diggs said, each word bearing no small amount of frustration. Tossing a thin stack of papers onto the table, he continued working at the skin of his forehead, oblivious to the pages spilling across the polished wood. "Are they serious with this shit?"

Unable to disagree, or to offer anything more on point than what he'd just said, I nodded twice in agreement, chin rocking atop my fingers.

For the better part of three days, I'd been sprinting headlong at this thing. At times feeling like a pinball bouncing around inside a machine, I had thrown myself from West Yellowstone to Snoqualmie and back. Had made a pitstop in Spokane, spent a few hours in the Beaverhead, and was now sitting outside of San Diego.

Sometimes it felt like I was bumping along without a flashlight in the dark, others like I was taking a chainsaw to anything in my path. Only in the last couple of hours were things starting to come together.

And now this.

A visit from Jones and Smith, and a trace on Ruiz's phone that put him standing in a damn vineyard. In the desert.

"Has to be a front, right?" I said. "I mean-"

"What are the odds somebody would go to the time and expense of putting something like that in the damn desert?" Diggs said without glancing over.

"It's also legit, though," Diaz said. Raising a couple of sheets of paper in her lap, she kept her gaze aimed down, scanning over what

321

Pally had sent. "They are fully incorporated in California. Pay their state and federal taxes on time."

All of this we had already been over twice before. Just as we had ascertained that the listed CEO of the organization was a man named Ramon Reyes, a moniker just generic enough in this part of the country to be legit or completely fraudulent.

No way of knowing either way, Pally digging away on it but thus far unable to find much of use.

The instant we had first gotten a location on both Ruiz and the number programmed into Salinas's cellphone, Diggs and my initial reaction had been to load up. To jump directly into whatever vehicle had brought Diggs to the headquarters and head out.

Take any firepower we could get our hands on and go pay the man a visit. Give him our answer to the unspoken challenge left on Martin's mantle. Show him what happened when he dared come after our team, eight years later or not.

Both so charged on adrenaline and anger, we were each already teetering on the line as was, the sight of one another being the nudge we needed to go charging off into the desert.

Fortunately for both of us, Diaz had been there to serve as a voice of reason.

To her credit, not once did she try to tell us we were wrong. She never claimed we shouldn't be upset about what had happened to Martin, shouldn't be seeking active retribution on the man that had come after us and had the audacity to leave a calling card behind to mock us.

What she had done was point out that in doing so, we would be going after a location we knew nothing about. Under the full light of day.

Pissed or not, neither of us were stupid. We'd survived in the lives we had for a long time by always doing our diligence, being prepared for whatever we walked into.

If this was going to go like all those previous missions, we had to approach it in the same way. We had to hang onto the angst and emotion of losing our friend, letting it simmer just beneath the surface without allowing it to become our primary fuel.

"Okay, let's come at this from a different angle," I said.

Unlacing my fingers before me, I extended a hand. Grabbing up the file on Ruiz again, I drew it over and flipped it open, snatching the photo and flinging it out in the center of the table.

Starting in on the small stack of pages affixed to the opposite flap of the folder, I riffled down through them, finding what I was looking for.

"Back when we were running surveillance on Ruiz, the power structure was set up with him obviously at the top," I said. "Beneath that, he split everything into two sides – shipping and production."

"Right," Diaz said. "On the shipping side, his guy was Jorge Martinez. After Ruiz got pinched, Martinez tried to get on with a different cartel in the area. Got caught in the crossfire."

Twisting his seat to get a better look at her, Diggs asked, "Literally, or figuratively?"

"Literally," Diaz replied. "Less than six months after Ruiz went away, he ended up in a ditch along the side of the road somewhere."

How she knew this, neither one of us bothered pressing. Unable to find the requisite empathy for such a disclosure, we moved on, my attention immediately going back to the pages before me.

"The other one, the one covering production, was Martine Valdez. Anything there?"

"Prison," Diaz replied. Clearly having had the same thought as me already, she consulted a printout on the table beside her, scanning it almost to the bottom before adding, "Pinched year before last."

"North or south of the line?" Diggs asked.

"South," Diaz answered. "One of those places where sentencing is just sort of left open-ended, because they don't really expect most people to make it out alive."

Over the years, Diggs and I both had seen exactly what she meant. While her assessment might have seemed harsh, it was in no way wrong.

Nor was the underlying assumption that whatever strings had been tugged to get Ruiz free would be extremely ineffective trying the same thing down there. Valdez was as good as done.

"Great," Diggs said. Rolling his focus over my way, the overhead lights glinted off his shaved head. "We still have no idea who Ramon Reyes is or why he was the first person Ruiz went to see when he got out."

With every word, I could sense what Diggs was getting at. Trying to decipher everything at play here was pointless. We weren't still with the DEA, weren't trying to build a case.

We knew where Junior Ruiz was. We knew he was responsible for killing Martin and for trying to kill me.

That was enough.

Or, at least it would be if we weren't currently sitting in a DEA facility, its acting director right beside us.

Shifting my focus back to the file, I pressed the middle and index fingers on my right hand together. Using them as a scanner, I made my way down the page before me. Not seeing what I was after, I moved to the next in order, finding it equally void of what I needed.

Same for the one after that.

"What are you looking for?" Diaz asked, her voice barely penetrating as I kept my focus downward.

Opting not to respond just yet, I made my way through the last pages in order. Seeing nothing, I flipped the stack back over to the beginning, lifting my face to see Diaz and Diggs both staring intently my way.

"There's a name we're missing in here."

"And you think they might be Reyes?" Diggs asked.

"No," I replied, "but I think they might be able to tell us who he is."

Chapter Seventy-One

The desk that Ramon Reyes had had specially manufactured was ridiculous. Not only was it a monument to opulence and excess, an infatuation with everything that didn't matter, it failed to perform the task for which it was designed.

Conducting business.

Long ago, Junior Ruiz had learned that in an industry such as theirs, the way a man presented himself was of paramount import. Not the way he dressed or the size of his home or the way he drank his damn coffee. Those were all the sorts of things someone as out of touch as Reyes would seize on.

What really mattered was the way he interacted with others. Not how they saw him, but how they perceived him to see *them*.

Only when someone felt they were being treated as an equal would they perform their best. Would they offer their loyalty.

It was how he had first gotten Burris to begin doing his bidding in Lompoc. The way he had managed to rise above the fray of the infighting in Baja, putting the drug wars on hold, getting all of the local heavyweights to back him as the one true *El Jefe*.

How he had managed to secure someone like Arlin Mejia to serve as his mole, secretly keeping an eye on things, keeping morale up among his loyalists while he was away.

And the reason he was currently seated on one of the sofas in the center of office. Eschewing the ridiculous desk nearby and the disparate heights of the chairs, he stared straight across, looking Mejia square.

In his hand was the remainder of the cigar he had started earlier, smoke curling up from the tip of it, a thin haze floating across the afternoon rays of sunshine angled in through the open windows nearby.

"So these men," Mejia said, "Jones and Smith-"

"Or so they said," Ruiz replied. Using the hand still gripping the cigar, he waved it in front of him, an unspoken signal that he knew the names were bunk.

The sort of thing everybody tended to revert to when they were trying to circumvent the truth, but names nobody actually used anymore.

"Right," Mejia agreed, "they were the ones that orchestrated your release."

"Yes," Ruiz replied. "Which is why when Esmera called, that's who I figured she meant."

Accepting the information, Mejia nodded once. "Any idea why?"

Again, Ruiz waved the cigar. He was fully aware of the reasoning behind springing him, though for the time being it would have to wait.

They had more pressing matters to discuss at the moment.

"We'll get to that later," he said.

"Okay," Mejia said, not offering the slightest pushback. Seated with one leg crossed over the other, his forearm extended atop the arm of the couch, his body was completely rigid. "But they weren't the ones that came to your sister's door?"

"No," Ruiz said. "A man and a woman. Badges, but no uniforms. She said they gave their names and organization, but she was shitting bullets, didn't catch them."

Grunting softly, the same click that Mejia always made when responding to something, he nodded once more. "DEA?"

"Almost definitely," Ruiz replied. "Description of the woman she gave me matches up with the agent in charge of the local head-quarters.

"The man, well..."

Raising the cigar to his mouth, Ruiz closed his lips around it, drawing in a long pull. Letting it fill his cheeks, he allowed the flavor to roll across his tongue before slowly pushing it out.

As he did so, he shifted his gaze toward the windows, the late afternoon sun coming in at an angle. Painting everything in a straw-colored hue, it promised that the sun's descent wasn't far off, just a couple of hours before dusk would be upon them.

"Tate," Mejia said.

Without the slightest bit of inflection on the end, there wasn't a hint of uncertainty. A statement rather than a question.

Picking up on the delivery, Ruiz flicked his gaze back to Mejia. Saying nothing, he sat and waited, knowing there was more forthcoming.

Perched in the same pose, a single muscle twitched in Mejia's cheek. His nostrils flared slightly as he pulled in air, his bony shoulders rising a fraction of an inch before slowly releasing.

"I got a call earlier this afternoon as well. A message from Tres."

The last Ruiz had heard, Tres was en route to clean up the other man that had been sent north and failed. Having checked in to report that it had been finished, he was said to be going silent until his return.

Throughout the events of the last twenty-four hours, Ruiz had forgotten all about the man, assuming he was still making his way south, per the reported plan.

A plan that had obviously been cut short somewhere along the way.

"A message?" Ruiz asked.

"Yes," Mejia replied. "Via a lawyer, some public defender out of Montana."

His grip on the cigar tightening, Ruiz felt his features harden. His eyes narrowed, his head turning a half inch to the side.

Sensing the shift, seeing the cues, Mejia raised his hand from the arm of the chair, flashing his palm.

"Tres knows the rules. He didn't reveal anything, would never think of cutting a deal."

Lowering the hand back into place, he added, "Bastards cut his phone privileges. It was the only way to get word back down here."

The statement did little to alleviate the clench in Ruiz's chest. With it went any taste for the cigar, his focus solely on the man across from him.

"What word?"

"He knows."

Simply two words, they were all the explanation Ruiz needed. In an instant, he knew both who was being referred to and what it was he knew.

"It seems Tres left something at the house of the team leader," Mejia said. Breaking eye contact for the first time, Mejia glanced out to the windows.

"He was there that night. In Baja, when you were taken away." Shifting his gaze back, he stared across at Ruiz. "He saw what happened, heard the offer you made to them."

He went no further, though he didn't need to.

Hundreds of times in the preceding years, Ruiz had played back that evening in his head. One time after another on loop, every detail forever ingrained in his memory, all of it in vivid color.

Memories he would carry with him to his grave, no matter how long he might live.

"And?" Ruiz asked.

"He left a bullet and a coin on the mantle in their living room."

The words were delivered as little more than a whisper. Brimming with pain, they matched the look that flashed behind Mejia's eyes, grief and realization mixed in equal parts.

The kind only a father realizing a fatal mistake had been made could have.

Chapter Seventy-Two

When Pally had first started digging into Tres Salinas, he hadn't found much of a backstory. No property holdings, not even a record of high school graduation. Nothing more than a birth certificate and then nineteen years later the driver's license that had enabled us to begin piecing things together.

The story behind his younger sister Juana was a bit more fleshed out.

Four years younger than her brother, she had been born in Mexico, never crossing north into America until a month after our raid. A minor at the time, she was granted temporary citizenship to live with her mother in the San Diego suburb of Chula Vista. There, she attended Olympian High School before moving just a few miles north to attend San Diego State University.

After graduating from there with a degree in finance, she had gone to work for a real estate firm in La Mesa, still residing in the apartment she'd used throughout her final three years of college.

The very same apartment that stood before us as Diaz and I exited the same sedan we'd used earlier in the day. Not wanting to arrive with too strong a display of force, or to have to explain away two former agents, it had been decided that Diggs would remain behind at the headquarters.

Intent to grab a quick shower in the locker room and wash off whatever lingered from his quick trip back from the jungle, from there the plan was for him to get with Pally and continue gleaning everything they could on all parties involved.

After that, hopefully we would add it to whatever Diaz and I were about to find and have a clear path moving forward.

Hopefully.

Otherwise, there was no guarantee that the concentrated angst Diggs and I were both feeling wouldn't cause us to simply go find the biggest guns we could and start mowing things down.

A plan I still wouldn't go as far as to have relegated to Plan B status.

"Just like last time?" I asked, falling in beside Diaz as we followed the sidewalk along the front of the small apartment building Juana Salinas called home. Making the corner, we hooked a right onto the concrete path leading up to the building, the place looking like a thousand similar structures throughout the area.

Two stories in height, the place was covered in wooden siding painted dark brown. Through the center of it rose a single staircase, a pair of entrances to either side at ground level, a matching set sitting at the top.

Encasing the walkway on both sides were small patches of grass in dire need of water, twin palm trees rising from the center of either one.

Tucked into a small lot off a side street, it wasn't hard to see why Salinas would have chosen the place. Several blocks away from the main SDSU campus, it was shielded from the sounds of the freeways nearby, well away from the usual foot traffic associated with the school.

Instead, the area looked like a pretty standard neighborhood, the place almost quaint as it began to transition toward evening.

"We'll start that way," Diaz said, answering without glancing my way. "How it goes from there..."

Leaving the statement to dangle on insinuation, she increased her pace slightly. Going straight for the staircase rising before us, she pounded straight ahead, the soles of her shoes thumping against the wooden planks.

Taking them two at a time beside her, we reached the top landing at the same time, both glancing either direction to check numbers before turning toward the unit on the left.

Matching the entrances on the ground level below, apartment C used a metal storm door. Behind it, a solid wooden inner door stood open, the latticed metal giving us a partial view inside. A standard living room for someone just a year removed from college, a futon and armchair were formed up around a coffee table, a television on a nightstand opposite them both.

That much we both saw and dismissed, instead focusing on the smell of cooked vegetables wafting our way.

And the accompanying sound of Latin music.

Or, more aptly, the young lady singing along to it.

"At least we know she's home," Diaz muttered.

Grunting a small response, I watched as Diaz leaned forward and lifted her fist, pounding it against the edge of the storm door. Setting it to rattling, she had no more than stepped back when a shadow crossed into the living room.

A moment later, a young woman appeared. Dishtowel clutched before her, she seemed to be drying her hands as she stared at each of us in order.

On sight, the smile she'd been wearing faded, a scowl twisting her lips into something approximating a snarl.

"Good evening," Diaz opened. "Are you Juana Salinas?"

Once more, the young lady flicked her gaze between us, the curl of her lips growing more pronounced.

"Aw, shit. What the hell did they do now?"

Chapter Seventy-Three

The young woman sitting before us seemed to be a bundle of contradictions. Her hair and makeup were fully done, applied with a touch that bordered on professional. Dark curls cascaded down onto her shoulders. Eyeliner and mascara accentuated chestnut colored eyes.

To look her full in the face, it appeared that the girl was a television newscaster, coiffed and ready to sit in front of the camera.

From the neck down though, she was dressed as if she had spent the day on the couch. A baggy SDSU Aztecs tank top hung from her slender shoulders, tilted to one side. Beneath it was a pair of cloth shorts, her tan feet bare and curled up under her.

Definitely fitting with the twenty-three years of age we knew her to be, her features were vibrant and youthful. No lines or blemishes marred her skin. Just the right amount of sunshine graced her visage.

Again, a harsh contrast to the scowl on her features.

A look that, for quite possibly the first time in the history of the DEA, didn't seem to be aimed directly at us.

Seated in the living room of Salinas's apartment, Diaz and I were perched on the front edge of the futon. Across from us, Salinas had taken the armchair. On the coffee table between us were a couple of bottles of water she had set out, though nobody had asked for or yet touched them. In the warmth of the apartment, condensation dripped down their sides, rings forming on the dark wood.

"Ms. Salinas," Diaz said, "it doesn't seem like you're that surprised to see us here."

It wasn't quite phrased as a question, though still it got a reaction. Snorting loudly, Salinas let her head rock back. Her eyes rolled to the side, her gaze fixing on the darkened television.

"Should I be?" she asked.

Employing arguably the best tool an interviewer had available, Diaz opted to remain silent, letting it settle between the three of us.

After a moment, Salinas pulled her focus back our direction, the scowl still very much in place.

"Look, I don't even know who you guys work for, but I know I didn't do anything. The only reason you could possibly have for banging on my door is them."

Pausing there, her eyes narrowed slightly. "Who *do* you guys work for?"

Even before she responded, I could sense a bit of hesitance from Diaz. The girl's initial comments alone were enough to establish lingering hostility.

Finding out who we were was only going to heighten that.

"DEA," Diaz replied.

On cue, the girl threw her hands up. Lifting her gaze with them, she raised all three toward the ceiling, letting them linger before dropping down, her hands slapping against her thighs.

"Well, hell. There you go. Eight years of this shit. Different name, different country, and still it comes and finds me."

Not yet had we asked a single question, and already she was dropping morsels too large to ignore. Open hints practically begging us to inquire further.

All things that my mind was already working to tie to our reason for being there. Tiny strands of connective tissue, fusing disparate bits of information in my mind.

"What do you mean by *different name, different country*?" Diaz asked.

Fixing her stare on Diaz, the look fast approaching a glare, Salinas let out a long sigh. "If you're DEA, then you've seen the file. You were there that night.

"You know it was my party you guys crashed."

Flicking her gaze between us, she added, "I mean, isn't that why you're here now? Something else has happened and you figured it worked once, why not try again?"

Scads of new questions floated to the fore. So many things I wanted to ask, the topics varied, almost too great to even know where to begin.

Beside me, Diaz seemed to be working through the same process in her head.

A combination that again led to our silence, Salinas attempting to wait us out before finally saying, "Okay, fine, play it dumb. Pretend that you didn't know that when my brother and I were born, my father was so concerned about our well-being that he had us take our mother's name. Or that after what happened at my *quinceañera*, he sent us both north to live with our mother - who had the good sense to leave his ass years before – even though it meant I had to apply for citizenship and *learn the damn language*."

Every word seemed to be tinged with bitterness. A faint sheen rose to the bottom side of her eyes as she shifted to face the black mirror of the TV screen again. Pausing, she waited until the bit of emotion passed before turning back to us.

When she did, gone was the momentary break in resolve, again returning to the same anger she'd carried since we arrived.

"Do you know what all that does to a person? A *quinceañera* is supposed to be a big deal. It's supposed to be the night a young girl becomes a woman.

"It was supposed to be my night to put on the white dress and walk out in front of everybody. Instead, it just became more of the same old shit."

"What shit is that?" Diaz asked, her voice lowered to match Salinas's.

The young woman's eyes bulged slightly as she replied, "The great Junior Ruiz. My life got turned upside down, but all anybody noticed was what happened to him."

Recalling what her brother had mentioned, the reason for us being there, I asked, "What was your connection to him?"

"To who?" Salinas asked, jerking her attention toward the sound of my voice, the first words I'd spoken since arriving.

"Ruiz," I replied.

"Me?" Salinas asked. "Absolutely nothing. That was all my father's doing. He worked for him, set the whole thing up.

"Kept going on about it being the biggest and best for his daughter, but that was such a crock. It was about him trying to curry favor with the man he practically worshipped."

Looking away again, she snorted softly. "Hell, still does, from what I hear."

Fireworks of various size and shape began exploding across my mind. Igniting behind my eyelids, they seemed to pulsate with every blink, the new information she was lobbing our way almost too much to process at once.

I had to give Tres Salinas credit. Two nights before, I had taken him out into the woods and done things that I wasn't quite proud of. Not one of them would I say I regretted, but I wouldn't readily admit to them if standing in front of my late wife and daughter either.

Throughout, he had given up plenty, but not once had he mentioned any of this.

"Your father?" Diaz asked. "He worked with Ruiz?"

Same look still in place, Salinas jerked her gaze over to Diaz. Pulling up short, her mouth formed into a circle, her eyes narrowing slightly.

"Not *with* him, *for* him." Flicking her gaze between us, a slow dawning seemed to set in. "But you guys didn't know that though, did you? That's not why you're here."

Any word of the father was completely new to me, but based on what she'd just shared, that wasn't surprising. Using different names, there would have been no reason for us to delve further in our previous surveillance.

"We're here about your brother," I said. "A couple nights ago, he was arrested in Montana."

It was clear there were questions Salinas wanted to fire in

response, but Diaz beat her there, adding, "For murder, in connection to Junior Ruiz."

Mouth open half an inch, Salinas dropped any pretense of trying to speak. Her eyelids fluttered shut, all air expelled from her lungs as she sat, accepting the information.

"That stupid, stupid son of a..."

Lifting her chin toward the ceiling, she remained that way for several moments. Like some sort of new yoga pose, she held the position, pushing and pulling air through her nose, before finally lowering her face.

Slowly opening her eyes, she whispered, "What can I do to help?"

Chapter Seventy-Four

It didn't seem to matter that it was the second time that day the young attorney was inside the interrogation room with Tres Salinas. Nor did it have any sway on him that Deputy Ferry was standing just inside the door. Having learned from his earlier mistakes, he had shed his jacket and stood with one hand on his weapon, holster unsnapped.

Not even the fact that Tres was back in handcuffs, clasped to the ring rising from the center of the table, his total range of movement no more than a few inches, managed to put the young man at ease. Barely able to contain his fidgeting, he was unable to so much as look at Tres for more than a few moments at a time.

A fact that was no doubt a mix of Tres's appearance and the full litany of charges that were being levied on him.

Both items that Tres could not care less about at the moment, his entire focus on feedback from their earlier meeting.

Much like the fact that he knew the kid had offered his name earlier, but he couldn't have been bothered to remember it. Not with something so much more pressing at the front of his mind.

"Were you able to get word out?" Tres asked, barely waiting until the young man had taken a seat across from him.

Ignoring the question, the young man positioned himself in the chair. Squaring the lapels of his jacket, he straightened his tie before reaching into the satchel on the floor by his feet. Drawing out a yellow legal pad, he placed it before him, a blue ink pen beside it.

Folding his hands atop the uneven writing scrawled across the page, he focused on the center of the table, careful to keep his eyes averted as much possible.

"Were you?" Tres asked a second time, careful to keep as much of the angst as he could from his voice.

To the side, he could hear the deputy take a step forward, his every movement punctuated by the groan of his belt.

"Yes," the attorney replied. Overhead lights shined off the sweat collecting on his forehead as he flicked his gaze up. Meeting Tres's glance for just an instant, he immediately pulled it back down.

Looking to the notebook before him, he pretended to be reading through things, lifting the top sheet before returning it.

"Though I don't know that it did a lot of good. Entire conversation didn't take much more than a minute or two."

The words Tres had opted to convey were meticulously chosen. Meant to be as innocuous as possible, he knew Ferry had likely gotten a copy of what was shared, attorney-client privilege be damned.

As had the DEA. And likely the bearded man from the woods a few nights before.

Each syllable was selected to be vague to the point of uselessness to anybody that wasn't privy to everything already happening. Barely enough to tell the story he needed them to.

Just as he knew that any message coming back the other direction would be much the same.

"But you were able to speak with him? And share exactly what I instructed you to?"

Again, the man chanced a quick glance.

"Yes."

"And did he have a response?"

Lifting his hands, the attorney studied his notes for a moment. A look that relayed pure dread passed over his features, his head remaining down for almost a full minute before finally he looked up.

"He said to tell you, farewell."

Chapter Seventy-Five

"Good God, she just told you all that?"

The surprise in Carl Diggs's voice pretty well matched what Diaz and I had felt sitting in Juana Salinas's living room. Once we'd gotten past the vitriol boiling just beneath the surface, had navigated a few tough moments in the opening, the proverbial gates had opened.

"Yeah," Diaz muttered, her chin working up and down in a quick nod. Laced through her tone was no small amount of astonishment, most likely for both the fact that such information was shared and the manner in which it was delivered.

"What was it Martin always told us?" I asked, raising my voice to be heard clearly by the phone balanced on my knee. "Just have to find the right leverage point.

"For her, that meant leaning on her brother. After we told her he'd been arrested and was looking at Murder One, she couldn't get it out fast enough."

While a bit of an oversimplification, it wasn't far from exactly the way it had played out.

In the wake of my bringing up her brother, it had taken a few more minutes for Salinas to completely calm down. A few tears had

340

managed to leak out and her voice cracked a bit each time she spoke, but the longer the discussion went, the calmer she became.

Almost as if tricking herself into believing what she was saying might in some way help us – and by extension her brother – she shared what she knew, providing the last bits of information we needed to bring the story together.

To hear her tell it, her father had two great devotions in his life.

His children, and Junior Ruiz.

Starting out as little more than a common hustler in the streets of Tijuana, he had met Ruiz in a chance encounter years before. With a wife at home and a child on the way, he had jumped at the chance to come and work for Ruiz, at the time still only a mid-level himself.

Entering on the low end of the cartel pecking order, he'd put his time in doing whatever was asked, ascending to warehouse foreman.

That much of the story Salinas had delivered as little more than background. Basic information of the sort that could be read from a Wikipedia page, as unremarkable as the daily weather report or sports scores.

It was from there that things began to get interesting.

It was no secret what generally happened for people like her father that worked the streets in Tijuana. The life was hard and fast, ending with either prison or a bullet, but there was little someone like him could do about it. He had people at home that needed him. No education. No clear path to ascension.

Because of that, the man always openly stated that Junior Ruiz had saved his life, and the lives of his family. It was the reason he had named his son Tres, a clear homage to someone that had earned his undying loyalty.

It was also why he worked so hard to cultivate a friendship, the sort of thing that would lead to Ruiz hosting a *quinceañera* for Juana.

In the wake of our raid on Ruiz, her father had sent his children north of the border. Years before, her mother had tired of having to fight for her husband's affection, throwing her hands up and fleeing the situation, knowing that relocating to America was the only way to escape the reach of Junior Ruiz.

Even then, though, her father had remained behind. Unable to shed his unflinching allegiance to Ruiz, he had remained in his post. He had weathered the storm, pretending to be nothing more than a low-level rube and taking up with the man that would become the cartel successor, even going to great lengths to quietly cultivate continued allegiance to someone that might never make it out of prison.

Among his converts apparently being his own son.

To hear Salinas tell it, the last she had heard from either her father or her brother was a few years before. On separate occasions, each had come to try and convince her to take up with the organization, though she had firmly told them both to go to hell.

The last experience she had had with such things was that night in Baja.

The longer it remained that way, the better.

Start to finish, it took her almost ten uninterrupted minutes to relay the tale. When she was done, she sat with her chest heaving just slightly, out of breath from sprinting straight through.

On her face was a mix of different thoughts and emotions, all of them dancing across her young features.

A cocktail I could readily recognize, many of them the same things I'd been feeling since Luis Mendoza showed up at my office several nights before.

"You say the name was Mejia?" Diggs asked, his voice piping in through the speaker.

"Yeah," I replied. "The kids both went by Salinas, but their old man's name was Arlin Mejia."

Several times since she'd first mentioned it, I'd gone back through my mind. I'd tried repeatedly to place it, to get it to shake something loose, though each of my attempts came up in vain.

Outside of Martinez and Valdez, there were precious few other names I could readily recall. One case of hundreds we worked together, most of the people that we tracked had managed to blend into a random amalgam, the passage of the years since doing nothing to keep them from becoming muddled in my mind.

"Don't remember the guy," Diggs muttered, seemingly coming to the same conclusion.

"No reason for you to," Diaz inserted. "Sounds like he was pretty low at the time, has made a point of keeping himself hidden ever since."

Grunting softly, I couldn't help but agree.

When we'd first arrived at Salinas's house, I'd expected to encounter something similar to what we'd gotten from Esmerelda Ruiz. I'd anticipated she would be cagey, clearly not enthused to see us standing on her doorstep. After a few minutes of back and forth, she'd find some reason to dismiss us before immediately running back to phone someone about what had happened.

Again, that seemed to be how most things went, in this business and in Latin culture.

What we had encountered was a different animal entirely. Someone that had been wronged badly enough in various ways to make her sidestep that thinking entirely.

No longer could she swear loyalty to someone that had clearly given his to someone else long before. Just as she couldn't pretend to overlook the turmoil such allegiance had caused in her own life, no matter that it appeared she had managed to come out okay on the back end.

"And I guess that leaves the biggest question," Diggs said. "Can we trust her?"

In the semi-darkness of the front seat, Diaz and I shared a glance.

The question was a fair one to ask, one I had already been considering, knew Diaz to likely be doing the same. Meeting each other's gaze, we considered it a moment before both nodding slightly.

"Yes," we said in unison.

"Good," Diggs replied. "Which brings me to my next question.

"These two white boys that just showed up – Jones and Smith. Can we trust them?"

Chapter Seventy-Six

Junior Ruiz's first inclination was to tell his sister to get out of the house. To pack a bag and go stay with one of her friends, or rent a hotel, or even take a short vacation.

No place that would require a flight. Nothing where her name would turn up in some database that the government might be monitoring.

Simply jump in the car, point it either due north or east, and start driving. When it got low on gas, stop and pay with cash. Keep going until she was far enough away that there was no chance at acting Director Diaz and Dead Man Walking Tate just stopping by to see her again.

For as fast as the thought materialized though, it disintegrated just as quickly.

Telling her to go anywhere would only alert anybody that might be keeping an eye on her. Never really good at hiding her emotions, they would easily spot her climbing into the car, a bag over her shoulder, tears likely streaming down her face.

Within minutes, a call would go up. Somebody would either stop her before she made it to the end of the street or they would put a tail on her. No matter that she had done nothing wrong, they would hound her for as long as it took, hoping she would lead them to him.

He'd seen similar things done too many times before to count. Had even employed the same tactics a time or two over the years himself.

"Sorry about this afternoon," Ruiz said. Standing just inside the rear of the office on the second floor, Ruiz leaned against the side of the desk, his legs were extended before him, crossed at the ankles.

Left arm folded over his stomach, his right elbow was propped against it, holding the phone to his face.

"Just a disconnect between the two teams," Ruiz assured her. "One of those *left hand doesn't know what the right is doing* sort of things."

He considered adding a joke about government workers, but decided against it. Already he was employing his best placating tone, knowing that pushing things much further would make what he was doing too obvious.

"You sure?" Esmera asked, her voice relaying the obvious uncertainty she still felt. "They were firing some pretty pointed questions this morning. Seemed like more than just a simple miscommunication."

A flicker of movement caught Ruiz's attention, drawing his gaze to the far side of the room. Standing rigid, he watched as the door swung inward, Arlin Mejia sliding through.

Arriving without a sound, he allowed the door to shut behind him, waiting with his hands clasped behind his back, his head bowed slightly.

"For sure," Ruiz replied. "You were there, you saw how it went. They opened the gate and let me walk right out. Would that have happened if everything wasn't copacetic?"

The explanation was far from being the truth - or even some sliver of it - but there was no way for Esmera to know that. At face value, it seemed plausible, the sort of thing that most people would believe.

Folks just don't walk right out of prison a fraction of the way through their sentence unless everything is on the up-and-up.

"Okay?" he pressed.

Ruiz could still sense a bit of hesitance over the line, though to his sister's credit, she didn't voice it.

"Okay," she eventually managed. "Give me a call tomorrow night? Just so I know everything is alright?"

A tiny jolt of annoyance passed through Ruiz as he leveraged himself up from the side of the desk. Extending his left hand, he motioned for Mejia to come closer.

"Will do," he said. "Bye."

Cutting the line before his sister had a chance to respond, Ruiz slid the phone onto the desk behind him. Rooted in place, he waited as Mejia came closer before falling in beside him. Together, the two men exited onto the balcony, going straight to the railing and peering out at the grounds below.

The house, the office, the various outbuildings, were all things Ruiz could do without.

In Baja - a place predicated as much on style as substance - having a majestic spread was a prerequisite. It was what set them apart from the various other organizations.

But even at that, every last piece was vital. There were no lavish costs sunk into faux businesses, no trying to irrigate a chunk of desert sand into a garden oasis.

Each time Ruiz stepped out onto the balcony, he couldn't help but feel his distaste spike for all that he was looking at. Nothing more than sunk investments, the single thought that kept entering his head was the enormous chunk of profits it was taking to maintain such a place.

A fact that was currently sitting second on his list of priorities, to be dealt with after their most pressing matter was properly addressed.

"What's the word?" Ruiz asked. Without looking over to Mejia, he stared straight ahead, gaze focused on an indeterminate point in the distance.

"It is done," Mejia replied. "The few that were fully in Reyes's camp have been removed. Those that remained were either already loyal to you or were easily convinced it was in their best interests to become so."

Allowing himself a small snort, Ruiz nodded, knowing exactly what Mejia meant. In their business, people tended to have allegiance to one of two things – either the people they worked for, or the money they made doing so.

The first group was preferable for obvious reasons, but it was never bad to have plenty of the second around as well.

"How many?" Ruiz asked.

"No more than a handful," Mejia replied.

"And where are they?"

Lifting a hand, Mejia gestured past the warehouse before them, pointing into the distance. "Same place as Reyes."

For the second time in as many minutes, Ruiz allowed himself to snort. He'd never known Mejia to be funny – if that was even his intent – but he couldn't help but find a bit of humor in the irony there.

"Anybody vital?"

"Not at all," Mejia answered. "All workers from the business side of things. Guys that saw their livelihood tied to the new direction Reyes was trying to take things."

Shaking his head slightly, Ruiz continued to stare out. Even in the gathering darkness, much of the land before them was still illuminated by the lights from the various buildings, long shadows playing out across the ground.

"Manny?" he asked.

"Ready to go," Mejia replied. Shifting slightly, he added, "In all the years working together, Reyes had no idea the man was on our side. Hell, he thought we hated each other."

Ruiz recognized that the comment was meant to elicit some form of response from him, though at the moment, he couldn't bring himself to provide it. Not with so much else seeming to be afoot, phone calls from his sister and Mejia's son both arriving earlier in the day.

The opportunity that Jones and Smith had provided for him was too good to pass up. For eight long years, he had lay in his cell and thought about what happened. He'd remembered the night in question, thought about how he'd been tackled to the ground and led out in handcuffs. Paraded past most of the guests in town like a common thug.

Untold times, he'd promised himself that if ever he got out, if ever he breathed free air again, he would make those responsible for his demise pay.

When the proposal had first been presented to him, the notion of waiting had occurred to him. He had considered settling into his new post, letting things get quiet before making a move.

After a few days though, that notion had shifted. There was no reason for him to pause. Never would he get a better chance, long before anybody even knew he was out.

There was nothing special about the date. No sort of anniversary, nobody outside of the three men in that basement room deep within Lompoc to even know an agreement had been made.

He could get to the men that arrested him without them having their guard up, using Burris as a conduit, trusting Mejia to put it together.

A plan that was made that much sweeter by Jones's agreement to wipe away everything that happened prior to the moment he stepped aside.

The only pitfall in the entire thing ended up being the execution of it, one lingering detail he needed to clean up before settling back into his post as *El Jefe*.

"And the guards?" Ruiz asked.

Jerking himself to attention, focus returning straight ahead, Mejia said, "Exactly as you requested. All still present, told to be on watch for an imminent threat."

Grunting softly, Ruiz kept himself planted in front of the railing. He swept his gaze over the assorted vegetation before him, again wishing that Reyes had been able to hem in his ego.

Instead, he'd created a damn jungle, replete with plenty of places to hide, innumerable angles from which to launch an assault.

"First thing tomorrow, I want the men to use some of that equipment and start knocking these trees out back here," he said.

"Of course," Mejia replied.

"Maybe take down a few of the smaller buildings we don't need, too."

Repeating the same throat click that he so often used, Mejia bowed the top of his head just slightly.

Already, he knew that Tate was in the area. More than that, it was clear he was hunting, earlier stopping by to see Esmera.

If what Ruiz remembered of the man was any indicator, there was little chance he would be letting up until one of them was dead.

And even if there was no way to know for certain when he might show, there was no point in making his task any easier.

Chapter Seventy-Seven

When I stepped away from the Administration six years before, weapons drop boxes were just starting to pop up. Positioned outside of prisons, courthouses, anyplace where a bit of extra firepower might be needed, they usually looked like a small bank of mailboxes. Inset into a brick or concrete wall, there were often a half-dozen or so stacked up, all capable of concealing handguns or assorted other small arms.

In our dealings, rarely did we ever go near any of those places. Never had I used them, but I knew many of the larger cities were installing them with increasing regularity.

Still, that was a far cry from what stood before us now.

"Just for the record, this never, ever happened," Diaz said. Swinging the door open, she stood to the side, letting the glow from our headlights illuminate the interior.

Designed to look like a regular electric transformer box, it was positioned just off the side of the road on the outer reaches of a suburb known as Lemon Grove. Standing four feet tall and three across, it was made from solid concrete painted tan on three sides. Across the front was a stainless-steel door in the same color on a pair of hinges.

Completely non-descript, it matched a thousand other similar structures positioned around the city, my mind immediately jumping to wonder how many of those were functional and how many were camouflaged to serve the same purpose as this one.

A few feet away, Diggs let out a low whistle. Bending at the waist, he peered past the open door to the stash filling the box, a small ammunition bunker squirreled away in plain sight.

"Nice," he muttered. Twisting his focus back our direction, a thin smile cracked his features. "Do I even want to know?"

"An idea we borrowed from *NCIS*, actually."

"Really?" Diggs asked, his eyebrows rising. "So all the government agencies have shit like this stashed around the city?"

"Not the agency, the TV show," Diaz corrected. Pulling the door open, she turned to stare in at the cache. Extending a finger, she said, "Handguns, couple of submachine guns, even some light explosives."

Looking back our way, she added, "All confiscated in prior raids."

She didn't add anything more, but the implication was clear.

Every single piece found here was something that had been lifted in the course of investigation. Items that weren't needed for evidence that had found their way into this hold, completely untraceable, to be used only in extreme circumstances.

Every weapon currently housed at the DEA headquarters was on file. Every serial number was recorded, every ballistic profile had been checked and entered into a database. Same for the evidence locker.

In no way could she just open up either and give us our pick. No matter how much she might want to, no matter how justified in principle it might be, doing so would be her job.

Or all three of us ending up in jail.

After speaking with Juana Salinas, the plan had been to go back to headquarters. To group up with Diggs, determine what he and Pally had been able to find, and put together a working outline.

A plan that had gotten completely obliterated the instant Diggs informed us Jones and Smith were back at headquarters waiting for us.

The men hadn't exactly told us earlier in the day who they worked for, though the implication was plenty clear. As was their intentions, warning us off of going near Junior Ruiz or anybody that might have been affiliated.

A warning that apparently extended to Juana Salinas. And the various online sources we had spent most of the afternoon digging through.

Actions that, no doubt, they were back to again tell us to stay away from.

This time probably being a lot less obtuse in their delivery.

Knowing that, the instant Diggs had uttered their names, we knew whatever wiggle room we had was gone. Any extra time for planning, any days to prepare ourselves, to let Ruiz sit and linger, on constant vigil for our arrival, had evaporated.

In response, Diaz had told Diggs to get out of there. To slip away the first chance he had and meet us at this exact location.

"Thank you for this," Diggs said, alternating glances between the locker and Diaz.

"For everything," I added, neither of saying another word.

Not that we needed to.

Diaz had gone well beyond anything we could have expected of her. Earlier today was the first time she and Diggs had ever met. She and I went back a year and a half, were what I would consider friends, but even at that, we couldn't ask her to put herself out there any further.

Just what she had done for us already went well beyond expectations. A play most likely mixed of respect for a fallen agent and not wanting to have the headache of Junior Ruiz ever cross her desk again. Added in I'm sure was no small bit of ego, not appreciating Jones and Smith walking in and telling her how to run things.

Still, she had to exercise some level of discretion. DEA policy didn't allow descent into vigilantism, and the justice system didn't look kindly on it either.

Everything up to this point was still cloaked in some level of plausible deniability. She could claim that she'd been looking into things adjacent to a case. Could possibly even state she had been doing a bit of research in connection to the death of a former agent.

But there was no way we could ask her to join us for what

happened next. Just as there was no way for her to sidestep a directive from another government agency.

Especially when all conventional forms of inquiry had turned up absolutely nothing.

The events of this week had started because of what happened eight years before. They were clearly targeted at our team, an effort for someone to exact revenge for some perceived wrong inflicted on them.

If it was going to end, it was only right that it be us that did it. And that nobody else got pulled down into the resulting jet wash as a result.

"We'll see you soon?" I asked.

"Definitely," Diaz responded. Taking a step to the side, it was clear she wasn't going to bother watching whatever we selected, one more thing she could deny with a clear conscious if ever it came to that.

"And be sure to say hi to those two boys in suits too, huh?" Diggs added, receiving nothing more than a snort as Diaz climbed into her sedan and pulled away.

Chapter Seventy-Eight

The vehicle Diggs had rented at the airport was a midsize-SUV. One of the newer models that used letters and numbers instead of giving it an actual name, it couldn't have had more than a couple of thousand miles on it. If not for the pair of giant coffees tucked into the cupholders separating the front seats, I'd have sworn it even still carried the proverbial new car smell.

Much roomier than Diaz's sedan that I'd been forced to fold myself into for a good chunk of the day, I sat in the passenger seat. Spread across my lap and over much of the dashboard was a flurry of white paper, everything Pally had sent over earlier in the day. Nabbed by Diggs when he made his escape a couple of hours earlier, every last detail available to us had been committed to memory, the sum total managing to point out the holes that remained more than provide any kind of working plan moving forward.

A fact we had already made peace with.

This wasn't a DEA raid and we weren't looking to make an arrest. We had one goal in what we were doing, one thing that needed to be done before we could both return to our respective lives.

One thing to both put our friend at rest and ensure we both

weren't perpetually on the lookout for Ruiz making an attempt to finish the job.

Reaching for my coffee, I flicked my gaze to the clock on the dashboard. The glowing green digits revealed it to be fast approaching midnight, the parking lot of the Wal-Mart we were in finally beginning to thin.

"This has got to be full-on amateur hour compared to what you're used to," I said. Taking in a long pull on what remained of my coffee, the lukewarm liquid washed over my tongue, the taste fast drifting toward acidic.

In no way did my body need the caffeine, the move one born of complete habit. Already surging on anticipation for what felt like days, adrenaline had started to leak into my system as well, setting my nerves on end.

An ingrained response, my body sensing that action was imminent. Heightened by the presence of Diggs beside me, the experiences we'd shared, every bit of me wanted to go tearing off into the night.

An eventuality that each passing second brought closer.

"Ha!" Diggs spat beside me, the single syllable rocking his head back a few inches. "You'd be amazed how many times we've had to make chicken shit into chicken salad out there."

It was an expression not far from one I'd heard him use often in our own time together. Moments of bemoaning where we were or what our end goal was.

Times when he didn't mind being the mouthpiece for the team, saying what we were all imminently aware of but didn't feel the need to vocalize.

"Kind of makes you wish just one time they'd start you with chicken salad, just to see what you could really do," I replied.

"Got that right," Diggs agreed.

The vast majority of what Pally had been able to pull was split into two even piles. On one side was the cumulative history of the various conversations that had occurred.

Junior Ruiz and his sister. Tres Salinas and his father. A handful of other interactions, all intersecting in a manner that coincided with the conversation Diaz and I had with Juana Salinas earlier in the night.

Eight years might have passed, but to look at what was laid out before us, it was time spent as little more than a holding pattern. Moments of waiting, looking for the day when somehow he would exit a free man and resume his prior activities.

Almost as if they knew it was coming.

On the other side was what had been pulled regarding the Fruit of the Desert Winery. SEC filings, tax information, what little there was regarding a recent start-up business still far from turning a profit.

None of it useful, little more than something to read, I considered taking it up one last time. Thinking better of it, I shuffled everything into a pile and tossed it onto the backseat. Lifting my backside a few inches, I tugged down the legs of my jeans before settling in, my focus aimed through the windshield.

Even at such an hour, a steady trickle of foot traffic moved across the brightly lit parking lot. Young twenty-somethings armed with cases of beer and families with small children were all represented in equal measure.

The occasional solo person was also thrown in, everybody moving fast, their eyes down. Somewhere else to be and little time to get there.

Beside me, Diggs attempted one last pass through his reading material before giving up as well. Forgoing putting anything into a pile, he simply tossed them over his shoulder, letting them land in a flurry behind us.

"Man, I hate this shit," he muttered. Gaze locked parallel to mine, he watched as an elderly couple toddled past, the old man pushing a cart with enormous sacks of dog food piled high.

The choices too numerous at the moment to even guess at what he was alluding to, I didn't even try.

"What's that?" I asked.

"Waiting," Diggs replied. "We know what he did. We know where he is."

It was obvious there was so many more things he could add, that maybe even he wanted to, though he managed to stop there.

Not that I didn't already know exactly what he meant.

Flicking my eyes to the dash again, I said, "Three minutes until Pally hits us back. Then we can move."

Diaz setting us up with the drop box was only half of what we needed. We might have been equipped with the firepower to make a move on Ruiz, but without some form of intel on where the man was holed up, it would have been nothing more than a kamikaze mission.

More or less exactly what he wanted.

"Look at this," Diggs said, jutting his chin forward to a man exiting the store. Pushing a cart loaded with plastic sacks, he was still dressed in a shirt and tie. Walking in barely more than a shuffle, he leaned forward with both forearms resting across the handle. "Poor bastard can barely keep his eyes open, not even home from work yet, having to stop and get groceries."

Feeling one corner of my mouth peel back, I watched as the man pulled up to a sedan on the opposite side of the lane we were parked in. Opening the rear door, he began unloading sacks, a stick figure family at least seven strong plastered across the rear windshield.

"Come on, you telling me that won't be you soon enough?" I asked. "You won't be off on one of these jaunts, find yourself some local woman?"

"What?" Diggs snapped, flashing a gaze over my direction. "And bring her back here? Start a family, get a dog, build a white picket fence?"

Meeting his glance, I let my smile grow a bit larger. "It could happen."

"Yeah, and I *could* meet Jessica Alba in the airport on my way back and decide to run off with her..."

A single chuckle escaped me as we watched the man finish unloading his sacks. Leaving the cart where it was, he climbed in and drove away, one less car providing cover for us as we waited for midnight.

Smile fading, I watched until the man's taillights faded before saying, "Seemed to be working for Martin."

"Yes, it was," Diggs agreed, his voice lowered to match mine. For a moment, he added nothing more, before saying, "Same for you for a while there, too."

Unable to disagree, to say anything more than what had already been stated, I opted to wait in silence, counting off the last thirty seconds until the sound of my phone erupted between us.

Chapter Seventy-Nine

The thin threadbare cotton of the sheet had ripped easily for Tres Salinas. Requiring little more than gnashing his incisors down in a few choice spots, he'd been able to tear chunks from the outer edge.

Once he had starting points, the weak material was no match, even for his weakened hands. Shearing away in jagged lines, he'd been able to tear the sheet into three semi-equal chunks.

From there, it had simply been a matter of calling on a most basic skill. Something most young girls are taught before they even reached elementary school.

Minute after minute of trying to find the patience he didn't really have, hoping that the same guard that had led him to the interrogation room twice before wouldn't feel the need to make yet another late-night jaunt down the hallway to check on him.

Taken alone, the sheet itself wasn't worth much. Whether intentional or through sheer neglect, there was no way the decrepit garment would ever perform what Tres needed it to. But by tearing it into thirds, he was able to twist each piece into tight rolls.

Weaving them together in a basic pattern, he could then form a braided rope, the cumulative tensile strength more than sufficient for what he was after.

In the wake of the public defender disclosing what Tres's father had shared earlier, there had been no need to further the conversation. No point in asking follow-up questions or beseeching him to perform any further tasks.

The instant the word was out, Tres had turned his attention to the guard and asked to be returned to his cell.

Fully aware of how it probably sounded, what the guard would probably think, Tres had positioned himself in the exact spot he'd been earlier in the day. Ignoring the continued pain in his feet and hands, the pickax jabbing into his ribs, the pounding that threatened to cause his head to explode, he had leaned himself against the wall and waited.

Counting off minutes, he'd remained completely motionless for more than two hours, watching as the guard made repeated trips down to check on him.

Three times, the man had shuffled forward, making it no further than the edge of the cell. Stopping, he'd leaned in, peering as if trying to catch Tres in the act of something.

Each time, seeing nothing out of the ordinary, he'd retreated back to the front of the building.

As close to a suicide watch as West Yellowstone ever got, Tres imagined.

Not until evening began to cede into night did Tres begin to work. Trusting that any interest in him would wane with the passage of time, he'd started in on the sheet. Moving as fast as his battered hands would allow, he threaded the uneven chunks together, droplets of blood oozing from his fingers, dotting the yellowed material.

The point in the second meeting with the public defender was not in hope that his father might have some new directive for him. He had known what he was doing when he volunteered for the assignment. Was fully aware of what would happen should it ever come to this.

Many times his father had tried to dissuade him, but Tres had insisted.

Everything their family was, everything they had ever been, was based on the kindness of Junior Ruiz. To serve him the way his father had was a singular honor Tres was glad to shoulder.

His mother had never understood such a thing. Neither had a sister. They'd never been able to understand why their father had lived the life he had, just as they didn't get it when this opportunity arose and Tres promptly left the life he'd built to help.

But he didn't expect them to. They were not of the same ilk as he and his father, did not understand how these things went. Too long they had been in America, assimilating into a new society, relishing the comforts they found there.

Just like he didn't expect them to understand what he was doing now.

The only reason in asking to see the attorney a second time was simply to ensure that the message had been received. To let it be known that he had made a mistake so that they could better prepare.

Once that was confirmed, his concerns allayed, he had made peace with what happened next.

Working his way to the end of the sheet, Tres tied a ragged knot. Looping it through three times, he pulled it tight, ensuring that the makeshift rope that was coiled around him would not unravel.

The first option for most people in his position was generally to attempt hanging. Having seen too many movies before, they assumed that there was some light fixture strong enough to hold their weight or something strong enough to use as a rope.

It had taken nothing more than a cursory glance around the cell to determine that wouldn't be an option here.

The ceiling above him was nothing but smooth concrete, all light coming from the bulbs lining the outer hall. The twin crosspieces on the front cage were at his knees and chin, neither tall enough to create the needed leverage to cause a clean break.

Even the rope he'd just braided, acceptable for his current plan, would not suffice for holding his body weight.

Instead, Tres had gone with the less obvious.

Keeping the end of the rope in hand, he formed a loose slip knot. Looping it over his head, he pulled it tight at the base of his neck, a macabre necktie cinched into place.

Spinning it around to the base of his hairline, he let the remainder of the rope trail down his back. Raising his knees beneath him, he brought his ankles together and tied the opposite end of the rope around them, allowing himself just barely enough slack to roll over onto his stomach.

Legs curled upward behind him, he could feel the tension of the rope across his windpipe, water coming to his eyes as he took one last long breath.

"Farewell," he whispered, extending his feet as far as he could, keeping them there as the world around him slowly faded to black.

Chapter Eighty

For no larger than the drop box was, it had held a cornucopia of small arms and tactile provisions. Far more than the two of us could ever hope to use and still survive, we'd left more than half of it behind as we locked up and drove away.

Even at that, it made for quite a spread stretched out across the back of the rented SUV.

"Just like old times, yeah?" Diggs asked.

Standing opposite me behind the rear bumper, Diggs finished strapping a thigh holster around his black canvas pants. Moving with practiced precision, it was clear it was still something he did with great frequency, the top of the rig falling just below his fingertips.

Textbook placement.

"Something like that," I replied, cinching a Velcro strap across my chest. Securing the body armor into place atop the t-shirt I wore, I swung my arms to either side, making sure it wasn't too tight, that I still had full range of motion.

"When was the last time you did something like this?" he asked. Lifting a Heckler & Koch MP5 submachine gun, he held it to his shoulder. Sighting down the length of it, he pulled the magazine and checked it was full before reinserting it.

Looping the shoulder strap over his right delt, he let it hang down, the body of it pressed along his ribcage.

Picking up a matching weapon, I took it in both hands. Tucking my chin to my shoulder, I pulled the gun in tight, the smell of oil wafting up off the barrel.

"Lot more recent than you'd probably believe."

Tightening the strap just slightly, I threaded my arm through the hole, letting it hang down by my side.

Reaching back into the rear hold, Diggs took up a small nylon duffel bag. Barely larger than a sack of potatoes, I could hear metal clinking inside, the explosives tucked within rattling against one another.

Looping it over his opposite shoulder, he slammed the rear hatch shut, the sound echoing across the sand before being swallowed up by the faint breeze blowing in from the west.

Without the faint glow of the interior dome light, the world grew darker instantly, my pupils dilating, adjusting to our surroundings.

The continued digging of Pally throughout the evening had revealed precious little. Nowhere in any databases were there any blueprints or schematics for the grounds of the Fruit of the Desert Winery. Same for any hope of using satellite imagery, the time of day making it impossible to get any sort of usable photos.

All we were left with was a handful of snapshots, images pulled from a real estate listing before the property was purchased years before. Done long before there was any thought of turning the place into a winery, it resembled most every estate in this part of the country.

A central structure surrounded by a small lawn and a whole lot of sand and hardscrabble plants.

Not nearly as much data as we'd want or need. The sort of thing we were doing only reluctantly, forced into action by the ongoing presence of Jones and Smith.

Curling his right hand up toward his armpit, Diggs grabbed his MP5. Pushing it across his chest, he took the opposite end in his left hand, the two barely more than ten inches apart, his elbows chicken-winged out to either side.

Dressed all in black, he was little more than a silhouette staring back at me.

"You think this has a chance in hell at working?"

Starting with my left hand, I grasped the barrel of my own MP5. Tugging it forward, I wrapped my right around the base, matching Diggs's pose.

"Pally said it wouldn't be an issue. These new cars are so auto-mated, it's like playing a damn video game."

Flicking his eyes over to the car, Diggs smirked. "Not what I meant. That's actually the only part of this whole damn thing I know will work."

Whether any of this would pan out, I didn't have a clue. Just as I had not the slightest what we were walking into. If Ruiz was waiting for us with an army, or if he was even here.

All I knew was that the more time we let expire, the greater his odds of disappearing. Of fortifying his position.

Of switching from defense to offense, getting antsy and deciding to come looking for us.

In no way was this how either one of us would prefer to be approaching things, but that was no longer in our control. We would finish what we had set out to, we would avenge our friend, ensure we didn't have to move forward constantly on the alert for Ruiz or his lackeys.

Or we wouldn't.

Either way, it ended here.

"Let's go."

Chapter Eighty-One

Sweat stung my eyes. It dripped down off my forehead, running over my cheeks and lips, the taste briny on my tongue.

Beneath the Kevlar vest I wore, I could feel my shirt clinging to my skin.

My lungs and thighs both were starting to burn, desert sand and lactic acid working through them respectively.

Without having any kind of overhead visual on the place we knew Ruiz to last be, the only thing we could go off of was a basic map. Nothing topographical, no sort of indication at all about the ground we were going to be covering.

Simply a generic road map.

Again, something neither one of us would have ever signed off on in a different life, but now were forced into, not having any other options. Because of that, any hope of infiltrating from the perimeter was dashed. As was the ability to use our numbers, splitting ourselves, coming in at them from different directions.

All we had was the road map, the simple schematic confirming the coordinates Pally had lifted from Ruiz and Mejia's phones and the address we had for Fruit of the Desert.

A spot in the sand well beyond the reach of greater San Diego. A place so remote no neighbors came up in any of the online searches.

A location meant to be beyond prying eyes, protected by the desert and a terrain that could not be trusted.

Taken as a whole, the sole hope for approach was to follow the road leading up to the place.

Leaving the SUV two miles out on the sand packed dense along the side of the asphalt, Diggs and I had fallen in beside one another. Submachine guns in hand, we'd started down the road, moving as quick as we could.

Side by side, we said not a word, the only sounds the occasional tapping of the grenades loaded into the bag Diggs carried.

Protected by the complete darkness of our location and a gradual rise in the road ahead, we'd been able to stand at full height, jogging without fear of being noticed. Both employing long strides, we'd worked our way down the unlined pavement, the road clearly one that didn't get much use.

For more than ten solid minutes, we continued on. Well after the SUV disappeared from behind us and on through the middle portion, when the only illumination was the stars and a waning gibbous moon above.

On further until we crested the small rise, spotting the dull glow of lights in the distance.

At the sight of them, we slowed our pace to a walk. Moving to the side of the road, we fell in one behind the other, Diggs taking point as I watched the rear. This we continued for five more minutes before lowering ourselves into a slight crouch. Even then, we kept our pace steady, watching as our destination grew ever closer.

As each step seemed to raise my heart rate, sweat continuing to seep from every pore.

Ahead of me, I saw as Diggs lowered his left hand from his weapon. Digging into his pants pocket, he buried everything from the wrist down into the dark material, his gait twisting slightly from the uneven stance.

"Alerting Pally now to our position," he whispered. "Five minutes out and closing."

Gaze fully locked on the orbs of light ahead, I kept my head twisted to the side, total focus on any sound that might make its way across the desert.

"Roger that."

Chapter Eighty-Two

We heard the SUV long before we saw it.

And even that wasn't until it was almost on us.

With the lights off and the black paint and dark window tint, it looked like little more than a dark turtle moving down the center of the road at us. Low and squat, it was positioned in the center of the asphalt strip, going at more than forty miles an hour.

Utilizing a hybrid engine, the sound was almost undetectable, the speed kept just short of engaging the engine, maintaining a point where it was still running entirely on electricity.

From the instant Diggs had reached into his pocket and pressed a single button on his cellphone, the signal sent for Pally to begin, we had increased our pace to almost a full sprint.

Having almost a half mile to cover, we had crossed over to the far side of the road. Abandoning some of our concern for moving in stealth, our chief concern became reaching the front gate, our best chance at success predicated on arriving at the same time as the SUV.

The idea was something Pally came up with, a practice he had employed a couple of times in his work in the private sector.

Apparently, many of the newer cars coming out today were governed by computer technology. What had started with only high-end models like Tesla or Lexus was now working its way down to less ostentatious vehicles, anything with a built-in video screen capable of being accessed remotely.

Or, more importantly for our purposes, accessed and operated.

How he knew that the SUV Diggs had rented was equipped with all this, I didn't bother inquiring. Just as I didn't need to know the particulars of how it worked.

Like so many things in the last couple of days − and over the last several years before that − I trusted him to do what he said he could.

Often, that meant getting us schematics or access to video feed.

In this instance, it meant providing us with a full-on battering ram, a way of penetrating the front gate and drawing attention, letting us slip in behind it.

Assuming, of course, that the gate that was shown in the old real estate photos still existed. If it didn't, Pally would simply find the closest inanimate target he could and aim for that.

From there, however things played out was on us.

Hearing the vehicle approaching fast behind us, we both increased our pace. Rising to full height, puffs of sand rose in our wake as we tore forward, the lights of our destination growing ever closer.

With each stride we took, more details emerged from the darkness. What we had thought was nothing more than a stretch of desert sand looked to be closer to a tropical oasis, a dense tangle of foliage rising upward.

Silhouetted by the bright glow of the security lights on the property, I could make out the jagged pattern of palm fronds. Mixed in were interspersed branches of other various trees, darkened fingers reaching upward, rising into the night sky.

Standing in a tight clump, it seemed to grow out of the desert fully formed. Reminding me of Devil's Tower in Wyoming, the spread seemed woefully out of place, springing up twenty-five feet higher than anything else in sight.

Around the rear perimeter of it, we could see most of the lights clustered, outbuildings forming a makeshift outer wall.

Gaze fixed on our target, trying to decipher every detail, we felt as the SUV blew by, warm air washing over us, the vehicle little more than a shadow moving past. Clutching submachine guns in either hand, the instant it was beyond us we both shoved out into the street, each of us falling in side by side.

Propelled by adrenaline, by anticipation, by wanton hatred of the man we were pursuing and everything he had done, we both hurtled forward as fast as we could.

Sweat poured from my body, my lungs clawed for air, as the brake lights on the SUV flared before us. A twin pair of bright red flashes, they ignited for no more than a second, an unspoken message from Pally.

It was time.

He was going in.

Pounding out another fifteen yards, we shifted our position once more. Reaching the outer edge of the foliage surrounding the estate, we fell back into a single file line along the right edge of the pavement, using the thick shadows of the trees for cover. As we did so, the humidity around us rose, the air becoming thicker, as ahead of us the SUV made the turn into the main drive.

No hesitation. No additional time for us to catch up.

Damned sure no warning to anybody waiting outside the gate.

Punching the gas hard, the squeal of tires rang out. A puff of smoke rose as the vehicle fishtailed from side to side, tires whirring atop the pavement before finally gaining purchase and shooting forward.

There and gone in nothing more than an instant, it disappeared from sight, folded into a gap ahead in the trees.

Behind it, we continued pushing on, never once slowing as we heard the sound of small arms fire begin to punctuate the night. Drawing metal, the distinctive pings could be heard as we continued moving forward, passing through the acrid smoke of the tires drifting back down the road toward us.

Sounds that were soon swallowed up by the sound of Pally doing just what he had promised.

Chapter Eighty-Three

The front gate we had spotted in the real estate photos had been removed in the years since, the classic black iron replaced by one that seemed to shine like gold. Much more for form than function, it barely served as a blockade to the SUV as it smashed into it, forced backward with an angry cry of metal against metal.

Shearing the hinges off on either side, the gate flipped end over end, the SUV barely slowing from the collision. Sparks flew into the night, their bright glow punctuated by handfuls of muzzle flashes, a half-dozen guards lining either side of the drive.

Not one of which was looking our way as we rounded the corner, Diggs taking the lead as I fanned out wide a few steps behind him.

Having no way of knowing what the grounds looked like, no clue what sort of manpower might be present, there hadn't been any chance for us to form a strategy. No way to know the best approach, everything from the moment Diaz had us convene at the drop box done completely on the fly.

So be it.

Sometimes the best plan is no plan.

Jerking the MP5 up in front of me, I took two steps out to the side from Diggs. Far enough to ensure I never fired his direction, but close enough that if anybody looked our way, I wouldn't be too exposed.

Nesting the submachine gun to my shoulder, I sighted in on the closest guard, the man's full attention on the vehicle that had just shouldered through the gate.

No more than twenty yards away, a quick three round burst all found center mass, his body jerking violently. Tossing his hands out before him, the Kalashnikov he carried clattered to the ground, the force of the shots tossing him sideways onto the driveway.

Beside me, I could hear Diggs's gun spitting out rounds in equal time, the scent of gunpowder rising around us, mixing with the lingering stench of the scorched tires.

Eyes stinging from the sweat coating my features, I jerked the muzzle of my gun a few inches to the side, the second guard in order just turning our direction as I unloaded another cluster.

From a greater distance and done on the fly, the aim was a bit more sporadic, the first drawing air, whizzing by to his right before the last two struck home. Smashing one into each side of his chest plate, his torso jerked straight back as he released his gun, weapon clattering to the ground by his feet.

Trusting he was finished, that the .40 caliber rounds had done their job, I moved on to the third and final in order. The furthest away, he'd had the most time to react, twisted back in our direction, his rifle raised to his shoulder.

Managing to squeeze off a pair of rounds, twin bright orange muzzle flashes erupted from the tip of his weapon, the rounds mashing into the dense leaves above us.

My stride even, I bore down on him, walking up the driveway. Keeping the same spacing from Diggs, I sighted in on the man, using the flicker of the muzzle flashes each time I blinked as a target before pushing out one final burst.

Stitching a ragged pattern across his torso, his body contorted in spastic movements, held upright by nothing more than muscle memory before gravity won out. Toppling to the ground, his body melted into a heap, not to move again.

After firing those last three rounds, I swept the front of the gun across the far side of the driveway. Checking every shadow, looking for any other sign of movement, I came to halt, only barely aware that Diggs had stopped firing beside me as well.

"You good?" I asked, focus still on the wall of trees nearby.

"Good," Diggs replied. "Three on my side. You?"

"Same."

Both keeping our weapons trained before us, I took a pair of steps forward. Drawing even with him, we stood peering the length of the driveway, the pale asphalt extending ahead of us before disappearing in a wide curve to the right.

Filling in the space on either side was more forestation, an odd mix of native and non-native plants.

Rising behind it in the distance was what I guessed to be the central home, lights peeking through the trees.

"Didn't my ass just leave the jungle?" Diggs whispered.

Thinking much the same, I raised a hand, wiping away some of the thick layer of sweat coating my forehead.

"How you want to play it?" I asked, ignoring his question.

In my periphery, I could see him glance my way, ambient light flashing against the perspiration covering his bald head.

"Well, I didn't carry this damn bag of explosives in here with us for nothing."

Chapter Eighty-Four

The stucco railing along the top of the balcony was cool to the touch. Hours removed from the last rays of sunlight for the day, all residual warmth had long since faded.

Even at that, it did little to lower Junior Ruiz's body temperature as he stood leaning forward, his palms pressed flat against it.

He was foolish to think he would be given even a day's head start. To consider that he could wait until the next morning before clearing some of the unnecessary clutter from the grounds.

Whatever lead they had, any element of surprise there might have been, had been wiped out when one of their assassins had fallen woefully short.

And then again when Mejia's son had decided to go off-script, leaving behind a calling card that was a neon arrow directly to his front door.

From that moment forward, he should have known that they were coming. That their visit to Esmera was only the beginning. That even if they didn't know exactly where he was, it was only a matter of time before they showed up.

These were the same people that had arrived in the middle of

Juana Salinas's *quinceañera*, had had no qualms about using the sacred event or the gathered crowd to nab him.

And that was long before he had taken out one of their own and made an attempt on another.

Seated on one of the sofas in his office, unable to even consider sleep, his subconscious refusing to shut down as it almost sensed what was surely coming, he had heard as the front gate was destroyed. Not quite certain what the noise was, he'd risen from his seat and walked outside, making it to the rail just in time to hear the gunfire begin.

A familiar din that instantly made everything clear.

"*El Jefe*," a voice said from behind him.

So deep in his thoughts, Ruiz hadn't heard the door to his office open. Not one footfall had penetrated his mind, the voice the first sign that he wasn't alone.

Feeling a spur of surprise roil through him, he pressed his fingertips hard against the top of the rail, a jolt passing through him before receding as recognition set in.

"I heard," Ruiz replied, not bothering to turn around to face Mejia behind him.

"You might want to consider coming inside," Mejia said. "Or at least turning off the lights behind you."

Head turned to the side, chin pressed to his shoulder, Ruiz grunted softly, as if considering the option.

Not that there was any point. Whoever had just entered the grounds had done so with the express purpose of finding him. Where he was standing, how much light was on him, didn't matter.

Which was why he wasn't now trying to run. He wasn't grabbing Mejia and whoever else was nearby and loading into a vehicle, hoping to steal away into the night.

Eventually, they would make their way to him. Or he would find them. Either way, this was a climax far too long in coming. Something that had to be finished before either side could ever move forward, free of the other.

Might as well be here and now. At least this way he could finish what had started eight years before, what he had spent many nights staring at the bunk above him thinking about.

A clean sweep, Reyes and Tate and whoever else, all in the first couple of days.

"How many men onsite tonight?" Ruiz asked.

"Twenty-two," Mejia said. Stepping up beside him, he extended a single hand, placing a gun atop the railing not ten inches from Ruiz's flattened palm. "Including us."

Chapter Eighty-Five

I have no idea why Junior Ruiz, or Ramon Reyes, or whoever the hell else was actually in charge, had decided to create a jungle twenty-five miles outside of San Diego. Whether it was to in some way bolster the fake business front they were running, or if it was some sort of vanity play gone overboard, or if it was something else entirely, I couldn't begin to fathom.

What I did know was that it made our job infinitely easier, giving us ample cover to work through as we made our way onward.

My knees flexed, submachine gun pressed tight to my shoulder, I moved one foot across the other. Body twisted slightly to the side to make myself as small a target as possible, I took the far side of the driveway, Diggs moving opposite me.

Under the heavy canopy of the palm fronds above, each step seemed to take me back into a different time. Missions conducted on separate continents, assignments handed down during my time with the DEA and the Navy before that.

At odds in every way with the desert setting just beyond us, the air was supersaturated with humidity. So thick it felt like breathing pure vapor, it clung to my skin and clothing. Beads of it lined the short hairs on my forearms, caused my bangs to hang damp and lank across my brow.

Underfoot, metric tons of topsoil had been brought in, the smell of damp earth rising to my nostrils.

There was no sound from my footfalls, the soft ground swallowing it up, bits of mud clinging to the soles of my boots.

Taking advantage of the thick tangle of forestation, I kept the driveway a few yards away to my right. Darting from the base of one tree to another, I was careful to avoid the low-hanging branches of fruit trees, instead sticking to the smooth trunks of the King Palm trees rising above.

Just barely visible was the glow of the main house, bits of light poking through narrow slits in the foliage, there and gone in a matter of moments.

Counting seconds in my head, I made it to one-hundred-and-ten, just shy of two minutes, before the telltale sound I'd been waiting on arrived.

Not yet had we come upon the remnants of the SUV. After ramming the front gate, it must have been in decent enough shape for Pally to keep going, no doubt finding a prime target and smashing the vehicle right into it.

Likely using it to take out some of the guards, or one of their rigs, or a chokepoint of some sort, the crash would have put whoever else was on the grounds scrambling.

An advantage that had allowed us to get inside, to tuck ourselves into the trees, before anybody else came looking.

But one I knew couldn't last forever, it only a matter of time before they were able to regroup and come looking for us.

Something that, if the sound of the engine ringing out into the night was any indicator, was now upon us.

Halting my forward progress, I moved back out to the edge of the driveway. Keeping the trunk of one of the towering palms lining it between myself and the sound of the approaching vehicle, I pressed my shoulder tight against it.

Lifting my chin, I pressed my tongue to the top of my mouth, pushing a hissing noise out as loud as I dared.

Catching it on the first pass, it took only a moment for Diggs to materialize from the opposite side of the drive. Completely at home in the jungle, barely a day removed from the real thing on the other side of the planet, he emerged five yards ahead of me, a bit of sweat shining from his head.

Using only hand gestures, I waved once to get his attention before pointing to my ear.

Nodding in agreement that he had heard it too, he pointed to me and then raised a single finger. Dropping his hand to clear the sequence, he then pointed to himself and raised a pair of fingers, ending with motioning to the bag still hanging from his shoulder.

Raising a closed fist in acknowledgment, I watched as he melted back into the trees, disappearing from sight.

The scheme was a simple one, something we had done a handful of times before in the past. Never before had we had the benefit of grenades with us at the time, but that didn't change the basic approach.

Keeping my position against the base of the tree, I lowered myself to a knee. Ear trained to the side, I waited, listening as the groan of an engine grew closer, seconds ticking by before a pair of headlights appeared through the brush.

Square and boxy, they set up high, appearing to be from a work truck of some sort. Moving as fast as the winding curve of the drive would allow, the engine revved and fell away.

Submachine gun tucked in tight, I watched as it grew steadily closer, waiting until it was just fifteen yards beyond where I knew Diggs to be before opening up.

At such a distance, with such an enormous target, there was virtually no way to miss. The first cluster of rounds all slammed into the engine, sparks flying from the collision of metal on metal.

Tugging back on the trigger a second time, I unleashed a second burst, this one aimed a few feet higher. Slapping across the front windshield, I could see sprays of crystalline glass rise up, spiderwebs spreading wide from a trio of impact points.

Careful to keep them on the passenger side of the truck, my goal wasn't to take out the driver. Of everybody, he was the only one I needed to ensure stayed alive, reacting with basic human instinct.

Which, a moment later, he did.

The truck was almost even with Diggs when the person behind the wheel slammed on the brakes. For the second time of the night, the squeal of tires on pavement rang out, the tang of burnt radials rising into the air.

Keeping my position, I unleashed one last trio, just barely getting it off before a pair of men rose from the bed of the truck. Standing over the front cab, they extended weapons my way, full focus on unloading at whoever was firing at them.

To the point they never even considered the ambush they had just driven into.

Back pressed to the base of the tree, I listened as Diggs's submachine gun opened up. Two quick sprays, I could just make out the pained grunts of his targets before hearing the distinctive clack of a grenade rolling across the concrete.

Tucked down tight, I put my head between my knees, waiting as the explosive ignited, a fiery wall of heat and shrapnel rushing past.

Chapter Eighty-Six

Most people would make the mistake of lobbing the grenade. They would have seen too many movies, would want that moment of seeing it silhouetted against the sky, tumbling end over end before landing in the bed of the truck.

Maybe even watching any opposition that might still be alive scrambling for cover, realizing what was about to happen.

Carl Diggs wasn't most people.

Following basic rules of physics, he had put it under the truck. Rolling it across the asphalt beneath the vehicle meant that all concentrated force was aimed upward, directly through the engine, with all of its various fuels and moving components. Igniting instantly, the explosion sent the rig skyward in a fiery pyre.

I remained tucked in my hiding spot. Four full seconds passed before it landed, the crash every bit as loud as the original detonation. Smashing down to the driveway, shattered remnants of the machine scattered in every direction. Twisted bits of metal and smoldering rubber pelted the trees, tearing through the thin leaves.

Waiting until both were past, until some portion of the concentrated heat and smoke had managed to slip upward into the atmosphere, I twisted myself free from the base of the tree. MP5 tucked back into position, I made a quick pass around the outside of the rig, checking for the unlikely event that someone had survived.

Seeing nothing that posed a threat, I kept my gun held tight, meeting Diggs on the backend of the wreck, his focus already turned to face down the length of the driveway.

"How many?" I asked.

"Three in the back, don't know about the front," he replied.

There had been six by the gate. Adding these, that put us at either ten or eleven, depending on if anybody was riding shotgun.

A solid start.

"How many you think are here?"

"This many buildings?" he asked. "Have to think fifteen or so."

"Yeah, but don't forget," I countered, "he knows I survived, and that I went to see his sister."

"Twenty or twenty-five anyway, then," he replied. Not one bit of mirth permeated the words, his attention squarely on the route ahead.

"We need to get off this driveway," I said.

There was no way at this point that every person on the property didn't know we were here. Not with what happened at the front gate and whatever Pally managed to do with the SUV.

That much was obvious.

Just as was the exact spot we were standing in, the explosion pinpointing our location.

"Right," he agreed. "Use the trees."

Not another word was said. No discussion about which way we should go, no further debate about how to proceed.

So many times over the years we had been drilled on the fact that a plan is only truly effective for approach and initial contact. After that, there was only a best-case scenario and then the hundreds of ways things usually ended up playing out.

None of them foreseeable, people's behavior in a fight being something there was no way of knowing in advance.

This time, we had arrived without so much as a plan, but that was irrelevant at this point. We had made it past the front gate, had now eliminated nearly a dozen of the opposition.

That's all we could ask for.

Pushing ourselves to the left of the drive, we set a course toward the house. Gone was any need to circle out wide, everybody present already knowing what we were here for. Any time we spent on the outbuildings, any further attempts at misdirection, were only going to give Ruiz time to better fortify.

Returning to our original stances, we settled in at double time. Keeping no more than a few yards between us, we picked a path over the forest floor, sweat and soot and humidity clinging to our skin.

Little by little, we made our way forward, the density of the forest thinning slightly around us. With every tree we passed, a bit more of the light from the main house became visible, the expanse of the structure stretching as far as the forest would let us see in both directions.

In the distance, we could make out the sound of a second engine turning over, a stray voice punctuating the air, dying away as fast as it had arrived.

Moving at a diagonal, we put as much ground as possible between us and the driveway. Sticking to the shadows, we pointed ourselves to the northeast, moving for more than two solid minutes before pulling up as a clear outline of the corner of the house could be seen peeking through the dense branches.

Inching toward it, we made our way to the edge of the tree line before pausing, waiting and listening.

Shoulders almost touching, Diggs whispered, "Looks like our big entrance pulled most of the patrols."

Grunting softly, I nodded in agreement.

Earlier in the night, not knowing when or even if we were coming, whatever coverage there was for the place would have been spread evenly over the grounds. More for surveillance than interaction, the moment our presence became known, they would have fallen back to key points.

Gates. Vehicles. Doorways.

Ruiz himself.

Where we were now had to be the least fortified spot on the grounds.

"How you want to play it?" I whispered.

Pausing a moment, I saw Diggs jerk his attention in either direction. Considering what we knew, where the points of contact were likely concentrated, he said, "Don't like the idea of splitting, but it may be our best bet."

I didn't like the idea either, but it was the same conclusion I had already drawn, the reason I had asked him what he thought before he did the same to me.

With only two of us, it would be too easy for them to evade on a property this size unless we somehow managed to funnel things inward.

"I'll swing down the side and around the back, meet you on the opposite corner in ten."

Chapter Eighty-Seven

C alling it a house wasn't just a misnomer, it was flat out wrong.
A house had normal dimensions. It had a number of bedrooms and bathrooms that could each be counted on one hand. It had windows lining the front and a garage on the end and a single kitchen and living room somewhere inside.

This place was nothing like that. It wasn't even what I would consider a mansion.

It was nothing short of a monstrosity.

When I'd suggested we meet on the far southwest corner of the spread in ten minutes, that was before realizing just how much ground that meant we both had to get across. Most of our time since arriving spent in the deep cover of trees, it had been impossible to get a full visual of what we were dealing with.

A fact that became apparent as it took me more than a minute walking fast just to get across the far end. Keeping to the trees, submachine gun with a half-magazine at the ready, every shadow, every rustle of the leaves, earned my attention.

Jerking the front tip of the muzzle from side to side, I left nothing uncovered, aware of the clock ticking steadily backward in my mind.

Several minutes had passed since the explosion on the front

driveway. A second response was no doubt being mobilized, every other guard onsite falling back into defense positions, placements meant to maximize visibility, to lessen any chance we had at getting to Ruiz.

Much like our first arrival - or even our being here at all tonight - the sooner we moved on them, the better. The more time they were afforded, the more entrenched they could become, hunkering down and waiting for us.

Swinging out wide, I circled around the southeast corner of the place. Dropping to a knee, I lined myself up with the backside of the house, finally getting a clear view the length of it.

Unlike the front, with trees butting as close to the structure as possible, meant to block everything from the road, a strip along the back of the structure had been left bare. Whatever effort had been made to fortify the area with orchards and grapevines had stopped short of the house, likely not wanting to have the irrigation and humidity so close to the residence.

Without it, a clear lane ran the length of it, a gentle bend in the middle giving it a slight boomerang shape, though still straight enough for me to get a full view.

Best bet, the place looked to be close to a hundred yards in length. On either side were matching wings, both bent back at an angle. Nothing but mulch beds and some shrubbery was tucked up against the house, plenty of light spilling out from the windows, illuminating everything.

In the center was an expansive patio, appearing to be made from paver stones, large planters filled with various flora set up at even intervals around the outside of it. In the center was a small tangle of furniture, all of it wrought iron and cushions.

Grouped into various clusters meant for dining or entertaining, tonight there was a far different crowd gathered, a trio of guards stationed along the back end of it. All dressed in black and carrying assault rifles, they were wearing sunglasses despite the hour, all appearing to be extras brought in from central casting more than men actually meant to serve a purpose.

Regardless of what had already transpired, the mess we had made out on the driveway, all three were rooted in place. Their rifles were held in either hand across their fronts, focus aimed outward.

Taking them in, committing their positioning to memory, I peeled back from the edge of the clearing. Receding further into the trees, I resumed my previous stance, looping wide out away from the house.

Within just a few strides, it became apparent that whatever had been planted on the front side of the spread was there for the express purpose of providing cover.

Out back, there appeared to be much more order, everything arranged into even rows. Irrigation had been taken to another level, puddles lining the ground, splashing up over the toes of my boots as I slipped ahead.

Somehow the humidity rose even higher, flies buzzing about.

Using the uniform grid of the trees around me, the cover of darkness beyond the reach of the lights of the house, I made my way across the back. Chewing up yards in short, choppy steps, I paused every few seconds. MP5 trained at the ready, I listened hard, hearing nothing more than the occasional rustle of leaves.

Two minutes passed, and then a third, as I steadily worked my way inward. Keeping the position of the back patio fixed in my mind, I moved in a small arc, bearing down on it.

By the time I drew even, five minutes – a full half of what I'd been allotted – had passed. Lowering myself into a crouch, I duckwalked my way forward, making it to within ten yards of the edge of the forest.

Dropping back to a knee, I felt water seep up through my jeans, soaking through to the skin. Around me, the smell of stagnant water was apparent, just one more scent of many I'd already encountered throughout the night I could do without.

Lowering myself so my elbows were only inches above the mud, I found a clear lane to the rear of the house. From such an angle, I was able to get a better fix on the guard's positions, working through the best way to approach when something caught my attention.

A quick flash of white, it pulled my focus upward, my grip on the submachine gun tightening as I stared at what appeared before me.

Pinpricks of sensation, of animosity, rippled the length of my body, every instinct I had telling me to burst forward.

For the briefest of instants, every other thought faded to the background, my entire focus on the balcony running the length of the patio on the second floor.

Pulled just as fast in the opposite direction by an explosion many, many times larger than what had happened on the driveway minutes before.

Chapter Eighty-Eight

The gun that Arlin Mejia had brought for Junior Ruiz was a Springfield XD. Small and compact, it fit easily within his grip, designed for ease of use.

Whether on purpose – a nod to his time away – or not, Ruiz didn't much care.

Standing on the balcony overlooking the grounds, he had not moved since hearing the front gate get torn away. Not as a few moments later there was a crash on the far end of the mansion, or again a couple of minutes after that when an explosion happened along the front drive.

But this was too much to ignore.

The sequence was three distinct parts, happening in such short order it was impossible not to be planned. Far more than just the lone agent that had managed to get away in Montana could pull off, it began with the sound of small arms fire near where the crash had occurred on the western end of the spread.

Arriving in quick bursts, it was soon met by the familiar pitch of automatic fire, the two sides going back and forth before an explosion infinitely larger than what had happened out front ripped through the night. Forceful enough to send a tremor the length the mansion, Ruiz snatched up his gun.

Rushing to the far end of the balcony, he clutched the small Springfield in both hands. Extending the front tip out over the railing, he leaned forward, peering down in time to see the outer half of a fireball rising beyond the edge of the house.

Orange flames encased in black smoke, he was barely able to make out what was happening before another volley of gunfire erupted. Much, much closer in proximity, the harsh crack of the rounds being fired jerked his attention downward, his focus turning to the patio below in time to see the first of his guards fall lifeless.

An instant later, a second plume of orange sprouted from the tree line just behind the house, a second guard jerking in short spasms. Barely lifting his rifle above his waist, his body pitched to the side, dark sprays of blood striping the stone.

Gun still squeezed tight in both hands, Ruiz extended the weapon before him. Turning his hips to the side, he walked straight back to the spot he'd been in most of the evening, the tip of the gun never wavering. Aimed at the spot where he'd seen the last bits of muzzle flash, he pulled back on the trigger, the easy pull of the semi-automatic barely kicking in his hand.

Less than a second later, it was cycled through and ready, Ruiz again pulling back on the trigger.

Oblivious to his presence, to the rounds he was squeezing off, a third burst sprang up from the tree line. Shifted a few feet to the side, their target was the third guard below, a single round finding flesh.

Tearing a chunk from his thigh, Ruiz heard the man cry out. Jerking his attention downward, he saw the man go to the ground, his weapon clattering down beside him.

A renewed bit of venom rising within, Ruiz jerked his weapon up to where the shots had originated. Taking aim again, twice more he fired off shots, bullets ripping into the heavy foliage.

The first time he had held a gun – much less fired one – in eight years, Ruiz smelled gunpowder rise to his nostrils. His hands absorbed the recoil of the shots, each one sending a tremor up through his arms, the absorbed energy seeming to embolden him.

Even without a face to look at, a clear view of who was out there, Ruiz kept the gun aimed. In no way did he hold any qualms about what he was doing, knowing this was likely just the first of many that would come for him.

Which was fine. If his time in prison had instilled anything, it was the need to always be on the offensive. To never ask, but to take.

That was why Jones and Smith had selected him for this task. Not because of his prior history with Reyes or the organization, but because he got things done.

Five yards to the west of where he was aiming, another trio of shots appeared. As if circling the wounded prey on the patio below, the shooter finished off the third guard, all three rounds finding center mass.

Blowing him flat to his back, it pushed blood spatter out across the ground, all three guards lying in twisted heaps, not one so much as getting off a shot.

Jerking his attention down, seeing what had happened, Ruiz felt another jolt of animosity rise within him. From deep in his core, a guttural cry rose up, rolling through his chest as he directed the gun to the spot of the last shots.

Tugging back on the trigger one time after another, he made it through four more rounds before one final pulse ignited from the darkened trees.

Of them, the first two drew the side of the house. Bits of stucco dust rose upward, spraying across his face, pelting the jacket of his linen suit.

The third managed to hit home.

Mashing into the soft tissue above his right hip, it was like a hot poker driving into his flesh, jerking his body backward. Under the force of it, his grip loosened on the handle of the Springfield, the weapon sliding from his fingers, tumbling over the edge of the railing to the ground below.

Chapter Eighty-Nine

The first time I'd seen Junior Ruiz standing at the top of the balcony, the sight had been so unexpected I was barely able to move. The singular goal I'd had for days on end, my senses had been preoccupied, focused on the trio of guards on the patio below.

Dressed all in white, he'd had almost an ethereal glow, adding to the shock of his sudden arrival.

When we'd rolled up on the place, I'd had reasonable certainty he'd be here. Twelve hours had passed since Pally had gotten a hard fix on his location, but we'd also been able to couple it with the cell-phone Arlin Mejia was using.

And match it to the Fruit of the Desert Winery, and Ramon Reyes, and a host of other things.

Still, never would I have thought he would merely stride out of the back door of the second floor into view.

If I were to have bet money, I would have figured him to have learned from what happened eight years ago in Baja. I would assume he'd be tucked away in a bunker somewhere, the door fortified with a team of guards and wired explosives and a host of other things that would make getting to him a suicide run.

Instead, his ego had seemed to be every bit as intact as the last time we encountered him.

Seeing him standing there, even for the briefest of moments, I had allowed my animosity for him to get the best of me. To pull my focus his way, forgetting about the guards below or Diggs nearby or anything else.

All I could think about was Kaylan hanging suspended in the air on the front porch of our guide business. And Serra Martin hugging me in the foyer of the Snoqualmie Police Department.

And the damn bullet and peso still wedged down in my pocket.

Very nearly rising from my post and aiming every round I had his way, fortunately I was drawn back to the task at hand by Diggs on the far end of the house.

The same location I was now running toward with everything I had, working my way down the back end of the mansion. Abandoning the cover of trees for the open expanse along the side of the structure, I lowered the submachine gun from my shoulder, pounding straight ahead.

Free from the dense cover of the forest, the ground beneath my feet was much firmer. My boots barely made any indent as I sprinted along, thick smoke lying close to the ground, a thin haze drifting through the beams of light extending from the windows beside me.

Making no effort to take cover, trusting that for the time being all attention would be aimed at the massive explosion that had just set the ground to quivering, I ran as hard as I could.

I ignored the rasp in my lungs and the burn of lactic acid in my thighs, my singular goal getting to the side of the house.

For twenty seconds, I ran as fast as I could, swinging out to my left and coming in tight on the southwest corner. Using the building for cover, I lowered myself into a crouch, raising the submachine gun back into place and peering out.

Serving as the end of the driveway, the entire western end of the place was cordoned into a parking lot. Lined across it was a handful of vehicles, the exact number indiscernible.

Directly in front of me sat a pair of trucks much like the one we'd encountered on the driveway. Next to it was a mid-sized SUV, an all-terrain model designed to move over the sand with minimal ease.

That much was easy to see.

It was after that that things got a bit tough to decipher.

From where I was standing, it looked like Pally had aimed the rental at the first vehicle in order. T-boning into the side of it, he had managed to push it up against the next car in order, some sort of small sedan.

A three-car melee that had been an optimal place for Diggs to drop a couple of grenades, all three of the rigs burning brightly. Most of the glass had been blown from each one, shards spread across the ground like fine diamonds, flames sparkling off them.

What remained of the vehicles were already black and charred, myriad chemical scents rising into the air, smoke biting at my nose and eyes.

Despite the vivid nature of the scene before me, all of that I was able to see and process in just a matter of moments. One quick sweep told me what I needed to know about the explosion, my gaze instead rising to the cluster of shadows just beyond them.

From where I was, it looked like Diggs had taken quarter in the forest on the far side of the drive. Every few moments, I could see a cluster of muzzle bursts flash from the dense cover.

Opposite him, there looked to be at least a handful of guards in black all inching forward.

Interspersed between them, at least as many lay prone on the driveway, their twisted positioning telling me they weren't a threat to rise again.

Scanning twice in both directions, I kept myself lowered into a crouch. Checking back the length of the house, I ensured nobody had come up behind me, that Ruiz hadn't reappeared along the balcony.

Turning to face forward, I pushed off my back foot, driving myself straight ahead, covering the short expanse between the corner of the house and the remaining vehicles parked in a row. Ducking between the last two, I rose onto my toes, making sure my footfalls were silent as I made my way to the rear bumper of the closest truck.

Returning the submachine gun to my shoulder, I waited for one more burst from the woods to check Diggs's position, making sure not to catch him in a crossfire.

The instant it appeared, I tugged on the trigger, keeping it pinned back until every remaining round I had was expended.

Chapter Ninety

"Longest damn ten minutes I ever saw," Carl Diggs said. Emerging on the far side of the twisted wreckage of the vehicles lining the side of the house, he had cast aside the nylon sack with the explosives and his submachine gun.

Most likely having expended both, he drew out his sidearm from the holster on his thigh, racking the slide before him.

"I saw Ruiz."

Tossing my MP5 into the vehicles burning bright beside us, I drew my own handgun, the much smaller weapon infinitely smaller and lighter in my hands.

"Ruiz?" Diggs said, jerking his attention up from the gun in his hand. "Where?"

Standing on the northwest corner of the house at the front of the driveway, I jerked my head back over my shoulder. "Second floor. Big ass balcony in the middle of the house, looks like an office or something.

"I put one in him, but don't think it was a kill shot."

Flicking his eyes in the direction I had motioned, Diggs returned his gaze to the scene before us.

In total, there looked to be just shy of a dozen men strewn across the blacktop. Coupled with those out by the gate, on the driveway, and that I had nabbed on the rear patio, I couldn't imagine there being many more on the grounds.

At most, Ruiz and a couple of personal protectors. Maybe one or two in some of the outbuildings.

"I only saw one entrance coming down the front," Diggs said. "Big central door, lots of stairs and columns and shit leading up to it."

Based on what I'd seen, the patio was a ground level entrance feeding straight into the house. Where it entered, there was no way to know, though I had to guess the front would be better for getting up to the office.

"Guessing anybody that's left will be coming from one of these buildings," I said.

Picking up on the insinuation, Diggs gave a nod. Scanning the area around us, he checked each of the bodies lying inert before spinning out in the opposite direction.

Falling in beside him, the two of us jogged in double time for the front. Free of having to run with two hands on our weapons and the extra weight of the MP5s and the explosives, not needing to be on such a constant vigil for guards, we moved easily.

Sticking to the narrow lane feeding from the main drive to front door, our boots slapped against the pavement, the two of us covering the short distance in under a minute.

As we reached the front steps, we each pulled our guns into two-handed shooting stances, Diggs focused on the area before us as I watched our rear. Panting slightly, my heart rate and adrenaline were both still redlined as we ascended the few stairs onto the front porch.

In the wake of the multiple explosions and without the staccato of automatic rifles, the world carried an almost eerie silence as we moved. In the air hung the assorted scents of battle, mixed signals that had my body jumping at every false start.

Backing our way across the porch, we both reached the front door at the same time. Accepting that the woods behind us was quiet, that we had stripped away any remaining threat, we turned in unison.

Extending a hand, I tugged on the handle of it just slightly. Feeling it pull back without opposition, I glanced to Diggs, nodding once.

Seeing him nod in return, I jerked the door open and stepped to the side, letting him push through first. Arms extended before him, he moved sideways to the right as I came in close behind him.

Matching his pose, I jerked my attention to the left.

Both of us finding nothing but silence.

Standing just inside the front door, we found ourselves on the largest foyer I had ever seen in my life. Rising two full floors above, a gigantic crystal chandelier hung from the ceiling, bright light casting a glow over a marble floor and a sweeping staircase. Rising from either side of the space, it wrapped around in one unending arc, a wrought iron railing running the full length of it.

On the walls were massive paintings in gold frames and various tables and vases, the single room we were in alone easily costing more than the entire building that comprised my office.

"I see the wine business is paying pretty well these days," Diggs whispered.

One corner of my mouth curled back at the crack, though nothing more. There would be a time for plenty of that in the very near future, but for the time being my focus was on Ruiz.

Once already I had seen him, been close enough to draw blood from him.

I was now into the fourth calendar day of chasing his ass.

It was time for it all to end.

"Layout would mean the office has to be at the top of those stairs," I said.

"Yeah," Diggs replied, "along with whoever he has waiting with him."

In the best of circumstances, we would still have a couple of those grenades left. Or a fully automatic weapon. Or a damned drone we could use to provide an image of whatever was at the top of the steps.

But we didn't.

All we had were a pair of handguns, each other, and twin staircases.

It would have to do.

Each nodding in agreement, we set off together. Fanning out in either direction, we both took one side of the stairwell.

Rising a single step at a time, we moved in complete silence, every stair heightening the anticipation I felt, bringing us closer to the guards I was certain were waiting for us at the top.

The higher we ascended, the slower our pace became. Pressing a shoulder into the wall, I peered up as far as I could, ready for whatever might be up ahead.

Not once did either one of us consider that it might come from behind.

Chapter Ninety-One

Never before had I seen Arlin Mejia. Prior to earlier in the day, I'd never even heard of him. But based on everything Juana Salinas had said about her father, about the unflinching loyalty he had to Ruiz and the role he played in the organization, I had not a single doubt that the fifty-something man in slacks and a dress shirt carrying a shotgun across the foyer floor below was Mejia.

Seeming to appear from nowhere, the first indicator we had of his presence was the unmistakable racking of a shell into the chamber.

The instant we both heard it, basic human instinct took over. The strongest of all innate traits rose to the fore, self-preservation shoving aside any thought of possible danger ahead.

Pushing straight ahead, I covered the top half of the staircase in four long strides, taking the steps two and a three at a time. Making it as far as a single step down from the top, I dove straight ahead onto the hardwood floor, my chest hitting first, body coasting atop my Kevlar vest.

Arriving no later than a half-step after me, Diggs hit a similar pose eight feet away, landing just before a shell tore an enormous gouge from the wall above him. Sending shards of plaster across the polished floor, dust still hung in the air as we heard the slide on the shotgun work a second time.

"Where the hell did that come from?" Diggs spat my direction, his features more annoyed than surprised. Remaining folded in his side, he switched his gun to his left hand, using his right and corresponding leg to pull himself across the floor.

"You good?" I hissed.

Flashing his eyes my direction, he replied, "I got this."

Lifting my pelvis a few inches, I crawled forward. For the first time, I took in the set of double doors standing closed before us. I saw the hall extended out in either direction, overhead lights revealing them to be completely empty.

"You sure?"

This time, Diggs didn't bother looking my way. "Just go get his ass."

Recognizing the tone, knowing better than to press it any further, I pushed myself a few feet further ahead. Making sure I was well beyond the vantage of Mejia below, I shifted my gaze to the doors before me.

One after another, I riffled through the various options I had, considering my approach.

Fifteen minutes earlier, he had stood on the balcony and fired down at me. Using a handgun, he hadn't a prayer at hitting anything, but he'd still unloaded the better part of a clip, proving he wasn't afraid to come at me if need be.

Hell, his actions at the estate in Baja years before had proved that much.

But I also knew that he had dropped that gun to ground when he took the bullet. And that it had been into the lower part of his torso, that entire area a mash of vital parts, an injury to any one of them enough to cause serious damage.

More than that though, I knew everything the man had done. I knew what had happened all those years before, just like I was fully aware of all that had occurred in the last couple of days.

Pushing myself to a standing position, I gripped the gun tight in my right hand. Abandoning any sort of crouched position, I made no attempt at making myself a smaller target. The noise of the fight between Diggs and Mejia behind me bled away.

On the other side of the doors could be damned near anything. I was aware of that, but this shit had gone on long enough.

Not once did I slow my pace as I strode forward.

Grabbing the handle of the left door, I jerked it open and stepped inside.

Chapter Ninety-Two

The inside of the office was even more ridiculous than the rest of the house, somehow infinitely more even than the grounds outside. Like a cross between a massage parlor, a Victorian castle, and the Oval Office, the place was a mishmash of styles and features, all of it aimed more at what someone thought the office of a drug kingpin should look like.

Style over substance.

The type of place that someone building an arboretum and a winery in the middle of the desert would put together.

Giving my surroundings nothing more than a cursory glance, making sure there were no other guards lurking nearby, I waited as the door to the hall swung shut behind me. With it fell away a fair bit of the noise from the hallway, only the occasion din of a gunshot punctuating the quiet.

"Ruiz," I muttered, my focus landing on the single person inside the room.

Twenty feet away, the man that hadn't crossed my mind in years but had somehow come to dominate my every thought in recent days sat staring back at me. Folded into a leather desk chair that appeared much too large for him, it rose above his head and behind either shoulder, giving him the appearance of a child playing businessman.

Wearing the same white linen suit he'd worn on the balcony, his shoulders were twisted a bit to the side, both hands pressed into his abdomen. Mashed into the space between his ribs and hip bone, both of them seemed to be stained red, blood continuing to seep out steadily beyond their reach.

"Tate," he muttered, the single word seeming already a bit slurred. As if the blood loss was already starting to get to him, his body already starting to shut down, he stared up at me with heavily lidded eyes. Sweat lined his face and forehead.

Whatever firepower he'd brought along for the evening seemed to have tumbled out over the railing minutes before, the desktop before him bare.

Not that it mattered, his current state appearing that he wouldn't have the strength to lift and fire a weapon even if he had one.

So often in the last couple of days, I'd been forced to sit and think. Multiple trips across Washington and Idaho, a flight from Bozeman to San Diego. Time to contemplate how this moment would play out.

What I would say to this man if given the chance.

Gun still clenched in my right hand, I started forward from the door. Splitting the sofas in the center of the room, I cut a direct path to the desk, his eyes tracking me the entire time.

"Do you remember what you said to us the night we brought you in?" I asked. Keeping my pace even, my boot heels echoed off the floorboards as I walked forward.

"I remember," Ruiz said. Grunting softly, he pulled himself up a few inches higher in his seat. "I also remember your partner telling me to shut the hell up, and when I wouldn't, he threw me to the ground in front of all my guests."

His eyes narrowed slightly as he looked up at me. "How's he doing now, by the way?"

Knowing that he was only trying to bait me, that he just wanted to put up the façade of being in control, hoping to mention Martin to get me to do something stupid, I forced myself to remain rigid as I stared at him. To bite back the jolt of ire that rose through me, the inclination to spring across the desk and bury my fist into his face, wrap my hands around his throat, until he was no more.

Digging into the left front pocket of my jeans, I drew out two items. Two things I had been carrying with me since leaving that house in Snoqualmie days before.

Placing both down side by side on the desk between us, I arranged them exactly as they had been on that mantle.

Sliding his gaze from me to the items and back up again, Ruiz remained motionless for a moment. Slowly, one corner of his mouth peeled back slightly, his lips and teeth glossy with saliva.

"*Plata o plomo*? Seriously? You're giving me a choice here?"

I met his gaze just long enough to see my features held no such mirth.

"No."

The smile had only just managed to fade, replaced by realization, as I lifted the gun to shoulder height and pulled the trigger.

Again.

And again.

Chapter Ninety-Three

The bottles of Powerade sitting in front of Carl Diggs and I seemed to be having little effect. After a night that had included a two-mile jog down a desert road, storming a home in the center of a tropical rainforest, enduring smoke and sweat and blood and everything else that had occurred, there was no way a couple of quarts of electrolytes could possibly return us to status quo.

The only things that even had a chance at beginning to make that a possibility were a shower and a few hours of sleep, both of which I knew to be waiting in the locker room in the back end of the DEA headquarters we now sat in. So close I could practically hear them calling to me, I forced myself to remain reclined in the leather rolling chair alongside the conference room table.

"Man, what the hell are we doing in here again?" Diggs asked, his voice relaying the same mix of thoughts I was currently working through.

Striking a pose similar to mine a few feet away, his legs were extended before him. Crossed at the ankles, his boots were propped on the edge of the table, his thumb and forefinger massaging his forehead.

With the exception of the clothes he now wore and the various scents of battle rolling off him, he was a very near copy to exactly how he'd appeared just eighteen hours before.

"Diaz asked us to give her a few more minutes."

In the wake of us finishing off Ruiz and Mejia respectively, Diggs and I had made quick pass over the grounds. Wanting to ensure that we had finished what we set out to, that we would never again have to worry about a Tres Salinas or someone like him showing up unexpectedly, we made a point of going through every last room and outbuilding.

A chore neither one of us had wanted to do, but ended up being damned glad we did.

Even if it did end up making our night much, much longer than originally anticipated.

"How much shit did they end up seizing?" Diggs asked, hand still working across his forehead, shielding his eyes from view.

"Last I heard, couple hundred kilos of pure product," I replied. "Plus, all that wine."

The process was something we'd started to hear about before I stepped away, the idea to dissolve cocaine into liquid and transport it that way. Supposedly much easier to move without detection, back then the whole thing was still pretty fledgling, working through a lot of snags.

Apparently, it had leaped forward a great deal in the time since, the massive warehouse on the back end of the property an operation designed entirely for its production.

"At least it makes a little more sense why they set up a damn winery way the hell out in the desert."

Snorting slightly, I gave no further response. Letting my features glaze, I stared off, thinking of everything that had transpired.

How a simple dinner of thanks for my friend and partner had ended with me now sitting here, on the back end of one of the largest busts in my life, bringing down someone I thought was in prison for a product I didn't know existed.

Wild.

Deep in thought, pondering what had happened, what still lay ahead, I barely noticed the light tapping at the door. Not until it cracked open, a puff of cool air from the hall flowing in, did I lift my gaze.

Beside me, Diggs did the same, both of us looking up expecting to see Diaz.

And seeing someone much, much different instead.

"Ah hell," Diggs muttered. "What do you two want?"

Filing through the door first was Agent Jones. His expression as affable as ever, he stepped through, his clothing without a wrinkle, his hair pushed neatly into place.

A far cry from us, it appeared he'd gotten a full night's sleep, just now arriving back for a new day.

A shoulder bag hitched into place, he stepped forward and lowered it to the ground beside his feet.

Entering behind him was Smith, his usual scowl locked in placed as he slid to the side, making a show of slamming the door a bit harder than necessary.

"Just going for coffee yesterday, Diggs?"

Keeping his feet extended before him, Diggs replied, "I didn't say where I was going. Had to hit my favorite spot, this joint up in LA called the Eat Shit Café."

The scowl on Smith's face grew a bit more pronounced as he stepped forward.

A move that we both knew he had no intention of following up on, was simply posturing, waiting for Jones to step back in.

More of the same practiced schadenfreude we'd seen from the day before.

"Gentlemen, please," Jones said. Raising his hands before him, he glanced between the two of them before working his way around to me. The diplomatic one of the pairing, he made a point of eye contact.

"There's been enough hostility for one night, I dare say."

Remaining in place, he kept his hands raised, waiting until Smith took a step back before lowering them to his sides. Glancing to Diggs, he waited until the man shifted his focus, returning his hand to his forehead, before sliding down into the closest seat.

"Now then," he said. Placing both forearms on the table, he laced his fingers before him. "It appears the four of us need to have a discussion."

"Like hell we do," Diggs muttered.

"Where's Diaz?" I added.

Ignoring Diggs's comment entirely, Jones shifted to me. "Agent Diaz is still overseeing things at Fruit of the Desert. That was quite a discovery you guys made out there last night."

The last few days had brought together quite a narrative, though it was still clear that there were a few pieces missing. Things that I hadn't quite been able to square yet, no matter how much I tried.

In spite of the man's word choice, it was clear that nothing that had happened out there was a surprise in the slightest.

Adding that bit to what I already knew, superimposing it onto the story we'd managed to cull together, I said, "You guys already knew what they were doing out there."

Across from me, Jones remained completely silent.

Even Smith, for his part, managed to keep his mouth shut.

"And that's why you sprung Ruiz. You wanted him there over-seeing it."

In my periphery, I saw Diggs pull his hand away from his fore-head. One at a time, he lowered his feet to the floor, turning his body to stare across the table as well.

"Not like that, exactly," Jones replied.

"Then like what, exactly?" Diggs shot back, his voice rising.

As if snapping back into action, remembering the role he was here to play, Smith took another step forward. Raising a finger before him, he snapped, "This is so, so much bigger than you two could ever hope to understand. Why the hell do you two think you were ordered to stay away from Ruiz?"

"Ordered?" Diggs spat back. Springing to his feet, he slapped both hands down onto the table, his body coiled, as if he might leap across it. "Who the hell do you think you're talking to? We're not soldiers, and we damned sure don't work for you."

The standoff between the two lasted the better part of a minute. Diggs on one side, appearing to want nothing more than to add one more tally to the night's list. Smith opposite him, playing the part, no matter how foolish such an attempt would be.

And again, it was Jones that managed to dispel things.

Bending at the waist, he took up the shoulder bag from the floor beside his chair. Pulling it onto his lap, he reached inside the top flap and drew out two thin stacks of printouts, both held together at the top by a binder clip.

Placing them side by side on the table before him, he returned the bag to the floor and again laced his fingers.

"Well, actually," he said, staring back at us, "that's what we're here to talk to you both about."

Chapter Ninety-Four

etween the two of us, Deputy Ferry looked like he'd had the worst week, but not by much. Seated in a padded chair outside of Kaylan's room, he stood as he saw me approaching, meeting me halfway down the hall. Across his nose was a padded metal splint held in place by white athletic tape. Peeking out from either side were concentric rings from the dark end of the color wheel, the entire area puffy and swollen.

All in all, a look that vaguely resembled a character from the old *Star Trek* series.

Not that I had any false pretenses of looking much better. Since the hatchet job I had done on my hair and beard a couple days ago, the total number of hours of sleep I'd gotten could be counted on one hand. My eyes still burned from the assortment of sweat and smoke and a hundred other things that had found their way in.

The stink of battle still clung to me, persisting even through a pair of the longest showers I'd ever taken. Added to it was the stench of the airplane, a toxic mix of tourists bathed in suntan lotion and the Mexican food the family sitting beside me had been kind enough to carry on with them.

Even at that, it wasn't like there was a single other place either one of us would be.

"Hawk," Ferry said, arriving with his hand outstretched.

"Deputy," I replied, returning the shake. Peeking over his right shoulder toward Kaylan's room down the hall, I asked, "How's she doing?"

Releasing his grip, Ferry turned over the same shoulder. His hands found his hips as he looked on a moment before turning back. "Better. Still sleeping most of the time, which the doctor said is normal with a head injury like hers."

In line with the carnage spread across his face, his voice was a bit distorted, his breathing extra loud.

"But she's been awake?" I pressed.

"Yeah," Ferry replied. "Couple different times, seems to be reasonably coherent too, which they say is a good sign."

On my last trip to visit Kaylan, she was still encased in gauze. Outside of her eyes, I hadn't been able to get any sort of read on the shape she was in, everything else hidden from view.

A mental image I'd carried to that jungle oasis in the desert and back. Had even had flash through my mind as Junior Ruiz asked if I would consider making him the same offer he'd posed to us so long ago.

"She's asked about you a couple of times," Ferry replied. Eyebrows rising slightly, he added, "I told her you'd been by, but were out helping apprehend the men that had done that to her."

As far as stories went, it wasn't the best I could hope for, but it damned sure wasn't the worst either.

My preference would have been that there was no need for such an explanation to be provided at all. As glad as I was that she was coming around, that some mental cognition was already present, I'd hoped to be back in time to be sitting there when she first opened her eyes.

Just one more thing to chalk up to what I wanted and what actually came to pass not quite matching up over the last week.

"Sorry about the extended guard duty," I said. "After that initial attack, I figured she was safe, but with everything else that ended up coming to light..."

Before leaving, I had only shared with Latham the bare minimum necessary for him to accept Tres Salinas and agree to look after Kaylan. Of that, I imagine he'd relayed even less to Ferry, leaving a pretty large gap between what had happened and what the man before me knew.

Not wanting to expend the time or energy on detailing it all out for him right now, I left it there, hoping he would accept my explanation as it was.

Given the current state of his features, I had a feeling he might.

"Glad to help," Ferry replied. "Appreciate what you did."

Much like me a moment before, I knew he was stopping well short of the full story. And like him, I was okay with letting it go at that.

There was no need to belabor that Salinas had gotten the better of him at the clinic a few days before, a random turn of luck being what had enabled me to nab him and bring him back. Or that Latham had called that morning to relay that they had found Salinas dead in his holding cell, apparently having used some sort of home-made strangulation device.

For days now, we had all been fumbling straight ahead, doing the best we could. No doubt mistakes had been made, things that we would all dwell on, berating ourselves over.

But with the exception of Martin, we had all made it.

Sometimes, that's all that can be asked for.

Lifting a hand, I patted Ferry on the shoulder. Turning myself to the side, I slid past him, moving down the hallway, neither of us saying another word.

Beside me, the late afternoon sun poured through the bank of windows lining the hall. Coming in at an angle, it bathed my entire left side in bright light, combining with my rising heart rate to lift my body temperature several degrees.

For the untold time over the last days, I could feel sweat appear on my brow, underscoring my beard, as I covered the last few steps to Kaylan's room. On approach, I considered raising a knuckle to knock before remembering Ferry's comment that she was still sleeping most of the time.

Not wanting to risk waking her, I instead slid sideways through the open doorway, pulling up at the foot of her bed. Compared to the hallway outside, the room was much darker, my eyes taking just a moment to adjust.

By the time they did, I could see she was awake, thin strips of pale blue irises peeking out at me.

Only two days had passed since I'd last been in this exact spot, though it felt like so much longer.

With more still yet to go.

"Hey there," I whispered, careful to keep my voice low.

Slight crinkles formed around her eyes, a bit of mirth finding her features. "Hi."

"How you feeling?" I asked.

The smile lingered for a moment before slowly fading. Her head lolled an inch to the side, her eyes narrowing. "Did you get him?"

Even knowing what she had gone through, the state she was in, I wasn't the least bit surprised she blew straight past my question. Much the same as I knew not to even try doing the same to hers.

"Yeah, we got him."

"Did you get everybody else?"

In the days or weeks ahead, I would sit down and tell Kaylan every last thing that she had missed. I'd start with the raid on Juana Salinas's *quinceañera* and finish with the trip to Fruit of the Desert, filling in every detail and answering every question I could.

She'd earned at least that much.

For the time being, though, I simply replied, "Yeah, we got them, too."

"Good," she whispered. Rolling her head back, she placed it in the center of the pillow beneath her, her gaze rising to the ceiling. "Hawk?"

Taking a step to the side, I slid around the corner of the bed. Dropping myself into the same hard plastic seat that had been my bed two days before, I leaned forward, elbows resting on my knees.

A post I had no intention of leaving until Kaylan was released.

"Yeah?"

"There's something I've been wanting to ask you."

Reaching out, I placed a hand atop her leg, the blankets she was wrapped in warm beneath my touch. The possibilities for what she was about to ask were infinite, a tiny clench appearing in my stomach as I braced for what might come next.

"What's that?"

Shifting her focus my way, she asked, "Next year, can we just get that fudge brownie sundae to go?"

Epilogue

A week had passed since sitting in the conference room of the DEA's Southwest Headquarters. Seven full days in which I'd sat vigil by Kaylan's bed until it was time to help her return home. In which I'd returned to my office and replaced the front door and casing that had been destroyed by Luis Mendoza and his makeshift explosives. Time when I'd finished up the last few things I needed to in West Yellowstone and made my way up to the cabin that served as my winter home outside of Glasgow.

One-hundred-and-sixty-eight hours of eating and sleeping and doing all of the other things a functional adult in modern society does.

Not one of them spent without thinking about the conversation that took place in the wee hours of dawn a week before.

And judging by the look on Carl Diggs's face beside me, the same exact state he had been in as well.

Standing shoulder to shoulder on the back deck of the home of Serra Martin's parents, we both stared out at the thick tangle of pine trees encroaching within ten yards of the house. Despite the time being just half past four in the afternoon, what little daylight the milky white sky had been able to produce was already starting to fade.

Barely enough to infiltrate the heavy boughs, we could just make a few tufts of white dotting the ground. In the air was the scent of pine and wood smoke, the latter pouring from the chimney behind us.

"Hell of a thing," Diggs said, the first words from either of us since stepping out onto the deck.

What exactly he was referring to, I couldn't be certain. Maybe it was the funeral of our friend that had just concluded a short time earlier, both of us still dressed in black suits. Perhaps it was what had transpired to bring us here, Junior Ruiz making an ill-fated attempt to right some perceived wrong from long ago.

Or, more likely, it was the same thing that had been nagging at me all week.

"Yeah," I agreed.

"You able to talk to Diaz?" he asked.

Glancing his way, I could see the lights from the interior of the home reflecting from the back of his shaved head. Flickering in uneven tones, the sight was punctuated by the sound of voices filtering out, nobody seeming to notice as the two of us stepped outside.

If they did, they didn't care enough to comment, Serra being only one of two people over the age of ten either of us had ever met before.

And she was tied up with her own responsibilities at the moment.

The other was currently squirreled away on the first floor, likely to join us whenever whatever had called him away was resolved.

"Couple times," I answered. "I guess we started a cascade of dominoes out there in the desert. The problem with Reyes trying to run things as a legitimate business was once the feds figured out what was actually in the wine-"

"They had a damn paper trail leading them to every single person that had ever bought the stuff," Diggs finished.

Hands shoved into the front pockets of my slacks, I shifted back to the trees. "Exactly. She was able to bring in field offices from all across the country. Biggest bust they've had on domestic soil in decades."

From the corner of my eye, I saw a tiny sliver of white flash, the first hint of a smile my friend had shown all day. "She keeps going like this, she won't be able to keep her ass out of D.C., no matter how hard she tries."

Snorting slightly, I felt my own mouth curl back into a smile. The assessment wasn't wrong, something she and I had both spoken of at length shortly before I'd gotten in the truck and headed back across the Northwest in time to be here.

The first time she and I ever met was working a case that had ended with a large international conglomerate being put out of business. At the time, D.C. had tried prying her out of the desert, but so new to the Southwest post, it had been easy for her to beg off.

Her biggest concern now was that they would force the issue, making her turn in her gun and badge to start working exclusively behind a desk.

Or, even worse, as a poster child.

"Could have easily gone the other way," I said, feeling the smile fade.

Beside me, Diggs glanced my way. His eyebrows raised, he nodded slightly, not needing to voice his agreement.

Diaz had gone out on a major limb for us with this one. The fact that it had yielded a large score that made her virtually bulletproof with both the Administration and the media was irrelevant, both of us knowing exactly how much we owed her for this.

"She say anything about the other...?" Diggs asked.

Falling silent, I let my eyes glaze, my mind again drifting back to the pair of very real agents with very fake names several days before.

The stack of papers that Jones and Smith handed over that morning had managed to answer one set of questions. They had detailed that they – acting on behalf of the very Agency that we had suspected all along – had been behind the release of Junior Ruiz. The goal in doing was so that he would do just as he was when we found him, returning to helm the organization that had brought him such notoriety a decade before.

That much hadn't come as much of a surprise. What did was the reasoning behind it.

Even more so the role they were hoping for us to play now in the wake of his death.

For decades, most of the cocaine production in the world was concentrated on the northern border of South America. Providing the perfect climate for the plant, growing had started in Colombia before eventually working its way next door into Ecuador. A single tight geographic region that was easy enough to monitor, the Agency and various other players from around the globe keeping a close watch on things without becoming too actively involved.

In recent years though, that had started to shift. Burgeoning methods of hydroponics and gene modification had allowed production to go widespread. Third world countries spanning the globe were now able to generate new and lucrative economies where they hadn't previously existed, the sudden influx of cash tilting power balances in ways they were never intended.

Places such as Peru, where the organization Ruiz had overseen for so long was now getting its product.

"Same as us," I replied. "Half shocked, half pissed at the whole thing."

The first part of the statement was clear enough. The back end was because neither one of the men had cared at all about the dope making it into America.

It was all about Peru and the concerns that were fast growing there.

The very same concerns they now wanted our help in quelling.

Grunting softly, Diggs fell silent as the door behind us opened. Bringing with it a spike in ambient noise, we both stood without turning. The smell of roast turkey and vegetables made its way out to us as the door closed quietly, followed by light footsteps across the wooden planks of the deck.

Just a moment after stepping outside, Mike Palinksy appeared along my left shoulder. His long hair pulled back into a ponytail, he had shed his ill-fitting sports coat, his usual baggy green sweater underscored by a white Oxford dress shirt.

Hands in his pockets, he glanced my way before assuming the same stance as us, his focus aimed at the trees out back.

"Sorry about that," he muttered. "Everybody always thinks everything is a damn emergency."

Leaning forward at the waist, Diggs peered past me to Pally. "Was it?"

"Yeah," Pally replied, sighing heavily, "but still..."

Diggs and I both let out a small chuckle as he returned to full height. For a moment, the three of us stood there, our first time together in more than half a decade.

The only thing missing being the friend we put to rest not two hours earlier.

Each lost in our thoughts, we remained that way for a long time. Past the ebb and flow of conversation behind us. Even beyond the sound of car doors opening and closing out front as people began to climb in and drive away.

Clear on to the point when Pally finally pulled in a deep breath through his nose, using it to lift his gaze toward the sky. Remaining there a moment, he slowly exhaled before asking, "What do you guys think?"

A week solid, I'd been asking myself that very same thing. Mulling what Jones and Smith had proposed, considering their motivations behind it. What they wanted from us, and how it might play out if we refused.

All of which was to say that after a solid week to think on it, I still had not one clue on how to best respond.

Thank You For Reading

Greetings y'all!

Per usual, I would be remiss if I didn't begin this letter with heartfelt thanks. This journey started for me a number of years ago, scratching out story ideas I'd been carrying around in my head, thoughts that just refused to go away. Fast forward nearly half a decade now (?!?!) and somehow I am still here getting to do this, something I would have never thought possible and have all of you to thank for.

Nowhere is that path more apparent than with this Hawk Tate series. Beginning five years ago with a single scene that came to me in a dream (no...seriously :), this is now the sixth entry in the canon, and if you've read this far, you know it won't be the last.

In each of his previous stories, I often allude to his past experiences, but with the exception of the vengeance he sought in *Cold Fire*, never have I made it a central aspect of the story. Feeling like it was a veritable treasure trove of ideas and possibilities that needed to be delved into, I started playing with different scenarios, eventually landing on this one.

I hope you enjoyed it.

Finally, if possible, I would like to ask one small favor from you. If you would be so kind as to leave a review – whether online or to me directly if you'd rather - I would greatly appreciate it. Every email I read personally, and do take all feedback very seriously.

As always, if you haven't yet, please accept as a token of appreciation for your reading and reviews a free download of my novel *21 Hours*, available HERE.

Thanks again!

Best,

Sneak Peek #1

HAM, A HAM NOVEL BOOK 1

Prologue

The ground absorbs any sound made by my footfalls. Walking heel-to-toe, I make sure each foot is placed down carefully, the thick bed of pine needles insulating the earth and masking my movements.

Moving in a serpentine pattern, I trace a path through the thin underbrush of the forest, this place one of the few in the world I have ever called home.

And right now, this man is here violating that. Not just with his mere presence but with everything he represents. Everybody he is associated with, every intention he has in mind.

With every thought, every realization, every moment, I am in his presence I can sense my animosity growing higher. I can feel as it raises my pulse, increases my body temperature, even tightens the grip on the rock in my hand.

To shoot this man would be easiest. To simply sight in on the back of his skull and ease back the trigger, knowing from this distance there is no possible way I can miss.

But the easiest path right now won't necessarily be the easiest moving forward.

And it would damned sure be far, far kinder than this man deserves.

Chapter One

THE LAST SLIVER of orange has just slid beneath the western horizon as the ring announcer steps through the ropes. It sends a thousand shards of shimmering light across the surface of the Pacific Ocean with its last gasps, the sudden absence plunging the world into a state of exaggerated darkness.

And just as they always do, the strands of bare bulbs strung high above the ring kick on a moment later, casting a straw-colored pallor over everything below.

The aging ring is built on pressure-treated 4x4's buried directly into the sand, spots of blood and assorted detritus dotting the canvas mat. The twin aluminum risers are on either end, both loaded with drunken revelers, their skins painted shades ranging from tomato red to dark tan. Beers in both hands, tobacco juice or sunflower seeds hang from their lips and the assorted forms of facial hair stuck to their chins.

Per usual, the overwhelming majority of onlookers are men, the few women that are mixed in serving clearly as accompaniment, still dressed in bikini tops from the day or already in leather anticipating the night ahead.

No in-between.

On the east and west ends of the ring are scads of wooden folding chairs, what were once even rows already a twisted jumble. Housing most of the regulars, they're grouped into random clusters, seats turned so they can see some combination of the sunset, the ring, or each other.

Considering that every last one of them had to pay to get in, I'm not sure anybody rightly gives a damn what they look at.

Least of all, me.

Despite the open-air venue, the recent sunset, the faint breeze pushing in from the sea, there is a palpable charge in the air. That familiar buzz that I've known for decades now, the unshakable feeling that seems to reach deep inside, igniting the parts of me I spend most of the week keeping tamped down.

For the last hour, the crowd has sat and watched the undercard for the night. Beginning with less than half of what is now on hand, the combination of buckets of beer and the cheap cover charge has managed to pull in enough to fill the bleachers, easily the largest crowd we've drawn in a while.

It also doesn't hurt that the first several bouts turned into little more than backyard brawls. Bloody affairs with over-muscled men that had once been high school athletes and can't let it go, so they come out here to the sand every weekend. Smaller guys that work the fields nearby, carrying resentment for damn near everything in their lives, entering the ring with something to prove.

And of course, a healthy sprinkling of fools that have watched a few too many MMA bouts on television and figured it didn't look that hard. Little more than chum for the crowd, they have done their part, sacrificial lambs for the maddened rabble.

With each passing bout, I sat in the back and felt the energy rising. Starting low, it worked steadily upward, cresting into a veritable hunger, bordering on lust, the feeling so strong I can feel it pushing in from every angle.

Goose pimples cover my exposed forearms and calves as I assume my stance in the corner, waiting as the ring announcer steps through the ropes. A cordless microphone in hand, he doesn't pretend to be some sort of Michael Buffer knockoff, showing up in the traditional attire of a tuxedo and polished wing tips.

Opting for little more than board shorts and a tank top, the tail of his unbuttoned Aloha shirt flaps to either side. No more than a couple of hours from the surf, his long hair is sun bleached and pulled back, a crooked grin on his face.

All in all, a look that holds no pretense, neither confirming nor denying the fact that he's a Los Angeles trust-fund baby down here hiding from his family and the real world and all the responsibility both brings with them.

Not that I give a shit. This isn't the place anybody ends up unless they're hiding from something.

Myself included.

"Ladies and gentlemen," he says, his sandals slapping against his heels as he saunters to the center of the ring. A quick squawk of feedback through the cheap mic echoes through the speakers, vocal displeasure sounding out from the audience.

Pretending not to notice, he pushes on. "Let's hear another round of applause for our last combatants, Charlie Reed and Eric Montrose!"

Calling the last two guys combatants is something like calling the Grand Canyon a ditch. Both big and beefy, the bout quickly devolved into a couple of gorillas trying to see who could withstand more haymakers.

It was like watching three rounds of the last forty seconds of every Rocky Balboa fight.

The crowd had loved it.

The reception to his request is weak at best, what clapping there is accompanied by a healthy smattering of boos. Already the crowd has moved on from the last spectacle, ready for the next in line. A small shower of peanut shells and paper napkins rain down, the items dotting the outer edges of the ring, some even landing within a few inches of my feet.

Not that the announcer seems to notice. Even with the top of my head buried into the corner pad, my gaze aimed straight down at the ground, I can imagine the look on his face. One corner of his mouth is rising higher, his grin growing ever more lopsided.

He lives for this shit, inciting the masses, feeling like he's some sort of ringmaster in his own personal circus.

All bought and paid for with his daddy's money.

Not that he — or any of us — have any delusions about where we are and what we're doing. The last guys beating the hell out of each other just means there are a few more stains on the mat going forward. Pelting the ring with garbage doesn't mean we're going to slow things down to sweep up. It's just that much more crap for me to now roll around in.

This isn't Las Vegas, or New York City, or even Rio. The people that have shown up to watch know that. Those of us that step inside the ring damned sure know it.

And here we are in spite of it.

Or, some might even argue, because of it.

"All right," the announcer says, a bit of his surfer accent sliding out, making him sound like McConaughey in *Dazed and Confused*. Rotating at the waist, he looks to either side before saying, "and with that, I'll get us straight to what we all came here to see tonight."

"*Ham!*" a stray voice calls out. "*Ham!*"

My eyes slide shut. This is the worst part. That damn chant that some drunken idiot always gets started.

"*Ham!*"

Ignoring him, the announcer calls, "For tonight's main event, we have one of the most anticipated bouts in Shakey Jake's history."

His voice cracks as he walks around the ring, pretending that he's trying to whip them up a bit more, though there's no need. The collective energy has continued to rise, the lack of walls or a roof having no negative effect on the tension brimming in the air.

No, this is about him siphoning off a little piece of things for himself, reminding everybody here who is responsible for all this.

Because it has been a whopping fifteen minutes since he last pointed it out.

"Two women, different in every way," he continues. "One Latina, the other white. One from South America, the other North. One making her Tijuana debut here tonight, the other putting her crown and perfect record on the line!"

The hype achieves some modest bit of effect, enough to at least push a swell of cheers and applause from the crowd.

Again, I hear the same inebriated bastard attempt to get a chant going, calling, "*Ham! Ham!*"

Once more, the announcer ignores him. My time will come. Right now, he's still milking his moment.

"In the blue corner," he continues, his voice rising and ebbing, "a woman coming to us straight from the underground club circuit of Colombia. Standing six foot two and weighing one hundred and sixty pounds, with a 38-2 record, the Bogota Brawler herself, Victoria Rosales!"

I don't bother moving from my spot in the corner, already knowing exactly what the woman looks like, her actual physical description enhanced the standard twenty percent by announcer hyperbole.

On a good day — in boots — she might go six feet even. Weigh maybe a pound or two above a buck forty. Striated muscle lines her arms and shoulders but her midsection is a bit softer, free of definition, with small bulges visible above her trunks.

Not that all of that is easy to see, most of it obscured by dark ink etched into much of her skin. Beginning around her ear, it wraps down one side of her neck before spreading over her back and, eventually, making it all the way to her calves.

With basic coloring and blurry lines, it's the sort of thing referred to in the States as *prison ink*, though I don't have enough knowledge of the girl or parlors in Colombia to know if she got hers inside or if that's just how tattoos look down there.

Not that it much matters, my lifetime interaction with her is about to come to an abrupt end in about ten minutes.

Perfunctory cheers ring out as a bit more debris lands in the ring. Right now, I imagine she has a fist or two raised into the air, making a small circle, the announcer remaining silent, extending the moment as long as he can.

Same cocksure smile on his face.

The first few times I was down here, I played the part. I stayed upright in the corner, responding to all the cues, doing what was expected.

That was long ago, well before I came to see that it went the same way every time, that the kid was more interested in playing out his own little fantasy than actually doing justice to the venue or the fighters.

Now, I just stay in my corner, wrists draped over the ropes, top of my head pressed into the pad, waiting it out.

"And her opponent," he eventually pushes out, "a woman that you all already know. Making her way down from just over the border and standing before you tonight with a perfect twenty-eight-and-oh record, your champion — Haaaaam!"

Click to download and continue reading *HAM* now!
dustinstevens.com/Hmwb

Sneak Peek #2

SHIPS PASSING, MY MIRA SAGA BOOK 4

Prologue

I'm not sure how I know. Like the words to a song I haven't heard in ages or the ending of a movie I stumble across late at night on cable, the pattern is already ingrained in my mind, the outcome sealed long before reaching the conclusion.

As if imprinted on me so long ago that the origin has ceased being of importance, cast aside into the ethereal abyss that the mind creates for all that it doesn't deem worthy of preserving.

The instant I hear the sound, the clear din of an engine approaching, every nerve ending in my body draws taut. My senses sharpen, picking up on the slightest shifts around me.

The diminishing light inside the room. The weak rattle of an air conditioning unit from next door. The smell of dust and cleaning product in the air.

Perched on the edge of the bed, I sit ramrod straight, counting off seconds. A sheen of sweat covers my skin, the residual light of day reflecting from it, though I am not nervous.

The point for that has come and gone.

Nor am I angry. Or sad. Or really feeling much of anything

433

beyond the tiniest bit of relief, knowing that this inevitability was coming. In a way, I'm just glad to get it over with, to put this behind me forever.

Fingers splayed over the tops of my thighs, I hear as the brakes moan slightly, bringing the approaching vehicle to a halt. As the engine cuts out a moment later.

As a door wrenches open and footsteps crunch across the parking lot, the mixture of dirt and gravel allowing each one to ring out. Hearing them, I am able to track my visitor's movement, imposing them on the images in my mind, knowing exactly where they stand at any given moment.

My breathing increases slightly, my pulse picking up, thrumming through my temples. Still, I remain motionless on the edge of the bed, watching as a shadow passes by the threadbare curtain hanging over the window at the front of the room.

It is time.

Finally.

―――

CHAPTER ONE

Hours have passed since I first showed up to see my home standing as a fiery pyre, oversized fingers of orange and yellow reaching ever higher into the night sky. In the time since, most of the commotion that was present when I first arrived has subsided.

Many of the first responders have now come and gone, nothing more than a pair of police cruisers sitting at either end of the street. To my right, a couple of officers lean against the front hood, glancing between the house and the adjoining thoroughfares, waving off the occasional rubbernecker on their way to work.

At the opposite end, the assigned pair has given up the task, instead retreating inside their vehicle, their heads silhouetted behind the windshield.

Not that I harbor any ill will toward them. They are right. There isn't anything more they can do.

Between the two cruisers, the quartet of fire engines that first showed up has shrunk to a single unit. A small cluster of men in over-sized fire-retardant pants and suspenders stand near the back end of it, their bare arms and faces smudged with soot. Spooled out alongside them is enough hose to ensure that the last dying gasps of the home don't somehow spring back to life, but it is clear at a glance that they expect nothing of the sort.

At this point, the fight has been fought and lost.

Just as has almost every earthly possession that remained of my Mira.

When the sun last set, it did so on the definition of a bucolic suburban Southern California neighborhood. Single family dwellings butted up tight to one another, both sides of the street filled with lots of equal size. Containing all the usual trappings, each had front lawns, side garages, a car or two parked outside.

A few had pets. A smaller handful even had the mythical white picket fence.

Only a matter of hours has passed since then, but already the sun is beginning to rise on a much different scene. No longer does the street look like it once did, an enormous black divot gouged into the center of it.

What was once my home, the first house my wife and I owned together, the place where we were seriously considering expanding our family, is now nothing but a pile of cinders, each passing moment further reducing all that remains.

By noon, I suspect it will be nothing more than ash, the Santa Ana winds carrying it into the distance.

I can feel the concrete curb beneath me biting into my tailbone as I sit on the opposite side of the street and stare. Disbelief, terror, shock, nostalgia, all run through my mind in equal measure. All so fierce, all so prescient, I don't know which to seize on first, my body numb.

For only the second time in my life – both coming in the last week - I have no idea how to process something.

"Here," a voice says, arriving a split second before a foil package taps against my shoulder. On contact, I can smell sausage and cheese, my hand reaching up to accept the intrusion without my mind truly grasping what it is.

"Breakfast burrito," Wendell Ross says, stepping down onto the street beside me and settling onto the curb.

A fellow Petty Officer, Ross has been by my side since we first went into SEAL training almost a decade before. A bit shorter than me, he is cut from corded muscle and sinew, his arms and chest broad plates achieved through hours of bodyweight calisthenics.

Dressed in gym shorts and a long-sleeve neoprene shirt, he places a brown paper bag between his feet as he settles in, though makes no move to open it.

Where he went or how long he's been gone, I can only guess at, the last several hours a menagerie of sights and sounds and thoughts, all of it contorted into one unending nightmare.

Just as the last week since my wife's death has been.

"You should eat something," Ross says, his voice low and composed. He doesn't bother looking my way as he says it, both of us staring at the shattered remnants of the last tangible vestige I had of my marriage.

Of course, he is right. Just as he has been a dozen times before over the years when we were together out in the shit. Moments when he would ensure the rest of us got the food or rest we needed.

A direct result of being one of the few among us that was also a father, the paternal instinct ingrained.

"Thanks," I manage, not knowing what else to say at the moment.

I do need food. And water. And sleep.

I need to push rewind, and go back to sitting in the corner booth at The Cartwright with Mira and Ross and our friends Emily Stapleton and Jeff Swinger. I need to take her directly home afterward, avoiding Balboa Park and the Wolves and anything else that might endanger her.

I need a lot of things right now. But just like every last one of them, I'm not sure my body can even handle the thought of eating at the moment.

"Jeff and Emily take off?" I whisper.

"Yeah," Ross replies. "They were both going to call in today, but I told them to go on. There's nothing more they can do here."

Again, he is right. There is nothing anybody can do here. In a couple of hours, the fire department will determine that there is no risk of reignition and the police will string crime scene tape across the front. Tomorrow, or the next day, an arson investigator will come out and take a look.

Not that I need to wait that long to know what happened here.

"Sonsabitches," I mutter.

Beside me, Ross grunts slightly. "Wolves?"

Just hearing the name draws my hand up into a fist. My jaw clenches as I stare straight ahead, the burning in my eyes becoming more pronounced.

"Who else?" I whisper.

This time, he doesn't bother to respond. There is no need to. We both know who is behind this, the bigger question being the one I've spent much of the last week trying to determine.

Why? Why had one of their members killed my wife in cold blood? Why were they targeting Fran Ogo and her granddaughter Valerie? Why did they search my house six days ago only to come back and burn the place to the ground now?

Why?

The smell of wood char hangs heavy in the air, overpowering even the breakfast in my hand. I haven't caught a glimpse of myself in hours, though I can only imagine how I must appear, with ash and soot staining my cheeks, rivulets streaming vertically through it, revealing where my tears have fallen.

Almost certainly my eyes and nostrils are both red-rimmed, all stinging in the aftermath of the fire.

At this point, I am well past caring.

"What are you thinking?" he asks.

He doesn't expound further, though I know exactly what he is trying to say. He wants to know the plan I'm putting together, wants to make sure I'm not about to do something incredibly stupid.

What he can't possibly understand is, I haven't even made it that far yet, my focus still on the remnants of my home before us.

"I have to go in this morning," I reply. "Another one of those damn sessions with the doc."

Pausing, I smirk slightly, the fact that every last thing I have to wear just burned up occurring to me. "Think she'll write me up for appearing out of uniform?"

━━

Look for Ships Passing , My Mira Book 4, in late 2019!

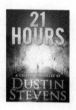

Free Book

_____

As thank you for reading, please enjoy a FREE copy of my first best-seller – and still one of my personal favorites – *21 Hours!*

Bookshelf

Bookshelf

The Zoo Crew
Dead Peasants
Tracer
The Glue Guy
Moonblink
The Shuffle
(Coming 2020)

Ham Novels:
HAM
EVEN

Standalone Thrillers:
Four
Ohana
Liberation Day
Twelve
21 Hours
Catastrophic
Scars and Stars
Motive
Going Viral
The Debt
One Last Day
The Subway
The Exchange

Standalone Dramas:
Just A Game
Be My Eyes
Quarterback

Children's Books w/ Maddie Stevens:
Danny the Daydreamer…Goes to the Grammy's
Danny the Daydreamer…Visits the Old West
Danny the Daydreamer…Goes to the Moon

Bookshelf

(Coming Soon)

Works Written by T.R. Kohler:
Shoot to Wound
Peeping Thoms
The Ring
The Hunter

My Mira Saga
Spare Change
Office Visit
Fair Trade

About the Author

Dustin Stevens is the author of more than 40 novels, the vast majority having become #1 Amazon bestsellers, including the Reed & Billie and Hawk Tate series. *The Boat Man*, the first release in the best-selling Reed & Billie series, was named the 2016 Indie Award winner for E-Book fiction. The freestanding work *The Debt* was named an Independent Author Network action/adventure novel of the year for 2017 and *The Exchange* was dubbed a fiction novel of the year for 2018.

He also writes thrillers and assorted other stories under the pseudonym T.R. Kohler, including *The Hunter, The Ring, Shoot to Wound*, and *Peeping Thoms*.

A member of the Mystery Writers of America and Thriller Writers International, he resides in Honolulu, Hawaii.

Let's Keep in Touch:
Website: dustinstevens.com
Facebook: dustinstevens.com/fcbk
Twitter: dustinstevens.com/tw
Instagram: dustinstevens.com/DSinsta

CPSIA information can be obtained
at www.ICGtesting.com
Printed in the USA
FSHW010706180421
80588FS